THE YORK CAT CRIME TRILOGY

THE YORK CAT CRIME TRILOGY

The Case of the Clementhorpe Killer
The Cat Who Knew Too Much
The Call of the Cat Basket

James Barrie

Severus House

CONTENTS

1

The Case of the
Clementhorpe Killer

Peter Morris was already dead when Theodore woke.

The dim hour before dawn was usually his favourite time of day. The birds are awake. Most cats are awake. Most people are asleep.

But this spring morning Theodore sensed something was not right. He blinked open his eyes and stretched. His ears twitched.

The birds tweeted. The pigeons cooed. A young German shepherd whined. A car engine started up a few streets away. In the distance a train rumbled on its way to Leeds. It sounded like any other morning. But why then did he feel something was not right?

He stirred from Emily's side. In the grey light he padded downstairs. He glanced at his food bowls. It would be at least an hour before they were filled. He exited through the cat flap, out into the yard.

A light breeze blew from the south. He tasted the damp morning air.

His own scent dominated the yard, he made sure of that. The potted herbs at the bottom of the boundary wall he sprayed on a daily basis. He caught whiffs of other cats from adjoining 'shared' territories. He made out the faint smell of cocoa hanging in the air.

He jumped up onto the boundary wall and made his way to the back wall.

He picked his way across the clematis, his ears twitching. He crossed the concrete plinth that spanned the back gate. He continued along the back walls, down the hill, until he was facing the house with the pigeon loft.

The house was on the corner of an access road to the back alley. The pigeon loft was fixed high up on the back gable wall. The yard was surrounded by a six-foot-high brick wall. On top of the wall was a wooden trellis, eighteen inches high. A single strand of rusted barbed wire was suspended two inches above the trellis.

Set into the wall was a wooden gate, coated black with creosote. The gate was never left open. Certainly not at this early hour, thought Theodore. But this morning the gate was open a few inches. Wide enough for a cat to slip through.

Theodore looked up and down the back alley, then jumped down from the wall. He padded over the blue hexagonal cobblestones. In front of the gate he paused. He looked up and down the alley. He saw a stocky black cat at the crest of the hill. Arthur licked his paws in the long shadows, his back to Theodore.

Theodore turned back to the gate and padded into the yard. He looked up at the pigeons perched on the eaves of the loft, cooing excitedly. He circled the yard. He looked up at the pigeons again.

They cooed down at him, a provocation to Theodore. 'You can't get at us. You can't get at us,' they called, their napes glistening green and blue in the early morning sun.

Pea-brainers, Theodore thought, miaowing up at them.

Again he circled the yard, his tail straight up.

'You can't get at us,' the pigeons cooed down. 'You can't get at us.'

Just you wait..., thought Theodore.

He turned and noticed the door to an outbuilding; it too was ajar. He approached and, in the shadows, made out a tartan slipper, its black shiny sole facing him. He went closer, and that was when he saw the body.

Peter Morris lay on his front. He wore brown corduroy trousers and a blue checked shirt, the upper part dyed maroon with blood. A dark pool extended from what had been his head, now a colourful mess of shattered bone, congealed blood and grey brain. Pigeon feed had spilled from an upturned sack. The little seeds coated the dead man's head like some horrific dessert.

Theodore had never seen a dead human before. His instinct was to turn tail and head home.

He was soon back on the bed he had left just minutes before. He stood on Emily's shoulder as she lay on her side. He dabbed at her face with the pads of his paws.

She pushed him away with a heavy groan. 'It's too early,' she complained. 'I'm not feeding you yet.'

He pressed his paws into her shoulder, digging his claws into warm flesh. She pushed him away again. But now she had her eyes open. She rolled onto her back and was met by Theodore's green stare. She turned and glanced at the digital figures on her radio alarm clock.

'It's not even six o'clock,' she groaned. 'It's too early.'

She rolled back over, pulling the duvet around her shoulders so only her face was exposed. 'There's no way I'm going to start getting up this early to feed you.'

Theodore jumped down and a minute later he was back in the Morris's yard. He ran to a corner, collected several grey feathers in his mouth and returned to Emily's side. He dropped the dirty grey feathers onto her face.

She spluttered, swiping the feathers away with her hand.

'What the!' she said, rubbing at her face before sitting up.

Her eyes opened wide as she examined the dirty feathers that lay on the bed sheet.

'Fiddlesticks! You've only gone and eaten one of his pigeons.'

Theodore jumped down from the bed. He made for the top of the stairs and paused, his tail held upright, making sure Emily was following before he went down. He didn't have to wait long. He soon heard her feet on the bare boards of the bedroom floor. He dashed down the stairs and through the dining room. He paused in the kitchen until he was sure she had reached the bottom of the stairs, then exited into the yard, the cat flap snapping shut behind him.

Emily grabbed her black woollen coat from the coat stand and pulled on her slippers before unlocking the backdoor.

She spotted Theodore standing on the back wall of the yard.

Theodore padded across the clematis, crossed the concrete plinth and jumped down into the alley.

'For heaven's sake!' Emily said, walking over to the back gate and doing up the two middle buttons of her coat as she went.

She unbolted the gate and entered the alley. In the grey light she saw Theodore approach the house with the pigeon loft.

'Get out of there,' she hissed.

But Theodore had already disappeared inside the yard.

She glanced up and down the back alley, did up another button on her coat and then walked down the hill. She pushed the gate open and entered the yard.

Theodore was standing in front of an outbuilding. A handful of pigeons took to the air and fluttered overhead, beating their grey wings.

She walked over and picked Theodore up and held him to her chest. Theodore let his body go limp. Then she saw the body. Theodore dropped to the ground.

Her scream was heard by over a hundred people, many dragged from their dreams by the shrill screech.

At that moment the bells of St Clement's at the bottom of the hill began to clang out six o'clock. They were shortly followed by the bells of York Minster, just over a mile away.

The next person to arrive at the murder scene was Michael Butler, whose house backed onto the Morris's. He entered the yard, dressed in tight running gear, saw Emily and approached the shed. At that moment the back door of the house swung open and the very recently widowed Wendy Morris marched out, tying the cord of her mauve towel dressing gown as she approached.

'What's going on out here?' she demanded.

Emily opened her mouth to speak but no words came out.

'It appears that Mr Morris has had an accident,' Michael said, halfway in the outbuilding.

'An accident?' Wendy said. 'Let me see.'

She approached the outbuilding but Michael stood in her way.

'You shouldn't look in there,' Michael said. 'I think he's dead.'

'Don't tell me what I can and can't do in my own yard.'

She pushed past him.

'Peter!' she cried, dropping to her knees. 'Oh, Peter...'

Emily started crying.

'He's dead,' Wendy said, stooping over the body of her husband.

'I'd better go and call the police,' Michael said.

He hurried out of the yard.

Wendy turned and faced Emily. 'How did you get in?' She pointed her forefinger at Emily's chest.

'Through the gate,' Emily said, sniffing. She wiped her nose on the sleeve of her coat, leaving a silvery trail behind. 'It was open...'

'He never leaves the gate open.'

'It was open this morning,' she blubbered. 'My cat...'

'Your cat?' Wendy asked. 'What's your cat got to do with this?'

Emily looked around for Theodore but she couldn't see him. 'My cat,' she said. 'He brought some feathers into my house. I thought...'

'You thought what?'

Wendy marched to the back of the yard. Several pigeons had settled up on the eaves of the slate-tiled roof. A further two fluttered overhead. 'One of his pigeons is missing,' she said. 'Ethel.'

Emily stared at her through red-rimmed eyes. 'Ethel?'

'Yes, Ethel...' Wendy said. 'She's one of his pigeons. I bet your cat's had it.'

Wendy looked at the door of the outbuilding, where her dead husband lay. She looked at her hands, smudged red with blood. She looked at the open gate.

'Peter would never have left that gate open,' she went on. 'Someone's murdered him and your cat has made off with one of his birds.' She put her hands on her hips.

Then Michael strode back into the yard. He was followed by his partner, Philip. 'The police are on their way,' Michael said.

Then, as if on cue, they heard the siren of a police car as it made its way from Fulford, on the other side of the River Ouse.

'What's happened?' Philip asked, wiping sleep from his eyes.

He crossed the yard to the outbuilding and peered in. 'Ugh,' he said, grimacing. 'That's not very nice.'

The police siren grew louder. Wendy pushed her hands into the pockets of her dressing gown, her fists clenched. 'Somebody's killed him,' she said. 'And her cat has had Ethel.'

'Ethel?' Philip asked.

'Yes, Ethel. One of his pigeons. A prize pigeon at that.'

Emily whimpered and began crying again.

Then there was a loud knocking at the front door.

'I'll go and let them in,' Michael said.

'I can get it,' Wendy said.

She turned and marched back inside.

From behind the wooden trellis that topped the back wall, Theodore saw that she was wearing slippers, large fur-lined slippers.

He hadn't eaten any pigeon. He didn't even know what one tasted like. Now I'm accused of killing one, he thought, looking up at the remaining birds.

He would prove them wrong. He would find out who or what had taken the pigeon. He would clear his name and, in doing so, find out who had killed Peter Morris.

In the distance he heard more sirens approaching. Two police officers were standing in front of the outbuilding. Wendy Morris, arms folded across her bosom, stood behind the police officers. Michael and Philip had retreated to the gate. Michael lifted his feet in turn and glanced at the white soles of his running shoes. Probably checking he hasn't stood in any blood, thought Theodore.

Emily stood near the back wall, unaware that Theodore was only a few yards from her.

Her hair was a tangled mess of strawberry blonde. Her black woollen coat ended mid-thigh, below which her baggy pink pyjama bottoms showed. On her feet she wore her old Garfield slippers. The ridiculous orange lasagne-loving cats looking a little worse for wear.

Not quite the Watson I had in mind, Theodore thought, blinking in the early morning sun.

2

Theodore's father was a Scottish Fold, his mother a Ragdoll. He hadn't inherited the folded ears of his father, but, like his father, his long silvery fur was streaked with charcoal, his chest and underside snow white. His emerald green eyes were underscored with white mascara and his nose was the colour of cooked liver.

Around his neck he wore a purple velvet collar, attached to the collar was a small silver disc bearing his name and Emily's mobile phone number.

'He's too pretty to be a boy,' said Michael.

Emily looked out of the window to see her cat sitting on the back wall staring across at her. 'What are you doing there?' she said.

Theodore widened his eyes at her, as if to say, 'What are *you* doing there?'

'Does he sit there often?' Emily asked.

'Sometimes,' Michael replied. 'He's an inquisitive one.'

'You can say that again,' Emily said, thinking of the events of that morning.

'I don't let him in,' Michael went on. 'I'm allergic to cats.' He got up. 'I'll go and get the tea.'

Emily, Michael and Philip had been taken to Fulford Police Station that morning to make statements. Having made her way home, she'd decided to call on Michael. She hadn't spoken to him much before, but she felt the need to talk about what had happened and not knowing anyone else on the street had called on Michael.

While he was in the kitchen making tea, Emily glanced around the room. There were several framed pencil drawings hanging on the wall, over a purple clad chaise longue. The pictures were all York street scenes – Stonegate, Goodramgate, Micklegate.

There was a sheet of paper pinned onto a drawing board at the back of the room. An anglepoise lamp lit up the white rectangle of paper. She could make out some faint pencil marks. Drawing equipment was laid out on a table beside the drawing board. Not a pencil out of place. Also on the table, there was a little wooden mallet, the sort used to tenderize steaks. I wonder what that's doing there, she thought.

From the back wall of Michael's house Theodore also wondered what the mallet was for.

Emily didn't know much about Michael. He was already living on Avondale Terrace when she'd moved in two years ago. He sometimes wore thick-rimmed tortoiseshell glasses, other times he must wear contact lenses, she thought.

Philip had only appeared recently. She wasn't sure if he lived with Michael, or just stayed over some nights.

'Did you know Peter Morris at all?' she asked Michael, when he returned. He was carrying a tray with a tea pot and two cups, all matching porcelain.

'Not really,' he said, putting the tea things down and arranging them on the table. 'I used to hear him on a night. He talked to his pigeons.'

'Really?'

'Yes. That's not so surprising, is it? I bet you talk to your cat.'

'Yes, but that's different,' Emily said, biting on her bottom lip. 'I mean Theodore is intelligent.'

Michael shrugged. 'Well, he used to talk to them... He had names for them too. Deirdre, Lily, Daisy, Ethel... I think Ethel must have been his favourite. "Oh, Ethel," he used to say, "You are a beauty..." Late at night when I was lying in bed I could hear him... I sleep with the window open... Didn't you ever hear him?'

'No. Never... I go to sleep with the radio on,' Emily said.

Emily sipped at her tea. It was slightly citrusy. 'What do you think she's going to do with the pigeons?' she said.

'Probably sell them. The police said to me that some of them may be worth a bit. Maybe whoever killed Peter did it over a pigeon.'

'Over a pigeon?' Emily said. 'I don't believe that.'

'Well, it would clear your cat – if someone had stolen the bird.'

On the back wall, Theodore pricked up his ears.

'Whoever killed Peter Morris had to have a reason,' Michael went on. 'A motive if you like... If someone had found out that those birds of his were worth a lot of money...'

'They might have broken into his yard to steal his birds,' Emily continued the chain of thought.

'And Peter surprised them...'

'And they bashed him over the head...' Emily said.

Theodore turned and looked at the pigeon loft on the gable wall. Now Ethel was gone, there were five pigeons; the day before there had been half a dozen.

He watched as a police officer cycled down the hill. She didn't notice Theodore on the wall. She was looking the other way. Towards Wendy Morris's house.

Theodore jumped down into the alley and up onto the other side, on top of Wendy's back wall.

The trellis had square openings, about two inches apart. Theodore peered through the trellis and spotted Wendy, sitting at her kitchen table, her back to the window. Dirty dishes soaked in the sink. The knuckle of a rolling pin stood proud of the greyish brown washing up water. An early evening soap opera was on; a small television tucked into the corner of the room. An advertisement break interrupted the programme.

'All this baking!' Irene said. 'I don't know how you can eat with what's happened... Poor Peter. I mean he had plenty more life in him, didn't he?'

'I can always freeze them,' Wendy said. 'Unless you'd like to take one. I've not got that much room in my freezer come to think of it.'

'Go on then,' Irene said. 'I don't mind if I do. If I don't eat it, Rocky will.'

'Best to keep busy,' Wendy said. 'That's what they say.'

'And they haven't found the murder weapon? I doubt they will now. I mean it could have been owt. A sledgehammer. A brick. A lump of concrete. I'll bet it's at the bottom of the Ouse by now. No doubt they'll be out searching people's backyards tomorrow morning. I doubt they will find owt though.'

'Emmerdale's back on,' Wendy said, nodding her head at the television in the corner.

'Oh, so it is.'

The two old ladies turned to face the television. However, Wendy did not follow the plot as it played out on the small screen. Instead the scenes from her own day replayed themselves in her head.

She remembered the scream and going downstairs. The silly girl sobbing in her yard; the man in tight running gear dashing off to call the police; another man. Then the police arriving.

They took away the two men and the girl to Fulford Police Station, and then she was also taken to make a statement. When she returned from Fulford several hours later Peter had gone and the shed floor had been scrubbed clean. Two young female officers had sat with her into the evening, asking questions. Wendy was not sure if she were being counselled or questioned.

She was told by the quietly spoken police officer, her hand on hers, that her husband had died instantly and would have felt no pain. Then the other asked quite bluntly if she had any idea what might have done such damage. Wendy said that she didn't know.

'He wouldn't have known what hit him,' the first officer said.

The young police officer asked her if she had anywhere else to spend the night. 'A relation you could stay with?' she suggested. 'It might be a good idea after what's happened...'

Wendy shook her head. 'I'll stay here,' she said. 'I have a friend who'll come and sit with me... Irene. She's only down the road.'

As evening set in, Theodore knew that the police investigation would be put on hold until the next day. Now his investigation could begin.

Night-time was a friend to the cat. While humans can only see darkness, a cat can pick out a thousand shades of grey. He walked along the back walls, inspecting the backyards and gardens, looking for anything out of place. Unlike the police, he didn't need to seek permission to enter a person's yard.

There was a neglected garden to the rear of No. 19 Avondale Terrace, the house next door to his own. The grass had not been cut in years. Every curtain in the house was closed. They were never opened as far as Theodore was aware. It began to spit with rain but Theodore did not feel it through his thick coat.

He jumped down into the overgrown rectangle of lawn. He had explored this garden numerous times in recent months. In among the long, wet undergrowth were crumpled beer cans, plastic bottles, crisp packets, sodden newspapers, a bicycle wheel, the remains of a takeaway tied up in a plastic bag and numerous little blue plastic bags of canine excrement.

Theodore sensed something foreign among the undergrowth, something that hadn't been there before.

He approached through the long, wet grass, his head close to the ground, sniffing. In front of him there lay a hexagonal-shaped cobblestone, just like the ones that paved the back alley. Its glazed blue surface was splashed with dried blood.

Wendy picked up Laura's mug of undrunk coffee and poured it down the sink.

Sitting herself down at the kitchen table, Irene said, 'I haven't seen her for so long...'

Wendy went over to the kitchen cupboard.

'Would you like a drink of something?'

'What have you got?'

Wendy peered into the cupboard.

'Malibu?'

'Go on then,' Irene said. 'I haven't had a Malibu for ages.'

'It's Peter's. He used to like a glass of Malibu. He's hardly going to finish it now.'

Wendy poured Irene a generous tumbler full. She poured herself a finger of whisky.

'They still think that Craig did it for the money?' Irene said.

Wendy took a sip of whisky. 'What other reason could there be?'

'The papers say he was an oddball.'

'You just don't know who's living next to you these days.'

'It's not like the old days,' Irene said. 'Everybody used to know everybody's business back then.'

'They did that.'

Both women had a drink.

'He's back again,' Wendy said, nodding to her kitchen window.

'Who's that?'

'That girl's cat. He's eyeing up those pigeons. What's left of them.'

'He can't get in, can he?'

'No. Only through the gate... And he'll have to be quick to get past me.'

Irene looked to the window but couldn't make out the cat crouching behind the trellis; she had cataracts.

Emily brought Jonathan back to hers shortly after eleven o'clock. They had with them a plastic carrier bag containing half a crispy duck from the Chinese takeaway.

She went to the kitchen and returned to the lounge with two plates, two glasses, knives, forks and spoons.

Theodore eyed the bag and sniffed its contents. A droplet of drool formed on his bottom lip.

'Is this your cat?' Jonathan said, patting Theodore heavily on the head.

'Yes. That's Theo,' Emily said, sitting down beside him.

Theodore stared up at Jonathan. He was sitting in his place... Where was he supposed to sit now? He paced the laminate floor, his tail raised, his ears folded flat.

Jonathan began to roll up a crispy duck pancake. Emily copied him, smearing plum sauce over a circular pancake, then added the dark brown crispy meat, spring onion and cucumber spears. Jonathan managed to roll his into a neat little cigar-shaped parcel. But when Emily tried, the pancake sprung apart, its filling spilling onto her lap.

She'd had three (or was it four?) glasses of wine at the Golden Ball. First date nerves, she'd reasoned.

'Here. I'll roll you one,' Jonathan offered. He quickly rolled her a pancake.

Emily ate the crispy duck roll in two mouthfuls, smearing her chin with plum sauce. 'That really is quite good,' she told him through a mouthful of food.

Theodore approached the plastic bag of food again. Just as he was about to stick his head inside to investigate, Jonathan pushed him away with the back of his hand.

'Hey,' he said. 'It's not for you.'

'You can have some later,' Emily said, picking the bag of food up and putting it up on the coffee table.

Theodore stared at the intruder. 'Why should *I* have to wait? I was here first...'

Theodore suddenly jumped up onto the coffee table. He spotted the dark brown meat in the tinfoil tray and made for it. But this time it was Emily who jumped up and grabbed him before he could snatch a sliver of crispy duck.

'No, you don't,' she told him. 'You've got your own food.'

Theodore let his body go limp, as she lifted him from the table.

Feel free to help yourself, he thought, retreating to a corner. What's mine is yours and all that...

After the duck pancakes had been eaten and a couple more glasses of wine had been drunk, Emily started crying.

'What is it?' Jonathan asked.

'Sorry,' Emily said. 'It's the wine...'

'Does wine make you cry?'

'That old man being murdered,' Emily said. 'I can't stop thinking about it.'

'Was that round here? I didn't realise.'

'Just behind,' Emily said, wiping her eyes. 'He lived on the corner opposite. I was the one who discovered the body. They think he was hit over the head with a cobblestone. And now my neighbour's been arrested. They think *he* did it...'

She nodded to the wall that separated her house from his.

'I didn't know.' Jonathan put his hand on her arm. 'You didn't say anything.'

'It's not really something you tell people when you first meet them... Oh, by the way, I discovered a dead body the other day. His head had been bashed in with a cobblestone...'

'Those blue cobblestones *are* heavy,' Jonathan said knowingly. 'They made them from slag from the old steelworks in Tyneside.'

'I didn't know that,' Emily said, rubbing her eyes.

After Emily and Jonathan went upstairs, Theodore jumped up onto the coffee table and finished off the last scraps of duck, then licked the droplets of grease from the silver carton.

When Theodore climbed the stairs up to bed, he found Jonathan on his side of the bed, his head bent back into the pillow, snoring.

Theodore tried to get into the space between the two bodies, but he could not get comfortable. He climbed over Emily but there was not enough room for him on the edge of the bed. He clambered over Jonathan but the intruder chose that moment to turn on his side – sending Theodore onto the floor.

He paced the bedroom. Who was this person who had gate-crashed their lives?

For all he knew Jonathan could be the Clementhorpe Killer.

The intruder's jeans and socks were lying in a heap by the doorway to the en-suite bathroom. His boots were discarded by the foot of the bed.

Theodore sniffed at the intruding objects, his tail wagging with irritation.

3

Jonathan woke at a quarter to seven and realised he was not in his own bed. Emily's alarm bleated from the corner of the room. She turned over, pulling the duvet with her, and silenced the alarm. She lay there and didn't say anything.

He rubbed his eyes and looked at his wristwatch, a much-scratched stainless steel Casio. 'I'd better get off,' he said. 'I'm on a site on the other side of Bradford. It's a nightmare to get to.'

Emily didn't say anything.

Jonathan got out of bed and pulled on his jeans. He felt at his stubble, picked off some cat fluff and dropped it onto the floor.

The alarm went off again and Emily snoozed it again.

Jonathan went into the bathroom and splashed cold water onto his face. He looked at himself in the mirror. Clumps of cat fur were stuck in his hair. He picked them out and dropped them into the washbasin. His t-shirt, an obscure American indie band, was covered in a mesh of silver, grey and white fur. He picked off some of the bigger clumps and threw them onto the overflowing bin. He swore out loud. Then he said, 'I am absolutely covered in cat fur.'

'Maybe you shouldn't have slept in your t-shirt,' Emily said from below the duvet.

Emily glanced at her alarm clock. She really should have got up by now but was waiting for Jonathan to leave. The top of her mouth was dry and tacky, and she had a strange taste in her mouth. It must be that plum sauce, she thought, before wondering if she had any mouthwash in the house.

She watched as Jonathan crossed the room and, sitting on the corner of the bed, pulled on his boots. He swore again.

'My boots are wet,' he said. He took them off and put them to his face. 'I think your cat has weed in my boots.'

'Sorry,' Emily murmured from beneath the duvet. She looked again at her clock and hoped he would hurry up and leave.

Jonathan pulled his boots back on. 'Think I'm going to walk back through Scarcroft allotments,' he said. 'Wouldn't want anybody seeing me in this state.'

'Suit yourself,' Emily said. 'Bye.'

'Bye,' Jonathan almost barked.

A few seconds later Emily heard the front door open and slam shut. She jumped out of bed and began to run a bath.

Only then did Theodore crawl out from under the bed and make his presence known. In the ensuing rush to leave the house, he didn't want Emily to forget to feed him. Otherwise it would be a long hungry day.

While sitting in early morning traffic on the ring road that morning, Emily wondered if she would see Jonathan again.

She didn't have to wonder long. That evening she received a text message.

As soon as her mobile beeped, she picked it up from the coffee table and read: 'Had a great time last night... Would you like to meet up again this Friday?'

It was only Tuesday. She questioned how keen he actually was.

She waited twenty minutes, until the television show she was watching had finished, and then responded: 'Yes. Free Friday. Really enjoyed those crispy duck pancakes!'

She then noticed that her telephone was blinking. She reached over and played the message.

It was her mother.

'They've let him go,' she said. 'There's still a killer on the loose. Make sure you lock all your doors and windows tonight. Your dad says you should put something behind your back gate in case they try to force their way in...

'Oh, your father wants to say hello.'

'Hello,' her father said, and the message ended with a beep.

She picked up her laptop. She entered the address of the local newspaper. The headline confirmed that Craig Foster had been released.

'Clementhorpe Killer Still on the Loose', the newspaper headline announced.

The police had found no evidence to link Craig to the death of Peter Morris. Following a check on his bank accounts, it was discovered that Craig spent less than half of what he earned. The other half remained in his bank account, accumulating interest. Craig Foster was not in any great need of money. The police could find no motive for him to have killed Peter Morris.

Emily shuddered to think that whoever had killed Peter Morris was still at large. And her neighbour, possibly the murderer, was probably back at home. Just the wall separating him from her, and not even a cavity wall at that.

'The police have stated that they are pursuing other lines of inquiry and if anybody has information they should contact them,' Emily read. They have no idea who did it.

Emily thought back to the night Peter Morris was killed. She remembered being woken by Theodore in the early morning. The feathers dropped on her pillow. She wondered if she had overheard anything in the night. Had she heard arguing in the early hours? She couldn't remember anything but then her radio had been on.

She felt uneasy. She called for Theodore but he did not come.

She paced the front room. She went and checked that her back door was locked. She picked up the heavy pan from the side and practised swinging it at an imaginary intruder.

Back in the lounge, she picked up a magazine from the coffee table. She took in the headlines. 'My ninja kitten left me for dead'. 'My psychic dog has healing powers. Can he help you?' 'Car jacked! Then force fed meat pies.'

She threw the magazine across the room. 'Give me a break!' she cried.

Theodore had heard Emily calling but chose to ignore her. He sat on the boundary wall with Craig's house. The parcel of grass was exposed, the white tent having been removed that morning.

He jumped down into Craig's garden and, arching his back, signed his signature across the spot where he'd discovered the murder weapon. Mid-wee the backdoor opened and Craig appeared.

Theodore tightened his bladder and the stream of wee came to an abrupt stop. He felt the fur on his back bristling.

Craig froze. They faced each other.

'Wait there,' Craig said.

He turned and went back into his house. Theodore remained standing in the garden, his bushy tail held aloft.

He heard Emily calling again from inside his house. He chose to ignore her.

It wasn't long before Craig returned. He placed a saucer of tuna on the edge of the lawn. Then he stood back into the kitchen doorway.

Theodore had never been given tuna to eat. Emily didn't even buy tuna-flavoured cat food. He sniffed the air and licked his lips.

Theodore approached. He wolfed down the saucer of tuna. He purred with thanks as Craig walked over. He rubbed himself against Craig's trousers, wondering if there was any tuna left. He let Craig pick him up and hold him to his chest.

Craig was soon overcome by emotion and began to cry. He sobbed into the cat's fur.

'Oh, mummy,' he cried. The tears streamed down his face. 'Why are they doing this to me?'

Theodore remained limp for a whole minute before writhing himself loose and jumping up onto the top of the boundary wall.

He watched as Craig returned inside his house and locked the door behind him.

Before Theodore returned home, he checked up on Wendy Morris. She was baking again.

Theodore sniffed the air. He picked out the savoury smells.

Meat pies, he thought. I wonder what meat?

Then Irene came down the alley, pulled along by her dog Rocky straining at his lead.

A solitary magpie was perched on a television aerial near the bottom of the hill.

Irene spotted the black and white bird and raised a hand in salute. 'Good evening Mr Magpie,' she called. 'And how is your lady wife today?'

Irene knew that magpies paired for life. The solitary magpie was a widower; she didn't want to remind him of his loss. Yes, better to pretend, she said to herself.

Then she was dragged further down the alley by her dog.

Theodore looked across at the pigeon loft. He counted four pigeons. He glanced up at the sky and then the eaves of the house and the neighbouring houses.

Another pigeon had gone.

4

Friday evening Emily and Jonathan had their second date. They returned in the early hours, Jonathan carrying a small knapsack over his shoulder. While Emily was in the bathroom, Jonathan changed his t-shirt and put on a pair of pyjama bottoms.

In the following weeks Theodore noted a change in the household dynamics. It began with Emily spending a lot more time in the bathroom a couple of evenings a week before disappearing outside, leaving Theodore to his own devices.

Half the time she would return with Jonathan and they would have a bottle of wine before going upstairs. Their antics in the bedroom were not conducive to a good night's rest. One Sunday he wasn't fed until nearly midday. It was completely unacceptable.

Other nights Emily would go out and not return. On these nights Theodore busied himself with his investigations. He had the double bed to himself, but he missed Emily and slept with one ear listening out for her return.

Theodore did not like Jonathan; did not like it when he stayed over and did not like it when Emily did not return home.

It was a Wednesday night and Emily was speaking to Jonathan on the phone. He was working away in Cumbria. Theodore sat purring on her lap. Jonathan could stay in Cumbria for all he cared.

Emily was telling Jonathan how she had been applying for jobs in the centre of York. 'I can't stand that bloody ring road any longer,' she told him.

Outside a girl called out.

'I'll call you back later,' she told Jonathan.

She went upstairs and looked out of the back bedroom window. She saw a dark-haired girl, heavily pregnant, walking along the back alley.

Zeynep was calling for her missing cat Bal. She still hadn't given up hope that she would return, or that she would find her trapped in someone's shed or garage. Weeks had passed and the urgency of finding him had not lessened but increased as her pregnancy had advanced.

'Bal!' she called out. 'Come here, Bal.'

Emily opened her back gate and approached the other woman. 'Hi,' she said. 'I was wondering what you were shouting.'

'Bal,' Zeynep said. 'It means 'honey' in Turkish. She's one of my cats. I have two. They are sisters. But Bal has gone missing. I am trying to find her.'

'My cat goes missing for a few hours but he always comes back,' Emily said. 'I'm sure yours will too.'

'Bal's been gone for weeks now. I've put posters up. I've looked all over for her... I can't find her anywhere. But I know she is alive. Somewhere.'

'Can I help you look for her?' Emily offered.

'Yes, of course... Please.'

Emily found out that Zeynep's husband Ahmet worked as a taxi driver, working split shifts: mornings and evenings. For over an hour they walked the streets, calling out the missing cat's name and chatting together.

They cut through the allotments, skirted the racecourse and passed by the Knavesmire pub, then back down Queen Victoria Street.

Emily noticed that Zeynep had slowed down. 'Shall we turn back?' she suggested.

'Yes, okay.' Zeynep sighed. 'I am so worried about Bal. It's so unlike her to disappear. She has never gone missing before. Maybe she has been stolen.'

'I'm sure she hasn't been stolen.'

'Or something has happened to her.' Zeynep stopped walking. 'She might be dead.'

Opening her front door, Emily picked up a brown envelope that had been pushed through. She removed the contents. There were two sheets of A4 paper. A pink post-it note was stuck on the top one.

'Thought these might be useful,' her mother had written on the heart-shaped post-it note.

One photocopied sheet contained a breakdown of the Cabbage Soup Diet, the other the Dukan Diet.

Evidently her mother had noticed that she'd put on a bit of weight in the last few weeks, since Peter Morris's death. She went and put the papers into the recycling bin.

Back in the front room, she noticed the red LED on her telephone flashing, telling her someone had left her a message. She knew it would be her mother.

She played the message: 'Did you get the leaflets I left you,' her mother said. 'I thought they might be useful. I went to the library today...

'This new boyfriend of yours,' she went on, 'I hope you have done a full police background check on him. You never know these days... Especially with that murderer on the loose. Oh your father wants to say hello.'

'Hello', her father said. The answer phone beeped. Then there was just the silence of her front room.

The uneasiness in her stomach had become a general dissatisfaction with her life. She hated her job. She was now ill at ease in her own house, and did not even feel comfortable in her own skin. She finished the bottle of wine, poured herself a glass of water and went upstairs.

She lay in bed and thought of her neighbour who had been arrested for killing the pigeon man and later released. He was probably sleeping on the other side of her bedroom wall contemplating who he was going to kill next. She thought of the Turkish woman, Zeynep, and her missing cat, Bal. She thought of her own cat Theodore, who had been accused of eating a pigeon by Wendy Morris. She thought of Peter Morris, who had had his head bashed in.

She wished Jonathan was with her. She texted him: 'Hello, are you awake?' and when he didn't respond after ten minutes, she understood that he must be sleeping in his hotel room on the other side of the country. She turned over and began to cry into her pillow.

Theodore padded upstairs.

'Oh, Theo,' Emily said, when he'd settled on the pillow beside her. 'I can't help thinking that there is a murderer out there. He could kill again...'

Theodore tried to reassure her. I'll find out, he purred. I'll find the killer.

5

Theodore was sitting on the boundary wall of Michael's house, within a tangle of overgrown ivy. The sash window at the back of the house was open a couple of inches, and Theodore could hear classical music. Michael was working on his drawing.

Theodore watched as Michael added tiny pencil marks to an incredibly detailed sketch of the back alley, looking down from the top of the hill to the church at the bottom. He was now working on the clematis that hung over Theodore and Emily's back wall. He used the little wooden mallet as a rest, so that he wouldn't smudge his work. So that's what the mallet's for, thought Theodore.

Michael took a break. In the kitchen he poured himself a glass of green liquid. He winced as he swallowed the wheatgrass and Theodore winced with him.

Neither man nor cat was meant to eat greens, thought Theodore. They were only good for clearing out your digestive tract. Even dogs knew that. He watched as Michael drained the contents of the small glass, his face screwed up.

Michael turned and faced the kitchen window, his face still contorted. He spotted Theodore perched in the ivy and hissed through his teeth at the cat.

Theodore closed his eyes. The feeling was reciprocal.

He opened his eyes again when he heard a door slam.

Michael swore. A thick black pencil line now extended from the clematis down to the hexagonal cobblestones outlined in the foreground. He took a deep breath, snapped his pencil into two and threw both pieces at the wall.

'What's up?' Philip said, entering the room.

'Look what you've made me do.'

'Oh dear,' said Philip, surveying the picture. 'It'll rub out, won't it?'

'Yes,' Michael said. 'I think I can fix it. But do you have to slam the door every time you come in?'

'Sorry Mikey,' Philip said. He walked into the kitchen and opened the fridge. 'Who's going to buy a drawing of a back alley, anyway?'

'Somebody who appreciates art,' Michael said. 'That's who.'

'So how many of these pictures have you actually sold?'

'It's not all about money,' Michael said. 'If it were, I'd be a stockbroker or something, you know, in the City...'

'I just can't see you becoming famous drawing pictures of back alleys.'

'It's about seeing the beauty in the mundane,' Michael said.

'Mundane being the appropriate word,' Philip said, pouring a glass of milk.

'One day I will be appreciated. You wait... They will know who I am.'

'I saw a nice pair of trainers in town,' Philip said, changing the subject. 'Two hundred pounds though.' He sucked in air through his teeth.

'You've got a new pair of trainers,' Michael said, looking down at Philip's feet.

Philip was wearing a pair of bright red trainers.

'Yes, but these were yellow,' Philip said. 'I don't have a pair of yellow ones.'

'Do you need a pair of yellow ones?'

'Well, I don't *need* a pair of yellow trainers,' Philip said. 'I just thought they looked good. They would go with that silk shirt you bought me the other week...'

Philip sat down at the table in the lounge. He took a drink of milk. He looked out of the back window.

'Every time I come round here,' he said, a thin milk moustache on his top lip, 'I think about what happened that morning. That poor old man being killed. They still haven't caught him, have they?'

'No,' Michael said, his pencil poised above the paper. 'It was a terrible thing to happen.'

'Yes, terrible,' Philip said. He looked again out of the window, his eyes narrowed to slits. 'A terrible thing to happen.'

From within the ivy Theodore yawned. He was wasting his time investigating this pair. He couldn't imagine either of them hurting a fly, let alone a little old man

6

As any seasoned detective will tell you, surveillance work is tedious and tiring. The endless hours spent listening to conversations. Never knowing when something pertinent might slip from an unguarded mouth. Never knowing when a fragment of conversation may become relevant to the investigation later. The hours spent enduring the shifting weather. Not being able to slip home for a bite of food or sip of water for fear of missing a slip of the tongue.

It was essential but dull work.

Anyone passing would think that Theodore was just a cat sitting on a wall, and not a detective carrying out covert surveillance. He understood that this was what made him superior to the police. If a police officer was sitting on your back wall, staring at you through your kitchen window, you would probably have something to say.

Theodore jumped down into the back alley and up onto the top of the wall on the other side. Through the trellis he saw the pigeon loft, its white paintwork glistening in the spring sun.

He counted only three pigeons. They flitted in and out of their roosts, fluttered over the yard and rested on the eaves of the houses. There had been half a dozen. Now there were only three. They were restless.

What was happening to the pigeons? Theodore wondered.

Through the trellis he watched as Irene and Wendy ate dinner at the kitchen table. A radio on the kitchen windowsill was tuned to Minster FM. The women chewed on their food as the news headlines were read out.

New plans had been announced for the old Terry's chocolate factory, located to the south of Clementhorpe; alcohol-fuelled violence had erupted in York city centre following yesterday's horse racing, and finally a multiple pile up on the A64 was causing delays on the eastbound carriageway, back to Tadcaster.

There was no mention of Peter Morris's murder, noted Theodore. There had been no developments. Nothing new. It was no longer news.

Wendy stood up and approached the window. She turned off the radio and returned to her dinner.

'Who'd have thought it?' Irene said. 'They'll be building houses at Terry's.'

'Better than it being left derelict,' Wendy said.

'Aye,' Irene said. 'It's been closed a few years now.'

'I knew the factory would close as soon as they stopped making them chocolate oranges,' Wendy said. 'It was only a matter of time.'

'Aye,' Irene agreed. 'It was only a matter of time.'

Irene's husband had been forced into redundancy before he'd reached sixty, after the production of chocolate oranges had moved to Poland. Too old to find another job, he'd idled around the house for a few months before breathing his last during a particularly eventful *Crimewatch*.

After they had finished their tea, Wendy took their mugs to the sink, and adding them to the greasy plates, filled the sink with hot water. She pulled on her pink rubber gloves. She took the chicken carcass from the fridge and, with the aid of a small, sharp knife, began to strip the remaining meat from the carcass. She added the chicken meat to a plastic margarine tub on the side. She then slid the carcass into her kitchen bin. She began to wash the dishes.

'So the police are no closer to finding out who did it?' Irene asked.

'There's no new leads,' Wendy said, her back to Irene. 'That's what they told me.'

'When they found the murder weapon I thought that would be it.'

'Maybe it *was* that Craig Foster. But there was no evidence to place him at the scene,' Wendy said. 'And no motive.'

'Sometimes people don't need a motive,' Irene said. 'They kill for the sake of it. There are some strange ones about these days.'

'Yes,' agreed Wendy.

'Whoever did it must have planned it,' Irene said. 'That's why they couldn't find any fingerprints. They would have worn gloves.'

Wendy Morris turned round. Suds fell from her pink rubber gloves onto the linoleum floor.

Theodore stared at the pink clad hands which continued to drip suds onto the floor. Had Wendy clobbered her husband wearing those pink rubber gloves?

'I think it's time for our soap,' Wendy said.

Theodore got to his paws and stretched. He walked along the wall. Ahead of him a stocky black cat blocked his path. Theodore stopped in his tracks and held the other cat's stare for a moment.

They knew each other by sight. They knew each other by scent. They were enemies, and always would be. Arthur, the black cat, was not going to make way for Theodore.

Arthur looked across at the remaining pigeons. He looked at Theodore.

Arthur was an unneutered tom. Like all civilized cats Theodore was neutered. He looked on Arthur as some sort of primitive species, driven by baser instincts. As Theodore held the intellectual high ground, he understood enough to make way for this coarse feline.

Theodore jumped down onto the cobbles of the back alley and padded towards his own house. Without turning round, he jumped up onto his back wall and a second later was back within the safety of his own territory.

From the front of the house he heard Emily's Beetle pull to an abrupt stop. A few seconds later he was at the front door, ready to greet her.

7

Ahmet Akbulut had a hobby. In the afternoons between his morning and evening shifts, he built miniature Ottoman houses.

Almost all of the elegant old timber houses back in his hometown of Zonguldak, on the Black Sea coast, had been burned down or bulldozed, only to be replaced by nondescript concrete apartment blocks, two to four storeys high.

As a boy he had dreamed of becoming an architect and reviving traditional forms of domestic building. But then he'd had to go out to work at fourteen, after his father's ill health meant he could no longer work at the local coal mine. Ahmet had left school and abandoned his dream.

But not quite.

In the intricate models he built in the spare bedroom, soon to be a nursery, his dream survived. At the moment, he was building a doll's house. He secretly hoped his wife was carrying a girl.

In the afternoons, he glued matchsticks to matchsticks with balsa cement, cut rectangular holes for windows in corrugated cardboard walls, and, with his trusty craft knife, cut out finger-nail-shaped roof tiles from thin sheets of balsa wood.

On six separate shelves in the back bedroom were six completed miniature Ottoman houses. Each house had taken him a year to construct. They represented six years of working in England: first delivering fast food for a pizza outlet and then as a taxi driver. Each month he sent money back to his family in Turkey.

When the baby arrived he would have to find somewhere else to build his houses, Zeynep had warned him; the table where he now worked would be for nappy changing. He would put a window into the sloping shed roof, he thought, gazing out across the yard and catching the stare of a large grey fluffy cat sitting on the back wall.

Theodore noticed Ahmet look up from his work and out of the window. Most times he looked in the same direction. To a house on the other side, a little further up the hill.

Zeynep carried a laundry basket out into the yard. Belle followed a moment later and lay down on the concrete, as Zeynep hung out the clothes to dry.

After a minute, she turned to the window of the back bedroom. 'Ahmet!' she shouted up.

'Yes, dear,' Ahmet shouted down.

'Have you been stealing my pegs?'

'Pegs? No, dear. What would I want with your pegs?'

He looked across the table to the shoebox where he stockpiled his materials. Inside he had acquired several wooden pegs that he was going to transform into a peg family. He had already drawn on faces and hair with a permanent marker. He had also swiped a couple of pairs of black lace knickers from Zeynep's underwear drawer. She hadn't noticed, as she hadn't been able to fit into them for some time. Ahmet planned to create a black silk dress for the peg grandmother and aunties. But he'd shied away from the task, thinking it may well be beyond his capabilities.

He turned his attention back to the balsa wood tiles and cut out another half dozen. He hoped to have one side of a roof tiled before he started his evening shift. His mobile beeped from within his jeans pocket. He read the message and, smiling to himself, looked outside.

Theodore followed his stare and noticed a pair of blue satin curtains twitch.

Ahmet responded to the text, replaced his mobile in his jeans, and then picked up his tube of balsa cement once more. But before he could glue another tile onto the roof, Zeynep shouted up at him once more, her voice edgier and higher pitched.

'Yes, dear?' he called down.

'Get down here now!'

As Ahmet came out of the back door, Theodore saw that Zeynep was holding up a pair of white underpants.

'What are these? she said, waving the pants at Ahmet.

'My underpants?' Ahmet said, palms outstretched.

'No, these?'

She plucked at the pants. In her fingers she held a pinch of short black hairs.

Ahmet looked at the hairs. 'They are little black hairs,' he said. 'So? I have black hair. They are my little hairs. Is it an offence to leave some little hairs in my underpants?'

'It's fur. Not hair,' Zeynep said. 'I do know the difference.'

'We have cats, don't we? It is just a bit of cat fur. Gets everywhere.'

'We have Belle,' Zeynep said. 'But she is not black. If you hadn't noticed.'

'What are you accusing me of?'

'I want to know how you got black fur on your underpants when we don't have a black cat.'

'Please, Zeynep,' Ahmet said. 'It is all in your head. Hormones because of the baby.'

Zeynep swore, then kicked over the laundry basket, sending its damp contents spilling onto the ground. Then she marched back inside the house, slamming the door behind her.

Ahmet picked up the basket and finished hanging out the washing – running out of pegs before he had finished.

Theodore watched him from the back wall. In the back bedroom window he spotted Belle looking down at Ahmet.

Then he sensed another presence. He turned round, and further up the hill, on the other side of the alley, he was met by Arthur's amber stare. Arthur was sitting on the back wall of the house with the blue satin curtains. It was his house.

The black cat did not blink instead its stare bore into Theodore.

Theodore looked away, down the hill.

How had Arthur's fur got on Ahmet's underpants? he wondered.

8

From on top of the chest in the bay window, Theodore could see to the end of the street. He spied Wendy crossing the road, on her way to the shops; her shopping trolley bumping along behind. Theodore glanced at the DVD player on the shelf below the television. 14:24.

At 15.07 he spotted Irene being pulled across the road by Rocky. Ahmet pulled away in his taxi at 16.15 to begin his evening shift. At 17.07 Craig Foster glided to a halt on his bicycle in front of his house. He glanced up and down the street before unlocking his door and pushing his bicycle inside.

Tuna time, Theodore thought.

He got to his paws, stretched and a minute later exited the cat flap.

Craig Foster usually arrived home before Emily by about twenty minutes. Before he met Theodore he'd only gone into his back garden on a Tuesday to put out his rubbish when he remembered, which wasn't very often. But now after arriving home each day, he opened the backdoor and took out a saucer of tuna for his neighbour's cat.

Theodore rubbed against Craig's legs, letting himself be patted on the head before wolfing down the tuna.

Craig took his tuna sandwich to the back room, where he sat at the table and ate it in the semi dark. After his sandwich, he went to the bathroom where he remained for ten minutes.

Theodore continued his search of Craig's house while Craig was in the bathroom. He'd searched most of the house but had yet to find anything to incriminate Craig with Peter Morris's murder. Not even a pigeon feather.

However, Theodore knew Craig was lying about one thing. He knew that he was not as interested in stargazing as he had made out to the police. If he hadn't been looking up at the stars, what had he been looking at?

He climbed the stairs in seconds and paused on the landing. The curtains in the bedrooms were permanently closed but the bathroom door was ajar and light leaked in through frosted glass. Yesterday Theodore had searched the bathroom: an unpleasant task he was glad to get over.

He went up the stairs to the attic room. Magazines and papers lay scattered across grey carpet tiles, many of which lay open to display photographs of the human anatomy, focussing primarily on the sexual organs. Theodore arched his eyebrows and continued his search.

There was a desk against the chimney breast on which sat a computer monitor, its screen blank. The computer stood on the floor beside the desk and whirred quietly to itself. A black metal waste paper bin, overflowing with used tissues stood next to the computer. Empty tissue boxes and toilet rolls lay scattered across the floor.

Human behaviour sometimes bemused Theodore; sometimes it just saddened him. He decided against a detailed examination of the contents of the bin.

He jumped up onto the desk and stood in front of the monitor. He dabbed at the mouse which sat next to the keyboard. Suddenly the screen sprang to life. *'SPANKING TIME!'* the website shouted in fat pink letters.

Three young females crouched in a row, their rear ends raised.

As a kitten Theodore had raised his behind to allow his mother to inspect his nether regions, an honour he now bestowed on his human Emily from time to time. However, he doubted Craig's interest in behinds was hygiene related.

A chair in the middle of the room faced a Velux window, set into the sloping roof. In front of the chair a telescope was attached to a tripod.

Theodore remembered Craig's astrological slip to the police officer when they were taking him away for questioning. He noted that the telescope was not pointing up towards the sky but below the horizon. He jumped across onto the chair seat and then up onto the back of the chair. Balancing on the thin chair back, he lined up his sight with the telescope. He made out the back bedroom window of a house on the other side of the alley, a few houses further up. The window had blue satin curtains.

Theodore noted that the curtains were halfway between open and closed, and the window was open a couple of inches at the bottom. From within the darkened room a pair of amber eyes stared back at him.

Downstairs the toilet flushed. Theodore jumped down from the chair and raced downstairs.

When Craig emerged from the toilet Theodore was by the door, licking the empty saucer. Craig picked him up and hugged him to his chest. 'See you tomorrow, little man,' he said.

He put Theodore back down and picked up the saucer.

He gave Theodore a little wave before going back into his house, closing and locking the backdoor behind him. He would not leave his house again until the next morning.

Theodore jumped up onto the boundary wall. He looked across at the houses opposite.

He understood that Craig was not interested in astronomy, but was undertaking his own surveillance. But why?

From the front of the house, Theodore heard Emily park her car. Michael Jackson came to an abrupt end ('Just to tell you once again, who's bad...'), and the car door slammed shut. At least she was in a good mood, he thought, jumping down into his yard.

Emily picked him up with a smile and gave him a hug. Then she held him up in front of her so he faced her. Her brow creased.

He blinked hello, purring loudly.

'Imperial Leather,' she said.

Theodore was confused.

'Carbolic soap,' she explained, pulling him closer. 'You smell of carbolic soap and...'

She inhaled deeply.

'Tuna!'

Theodore tried to wriggle free.

She held onto him tightly. 'Someone's been feeding you, haven't they?' she said. 'I wonder... 'Who still uses Imperial Leather?'

Theodore struggled in her grasp.

'Someone who uses carbolic soap has been feeding you tuna,' she said, her eyes wide.

There was nothing wrong with Emily's powers of deduction, thought Theodore. Perhaps he'd underestimated her, he thought, as he was dropped to the floor.

9

Theodore watched from the front window as she marched up the street; she was going to be gone some time. He exited through the cat flap and a few seconds later approached Wendy Morris's house.

Arthur was sitting in Theodore's preferred surveillance location, behind the trellis fence. Theodore jumped up onto the wall on the opposite side of the alley. He counted two pigeons, both perched up on the gutter. From this side of the back alley, Theodore could not see into the kitchen. He paced the wall with agitation.

At least he knew where Arthur was, he thought; now might be a good time to check up on his house and find out why Craig's telescope was pointing at the window with the blue curtains.

He jumped back down into the alley and trotted up the hill, his tail held aloft. He kept going past his own house until he was facing the house with the blue satin curtains. He glanced down the alleyway and saw in the distance Arthur's black silhouette. He was still watching the pigeons.

Theodore jumped up onto the back wall of Arthur's house. He glanced back down the hill but could not see the black cat from this position. He made his way along the boundary wall towards the house, his ears folded back, tail held straight up. He was in enemy territory.

Below him was an overgrown raised garden area that Arthur apparently used as his toilet; Theodore noted that he wasn't one to cover. The rest of the yard was concreted over. It looked like Arthur's owner did not sweep the yard often, if at all.

Theodore jumped down and began to examine a mound of brown mulch in a drain.

He fished out a feather with his paw. It might be a pigeon feather. It might be from Peter Morris's prize pigeon, Ethel, or one of the others that had disappeared. But then again it might just have blown in. He surveyed the raised garden area but didn't venture in. He would return and search the yard in more detail later, he decided.

He glanced up at the window with the blue curtains. He jumped back onto the boundary wall, then onto the felted roof of the extension. He made his way across the flat roof; then jumped up onto the bedroom windowsill.

He looked back across the yard, to the houses opposite; he wondered if Craig had his telescope trained on him at that moment.

The sash window was still open a couple of inches and from inside Theodore made out the moans and groans of human copulation. The smell of sex mixed with musky aftershave came from the room.

He edged along the windowsill and peered into the dark room. It was as he had suspected: Ahmet lay on top of Arthur's owner.

Theodore recognized the woman. She was the blue Fiat driver who had almost run him over.

Diane Banks's face was turned towards the window, her mouth parted. But in the gloom of the bedroom Theodore did not know if she was looking at him, past him or just staring into space. Meanwhile Ahmet pounded away on top of her. After a short while, the two bodies lay still. A minute later Diane lit a cigarette.

'I am worried,' Ahmet said, still catching his breath. 'Zeynep... She suspects.'

'She doesn't know anything,' Diane said, blowing out smoke.

'I tell you – she found black cat hairs in my underpants.'

'Just roller them before you go home, darling.'

'Then there was the old man,' Ahmet said. 'Peter Morris... He saw me coming out of the back gate.'

Theodore's ears pricked up at the mention of Peter.

'Big deal,' Diane said. 'He's dead. Dead men don't talk...'

'He said to me... I know what you've been up to.'

'So you killed him?' Diane laughed.

'It is not a joking matter,' Ahmet said. 'He knew... He knew about us. And if he knew, maybe he told others. He might have told his wife. You know what people are like... Zeynep must not know about us.'

Diane stubbed out her cigarette. 'Don't worry so much,' she said. 'Nobody will find out.'

'I am worried,' Ahmet said again. 'Maybe we shouldn't see each other for some time.'

'You don't mean that,' Diane said, reaching under the duvet.

'Zeynep,' Ahmet said. 'She is suspicious.'

'Don't worry about your little wife,' Diane said. She ducked under the duvet, and a minute later her head began to bob up and down.

Ahmet began to groan, his head bent into the pillow.

Theodore turned and jumped back down onto the felted flat roof of the extension; he had seen enough.

Then he noticed Arthur on the rear wall. The black cat's back was arched, his fur bristling. His baleful stare met Theodore's.

Theodore jumped down onto the boundary wall and Arthur proceeded along the back wall to cut off his escape.

The cats stopped a few feet apart.

Theodore jumped down into the yard.

Arthur jumped down too. He stood opposite Theodore. His tail swished from side to side.

Theodore retreated towards the house. He crouched down, his eyes half closed, ears flattened to the side of his head. The tip of his tail tapped the ground. Should he flee or make a stand?

Arthur advanced, growling.

Theodore growled back and arched his tail.

He turned sideways and arched his back to look bigger. His pupils dilated. His fur stood on end.

Arthur took a step towards him.

Theodore bared his teeth and hissed.

Then Arthur launched himself at Theodore.

Theodore rolled onto his back, all four legs out, claws extended. Ready. Then he kicked out with his hind legs as Arthur landed on him.

10

Theodore was woken by an angel. Her bright blue eyes stared into his. Her nose was a pale pink T. She was surrounded by the golden aura cast by a street light further up the back alley. She licked at his face, like his mother had once done.

As his eyes focussed, he noticed she had a tabby face. An angel with a tabby face, he thought: he must be dreaming.

He closed his eyes, trying to remember what had happened. When he opened them again, the angelic tabby-faced cat was still there, slowly coming into focus.

It's time to go home, she purred softly.

Home?

Yes. It's time that you went home, she purred. *You need to rest. You had a fight... Don't you remember?*

Of course the angel cat did not actually speak to Theodore, the way that humans do. She conveyed her meaning through purring, her eyes and the gentle movements of her tongue as it glided over his fur.

Theodore tried to raise himself from the ground but his back legs were too weak. He remembered the fight with Arthur, his back legs kicking and pushing the black cat away, not allowing his opponent the opportunity to get at his neck.

He remembered the other cat's teeth fastening on his ear, then pulling, the cartilage tearing. Arthur chewing on the gristly morsel. Then Theodore fleeing over the wall, down into the back alley. Arthur chasing him, his mouth red with Theodore's blood. Running blindly towards home. Arthur catching up. Jumping up onto a back wall. Then a mighty blow to his side and falling...

It was night but the moon was almost full. Belle the Birman cat licked his face.

How long had he been lying there?

On one side of him there was a brick wall; on the other the side of a shed. He must be in the Turkish couple's yard, he realised.

He tried to get to his feet again and this time managed, his limbs aching from the fight. He walked a few trembling yards.

There was a cat flap at the bottom of the gate. He turned and blinked goodbye to Belle before exiting into the back alley.

He staggered down the alley until he was at his own gate. He didn't have the strength to jump up onto the back wall. He miaowed at the gate hoping that Emily would hear. He waited but she didn't come. He rested and then miaowed again.

He lay on the ground in front of the gate. He could smell the safety of his own yard but couldn't enter it.

He listened to the hustle and bustle of other cats going about their business. He heard the wail of a female in heat. The rustle of leaves as another cat followed the trail of a mouse. The soft padding of a thousand paws in the night. He closed his eyes.

What had he achieved this evening besides being beaten up by a thug of a cat?

He'd discovered that a middle-aged divorcee was having an affair with a Turkish taxi driver. He'd discovered that Craig Foster liked to watch them have sexual intercourse through his telescope.

But what did any of that have to do with who killed Peter Morris and who or what was taking his pigeons?

As night began to turn to the grey of morning and the birds began to call out for the dawn to come, he stirred from his spot by the gate. He jumped up onto the top of the back wall and made his way to his back door. His whole body trembled, from his whiskers to the tip of his tail.

He paused in the kitchen. Snoring was coming from the front room.

Emily was lying on the sofa. An empty bottle of Chardonnay stood beside a wine glass on the table.

Emily woke some hours later. She glanced at the clock on the mantelpiece, then at her wristwatch. She picked Theodore up from her stomach and put him on the floor. Then she swung herself round.

She turned to Theodore. She took a quick breath. 'Oh, my God. What happened to you?'

Theodore remembered that he'd lost part of his ear in the fight with Arthur. A triangle was missing from the middle. The upper part of what remained was now folded down over itself. What was left of the lower part was a mess of cartilage, fur and scab.

'Pooh sticks,' Emily said. She picked Theodore up. 'We're going to the vet's.'

11

Theodore heard Jonathan's footsteps on the pavement outside. Then there were his familiar three sharp knocks on the door.

'I wasn't expecting you so early,' Emily said, opening the door.

'I got off work early for once,' Jonathan said. 'Thought I'd surprise you.' He walked into the house and bent down to give her a kiss.

Theodore exited the cat flap. In the yard he circled the bin. It was galvanized steel and even if he managed to push it over, it would make such a clatter, Emily would be out of the house in seconds. Grey cloud gathered over the yard.

He felt cheated. Life would be so much better if Jonathan wasn't around. He schemed silently, dreaming up ways of annoying the intruder to the point he would give up on Emily and find someone without the complications. Someone without a cat...

People want a simple life, Theodore philosophised. They just don't realise it.

'I wish I could lie in bed all day,' Emily had told him on more than one occasion.

Well, why don't you? Theodore thought back.

All this rushing around, sitting in cars in traffic jams, going to jobs that you don't even like, just so you have the money to pay for the fuel to get to work and the sandwich you cram into your mouth in the ten minute lunch break (if you're lucky), and then driving home, where you fritter away your money online on products which you don't need. People needed to do less, Theodore concluded; they just didn't realise it.

As long as he continued to annoy Jonathan, Theodore reasoned, it was only a matter of time until he signed back on that dating website and found someone else. Then it would be Theodore and Emily again. It was only a matter of time.

He returned inside. Jonathan's rucksack was at the foot of the stairs. Evidently he was planning to stay over. He raised his rear end and shot a jet of urine over the bag. Then he went outside again.

On the table in front of the back window, Michael had lit candles. In the kitchen Theodore watched as Michael tapped purplish red steaks with his little wooden mallet.

It was Philip's birthday and Michael was cooking him a special meal. Philip's present was waiting on the table. A cube wrapped carefully in pink crepe paper.

Philip walked in. 'Bit dark in here,' he said, flicking on the lights.

Michael walked over to the table and blew out the candles, sending wisps of smoke into the air.

'Oh, candles,' Philip said. 'I didn't realise. Sorry.'

'Never mind,' Michael said. 'I got you a little present.'

Philip tore open the cube. 'A new watch,' he said, his voice not trying to hide his disappointment. He opened the box and removed the grey Swatch. 'I really wanted a Rolex,' he said, putting the watch back in its display case.

'It will go with your shirt,' Michael said. 'The shirt I bought you last week. Grey's all the rage at the moment...'

Philip shrugged. 'If you say so,' he said.

Theodore yawned. Why Michael put up with Philip was beyond his comprehension. He jumped down into the alley and then back up the other side, on top of Wendy Morris's wall.

Wendy and Irene had just finished dinner.

'I never knew you were keen on pizza,' he heard Irene say.

'Peter never liked foreign food,' Wendy said. 'He would never try anything new. Now he's not here, I thought I'd have a go at something a bit different.'

'Well, I've had a few pizzas in my time,' Irene went on, 'but roast beef and peas are new toppings on me.' She laughed.

'Just using up a few bits,' Wendy said.

She took their plates over to the kitchen sink and dumped them into the water.

Zeynep entered the alley further up the hill. She began shouting for her cat. She walked down the alley, a thin coat buttoned over her bulging belly.

She hadn't yet given up on Bal, Theodore realised. He jumped down from the wall and followed behind Zeynep. They exited the access alley and out onto the next street.

Zeynep paused on the pavement, in front of Diane's house. A taxi was parked outside. Ahmet's taxi.

She took her mobile phone from her coat pocket. She pressed the touch screen and then held the phone to her ear.

A moment later a faint tune could be heard from within the house. Zeynep thrust the mobile phone back into her pocket.

She marched back into the alley. She didn't stop until she reached her own gate.

Theodore followed her as far as her yard. He took up a position on the back wall. He spied Belle sitting on the kitchen table.

Zeynep went straight up to the back bedroom. She swept the unfinished Ottoman dolls house from the table with her forearm. She stamped on its roof. She grabbed the shoebox and emptied its contents onto the floor.

'Pervert! she screamed, spying a pair of her black lace knickers.

She pulled the completed models from the shelves around the room and stamped on them, balsa wood crumpling beneath her shoes.

She came back downstairs and paced the kitchen. She took her mobile phone from her pocket again and began to jab at the screen.

She pressed the phone to her ear.

'Hello... Yes... Police...,' she said.

A few seconds went by.

'Hello. Yes... Is that the police? Yes.'

Another silence and then: 'I have information about the Clementhorpe murder... My husband. He was very late coming home that night... And when he did, he washed his clothing... It is very unlike him to wash his own clothes. Especially late at night...'

Theodore's ears twitched.

'I think he is acting differently since what happened... His name? It is Ahmet. Ahmet Akbulut. He works for Crow Line taxis.'

There was a pause.

Then: 'He is at work now. Crow Line taxis. His car is white. A white Toyota Avensis.

And then: 'You should know he has a temper.'

Theodore's brow furrowed. Ahmet? A liar and a cheat perhaps, but a murderer?

He jumped down from the wall and trotted back round to where Ahmet's taxi was parked in front of Diane's house.

He sat below the still warm engine and waited for the police to arrive. He didn't have to wait long.

12

The police had knocked on Diane's door following Zeynep's phone call and had taken Ahmet back to Fulford Police Station for questioning. They had kept him in custody overnight. In the morning they'd collected Zeynep and then shortly afterwards Diane.

'I was out with Rocky,' Irene said. 'Diane was still wearing her nightgown when they took her away. They must have got her out of bed...'

'You'd have thought they'd have let her get dressed,' Wendy said.

'I wonder what she has to do with it,' Irene said.

'She had a thing for that taxi driver,' Wendy said. 'Peter told me about them. He'd seen him coming out of her back gate one evening.'

'Did he now? They took away some bin bags from the Turkish couple's. I reckon they were his clothes. Evidence, you know.'

'But why would he want to harm Peter?' Wendy asked. 'They didn't even know each other.' She was standing in front of the kitchen window, rolling out dough. Her navy blue apron was grey across her bosom from decades of flour and grease. She'd had her greying hair dyed red that morning. It looked more carroty than she'd hoped.

'There must be something in it,' Irene said. 'They wouldn't have taken him in for no reason now, would they?'

'No, I suppose not.'

Wendy laid the dough into a pie dish and thumbed the edges.

'But why would he want to harm Peter?' she said again.

From the back wall of Wendy's yard, Theodore also pondered this question. Peter Morris had known that Ahmet was sleeping with Diane. Had Ahmet killed Peter Morris because he knew about the affair? He could have used the pretext of asking after the missing cat, and when Peter had opened the gate, Ahmet had clobbered him.

Theodore looked across at the pigeon loft. One solitary bird perched on its roof. He inspected the sky for its companions but there was none. He turned his attention back to the kitchen window and saw Wendy washing dishes at the kitchen sink.

'Have you heard from Laura?' Irene asked. 'Since the funeral.'

'No,' Wendy said. 'Not a peep.'

'Such a shame,' Irene said. 'If I were you, I'd be round there. He's your grandchild, you know.'

'It's all because of what happened between her and Peter... They never saw eye to eye... But Peter was set in his ways. He had his opinions and he stuck to them.'

'I know that,' Irene said bluntly. 'But Peter's not around anymore. You have a chance to set things right. You have a beautiful grandson. You don't want to miss out on that...'

Then Theodore sensed another animal approach. He turned to see Arthur padding along the back alley, his tail up straight. The black cat stopped directly below Theodore and miaowed up at him. It was an order: 'Get out of the way or else!'

Theodore backed away, further down the wall.

Arthur jumped up onto the wall and took up Theodore's spot, behind the barbed wire topped trellis that surrounded the Morris's yard. He hadn't eaten that morning. Diane had been whisked off to the police station to be interviewed before she'd had chance to feed him.

Theodore watched as he eyed the last remaining pigeon, the tip of his tongue showing.

He doesn't have a chance, Theodore thought, watching as Arthur paced backwards and forwards, up and down the length of wall.

The eighteen-inch-high trellis was fixed in the middle of the wall, a slight gap on either side. Arthur paced on the outside of the trellis. He went beyond the Morris's yard, towards Theodore, who retreated further along the wall.

Then Arthur began to run towards Wendy Morris's yard. When he reached the trellis he jumped two feet into the air before landing on the inside of the trellis, three yards further along.

Theodore blinked in astonishment. Arthur was inside the Morris's yard.

The black cat stalked up and down along the wall, his eyes fixed on the pigeon, his ears folded flat.

The pigeon launched itself into the air and flapped about the yard. It was making for the safety of the loft when Arthur jumped. They met in mid-air. Arthur's teeth sunk into the bird's nape. By the time they hit the ground, the bird was dead. Arthur shook it for good measure.

He turned around, the bird held firmly in his mouth, looking for an escape.

The stepladder Peter Morris had used to clean out the pigeon loft was leant against the back wall. Arthur was soon up the ladder and back on top of the wall, the dead pigeon clasped in his mouth. He paced along the wall once more. Then, breaking into a run, he jumped into the air.

Then Theodore saw Wendy Morris out in her yard, rolling pin in hand. She raised the wooden cylinder, then threw it.

It flipped through the air before cracking Arthur's skull.

Arthur landed in the back alley with a soft thud. The pigeon dropped a few feet away. The rolling pin landed a moment later.

Theodore saw a small pool of blood begin to form on the cobbles around Arthur's head. He heard a bolt being pulled and then slippered steps across the cobblestones.

He hurried further along the wall seeking the cover of an overgrown privet hedge. When he turned, he saw Wendy leaning over the dead cat.

She picked him up and carried him at arm's length into her yard. Arthur hung limp. A moment later she returned with a sheet of newspaper for the pigeon.

Theodore listened as the back gate was bolted behind her. He looked up and down the back alley. There was no one... No one to have witnessed the felinicide.

He approached Wendy's yard, stopping short of the trellis. He glanced at the splash of blood on the cobbles and the few flecks from the pigeon a few feet away.

Theodore had not been friends with Arthur but he would never wish such a brutal end to one of his own kind.

Arthur had been acting in accordance with his baser instinct. He hadn't been fed that morning. He'd been hungry. Food had presented itself in the form of a pigeon. He had risked his life in killing the bird and, as a result, he was dead. Arthur had taken a gamble, Theodore thought, and had lost.

Theodore looked down into the yard. Arthur lay on the concrete beneath the pigeon loft. On the chimney of the Morris house a crow cawed out the death.

Wendy was in the outbuilding. She came out with a bucket and mop.

Irene was standing by the back door. 'I can't believe you've gone and killed Diane's cat,' she said, clucking her tongue.

'Well, I did,' Wendy said. 'It had one of his birds.'

'But you killed Diane's cat...'

Wendy pushed past Irene and filled the bucket at the kitchen sink.

'Those cats are always killing things,' she said.

'Diane thought the world of that cat,' Irene said.

'I didn't *mean* to kill him,' Wendy said. 'I only meant to scare him off.'

She turned off the kitchen tap. She went out the back door carrying her plastic bucket of soapy water.

Irene followed. 'I'd better be getting along,' she said. 'I need to take Rocky out for his walk.'

'Don't you go telling to Diane about this,' Wendy said.

Irene didn't respond. She hurried down the back alley to her own gate.

Theodore watched as Wendy washed the cobbles of blood.

Then she went back inside her house. She took a bin bag from a kitchen drawer. She came outside again and pushed Arthur's body inside the bin bag. Then she went back inside.

A few minutes later Theodore watched as Wendy Morris pulled her shopping trolley along the back alley.

Theodore looked back down into the yard. There was a dark stain where Arthur had been. He jumped down into the alley. He raced out into the street. He spied Wendy, her shopping trolley bumping along behind her, as she turned onto Scarcroft Road. Then she disappeared from sight.

He raced down Alcuin Terrace and spotted Wendy hurrying along the road. Then she disappeared.

When he arrived at the spot where she'd disappeared, he noticed a gate set into the hedge. He ducked under and began to pad along the path that extended up through the allotments.

Wendy was further up the path, dragging the shopping trolley along behind her over the rough ground.

Theodore trotted behind, keeping to the sides of the path. Several times she glanced behind her but Theodore darted into the undergrowth.

Wendy stopped in a small clearing beside a large mound of decomposing grass clippings. Theodore watched as she undid a zip and took from her shopping trolley the black bin bag. She made a hole in the brown mulch and pushed the bag inside. Then she pushed the moulding grass back over. A moment later she continued along the path, over Scarcroft Hill towards the Knavesmire.

Theodore approached the mound. He inspected the place where she'd replaced the brown grass. Then he dug out the grass with his front paws, sending it flying behind him. He soon exposed the black bin liner. With a claw he split the thin black plastic.

A lifeless amber eye stared back at him.

13

Jonathan was watching television while Emily was upstairs having a bath.

Suddenly Theodore darted in, carrying a plastic bag in his mouth. He rolled over, wrapping the bag around himself.

'What an earth are you up to?' Jonathan said, removing his feet from the table. 'Don't you know it's dangerous to play with plastic bags?'

Theodore rolled onto his back, paws in the air, the plastic bag below him.

Arthur's been killed by Wendy, wrapped in a bin liner and buried in the allotments, he wanted to say.

Jonathan lent over. He pulled the plastic bag from beneath the cat. 'You want your tummy tickling, Theo?' he said, digging his fingers into Theodore's stomach.

Theodore got to his feet and exited the front room.

Jonathan put his feet back up on the coffee table and tried to watch his programme again. But a minute later he heard a miaow from outside. He stood up and went over to the front window. He saw Theodore sitting on the front wall. He returned to the sofa, determined to watch his programme.

Theodore miaowed again. He miaowed as loudly as he could. It was some minutes before Jonathan's face appeared again at the window.

He jumped down and marched into the middle of the road. He stretched out on the warm tarmac. It was not a busy street but it wouldn't be too long before a car came.

He heard Jonathan shouting up to the bathroom: 'Your cat's in the road.'

Theodore did not hear Emily's muffled response, but a moment later the front door opened and Jonathan appeared, shaking his head.

Theodore stood up and began to walk down the middle of the street, between the parked cars, his tail held up behind him.

'Do you have a death wish?' Jonathan asked Theodore's retreating fluffy rear end.

He began to follow Theodore down the middle of Avondale Terrace, calling his name. He broke into a short sprint in an attempt to grab him, but Theodore was too quick for him.

Theodore turned left at the bottom of the street and waited for Jonathan to catch up with him. As soon as he saw Jonathan rounding the corner, he trotted ahead, turning every once in a while to make sure he was still being followed.

Twenty minutes later Theodore led Jonathan back to the house. In his arms he carried Arthur, still partly wrapped in the bin liner.

The front door had been left open while they'd been gone. Emily now stood in the doorway, her wet hair tied back.

'Where have you two been?' she said. 'I was worried.'

'Scarcroft Allotments,' Jonathan said. 'Theodore wanted to show me something.'

He held up the black bag and grimaced.

'What is it?'

He opened the bag to show her the dead cat. 'It looks like he's been whacked over the head,' he said, pointing to the black fur matted with blood.

Theodore circled his legs. He's not so stupid after all, he thought.

'Why have you brought a dead cat in here?' Emily suddenly shouted. 'If you think you are going to bring that thing into my house, you've got another thing coming.'

'But your cat led me to it,' he said. 'I think someone's killed it.'

'I don't want a dead cat in my house!'

'I found it in the allotments,' Jonathan went on. 'It doesn't have a collar... Somebody must have killed it and hid it in the allotments.'

'Don't be stupid,' Emily said, hands on hips. 'It'll have been knocked down by a car and crawled into the allotments to die. Cats do that...'

'But it was in a bin liner.'

'Maybe the car driver put it in a bin liner and hid it in the allotments rather than owning up to it... I just don't want a dead cat in my house.'

'Well,' Jonathan said, holding the bag out in front of him, 'what do you suggest I do with it?'

'I don't care what you do with it. Just get it out of here.'

The black cat Jonathan had found in the allotments had reminded him of his own cat that had died the year before. Perhaps that was why he had not hesitated to pick it up. He didn't mention this to Emily. He shook his head.

Theodore stared up at him. What are you going to do now? his eyes asked.

'I'll take it back to mine and bury it,' Jonathan said, matter-of-factly. 'I'll be back later and then we can go out and get something to eat.'

'Sounds like a plan,' Emily said. 'It'll give me time to dry my hair.'

As soon as the front door had closed behind Jonathan, Emily went upstairs, and Theodore heard the whir of the hairdryer. He padded through the dining room and back out into the yard.

He jumped onto the back wall of his yard and looked down into the alley. The blue cobbles looked polished where Wendy had washed them of blood. He pondered the scene a moment. The rolling pin!

Wendy had removed the dead cat. She had come back for the pigeon. But what had happened to the rolling pin?

He replayed Arthur's last seconds. The moment the rolling pin hit Arthur's head with a crack. Wood on bone. Arthur hitting the ground with a soft thud. The hollow sound of the rolling pin landing and then another hollow noise as it bounced off down the alley.

The rolling pin had bounced, then rolled down the hill, Theodore concluded.

He looked down the alley. The rolling pin was nowhere to be seen. He jumped down.

Each house had a gate recessed into the back wall. The rolling pin must have rolled down the hill and come to rest against a gate.

Theodore trotted down the alley, inspecting each gateway in turn. He was almost at the bottom when he spotted the rolling pin lying flush against a gate.

With his front paws he rolled it back out into the middle of the alley and then up the hill towards home. Murderers always miss something, he reflected, as he patted the rolling pin up the hill.

The rolling pin was still dotted with flour. He noted some specks of dark red. Theodore smiled to himself. He had all the proof he needed. Emily surely would be able to put two and two together.

He arrived at his back gate. He rolled the rolling pin up against it. He miaowed. He could hear Emily's hairdryer whirring from upstairs. He miaowed again.

He heard a backdoor open down the alley. A loose pane of glass rattled in its frame as the door closed. It was Wendy's backdoor.

The hair dryer stopped. Theodore miaowed.

He heard steps on the stairs. A moment later the kitchen door was opened. At the same time the bolt of Wendy's back gate was pulled back.

Murderers always returned to the scene of the crime, Theodore remembered, his front paws still holding the rolling pin up against his gate.

He pulled the rolling pin back towards him, then against the gate as hard as he could.

He heard steps coming towards him from inside his yard. He heard steps coming towards him from down the hill.

'Is that you Theodore?' he heard Emily say.

He miaowed back. Let me in.

'Why can't you just jump over the wall?' she said. 'You usually do.'

The bolt was pulled back and the gate swung open.

Theodore pushed the rolling pin into the safety of his yard, then followed after.

'What's this?' Emily asked, picking up the rolling pin.

'It's mine,' Wendy Morris said.

Theodore looked on as Emily handed the rolling pin to Wendy.

'I've been looking for it all over,' Wendy said.

'I just opened my gate and there it was,' Emily said, smiling nervously.

'I heard him miaowing in the alley,' Wendy went on. 'And when I came out to see what the matter was, I saw him with it.'

'He's always bringing things in.'

'Yes,' Wendy said, smiling. 'I suppose he is.'

Emily thought of the pigeon feathers Theodore had dropped on her pillow. 'Well, I'm glad Theodore managed to find your rolling pin,' she said.

'Goodness knows how it came to be in the back alley,' Wendy said.

Emily noticed that Wendy had had her hair dyed red and had lost several pounds since she had last seen her.

'Are you managing all right?' she asked.

'I'm coping,' Wendy said. 'What else do you do?'

'If I can do anything?'

Emily felt Theodore rubbing against her calves. She remembered that she still had to paint her toenails. 'Well, I'm glad you got your rolling pin back.'

Wendy said, 'I would have been lost without it.' She bent down and reached out to pat Theodore.

Theodore backed away and hissed up at her.

'Theodore!' Emily said.

'Not to worry,' Wendy said. 'I'd better be off. I've got a pie in the oven.'

Emily stood in the gateway and watched as Wendy marched back down the hill, rolling pin in hand. She shut the gate, scooped Theodore up and pressed him to her.

'What am I going to do with you?' she said. 'Stealing people's rolling pins... Whatever next?'

She carried him upstairs and placed him on the bed while she painted her toenails.

As they ate the Chinese takeaway, drank the Italian wine and watched an American film, Emily asked Jonathan if he had buried the cat.

Jonathan said that he hadn't. He had intended to, but on his way home he'd passed a green wheelie bin left conveniently next to the footpath and had dropped the dead cat inside.

'You put the cat in a wheelie bin?'

Emily, who was on her second glass of wine, began to giggle.

'It was *dead*,' Jonathan said. 'I don't see that it really matters.'

'Was it empty... the wheelie bin?' Emily asked, laughing.

'Yes.'

'Well, it's going to be a fortnight until it gets buried now.'

14

Saturday morning, as Emily and Jonathan lay in bed, there was a knock at the door.

'Can you get that?' Emily said. 'I'm expecting a parcel.'

Jonathan got out of bed and hurried downstairs, Theodore following at his heels. When he opened the front door, there was no parcel but a woman with short dark hair standing on the doorstep.

Theodore eyed her from behind Jonathan's. It was the woman who had almost run him over. Arthur's owner and Ahmet's lover Diane.

'Can I help?' Jonathan asked, rubbing his eyes.

'You haven't seen a black cat, have you?' Diane asked. 'He hasn't had his breakfast this morning. He never misses his breakfast. And he didn't come home last night. I think something might have happened to him... He answers to Arthur... I was wondering if you could check your shed. Make sure he hasn't got in.'

Jonathan's brain had yet to awake fully. Rather than telling Diane that he hadn't seen her cat and promising to check the shed, he told her the truth.

'I'm afraid your cat's dead,' he said.

'Dead?' Diane opened her mouth to show a piece of white chewing gum.

'Yes. I found him in the allotments. I think he'd been hit...'

'Hit? Hit by a car?'

Jonathan paused. His head pounded. 'Yes,' he said. 'He'd been hit by a car. He must have dragged himself into the allotments.'

He didn't tell her about Theodore leading him to the compost heap or the bin liner in which he'd been buried.

Instead he said, 'Yes, he'd been hit by a car. I didn't want to leave him there in the allotments, so I brought him back here.'

Diane began to cry. She wiped tears from her reddened cheeks. She chewed vigorously on her chewing gum, taking it all in.

'I can't believe it,' she said.

'I went and buried him,' Jonathan went on. Lying was easy, he thought, once you got going. 'In my garden...'

'That was thoughtful,' she said, sniffing. 'Can I see?'

'He's not here,' Jonathan said. 'You see I don't live here... This is my girlfriend's house. She doesn't have a garden. So I took the cat back to my house and buried him there... Under a tree.'

'Under a tree?' Diane said. A tear ran down her cheek at this minor detail. She blew her nose noisily.

They stood staring at each a minute.

'Could I visit his grave?'

Jonathan looked down at his tartan pyjama bottoms and wrinkled Ramones t-shirt. He noted a dried smear of grease across his chest. He felt Theodore's tail against his ankle. He wanted to scratch the place but restrained himself. 'I'm not really dressed at the moment,' he said.

'Perhaps later then?' Diane said, wiping a tear from her cheek. 'I believe closure is important.'

'Yes, of course,' Jonathan said warily. 'Closure... of course.'

'This afternoon?'

'I'll write down my address.'

He left Diane at the front door while he went inside and scribbled his address on a scrap of paper.

'Say two o'clock,' he said, handing over his address.

'See you at two,' Diane said, smiling, her eyes red lined and bleary.

When he returned upstairs, Theodore had stolen his side of the bed. He lifted him up, placed him at the bottom of the bed and climbed back in.

He explained to Emily that a woman called Diane was going to go to his house to pay her respects at her cat's grave.

'But you put it in a wheelie bin,' Emily said, sitting up and slurping her tea.

'I know.'

'What are you going to do?'

'I'll sort something out,' Jonathan said.

Mid-morning there was another knock on the door. This time Emily got it. It was the parcel that she'd been expecting. 'Theo!' she called. 'I have a present for you.'

Theodore jumped down from the chest in the front room and went through to the dining room.

Emily had opened the package by the time Theodore arrived on the scene. He jumped up onto the dining room table.

Inside the package there was a tracking device. She fixed it to Theodore's purple collar.

Jonathan put down his newspaper and began reading the instructions.

Soon he had managed to set the handset to recognize the tracker. 'I don't know why you feel the need for this,' he said. 'It's not as if he's always disappearing.'

'I want to know where he gets to,' Emily said. 'He's always going off these days. Didn't he take you on a trip to the allotments yesterday? And there's cats going missing around here...'

She pressed a button on the handset and the pendant sitting on the crown of Theodore's chest began to flash red.

'I don't know what I'd do if anything happened to Theo,' she said.

After Jonathan had gone back to his own house to shower, get changed and prepare Arthur's grave, there was another knock at the Emily's door.

This time it was Wendy. Her carrot red hair was tied back. She'd coated her lips with red lipstick that morning and was wearing blue jeans and a baggy red blouse. In her hands she held out a pie.

She handed it to Emily, saying with a smile: 'A little thank you for finding my rolling pin.'

Emily took the pie and said, 'Thank you... But you really didn't need to.'

'I still cook for two,' Wendy said. 'And now's there's just the one of me. I have a freezer full of food that I'm never going to get through!'

'It looks tasty,' Emily said. 'We'll have it for dinner tomorrow.'

'I'll be off then.'

'Thanks again.'

Emily carried the pie through to the kitchen and slid it onto an empty shelf in the fridge. She closed the door and then realised she had not asked what was in the pie.

Oh, well, she thought. It'll be a surprise... A surprise pie!

15

Shortly after two o'clock that afternoon, there was a knock at Jonathan's front door. When he opened it, there was Diane in a black blouse and skirt. She held a posy of yellow pansies. She chewed on a piece of gum.

Jonathan suddenly felt underdressed for the occasion in his white t-shirt and jeans. He invited her in and told her to go through to the yard.

'Quite the bachelor's den you've got here,' she commented, as she walked through the front room.

Jonathan glanced about the room. He noticed the pizza box lying on the sofa, the remains of a pepperoni pizza peeping out.

'Not quite,' he said, wishing he'd tidied up.

He followed her through to the back door, noticing her black skirt stopped short of her knees.

In the yard there was a small garden area against the back wall. A red-leaved dwarf sycamore grew in the corner. A rectangle of soil under the sycamore had been recently turned over. As an added touch, Jonathan had tied two lollipop sticks into a cross using green twine and planted it at one end of the turned over patch.

Diane removed her gum from her mouth and held it between thumb and forefinger. She stood before the mock grave, her back to Jonathan. She bent down and placed the pansies onto the recently turned over soil. 'I will miss you, dear Arthur,' she said.

Jonathan backed away. 'Maybe I should leave you alone for a minute,' he said.

She turned to face him.

Charcoal rivulets of mascara had streaked down her cheeks. Her bleary eyes looked into his. 'It's just so horrible,' she said. 'I just can't believe that Arthur's there. Under the ground... In the soil.'

'No?'

'I just can't believe that he's dead and never coming back.'

'He's definitely dead and not coming back,' Jonathan said.

Diane cried harder.

Jonathan approached. He put his arms around her, and Diane turned and sobbed onto his chest.

He looked over at the back windows of the houses opposite. He felt Diane's face pressing against him, her hot tears piercing his thin cotton t-shirt, her hot breath against his chest. Her breasts pushed against his abdomen through her thin silk blouse. He felt her hands wrapping around his lower back. Her hands slipped down. He took a step backwards and she took a step forwards.

'Diane,' he said.

'Yes?'

She looked up at him, her eyes glazed, her mouth parted.

'I don't think this is really appropriate,' Jonathan said.

He felt her hands squeezing his bottom, her body pushing against him.

'I have a girlfriend,' he said.

'I know,' she said. 'But I'm not going to tell.'

'That's not the point,' Jonathan said, trying to pull away.

'You don't remember me, do you?' Diane said. 'I was the one who nearly ran over your cat. Then you find my cat run over. That's some coincidence, isn't it?'

'A coincidence, I suppose.'

'We are connected,' Diane said, pushing into him. 'Don't you see we are connected?'

'I just don't find you attractive,' Jonathan said.

Diane took a step backwards. 'She's just a silly girl,' Diane said. 'You can do better than that.'

Jonathan shook his head. 'I think you should say goodbye to your cat and leave.'

'I thought you were different,' Diane said. 'But you're just *boring*.'

'Let yourself out when you've done with your *closure*,' Jonathan said.

He turned and walked back into his house.

His t-shirt was sodden with Diane's tears and smudged with mascara and lipstick. He pulled it over his head and fed it into the washing machine. He turned and locked the door before going to have his second shower of the day.

Theodore peered down at Diane from between the branches of the little sycamore tree.

Although Jonathan had replaced the insoles in his boots following their first encounter, Theodore's scent had impregnated the boots, and every time he had walked from his house to Emily's and back again, he had reinforced the trail which Theodore had followed that afternoon across South Bank.

Diane stood in front of the mock grave. She dabbed at her face with the cuffs of her blouse.

She thought of Ahmet. She was still angry with him for telling the police about them.

She looked down at her cat's grave once more. Then she took a step towards the gate.

Something grey caught her eye. She looked up and saw a pair of green eyes looking down at her from between the leafy limbs of the sycamore. She took a step towards the tree and made out a grey cat sitting on a branch.

Theodore stared back at her.

'What do you think you're looking at?' she said, not expecting a response.

Theodore met her stare. His eyes bore into hers.

'It was just a wind up,' Diane said. 'Just a bit of fun.'

Theodore continued to stare at her.

'Who do you think you are to judge me? If you must know, my husband ran off with his secretary. Ten years younger than me... I was left with nothing... Only Arthur. And I had to fight to keep him... Now he's gone too. I've got nothing.

'Nothing... I might as well move back to Lancashire,' she said with an air of finality.

You might as well, thought back Theodore.

Diane wiped a fresh tear from her cheek. Then she bent down and grabbed a handful of soil and threw it at Theodore.

'Sod off!' she cried.

But Theodore was already on the other side of the wall.

'That's right... You run home!' she shouted after him.

The sound of water from the bathroom had stopped.

Diane wiped her hands on her skirt.

'Goodbye Arthur,' she said sniffing.

Then she opened the gate and, entering the alley, slammed it shut behind her.

16

'What's in the pie?' Jonathan asked, chewing on a piece of chewy meat.

It was Sunday evening. Emily had warmed the pie that Wendy had given her. She examined the reddish-brown piece of meat at the end of her fork. 'It's certainly not chicken,' she said.

'I know that,' Jonathan said, still chewing on the same piece of meat. 'It's a bit tough...'

'Wendy gave it to us... Theodore found her rolling pin. She wanted to thank us. So she gave us this pie. I forgot to ask what was in it.'

'It's a bit tough,' Jonathan repeated.

'It's different,' Emily said, poking pieces of food around her plate.

They both ate in silence for a couple of minutes.

Then Emily put down her knife and fork and stood up. 'Where is Theo?' she said. 'I'm surprised he's not sniffing about when there's food about.'

She took the remote control for the tracker from the side and turned it on. She went into each room carrying the tracker in front of her. Returning to the dining room, she said, 'I'm not sure this tracker thing is working.'

'When was the last time you saw him?'

'Come to think of it, I'm not sure I've seen him since this morning.'

She hurried out of the back door and made a quick inspection of the yard.

'He's not out here,' she shouted back at the house.

Jonathan joined her in the backyard as she struggled with the bolt to the gate.

Once in the back alley, she consulted the tracker's remote control again, pointing it up and down the alley.

'I've got something,' she said. Two, three, four LEDs lit up. 'He's this way.'

'There he is,' Jonathan said, pointing. 'He's up on top of Wendy's wall.'

'Come here, Theodore,' Emily called. 'Come to Mummy!'

The pendant sitting on the crown of Theodore's chest was blinking frantically and the little device was emitting a series of beeps. His cover was blown... Theodore turned his back to the pair.

'He'll come home when he's ready,' Jonathan said. 'At least we know the tracker works... Let's get back to our dinner.'

'All right,' Emily said. 'But I don't like that pie. I might put a pizza in the oven.'

'Pepperoni?'

'Yes. I think I've got one in the freezer,' Emily said.

Theodore watched as they walked away. Then he turned his attention back to Wendy's kitchen window.

Wendy and Irene were sitting at the kitchen table. Wendy held a turkey drumstick in her hand and was working her way round it. Irene was forking chips into her mouth.

'One pound forty nine pence,' Wendy said.

'That's not bad,' Irene said. She trimmed some meat from the bone with her knife and fork, her head bent over her meal. 'Not bad at all. They've got a lot of meat on them.'

Wendy took a gulp of tea.

'Do you want to take these turkey bones with you? I can wrap them up.'

'Rocky doesn't eat poultry bones,' Irene said. 'They give him the runs.'

Theodore wandered back up the hill, past his own house and noticed Belle, sitting on the back wall of Zeynep and Ahmet's house. The two cats sat together while the Turkish couple watched television. Zeynep was sitting with her hands on top of her belly, fingers interlocked. In the corner of the room Theodore noted a leather holdall.

The holdall had been packed and repacked several times in the last days. It contained Zeynep's overnight essentials for when she was taken to hospital. The due date was looming, and the women in her family were not ones for being late.

'I cannot believe that you were having sex with that woman,' Zeynep said. 'When I am expecting your baby...'

Ahmet held his hands out before him. 'OK, OK,' he said. 'I was with her. Is it so hard to understand? We haven't had sex for months.'

'It was uncomfortable for me,' Zeynep said. 'It's not my fault.'

'Yes, I understand. But I have needs.'

'You have needs! You are not supposed to go sleeping with the neighbours when your wife is pregnant with your baby. You disgust me. I wish you would just leave.'

'But I pay the rent. I pay the bills. You need me. The baby needs me.'

'You should have thought about that before you slept with that woman.'

'She means nothing to me. It was just a mistake,' Ahmet said. 'It is over. Can you forgive me?'

'I'm not sure if I can. Or want to.'

'I will make up for it... I will. I will be the perfect father.'

'Do you realise how unhappy I have been,' Zeynep said, beginning to cry. 'Ever since Bal went missing, everything has been just terrible.'

'I promise I will change,' Ahmet said. 'I can make things better.'

Zeynep glared at him.

'I hate you,' she told Ahmet. 'I wish I had never married you.'

'Zeynep. Please.'

A tear slid down her cheek. 'Bal is dead and I might as well be.'

'She will return,' Ahmet said. 'Do not give up hope.'

'No,' Zeynep said. 'She is dead; I know it.'

17

Theodore spent the next day catching up on some sleep. He did not wake till he heard Craig unlocking his front door. Time for some tuna, he thought, getting to his feet and stretching.

The tuna dinners had become part of his daily routine. After he had wolfed down his saucer of tuna, he entered the house.

Satisfied that Craig was in the toilet, he hurried upstairs. He had completed his search of Craig's house but had failed to find any incriminating evidence. In the attic he noted that the telescope was still pointing at Diane's bedroom window. The blue curtains were pulled shut even though it was still daylight.

From downstairs, he heard three sharp raps on the front door. He flattened back his ears. In all the weeks of visiting Craig's house, Theodore had never known him have a visitor.

He heard the toilet flush. He jumped down from the back of the chair and raced down the stairs. As he reached the final flight, he saw Craig enter the hallway and approach the front door. Theodore stopped in his tracks halfway down the final flight. If Craig turned round now, he would see Theodore.

Craig inched the front door open.

Emily was on the other side, the remote control for the tracking device pointing at his chest. 'Where is he?' she demanded.

Theodore's tracker was beeping and flashing.

Craig was speechless.

'I know he's in here.'

'Nobody is here except me,' Craig said, staring at the little black box his neighbour was holding. 'I don't know what you're talking about.'

'My cat,' Emily said. 'You've got him in here.'

'I haven't,' Craig began.

'I can see him,' Emily cried. 'He's right behind you.'

Craig turned round to see Theodore on the stairs, his front paws on a lower step to his rear ones.

'I didn't know he was in here,' Craig stuttered. 'I was in the bathroom. I must have left the backdoor open and he wandered in... I just gave him a little bit of tuna.'

'Tuna!' Emily screamed. 'He doesn't eat tuna... 'It gives cats Yellow Fat Disease!'

Emily pushed past Craig and grabbed Theodore up from the stairs. On her way out, she said, 'If you want a cat, go buy your own... Just keep away from mine.'

Once back home, she petted Theodore while Jonathan made two mugs of tea. Her heart was still pounding.

'I'm not going to let him out again,' Emily said. 'He's going to be kept inside from now on.'

Theodore dug his claws into Emily's thighs in protest.

'You can't do that to Theodore,' Jonathan said. 'He loves it outside. He's always in that back alley.'

Emily inspected the tracking device that was fastened to his collar, glad that it had done its job.

'I know what you mean,' she said. 'It would be mean to keep him locked inside all day. I just hope that that guy next door has learned that it's not all right to feed someone else's cat and let it in your house.'

Theodore jumped down from Emily's lap and padded through to the kitchen, before she could change her mind.

Before jumping up onto the back wall, he sharpened his claws on the trunk of the clematis. He worked the bark for some minutes, the shreds joining the growing pile at the foot of the plant.

18

The smoke from a dozen barbeques fused in the warm evening air. From the backyards came the smell of chicken wings, steaks, burgers, kebabs and sausages cooking over charcoal. The men stood by the makeshift grills, closely monitoring the cooking operation. Cans or little bottles of cold lager within easy reach.

Michael and Philip also had a barbecue in their backyard that evening, and Theodore knew that their sausages were of a superior quality. Michael had bought a selection from a speciality butcher's he had come across at the food fair in Parliament Street that afternoon. He'd opted for ostrich, venison with goose fat, wild boar, and rabbit with jalapeno.

He was wearing a spotless blue and white striped apron over his clothes. He'd had his hair cut that day. Prematurely balding, he now had his hair clipped to within a millimetre of his head at least once a week. He had taken the precaution of smearing sun cream over his stubbly head before lighting the barbeque, but he could still feel his skin turning pink from the sun and heat from the charcoal.

In his hand he held a pair of stainless steel tongs. He turned the spitting sausages and took a sip from his bottle of Belgian beer, a wedge of lime lodged in the neck.

'I think this picture is going to be my breakthrough piece,' he told Philip.

'It's just a drawing of the back alley,' Philip said, taking a swig of beer. He had already downed two bottles while Michael was still on his first.

'Well, you don't look closely enough,' Michael told him, turning a little pinker. 'It's all in the detail.'

'I think your problem is that you can't draw people... People don't want empty streets and alleys. They need to be populated. They need to have human interest.'

'I *can* draw people!' Michael almost shouted.

'I sat for you that time,' Philip said, 'and it looked nothing like me.'

'You kept fidgeting,' Michael said, his cheeks burning. 'You wouldn't keep still... How am I expected to draw someone when they're moving about all the time?'

Deciding to change the subject, Philip said, 'How do you know which sausage is which?'

'I put them in alphabetical order,' Michael said. 'The ostrich on the left. The wild boar on the right...'

'Oh,' Philip said.

Theodore was sitting in the overgrown ivy on top of Michael's wall. He had formed a nest within the plant, so that he was hidden from view. Below him was the barbeque. He eyed the four sausages, neatly lined up.

'I'm going to have the ostrich and the wild boar,' Michael told Philip.

'Looks like I'm having the rabbit and the venison,' Philip said.

'Are you complaining?'

'Of course not... I was just saying.'

'Well, can you keep an eye on them while I go in and butter some baps? They'll be done in a couple of minutes... Just make sure you don't burn them.'

'No problem,' Philip said, taking Michael's place in front of the barbeque.

As soon as Michael was in the kitchen, Philip took from the pocket of his jeans a packet of cigarettes and lit one. He fiddled with the spitting sausages and then went to the corner of the yard, so that he could not be seen from the kitchen window. He was wearing a pair of bright yellow trainers and on his wrist he wore a gold watch which glistened in the sun.

Theodore watched as Philip puffed on his cigarette and swigged from his bottle of beer, gazing up at the cloudless sky. Now was the time to strike.

He got to his paws, jumped silently down into the yard and a second later was standing in front of the barbeque. He singled out the wild boar.

He looked back across the yard. Philip was still smoking, his back to him.

Theodore raised himself up onto his hind legs and, ignoring the fierce heat from the charcoal, dabbed at the end sausage so that it dropped onto the ground. It was still spitting fat as he bit into it. The sausage between his jaws, Theodore jumped back up onto the wall and down the other side. He dropped the sausage to the ground.

It was too hot to eat, so he pawed it across the yard. The old couple who lived in the house next to Michael's were nowhere to be seen, so Theodore decided to let it cool before transporting it to the safety of his own yard. From the other side of the wall, he heard Michael say, 'What's happened to my wild boar?'

'I don't know,' Philip said. 'I really don't know. I was standing over there, and when I looked round there were only three.'

'You've eaten it, haven't you?'

'I haven't. It's just disappeared.'

'Just disappeared? Do you think I'm stupid? Sausages don't just disappear. I told you that I was going to have the wild boar. It was mine.'

'But I didn't touch your sausage,' Philip protested. 'Look Mikey... Someone must have sneaked in and taken it when I wasn't looking.'

'And don't call me Mikey,' Michael said. 'You know I don't like it.'

'Sorry, I forgot,' Philip said. 'But I really didn't take it, Michael. Somebody must have sneaked in and stolen it.'

Theodore heard footsteps approach the back gate, and then the scraping of wood on concrete as the gate was pulled open.

'There's no one out here,' Philip said, scraping the gate closed.

'What a surprise,' Theodore heard Michael mutter.

While the two men were arguing over the missing sausage, Theodore took a bite from the end and began to chew. He had never eaten wild boar before. He wondered momentarily over the ethics of eating animals much larger than himself. Well, he hadn't killed it, he thought, swallowing a piece of sausage.

Next door he heard Michael say loudly: 'It comes down to trust.'

'I really didn't take your sausage, Mikey.'

'Don't call me that!'

Ten minutes later Theodore carried what remained of the sausage through the cat flap. Jonathan was sitting at the dining room table, a newspaper laid out in front of him.

Theodore jumped up and dropped the remaining piece of sausage onto the newspaper.

'A present? For me?' Jonathan said smiling. 'That's very kind of you,' he said, patting Theodore on the head.

Theodore pawed the sausage, so that it rolled towards Jonathan. He had decided that wild boar wasn't for him. He should have gone for the ostrich...

'But it looks like you've singed your fur,' Jonathan said. 'And you've got a pink nose.'

When Emily came downstairs five minutes later, Theodore was still sitting on the table in front of Jonathan.

'Are you two friends now?' she asked.

'Yes, I think we are,' Jonathan said, rubbing Theodore's ears. 'Look he brought me a present.'

He lifted up the grubby sausage to show Emily.

'He brought you a sausage?'

'Yes, he brought it in and dropped it on the paper. He must have raided someone's barbeque. And look: he's singed his fur and burnt his nose.'

Emily picked Theodore up and examined him.

'It does look a bit sore.'

'He's a very brave cat,' Jonathan said.

'Well, I think he likes you now.'

Emily hugged Theodore to her. 'It took a little bit of time for him to get used to you,' she said, 'but he likes you now.'

'Well, I'm glad I've passed the Theodore Test,' Jonathan said.

He picked up the sausage and carried it out to the backyard.

Smoke from barbeques still hung heavy in the air. He checked that Theodore was not watching as he put the sausage in the outside bin. From down the hill he heard two men arguing.

A lovers' quarrel, he thought, as he gently replaced the bin lid.

19

As summer progressed there was little development in the murder case by the police. While the case file was kept open and any new leads followed up, it seemed more and more unlikely that they would ever catch the Clementhorpe Killer. It was left to Theodore to carry on the investigation on his own.

He was sitting on the back wall of Wendy Morris's house, eavesdropping as Wendy chatted to her friend Irene.

'Have another biscuit,' Wendy said.

'Don't mind if I do,' Irene said, taking a Viscount. 'I do like a Viscount,' she said, pronouncing the 's'.

'There was a thing on the radio this morning about a dead pigeon,' Irene said, her mouth full of biscuit. 'They went and found a dead pigeon down a chimney somewhere down south. Well, the pigeon had a message strapped to its leg in a little canister or something. But the message was in code so they don't know what it said... They reckon it had been there since the war.'

'Let's hope the message wasn't important,' Wendy said.

She took a gulp of tea and looked out of her kitchen window. Her eyes met Theodore's.

'That girl's cat is back,' she said. 'I don't know why it bothers now. There's no pigeons left. That black cat had the last one.'

'It's just curious,' Irene said.

'Well, you know what they say,' Wendy said. 'Curiosity...'

'Yes, I know,' Irene interrupted before Wendy could continue.

'Talking of which – I think you should tell Diane,' Irene said. 'Tell her what happened to Arthur. It might put her mind to rest. For all you know she might be thinking he's going to come back some day.'

'I'm not going to tell her,' Wendy said. 'That cat of hers was a menace.'

'It's not right though, and you know it. If you don't tell her, I will.'

'Don't you go telling her,' Wendy said. 'That would really put the cat among the pigeons.' She laughed unconvincingly.

'It's the right thing to do,' Irene said.

Wendy stopped laughing. 'I'll pop round later,' she said. 'I'll tell her myself what happened. Just you keep your nose out of it.'

'You will?'

'Yes, that's what I said. I'll tell her he was knocked down. Then at least she'll know he's not going to come back.'

From across the alley, Theodore heard a gate scrape open, and then Michael appeared togged out in a bright pink top and tight black Lycra shorts. He did a few stretches and then began to jog up the hill.

Ten minutes later, Wendy came out of her back door. She walked up the hill and stopped in front of Diane's back gate. She rapped on the gate. 'Hullo,' she called out. 'Anyone in?'

Shortly the gate was opened and Wendy disappeared inside Diane's yard.

Theodore hurried up to Diane's.

The two women were standing in the kitchen, facing each other.

'I thought you should know,' Wendy said. 'Your cat is not coming back.'

'I know that,' Diane said.

'You do?'

'Yes.'

Diane reached for her packet of cigarettes.

'He was by the side of Scarcroft Road,' Wendy lied. 'Must have been hit by a car.'

Diane lit a cigarette.

'I buried him there in the allotments. I wasn't sure whose cat it was. And I didn't want to leave him lying there.'

'You buried him?' Diane said, blowing out smoke.

'Yes,' Wendy said. 'That's what I said. In the allotments. I didn't want to leave him by the side of the road.'

'That's strange,' Diane said, frowning.

Wendy backed away from the cloud of smoke.

'I buried him in the allotments,' Wendy said. 'I could hardly bury him in my yard... There's no soil in it. I didn't know he was yours, you see. He didn't have a collar on.'

Diane blew more smoke at Wendy. 'And then someone dug him up and buried him in their garden?' she said.

'What do you mean?'

'Some guy said that he'd found Arthur in the allotments. He'd taken him and buried him in his garden.'

'I don't know about that,' Wendy said, backing towards the door. 'I just thought you should know. In case you were wondering what had happened to him. I'd better be going.'

Diane said, 'You told me you buried him in the allotments. Then someone tells me they found him in the allotments and buried him in their garden. Someone's lying. I just don't understand why.'

20

Zeynep was telephoned by a vet in Leeds.

Bal had been found by the side of the road. She had been taken to a nearby vets, where she was identified by her microchip. Although she had been hit by a car, she had no bones broken. A slight concussion, the vet had told Zeynep. She had been lucky.

As they drove back to York along the A64, Zeynep was speechless, only murmuring now and again to the plastic cat carrier on her lap. It was only later that evening, after Ahmet had returned to work, that she broke down.

Theodore took up position on the back wall and was joined by Belle. They watched as Zeynep sat down at her kitchen table, holding Bal beneath her chin, the cat resting on top of her bulge.

'I thought that pigeon man had done something to you,' Zeynep said, wiping tears from her cheeks. Then she told Bal what she had done.

Ahmet had been out at work, doing his evening shift, so Zeynep had gone out to look for Bal. She had walked down the alley and near the bottom she heard a murmuring from a yard. She realised it must be the pigeon man talking to his birds. She approached the back gate. Standing in the glare cast by the security light, she listened to the man mumbling away to his birds from behind the wall. She would ask him if he'd seen her cat. She would ask him if he could check his shed. She would find out if he had done something to Bal. She rapped on the gate. Peter Morris went quiet. She rapped again, a little louder. Then she heard soft-slippered footsteps approach the gate.

'Hullo?' he said from the other side.

'Hello,' Zeynep said. 'I live up the street.'

'How can I help?' Peter said.

'Can I speak to you for a moment?'

A moment passed and then the gate opened.

Peter Morris stood in the gateway. In his hands he held a plump pigeon.

'Yes?' he said. 'What is it?'

'My cat has gone missing,' Zeynep began, 'and I was wondering...'

Peter sucked in the cool night air between his teeth.

'I thought she may be in your shed,' Zeynep went on. 'She might have got locked in.'

'Look,' Peter said, stepping aside, so that Zeynep could see past him and into the outbuilding, 'there's no cat in there. See for yourself.'

Zeynep looked into the outbuilding. There was no cat.

'Just because I keep pigeons,' Peter muttered, 'doesn't mean I've done something to your bloody cat.'

'I didn't say you did.'

Peter shook his head from side to side.

'I know you,' he said. 'You're married to that taxi driver fellow, aren't you? I've seen him coming out of No.24. He's been having it off with that Lancashire hotpot. That's what he's been up to...'

'Excuse me?' Zeynep said.

'You heard... He's been having sex with that tart from No.24. Don't you understand English?'

'Tart?'

'Diane,' Peter said. 'Her from the wrong side of the Pennines. He's been having it off with her.'

Zeynep was stunned into silence. Then she said slowly, 'What's it got to do with you?'

'What's it got to do with me?' Peter said excitedly. 'I live here, that's what.'

'I live here too. Here is my home.'

'You don't understand. I live here. I was born here. You lot should go and clear off back where you came from.'

'You lot?' Zeynep's cheeks glowed with anger.

Peter began to close the gate on her. 'Yes, you lot!'

Zeynep pushed back against the gate, sending Peter falling backwards into his outbuilding. The events that followed were a bit of blur in her mind; it happened so quickly.

She remembered the pigeon scrabbling about on the floor of the yard. She remembered the old man's grunts as he lay on the floor of his outbuilding, seed spilling onto him from an up-turned sack. He was on his hands and knees, trying to get to his feet, his back to Zeynep.

She spotted the cobblestone holding the door open. She picked it up. Then she hit him on the back of the head with it before he could get to his feet.

Pigeons scattered into the night, their wings beating white against the dark sky.

'He was groaning in pain,' Zeynep gasped into Bal's fur. 'I ran up the alley, I threw the cobblestone over a wall as I passed. I got home. I sat here at the kitchen table... Waiting for Ahmet to come home. I was going to tell him everything. I waited and he didn't come... I was going to tell him what I'd done, but he didn't come home...

'Hours passed and I went up to bed... I couldn't sleep. Then I heard him come in. And I thought he would come up and check on me, but he didn't. He started doing laundry. Then I knew it was true. He had been with her. I decided not to tell him what I'd done...

'But I killed him. That horrible old man.'

Zeynep's face was buried in Bal's fur.

'I did it,' she spluttered. 'I killed him. I killed Peter Morris.'

She looked down to where a pool was growing on the linoleum between her feet. She placed Bal on the table and reached for her mobile.

'Ahmet,' she said into her phone. 'It is time.'

21

Theodore listened as Ahmet's taxi started up and the Turkish couple departed for York Hospital. The two Birman cats, Bal and Belle, sat on the dining table and waited. They weren't aware that the peace of their home was about to be shattered by a squalling usurper. Rather you than me, thought Theodore.

He jumped down into the back alley. He now knew who had killed Peter Morris. He padded across the cobbles. He just needed to prove that he hadn't eaten any pigeon.

He jumped up on the back wall of Diane's house. Her bedroom curtains were drawn. She was still in bed. It was Sunday morning after all, and she had no cat to get her out of bed.

In the undergrowth among Arthur's dried turds, he discovered the bones of a pigeon's leg encircled in a hard plastic ring. A string of letters and numbers carved into the ring could prove that the leg had once belonged to a certain pigeon that had gone missing at the start of summer.

Theodore cast his mind back to the morning he had discovered Peter Morris's body in the shed. Arthur had been cleaning himself in the back alley by his back gate. Evidently he had eaten the bird while Theodore had still been asleep. He recalled something his mother had once said to him about the early cat catching the bird.

Theodore took the thin bones encircled in plastic and carried them home. As he entered the kitchen, Emily jumped up from the dining room table.

'Theodore,' she cried. 'Where have you been?'

She grabbed him up and hugged him to her. 'I've been up half the night worrying.'

'I told you he'd come back,' Jonathan said, not looking up from the Sunday papers.

Theodore dropped his package of bones onto the Review.

'Ugh!' Jonathan said with a grimace. 'Look what he's brought in...'

'Eh!' Emily said. 'What is it?'

'I think it's part of a dead bird,' Jonathan said, prodding the bones with his forefinger. 'And there's a plastic ring.'

'Not again,' Emily said. 'Just put it in the bin... Outside.'

Theodore looked on as Jonathan carried the newspaper supplement with the pigeon remains outside.

It was definitely time for a nap, he thought, as he heard the bin lid being replaced with a clatter.

22

Theodore went to sleep on Emily's bed sound in the knowledge that he had solved the case. He knew that Zeynep had killed Peter Morris and Arthur had eaten Ethel. What he would do with the information was another matter.

It was late afternoon when he stirred. Through the open window, he could hear voices. One voice he recognized straight-away as Emily's. The other he soon realised was Michael's.

He heard Michael say, 'Haven't seen you in a while... Not since...'

'No,' Emily said. 'Not since *that* morning.'

Every few seconds Michael took a sharp intake of breath, and Theodore understood that he was running on the spot.

'How's the drawing going?' Emily asked.

'Good,' Michael said. 'I've started on a new series.'

'Oh, yes?'

'Portraiture...'

'How exciting!'

'I'm looking for a new model actually.'

'Oh, yes?' Emily said. 'What happened to the last one?'

She laughed but Michael didn't.

'You have quite an interesting face,' he said, breathing hard. 'Some interesting curves.'

'Well, no one's said that about it before!'

'Perhaps you can sit for me sometime?'

'Like model?'

'Yes, like model,' Michael said. 'Though you'll just have to sit still... No fidgeting!'

'Modelling?' Emily said. 'Why not?'

'That's great.'

'Me a model!' Emily said and laughed. 'When?'

'This evening?' Michael said, 'If you don't have anything else planned.'

'I've got no plans for this evening.'

'Well, I'll see you later then. Say seven? I'd better get on... I want to do two laps round the racecourse before dinner...'

'All right,' Emily said. 'See you at seven.'

Theodore listened as Michael panted off up the back alley and Emily returned inside.

Theodore tried to go back to sleep but something nagged at his mind. When he had gone to sleep he had been confident that the case was solved. Now he wasn't so sure. He began to think over the facts.

Peter Morris, it transpired, hadn't been a particularly nice man. He'd told Zeynep that her husband had been having an affair. He had made a racist remark to her. Zeynep had hit him over the head with a cobblestone. She had fled the scene. She had thrown the cobblestone in Craig's garden as she dashed by.

So far, so good.

Theodore did not doubt for a moment what Zeynep had confessed to Bal. What owner would lie to their cat?

But something did not add up.

He cast his mind back, searching for clues, thinking over the details. He went right back to the beginning, before he'd discovered the body of Peter Morris.

He had entered the back alley, smelling the morning air.

There were the smells of other cats, the fragrance from what flora grew, the human generated waste that lay decomposing in rubbish bins, the faint smell of cocoa hanging in the air...

He knew that the local chocolate factory, Terry's, had closed down some years earlier, and they were starting to build houses on the site. The other chocolate factory, Rowntrees, was located on the northern side of York.

Had the wind blown the smell of cocoa across the city? he wondered.

He remembered the wind had blown the feathers and other debris in Peter Morris's yard mainly towards the wall opposite the gate and not the other way. The wind had been blowing from the south that morning. Theodore realised that it couldn't have been the Rowntrees factory that he had smelled that morning.

The only other explanation was that someone had been up and made cocoa before the sun had risen.

Who drank cocoa?

'Me, I like a mug of cocoa in the morning,' Wendy had told Laura after Peter's funeral.

So Wendy was already awake when he had entered the yard and discovered Peter's body. She hadn't been woken by Emily's scream, as she'd claimed.

He remembered Wendy unlocking her back door and entering her yard. She had on her fur-lined slippers. If someone screamed in your yard, would you stop to put on your slippers? No, Wendy had been awake; awake and waiting.

Theodore got to his paws. If Wendy had already been awake, why did she claim that she'd been woken by Emily's scream?

He then remembered Zeynep's confession. 'He was groaning in pain,' she'd told Bal.

So when Zeynep fled the scene, Peter was still alive, and when Theodore discovered the body, Wendy was already awake.

'He wouldn't have known what hit him,' the police officer had told Wendy.

Theodore remembered the state of Peter Morris's head that morning. He wouldn't have been lying groaning in pain with an injury like that.

Zeynep might have hit him on the head with a cobblestone, but someone else had finished him off with something else.

That someone had to be his wife, Wendy, Theodore concluded. She had whacked him over the back of the head with her rolling pin.

He stirred from the bed, got to his paws and stretched.

The case is definitely altered, he thought.

23

Shortly after six o'clock, Wendy put out her rubbish. She opened her back gate and carried her two black bin bags outside and placed them against the side wall of her house.

Theodore knew from his reconnaissance that he only had a few seconds. As soon as her back was turned he dashed from the corner of the alley and through the open gate.

He was inside the house. He made for the stairs. He paused on the landing.

The front bedroom was painted salmon pink, a double bed with pink duvet. The back bedroom was magnolia with a single bed up against the window. Theodore understood that Peter and Wendy had slept in separate bedrooms, and the back bedroom was where Peter had slept.

'If owt got into the yard, he'd be out there in a flash,' Wendy had said.

From the windowsill Theodore peered outside.

Michael's house was directly behind. He looked across into the back bedroom.

Philip was lying in bed. He was wearing his yellow trainers and his arm was laid over the duvet cover, his gold watch on his wrist. The duvet obscured his face.

Theodore glanced down at the yard below. Wendy Morris had shut the gate and was walking to the back door. She glanced up as she passed below.

Theodore jumped down onto the bed. On the bedside table he noticed a mug. He looked inside. There was an inch of greyish brown solidified hot chocolate in the bottom of the mug.

'Your dad never liked hot chocolate either,' Wendy had said to Laura.

It had been Wendy who had brought the mug of hot chocolate upstairs on the morning of the murder, thought Theodore, before he had discovered the body. She had sat on his bed and waited. She had sipped at her hot chocolate, knowing that her husband was not coming back up to bed; waiting for a reasonable hour to go downstairs and discover her husband's body. Then she would phone the police and let them know that someone had been in her yard in the night and killed her husband. But before she could call the police, Theodore had discovered the murder scene.

Downstairs he heard the back door being shut and then locked. A moment later there were heavy footsteps on the stairs.

He made for the landing at the top of the stairs but Wendy was already half way up. In her right hand she held her rolling pin.

Theodore raced down the stairs on the banister side, keeping to the wall.

As he passed, the rolling pin came down, sending a lump of plaster from the wall.

Reaching the bottom, he turned to see Wendy turning mid-flight, rolling pin in hand.

He made for the back door. It was closed. There was no cat flap. He carried on, into the downstairs bathroom. There was nowhere to hide. He ran back into the kitchen, but Wendy was blocking the door. He ran into the corner, by the sink. As far from Wendy as he could get.

Wendy stood in the middle of the kitchen, holding up the rolling pin. She slapped the rolling pin into the palm of her other hand.

Theodore backed as far back into the corner as he could. There was no escape.

Wendy raised her rolling pin.

Theodore cowered. He closed his eyes, and braced himself for the blow. His end would be the same as Peter Morris's, he realised. He braced himself, ready for the final blow.

Then there was a sharp rapping on the window.

He opened his eyes and saw Irene's face pushed up against the kitchen window.

'You leave that cat alone!' Irene shouted through the glass.

24

'I'll make us a nice mug of tea,' Irene said, filling the kettle at the kitchen sink.

'I don't know what came over me,' Wendy said. She was sitting at the kitchen table, wringing her hands. 'It's like he knew all along,' she said. 'He knew and he wasn't going to let it drop. He knew, I tell you.'

'He's just a cat,' Irene said, switching the kettle on, and then turning to her friend: 'An inquisitive one, I grant you that. But just a cat at the end of the day.'

Wendy shook her head. 'He was like a dog with the scent of a fox,' she said.

Irene tutted. 'It's all in your head.'

'I'm going to call Fulford police station first thing in the morning. I'm going to tell the police everything.'

'You're going to tell them you did it?'

'Me?' Wendy said, clucking her tongue. 'I didn't do it.' She shook her head. 'But I know who did.'

Irene leant forward. 'Who did it then?'

'I heard everything,' Wendy said. 'Everything that went on that night... First it was that foreign girl. I heard them arguing... She hit him, but she didn't kill him. He was hurt all right. Lying there, groaning in pain. But I didn't go out to him... I sat there in the back bedroom and I waited.

'Then I heard a gate open and a minute later someone else came into the yard. There was a sharp crack.

'I heard a gate scrape closed. Then it was quiet. Dead quiet. I sat there. I didn't go back to bed. I sat there, on his bed by the window and I waited.

'With the first light, I crept downstairs. I didn't go out. I made myself a hot chocolate and went back upstairs. I sat on his bed and waited... The funny thing was: I felt relief.'

'Relief?' Irene said.

'Yes, relief,' Wendy said. 'Relief it was over. Relief he was gone and never coming back.'

'I knew there was more to it,' Irene said, handing her a mug of tea.

Wendy began to cry, big sobs from deep inside.

'Come on,' Irene said, putting a hand on Wendy's shoulder and patting her.

'You have no idea,' she spluttered. 'You have no idea what he was like.'

'I knew,' said Irene. 'I knew.'

'He cared more about his pigeons than me,' Wendy went on. 'For years I washed his socks and made his meals... and never any thanks. He even named his pigeons after girls he'd courted before me... Deirdre, Helen, Daisy, Ethel... I could hear him on a night, "Oh Ethel, you're such a pretty girl," or "Helen, I love you so much."'

'And then when Laura started seeing David he wouldn't even let me mention his name in the house. I thought maybe he would change his ideas when he knew Laura was serious about him. But when the baby came, he got even worse... He even went off his Jamaican Ginger Cake... Said it tasted foreign.

'All those years I'd had to listen to him and nod my head and say "Yes, dear". Well, no more. Is that so bad?'

'But if you didn't finish him off,' Irene said. 'Who did?'

Wendy sucked in a mouthful of air. 'It was him behind.'

She nodded to the kitchen window and the house behind. 'I don't know why he did it,' she said. 'But the way I see it, he did me a favour. That's why I didn't say owt to them about it. He'd done me a favour.

'But that cat knew something was up. And he wouldn't let it lie.'

Theodore, sitting on the back wall, looked from Wendy's kitchen window to the house behind. He noticed the bottom of the gate sitting on the concrete. He remembered Philip opening the gate to check if some sausage-stealing intruder was lurking on the other side. He remembered the gate scraping closed. Then he remembered Michael checking the soles of his trainers for blood on the morning of the murder.

The murderer always returned to the scene of the crime.

25

The picture of the back alley was complete. It was rich in detail. Theodore picked out Craig's house, where a cobblestone lay waiting to be discovered in the overgrown grass. He examined the back of his own house. The curtains in the back bedroom were closed, Emily still sleeping in bed.

Then there was Michael's own house. The curtains of the back bedroom were open a couple of inches.

Theodore's eyes were then drawn to the house on the corner. He noted the pigeons, five of them, perched on the eaves. The door to the outbuilding was open and Peter Morris's slippered foot was visible, the concrete stained dark beneath.

In the centre of the picture, coming up the alley, was Arthur, a pigeon in his mouth, its head hanging to the side. Specks of blood dotted the cobblestones indicating where it had come from. It was all in the details, Theodore understood.

Michael had given the drawing a title: "The Morning of the Murder", and signed it, Michael Butler.

Theodore should have known. The clues had been there all along, he realised.

Michael had finished off Peter Morris; then returned home. He had been unable to sleep. Had he left a bloody footprint behind at the murder scene? He checked his trainers. There was a faint smear of blood. He took them off his and washed them in the kitchen sink. He scrubbed at them frantically. Upstairs Philip slept on, unaware of what his boyfriend had done, or so he thought.

Michael realised what he had to do. When the wife discovered her husband's body, she would scream. He would be up, about to set off on an early morning run. He would dash in to see what was going on. He would trample over any evidence he might have left behind. He put on his running gear and waited, pacing his kitchen, waiting for a scream.

There was a tapping at Michael's front door. The bells of York Minster rang out seven o'clock.

Theodore's ears folded back. 'Me a model!' Emily had said. She was actually on time for once, Theodore realised.

Michael went to let her in.

A moment later, Theodore's eyes widened as he saw Emily enter the back living room. She was dressed in a pair of tight blue jeans and one of Jonathan's old checked shirts. 'You didn't forget our modelling date?' she said.

'How could I forget?' Michael said with a smile.

He indicated the purple chaise longue pushed up against the wall.

'How shabby chic,' Emily said, laughing nervously.

'Shall I get us a cup of tea before we start?' Michael said, walking into the kitchen and putting the kettle on; not waiting for a response.

Emily didn't sit down on the chaise longue straightaway. Instead she looked at some of the pictures on the walls. She paused in front of the picture of the back alley, not noticing the details. Then she examined the portrait of Philip, painted in acrylics. He stared lifelessly out from of the canvas.

'Is that supposed to be Philip?'

'Yes,' Michael said from the kitchen. 'Just a study I was working on.'

'I haven't seen him for a while...'

'No,' Michael said, the kettle reaching the boil. 'We're no longer an item.'

'Oh. I am sorry,' Emily said. She sat down on the chaise longue, her knees tightly together. Theodore watched as she undid a button of Jonathan's shirt.

He looked to the kitchen, where Michael was crushing little white tablets with the back of a teaspoon. He spooned the white powder into Emily's cup of tea and stirred it in.

Michael put the two cups of tea onto the tray and carried it through into the living room. He placed the tray on a little side table beside the chaise longue. For the next few minutes the pair chatted.

'What type of tea is this?' Emily asked. 'It has a strange edge to it.'

'It's Yamamotoyama, said Michael.

'I don't think I've ever had that one before...'

She began to giggle.

'What did you say it's called again? Yamma... mamma.'

Michael laughed too. 'Yamamotoyama,' he said.

'Yammamammayammamamma...' said Emily, before collapsing into giggles.

Michael stood up and from behind the easel he picked up the little wooden mallet.

He glanced out of the kitchen window. He spotted Theodore eyeing him from within the ivy that hung over the wall.

'They will know my name,' he mouthed silently at the cat.

Theodore realised that Michael was intent on tidying up any loose ends.

He jumped down from the wall, then up onto the windowsill. It was a sash window. It was open at the top a couple of inches but not enough for him to get through. He peered through the glass into the room.

Emily was reclined on the chaise longue, another button on her shirt undone.

'So how would you like me?' she said, giggling. 'Is this all right?'

'I can always arrange you later,' said Michael and laughed.

Emily giggled. 'I like this tea,' she said, still giggling. 'It's very nice.'

'A nice cup of tea!' Michael said, clapping his hands together.

Emily reached over and took her cup of tea. 'Yammamamma...' she slurred, raising the cup to her lips.

'You drink it all up now,' Michael said, clutching the mallet behind the drawing board.

Theodore jumped up at the top of the window. He managed to get his paws into the gap. He pushed down and pushed himself forward as the window dropped under his weight. He landed in the middle of the room. He skidded to a halt between Emily and Michael.

'It's Theo!' Emily cried, clapping her hands together. 'It's my cat!'

Michael still had the small mallet in his hand, held behind the drawing board. Theodore dashed towards Emily, knocking the tea cup from her hand. It fell to the floor and smashed. The half-drunk tea spilled onto the parquet floor.

'Get out of here!' Michael shouted.

'Hey! Don't shout at my cat!'

'I'm allergic to cats!'

Theodore made it through the door into the hallway. He looked at the closed front door and then dashed up the stairs and into the back bedroom.

He jumped onto the double bed. The duvet fell away from Philip's face. A red pulp, with black scabs and shards of bone. It was more like a giant red lollipop that had been rolled in a grate of ashes than a human head.

Behind him he heard footsteps pounding up the stairs. He dived under the bed.

'I know you're in there,' Michael said from the doorway.

Theodore positioned himself under the middle of the bed.

'I'm going to get you now,' he snarled.

He watched as Michael's face appeared at his own level, contorted into a grimace.

'I'm going to cut you in half and put you in formaldehyde.'

Theodore wasn't quite sure what formaldehyde was, having little interest in modern art. He edged backwards. He pushed up against something. It rolled away from him. He turned and inspected the object.

It was a wooden cylinder, about two feet long. A baseball bat. *Greetings from Louisville,* it said in cursive script down the side. He examined the end of the bat. It was caked in dried blood.

This is what Michael had used to finish Peter Morris off, realised Theodore, and then Philip. The murder weapon.

'Get out from there!' Michael hissed, his voice laced with anger. He swung his fist in a wide arc below the bed.

Theodore pressed himself into the corner. Just out of reach.

'Is everything all right up there?' Emily slurred from downstairs.

We are both for it now, thought Theodore.

'It's all right,' Michael said, 'I can manage. Just trying to get him out from under the bed.'

Michael approached the bottom of the bed. He yanked it away from the wall.

Theodore, exposed, dived back under the bed and out the other side. He ran through the door, before Michael could block him off, then back downstairs, past Emily, and into the kitchen.

'There,' Emily said. 'He's found his way out!'

Michael appeared at the top of the stairs, panting, the baseball bat held behind his back. 'I'm going to have to fumigate the house,' he said, coming back downstairs, breathing hard.

'I'm sorry,' Emily said.

Theodore miaowed at the back door.

'I'll let him out,' Emily said, making her way into the kitchen. 'I think it might be best if we both left.'

Theodore miaowed in agreement.

Emily tried the back door. It was locked. There was no key in the lock.

She turned and noticed the white powder smeared on the kitchen side. 'The door's locked,' Emily said slowly.

'I know,' said Michael.

Emily raised a hand to her temple. 'I feel very tired... after... all the... excitement,' she said. 'My head...'

She turned and fell to the floor.

Theodore watched from the corner, as Michael carried her back to the chaise longue and arranged her. Returning to his drawing board he picked up the meat tenderising mallet.

'Now we are going to see what cat brains look like!' Michael snarled, brandishing the mallet at Theodore.

Theodore ran past Michael, just avoiding a swipe from the mallet. He dashed into the hall and then back upstairs. This time, instead of making for the back bedroom, he ran into the front bedroom. There was a double bed. On top of one of the pillows there was a set of pink pyjamas, neatly folded.

The bedroom window was open, the sash pushed down. He jumped onto the bed and then up into the opening, balancing on the top of the window. The window dropped another inch under his weight.

He looked down. It was a twenty foot drop to the gravel forecourt below.

He looked up. There was the plastic gutter and then the eaves of the house.

He looked back and saw Michael standing in the doorway, clutching his mallet and grinning insanely.

He looked down once more. Then jumped.

26

Cats were designed to live in trees, so they know how to fall out of them.

They spread their legs out to increase their surface area and slow their fall. Their springy legs act as shock absorbers, cushioning the blow when they hit the ground. They rotate their bodies to make sure they land on their paws. Cats were designed to fall. Throw a cow out of a window and it would be another story.

Theodore landed in the limestone gravel of Michael's forecourt. He looked back up at the window.

Michael stared down at him, his face red, his eyes wide.

Theodore exited through the open front gate and sprinted down the street and into the safety of the back alley.

His own house was empty. He paused in front of his empty food bowls. If Michael killed Emily, his bowls may never be filled again.

He would be destitute. A stray. Having to survive on a diet of rodents and whatever else he could catch.

He paced the kitchen floor, swishing his tail from side to side. He glanced at the clock on the kitchen wall. It was nearly eight o'clock. He wondered if Jonathan was on his way round. He entered the front room and looked out of the window and up the street. No Jonathan.

He paced the front room. Theodore didn't even know if Jonathan had arranged to come round that evening. But Jonathan was their only hope.

Theodore stared at his paws a moment.

Why couldn't Emily have dated a soldier, a professional wrestler, a bodyguard? Her only hope was a geologist...

He looked again at his empty food bowls.

There was no one else.

He would have to go and find him.

Jonathan was having his dinner when Theodore appeared at his kitchen window. A pizza on the table in front of him.

'Theodore!' he said, getting to his feet. 'What are you doing here?'

He opened the back door but Theodore did not enter the house. He jumped down onto the ground and miaowed at Jonathan.

Your girlfriend's been drugged by a psychopathic homicidal killer, he wanted to say.

'What is it, Theodore?' Jonathan said. 'How did you find me here?'

She's probably being cut up into little pieces by now.

'We didn't arrange anything for tonight,' Jonathan said, patting Theodore on the head.

If you don't come now, you're going to be looking for a new girlfriend...

'I'm in the middle of eating my dinner,' Jonathan said. 'I don't want it to get cold.'

Theodore made his way to the back gate, miaowing the whole time.

Jonathan returned to his pepperoni pizza. He bit into a slice and chewed. He could hear Theodore miaowing from his back-yard. He got up and looked out of his kitchen window. Theodore was sitting on his back wall, staring back at him. When the cat saw him looking, it miaowed.

He reached for his mobile phone and called Emily's phone. She did not answer. He looked again out of his kitchen window at the grey cat.

A minute later Jonathan pushed the remains of his pizza into the kitchen bin and locked the back door behind him.

'This had better not be another dead cat in the allotments,' he said, as he shut his gate and followed Theodore's raised tail.

It might well be a dead girlfriend on the chaise longue, thought Theodore, as he trotted down the alley.

Back at No.17 Avondale Terrace, Jonathan discovered an empty house. There was Emily's mobile phone left on the arm of the sofa. There was one missed call. From him.

'She's probably just gone to the shops,' Jonathan said, following Theodore through to the kitchen.

He noticed Theodore's empty food bowls.

'So is that it?' he said. 'She went out without feeding you...'

Jonathan poured some biscuits into a bowl. But Theodore turned his tailed up at them. He went over to the back door and miaowed.

Jonathan unlocked the door and followed Theodore out into the yard. The cat walked to the back gate. Jonathan noticed the back gate was unbolted. Perhaps Emily had gone out. If she had gone out of the back gate, she couldn't have gone far. He opened the gate and followed Theodore down the alley.

Theodore stopped in front of a back gate, opposite the house where Peter Morris had been killed. Reminded of the murder, Jonathan began to worry about his girlfriend. He stood in front of the gate.

Theodore looked up at him and then miaowed at the gate.

Jonathan hesitated. He didn't know who lived in this house. Emily had not mentioned being friends with anyone on the street. She kept herself to herself; more so after the murder of her neighbour.

'Are you sure about this?' he said to Theodore.

The cat miaowed back at him. *Just get a move on.*

'You'd better be.'

Suddenly Diane appeared out of nowhere.

'I want a word with you,' she said, prodding her forefinger at his chest.

'Now's not a good time,' Jonathan said. 'I'm a bit busy.'

'I want to know about my cat,' Diane said. 'You didn't bury him in your garden, did you?'

'No,' Jonathan said. 'Not exactly.'

'I didn't think so.'

'I was going to,' Jonathan said. 'But then I threw him in a wheelie bin.'

'You did what?'

'Look, does it really matter now? He was dead. It was a little white lie.'

'You put my cat in a wheelie bin!' Diane screamed.

A piece of chewing gum dropped from her mouth onto the ground.

Jonathan took a step backwards.

'A little white lie!'

'It's a long story and I really don't have time to tell it now.'

'You threw Arthur into a wheelie bin?' Diane screamed.

She pushed Jonathan in the chest with her fingers.

'I have to go,' Jonathan said, but Diane was blocking his path, her face in his.

He tried to step round her but she moved too, her fingers poking at his chest.

Craig Foster had been watching the altercation from the window of his attic room. He rushed downstairs and out into the back alley.

'What's going on?' he gasped. 'Are you all right?'

Diane turned to face him. 'What's it to you?' she said. 'You ginger nutter.'

'I saw you arguing,' Craig panted. 'I came to help.'

'I don't need any help from you,' Diane barked.

Craig's face dropped. 'But...'

'But what? How are you going to help? Are you going to bring my cat back? Are you going to bring my husband back? Well?'

'Well, no,' Craig said.

'I really need to get going,' Jonathan interrupted.

'You're not going anywhere,' Diane said. 'Not until you tell me why you dropped my cat in a wheelie bin.'

'Look, now's not a good time,' Jonathan said and barged past her.

'You haven't heard the last of this,' Diane screamed after him.

Jonathan carried on down the hill, not looking round. Then Theodore emerged from his hiding place beneath a hedge and trotted after him.

Craig stood next to Diane and watched them go, tears in his eyes. 'I came to help,' he blubbed.

'Well, you weren't much help, were you?' Diane said.

Jonathan and Theodore exited the alley onto Avondale Terrace and then counted the houses back up the hill. He stopped in front of No.7. The front door was painted glossy black with a shiny brass knocker. He knocked on the door. He waited. He knocked again. Finally the door opened a couple of inches.

'This might sound stupid,' Jonathan said into the gap, 'but is my girlfriend here?'

'Your girlfriend?' Michael said.

'Yes. Emily Blenkin. She lives up the street.'

There was a pause, and then Michael said, 'Yes. Emily's modelling for me...'

'Modelling?' Jonathan said. 'She didn't mention it... I was worried.'

'I am working on her portrait,' Michael said. 'Didn't she say?'

Through the gap in the door, Jonathan noticed that Michael was indeed holding a pencil.

'I didn't know,' Jonathan said. 'She didn't say anything about modelling.'

'Yes, modelling,' Michael said. 'I'll get back to it if there's nothing else. Wouldn't want to lose the flow, you know.'

From behind Jonathan, Theodore miaowed.

Michael was about to close the door.

'I need to speak to her a minute,' Jonathan said. 'It's important. It's about her cat...'

'I'm afraid you can't at the moment,' Michael said.

'Excuse me?'

'She fell asleep,' Michael explained.

'Asleep? But I really need to speak to her.'

Jonathan moved towards the front door.

'You can come in a minute,' Michael said, 'but she's fast asleep...'

Theodore watched as Jonathan entered Michael's house and the door was shut behind him. He raced back into the alley and returned to the boundary wall of Michael's house. Inside, he saw Jonathan enter the lounge. Emily was laid out provocatively on the chaise longue. He looked at the parquet floor. The broken tea cup and its contents had been cleared away and cleaned up.

Jonathan put his hand on Emily's shoulder.

'Emily,' he said, shaking her. 'You need to wake up.'

Michael returned to his drawing board and picked up the little wooden mallet.

Theodore dropped down to the ground and then jumped up onto the windowsill. The sash window had been closed.

Michael approached, the mallet raised over Jonathan's head.

Theodore miaowed through the glass as loudly as he could.

Jonathan looked round and saw Theodore on the windowsill. He turned and saw Michael, a wooden mallet in his hand.

'What's that?' Jonathan said, squaring up to Michael.

'It's a mallet,' Michael said. 'You know for tenderising steaks.'

'But what are you doing with it?'

Michael hesitated.

Jonathan glanced back at his prone girlfriend, then back to Michael.

'Well?'

'I use it,' Michael said. 'As a rest. You know, so I don't smudge my work.'

'Well,' Jonathan said, turning back to Emily, 'I think I'd better get her home.'

Jonathan lifted her up from the chaise longue and placed her over his shoulder in a fireman's lift. As he shut the front door behind him, he murmured into Emily's ear, 'Let's get you home...'

27

Jonathan put Emily to bed. Theodore settled by her side and reassured himself that she was going to be fine. In her drug-induced sleep, he heard her say: 'I don't want to model for you anymore.'

Downstairs Jonathan watched television. He had opened a bottle of red wine and had found a Swedish crime drama on the television.

When he saw Theodore enter the front room, he said, 'Looks like it's me and you tonight.'

Theodore sat on his lap but couldn't settle.

'That guy gave me the creeps,' Jonathan said to Theodore.

Theodore purred in agreement. Jonathan took a large drink from his glass of wine. Then there was a knock at the door. Theodore followed Jonathan. There were two police officers.

'Are you Jonathan?' one of them said. 'Jonathan Fielder?'

'Yes,' said Jonathan.

'Do you know a Diane Banks?'

'Diane?' Jonathan said. 'I know someone called Diane.'

'Did you have an altercation with her this evening? In the alley behind?'

'An altercation? Not really. She was upset and I tried to get past her.'

'Did you push her?'

'She was in my way.'

'Did you push her?'

'I pushed past her.'

'So you pushed her.'

'I suppose I did. But she pushed me first.'

'She says that you threw her dead cat into a wheelie bin.'

'Yes. I did. It's a long story, but I didn't know it was hers. I found it and brought it back here.'

'I think you are going to have to come with us and make a statement. She is quite upset about it all.'

'Really? Now? Can't it wait until morning. My girlfriend is upstairs asleep.'

'I'm sure she'll still be here when you get back.'

'I think it best if you come with us now,' the other police officer said. 'These are quite serious allegations.'

Jonathan shook his head. 'I'll get my jacket,' he said.

Theodore watched from the front window as Jonathan got into the back of the police van, which had stopped in the middle of the street, lights flashing. After a minute or two the van pulled away. He went upstairs and checked on Emily. She was fast asleep. He dabbed at her face but she didn't wake.

As the light began to fade and the air grew cold, Theodore took up position in the ivy that grew over the boundary wall of Michael's house. Michael was doing the washing up in the kitchen. When he brought his kitchen bin out and emptied it into the bin in the yard, he spotted Theodore.

'So you want to know why?' he asked.

'Well, I could tell you how he muttered "Your sort disgusts me," as I was putting my rubbish out one night,' Michael said. 'I could tell you how he drove a wedge between mother and daughter because of his racist views... Yes. I've had my eye on the old bigot for years.'

Theodore stared into Michael's eyes. 'And what about Philip?' he wanted to say.

'Philip suspected that I'd done it but he didn't know for sure. I'd told him how much I hated the old codger.'

Theodore continued staring down at Michael.

'He began making demands... A new pair of trainers, an expensive watch, a meal out. It all adds up... I'm a struggling artist, you know. I don't have that sort of money. I had to deal with him before he said something.'

Theodore's eyes widened further.

'And Emily? Well, I was getting into the swing of it... Get it? The swing of it!' Michael mimicked swinging a baseball bat, a sick grin on his face. 'Then I have my reputation to think about,' he went on. 'One day my pictures will be priceless. Once people know the background...'

He replaced the cover to the metal bin with a clatter. 'It's a pity I don't do pets...' he said, grinning. He turned to go back inside but paused.

Then he turned back to Theodore. 'So, now you know the truth, what are you going to do about it, little pussy cat?'

Theodore considered attempting a feline arrest but knew it would be futile. He wanted to say that there was just one more thing, as he had heard his hero Lieutenant Columbo quip before delivering the killer line and nailing the criminal. But he did not say anything. He was just a cat after all.

'Well, if there's nothing else,' Michael said. 'I need to get on. I'm going down to London tomorrow. Business...' He turned and went back into his house, shutting the door behind him.

In the kitchen Michael took his mobile phone from his pocket and made a call.

'Henry?' he said. 'It's Michael... You know, Mikey from Yorkshire... Yes, I know it's late... But I'm coming down to London tomorrow... I've got something for you.'

He paused, listening to Henry talk.

'I know the last pictures didn't sell well,' he said. Then: 'These will make my name... I can promise you that. They will be priceless one day... I just need a bit of an advance on them. That's all. You see I'm planning a trip abroad.'

He paced the kitchen, his mobile held tightly to his ear, his pink head glistening beneath the fluorescent kitchen light.

'Look. I'll see you tomorrow. You won't be disappointed. Not when I tell you the story behind them...'

He finished the phone call. Then, from on top of a cupboard, he got down a brown suitcase. He began taking his pictures down from the walls and putting them into the suitcase. Once his suitcase was packed, Michael returned to the kitchen and from a cupboard he took a handheld electric circular saw he had bought that morning from B&Q and went upstairs.

Moments later the bathroom light was turned on. Theodore heard both bath taps turned on and water began to run from the bottom of a pipe into the drain. From the bathroom there came a whirring, and then the whine as metal cut bone.

Water gushed into the drain, through the round metal grate. Theodore watched as the water turned red.

Froth formed on the drain grate.

Theodore looked up at the bathroom window and the shadows dancing behind the mottled glass.

28

The dim hour before dawn is a magical time, if you are a cat. The birds are awake. Most cats are awake. Most people are asleep. Michael, however, was wide awake.

The night before bin day, people put their bin bags against their back walls. As the access into the back alley is too tight for the bin lorry to enter, a man gathers all the bags and stacks them in a big pile against the side of Wendy Morris's house. The lorry parks next to the access to the alley and the bin men heft the bags into the back of the bin lorry.

Michael waited until first light before putting out his rubbish. He had placed his bags in a neat row at the base of Wendy's wall. Now he stood in front of his bedroom window and waited.

Another person was also up early that morning. In her mauve dressing gown and fur-lined slippers, Wendy Morris paced her kitchen, glancing now and again at the telephone on the side and then to the clock on the wall. Waiting for a reasonable hour to call the police. She put the kettle on and made herself a hot chocolate.

Theodore lay on the pillow beside Emily. His ears twitched as he listened to the early morning noises from outside. His thoughts flicked back to the evening before. He remembered the red water that had gushed out into the drain, leaving pink and yellow scum over the grate.

There was no way he could prove that Michael had killed Peter Morris, but perhaps he could get him for Philip's murder.

Theodore got to his paws and jumped down onto the floor. He crossed to the window and, standing up on his hind legs, poked his head up behind the closed curtains.

Against Wendy's wall there was a line of three full bin liners, each closed at the top with parcel tape. He knew they did not belong to Wendy. Her bin bags were further up the wall of her house, nearer the street. He watched as a bin man added a dozen more bags to the bottom of the wall. No doubt the three ominous black bags would soon be beneath a mountain of rubbish, Theodore realised. His thoughts returned to the dancing silhouette behind the bathroom window.

He returned to his pillow and tried to wake Emily, dabbing at her face with the pads of his paws, but she was sound asleep, her mouth open. Jonathan had yet to return from Fulford Police Station. He was by himself, he realised.

In the grey light, he padded down the stairs and made for the cat flap.

From the back wall, he glanced up at Michael's bedroom window. The curtains were open; a dark silhouette behind the glass. He saw the bin man further up the hill, half a dozen bin bags in each hand, carrying them to the bottom to add to the ones already piled up against Wendy's wall; he whistled as he worked. He threw the bags onto the pile and then returned up the hill to gather more.

Theodore peered into Wendy's kitchen. Wendy was sitting at the kitchen table, the telephone in front of her, a mug of cocoa in her hand. Every minute or so she glanced at the clock on the wall.

The bin man was halfway up the hill, his back to Theodore. Theodore jumped down into the alley and dashed across to the bin bags piled up against Wendy's wall.

He slid a claw across the tight shiny black surface. The bag split open to reveal a second shiny black surface. Double-bagged!

He heard footsteps approach the corner. He swiped at the black shiny plastic again.

'Get out of it,' the bin man shouted, stamping his feet theatrically at the cat.

Theodore turned and dashed past the bin man, side stepping him, then raced back up the hill.

Back upstairs in the bedroom, Emily was still asleep. Theodore stood up behind the curtain once more. The three bin liners were now hidden by the ever growing pile of rubbish. In the distance he heard the bin lorry approach. The bin man who had seen Theodore off stood waiting beside the mountain of rubbish for his colleagues to join him.

An orange light began to flash against the side of Wendy's house, and soon two other men entered the back alley and began shifting the bin bags, tossing them into the back of the waiting lorry. Finally they got to the bottom of the pile.

A bin man picked up the last bag and began to carry it out into the street.

'You've lost something,' one of his colleagues shouted back at him.

On the ground lay a fingerless hand and forearm, wrapped in cling film. On the wrist there was a gold Rolex.

Theodore watched as one of the bin men shook his bald head slowly from side to side. 'Now I've seen it all,' he said.

The bin man took out his mobile phone and called the police.

At the same time Wendy took a last sip of hot chocolate, put down her mug; then picked up her phone and called the police.

The alarm clock went off. Emily rolled over and snoozed it. 'Too early,' she mumbled sleepily.

Theodore walked past the bed and into the front bedroom. He jumped up onto the table in front of the window. From down the street, he heard a door open and then close. In the distance he heard a police siren.

Michael walked to the pavement and placed his suitcase by the kerb. He glanced at his watch. He took out his mobile phone. Sweat beaded on his pink forehead.

Then a taxi appeared at the bottom of the hill. It pulled up against the kerb. He read the insignia on the side: Crow Line Taxis.

Ahmet swung open the taxi door and got out to help his first customer of the day with his luggage.

'Morning,' he said to Michael, recognising him as the artistic type who lived several doors down the hill from his own house.

Michael already had his suitcase in his hand as Ahmet approached.

'I can manage,' he said.

Ahmet opened the boot and Michael pushed the suitcase inside.

'I'm in a hurry,' Michael said, getting into the back of the taxi.

Ahmet closed the boot and got into the driving seat.

Michael looked out of the car window.

He saw the large grey cat staring down at him from a window. The cat blinked at him. He waved goodbye to the cat and mouthed, 'Bye, bye Pussy Cat.'

The sirens grew louder.

Theodore jumped down from the windowsill and headed downstairs.

'You know, I live on this street,' Ahmet said, getting in the driver's seat. 'Just up there... First customer of the morning and it's one of my neighbours. What a coincidence!'

'The station,' Michael said. 'I'm going to the railway station.'

'Business or pleasure?' Ahmet said, putting the car into gear.

He pulled the car into the middle of the road, between the lines of parked cars.

'Just drive,' Michael said. 'I'm not in the mood for small talk.'

Ahmet drove up the hill, not shifting up from second gear. As they neared the top of the road, a police car turned in, preventing them from exiting. Ahmet began to reverse into a gap in the parked cars to allow the police car to pass.

'Keep going!' Michael shouted. 'I have a train to catch.'

Ahmet glanced back down the street and saw another police car begin to ascend the hill, its siren turned on. He glanced at the police car in front, its siren now turned on. He glanced at his backseat passenger, his face red and dripping sweat.

'You're going to miss your train,' Ahmet said. He put the handbrake on and took the key from the ignition. Then he stepped out of his taxi and locked the doors.

The police car stopped in front and two officers got out.

Michael slapped his hands uselessly against the car window.

'Let me out!' he screamed from behind the glass.

'What seems to be the problem here?' one of the officers asked Ahmet.

'This gentleman appears to be in a rush this morning,' Ahmet said. 'With all the sirens, I thought I'd better stop.'

'We'd better have a word with him,' a police officer said. 'If you could unlock the doors...'

Ahmet clicked his car key and the passenger door swung open, across the pavement.

Michael jumped out of the taxi and faced the police officer.

'In a hurry?' the police officer said.

'Yes,' Michael said, and turned and began to run down the street.

As he passed the access into the back alley, he spotted the grey fluffy cat crouching against the wall.

And Theodore spotted the red-faced Michael as he flashed past. He saw Irene and Rocky crossing the road at the bottom of the hill, Rocky straining on his lead; out for his early morning walk.

Theodore dashed out onto the pavement, turned and caught the German shepherd's eye. Then he ran up the hill.

Rocky broke free of his lead and bolted up the hill after the big grey cat. Unfortunately Michael was in his way.

Michael's legs were taken out by the German shepherd. He was sent sprawling onto the pavement. Within seconds police officers were over him, one of them with his knee on his back.

'I think you've got some explaining to do,' he said, cuffing him.

Theodore watched from the forecourt of a house as Michael was dragged to his feet and walked towards a police car. Rocky was trotting up and down the street, his tongue lolling, while Irene called for him, 'Get here now!'

Theodore watched as Michael was put in the back of a police car. More police cars and vans had arrived; their sirens blaring out a symphony.

Later the police would discover Philip's dismembered body in the bin bags in the back alley. Later, his bashed-in head would be fished out of the muddy waters of the Ouse, tied up in a Waitrose bag-for-life.

His fingers and teeth would never be recovered.

29

'Clementhorpe Killer Caught!' the headline in *The Press* shouted the next day from Wendy's kitchen table.

'Well, at least you can move on now,' Irene said.

'Aye suppose so,' Wendy said. 'Talking of moving on, I saw a For Sale sign outside Diane's. Reckon she's moving back to Lancashire.'

'It'll be bought and let out like the rest of them.'

'Craig Foster's house too. He must have decided to move on too.'

'Investors,' Irene muttered. 'They'll soon snap them up. They keep putting leaflets through my door. Can't wait for me to pop my clogs.'

'You've got a good few years left in you,' Wendy said.

'I've got my dog to look after,' Irene said. 'I have to keep going for him.'

After Irene had left, Wendy had another visitor.

Her daughter pushed her pram through into the kitchen. On top of the pram was wedged a cat carrier.

'What's that you've got in there?' Wendy asked.

'What do you think it is? It's a kitten,' Laura said. 'It's for you.'

'But I don't like cats,' Wendy said. 'You know that.'

'Dad never liked cats,' Laura said. 'But that doesn't mean that you can't like them.'

Wendy shook her head.

'It'll keep you company,' Laura said. 'Go on.'

'You'd better get him out so I can have a look at him.'

Laura parked the pram in the backyard and made herself a coffee, the kitten purring on Wendy's lap the whole time.

They sat at the kitchen table.

'Joseph will be waking shortly,' Laura said, 'and I don't have any food with me.'

'I'm sure I've got something here you could give him. Porridge oats. I could make up some porridge for him.'

At that moment Joseph began to cry.

'I should really get going,' Laura said. 'But I'll call round tomorrow to see how you and the kitten are getting on.'

She turned to her mother: 'Best to let bygones be bygones.'

'Aye,' Wendy said. 'Best to let sleeping dogs lie.'

Later, Theodore watched as the kitten kneaded Wendy's stomach, purring loudly. It was a tortoiseshell: a mishmash of colours: white, marmalade, grey and black. Wendy stroked the kitten as she watched her soap opera. 'I'll call you Splodge,' she said.

Theodore got to his paws and stretched. Before returning home, he paid a visit to Zeynep and Ahmet's. From inside the house, the new baby cried.

Ahmet was standing over the Moses basket.

'You can pick him up, you know,' Zeynep said.

'I'm afraid to,' Ahmet said, peering down at the pink shrivelled baby with bruised eyes. 'He's so small.'

'It'll be fine,' Zeynep said. 'Just don't drop him!'

Ahmet picked the baby up and held him to his chest. He thought of the dolls' house he had made for the baby. The little house that Zeynep had smashed up.

'I will make him a railway set,' Ahmet said. 'For when he is bigger. It will have tunnels and bridges, and a station and station master...'

'You can make it in your shed,' Zeynep said and smiled.

From the back bedroom window Bal and Belle peered out. They would soon be removed from the bedroom which would become a nursery. They blinked hello at Theodore.

Theodore blinked back. He understood that Bal had been the key to unlocking the mystery. Zeynep had hit Peter Morris over the head but had not killed him.

Theodore closed his eyes. Who was ultimately responsible for killing Peter Morris?

Zeynep had hit him with the cobblestone. Wendy had ignored his cries for help. Then Michael had finished him off with his baseball bat, a Souvenir from Louisville, wherever that was.

But if Peter Morris had not made the racist remark to Zeynep, he might still be alive. If he had been a little nicer to his wife, Wendy, he might still be alive. If he had not insulted Michael, he might still be alive. So, in a way, Peter Morris had been responsible for his own ending. He just hadn't reckoned on having a psychopathic killer living behind. Who does?

Michael Butler had stored up his grievances inside. He had wanted fame and fortune for his art but they had not been forthcoming. He had spent his hours dwelling on the unfairness of life. Hatred for his fellow man festered inside with no outlet. Now, in a high security prison, he would get the therapy he needed through his art. He would produce masterworks which would never be seen outside Her Majesty's Prisons.

Then Theodore realised that he had been blinded by his own impressions of Michael. His own prejudice had shielded Michael. If Theodore had acted sooner, he might have put an end to Michael's murderous ways before he had killed Philip. Dried leaves blew down the back alley. Theodore wandered restlessly home.

Jonathan and Emily were in the front room.

'To think I modelled for him!' Emily said.

'I think you had a narrow escape,' Jonathan said, putting the newspaper down. 'We both did.'

'Don't you mean all three of us?' Emily said, nodding and smiling at Theodore, now standing in the middle of the room.

'Yes,' Jonathan said. 'I'm not sure what would have happened the other night if he hadn't turned up.'

The telephone in the corner began ringing.

'It'll be my mother,' said Emily.

They let it go to the answerphone.

'I can't believe it was the man from down the hill who did it,' Emily's mother said into the machine. 'I heard on the news that he's homosexual too. Well, I never thought you could get homicidal homosexuals!'

Emily snatched up the telephone. 'What about Ted Bundy?' she said.

'Pardon?' her mother said, surprised that the telephone had been answered. 'Who's this Ted Bundy?'

'He was a gay serial killer,' Emily said. 'Targeted young men. He used to dress up as a clown too.'

'Did he now?' her mother said. 'Well, I guess it takes all sorts.'

'Yes, Mum,' Emily said. 'I guess it does.'

'Don't they say: it's always the ones you don't suspect?'

After Emily had finished speaking to her mum and had said hello to her dad, she turned to Jonathan.

'After everything that's happened here,' she said, 'I think it might be an idea to move. After everything that's happened, I don't think I'm ever going to be comfortable round here again.'

'What do you mean move?' Jonathan said. 'When were you going to tell me?'

'Well, I'm asking?'

'Asking?'

'Asking if you'd like to move in together. With me and Theodore. It makes sense. We need somewhere bigger... You're paying rent for your place and spending half the time round here anyway. It just makes sense.

'And I'm sure Theodore would love a garden. He might not get into such mischief if he had a garden to play in.'

'So, you think we should all move in together and play happy families?'

'Why not?' Emily said, chewing on her thumbnail.

'Sounds like a plan,' Jonathan said. 'Where were you thinking?'

'I think a different area,' Emily said. 'After everything that's happened in Clementhorpe, I think we should move somewhere different. A new start... I hear Acomb is up-and-coming.'

Theodore slunk outside. He sat on the back wall. He gazed over at the brick walls of the alleys and houses. Further up the hill they had begun to lay tarmac over the cobbles, the black blanket covering over a hundred years of history. Further down the hill a street lamp bathed the remaining blue cobblestones in golden light.

Theodore knew that it would soon be gone. The back alley would be gone. The people he knew on the street would be gone. He would be yanked out of this world and plonked down in another.

He raised his head and began a low mewling, becoming higher pitched before breaking into full wail.

He sang his lament to the cobbles of the back alleys; the weathered bricks that made up the walls; the worn slate roof tiles; the satellite dishes perched under eaves pointing south; the old ladies nattering over tea and biscuits; the men busy in their sheds or jogging up and down the street; the cats sleeping under hedges or basking in the sun on flat felt roofs; the dogs whining for walks in backyards; the pigeons gathered on the ridges; the black and white geese flying over, en route to Rowntree Park, the solitary magpie perched on a television aerial...

He sang his song: his farewell to Clementhorpe. His home.

Windows up and down the street were abruptly pulled shut. As everyone knows, the singing of cats is not to everybody's taste.

2

The Cat Who Knew Too Much

She takes a last drag on the cigarette and drops it from her bedroom window, down the gap between the house and the shed, like she has done a thousand times or more, but this time, rather than smouldering out with the rest of the butts, the shed explodes with a bang.

Her dad staggers out. He's on fire. He stands in the middle of the lawn. He flaps his hands against his clothes, trying to put out the flames. He turns and faces the back of his house. He looks up at her bedroom window. 'Hell,' he shouts. 'Hell fire!'

She is 14 years old. She has unicorns and princesses on her curtains, pink and blue. She has grown out of them but her dad has promised her new curtains, yellow ones. She wonders if she'll get the yellow curtains now.

From the bedroom next to hers, she hears her sister scream. She is three years older, about to go off to university.

Then she sees her mum run outside, wet tea towels in her hands. 'Get down on the lawn,' her mum shouts at her dad.

Her dad lies down on the lawn and her mum pushes the wet tea towels against the flames and smouldering clothing. Her dad has stopped screaming and she knows he is dead. His mouth is open; his gums peeled back to show off his yellow teeth.

There is a corpse, with blackened, blistered skin, clothes burnt onto flesh, lying in the middle of the neatly trimmed lawn.

Her mum shakes out one of the tea towels. It is streaked with soot. She lays it over her dad's face.

The tea towel has rolling green hills and winding blue streams on it, and bares the slogan: 'Welcome to God's Own County'.

2

He had already been incarcerated for several days, or so it seemed. He had no way of knowing for sure. There was no clock on the wall and he had no means to tell the time.

His cell was a carpeted room, five feet by six. A small window without curtains, too high for him to look out of, was set into the wall. The door was shut. There was no way of escape.

He'd been left water and biscuits by his captors. He turned his nose up at the paltry offerings. He paced the room. At least they wanted to keep him alive, he thought, for the time being at least.

After pacing the carpeted floor for what seemed like hours, and relieving himself in a corner of the room, he settled on a makeshift bed in the opposite corner. He soon fell asleep.

When he woke the door was ajar. He stood in front of it for some minutes. It might be a trick.

Then he nudged it further open.

There was a landing, in the same mauve carpet as the room in which he'd been held. As he headed to the top of the stairs, he saw a cat. He turned to face it.

Its fur was silver and white, tinted charcoal. Its eyes were emerald green. Its nose was the brown of cooked liver. Its left ear was curled over, the result of a fight with another cat.

He stared at the cat and the cat stared back. The hair along his spine bristled and his tail stood up straight. The other cat did likewise.

Theodore approached, hissing, and the other cat approached, hissing back at him. It was quite a formidable foe, Theodore thought, and quite a handsome specimen.

It was him after all, he realised, as he came nose to nose with his reflection. He glanced behind the mirror, leaning against the landing wall, just to make sure. He raised his tail and carried on along the landing.

He examined the mauve pile of the carpet; noted the strange odours left by previous occupants, the dark stains, the strange brown sticky patches. Then he padded downstairs to investigate this new domain further.

In the kitchen he discovered his water bowl and a fresh bowl of cat biscuits in the corner. He ate several. They tasted no different to how they had tasted that morning, back at his old home in Clementhorpe. At least somethings did not change, he thought, approaching the back door.

There was no cat flap. He stared for a moment at the lack of an opening in the door, his tail raised high. He miaowed.

'You're not going anywhere, Theo,' Emily said. 'You've a litter tray over there.'

Theodore looked over at the covered tray in the corner. He swished his tail from side to side. For Bastet's sake, he swore under his breath, invoking the name of the Cat Goddess. How was he to maintain his dignity while having to relieve himself in a plastic tray with a see-through flap? How would a human like it?

'It's only for a couple of weeks,' Emily said, arms folded across her chest and shaking her head.

Emily's attention was then drawn to the litter tray and its contents. 'Jonathan,' she said. 'You bought the wrong type of litter...'

'The wrong type?' Jonathan said, looking up from his mobile phone. 'I just bought the cheapest one.'

'I can see that,' Emily said. 'It turns to sludge.'

Theodore miaowed in agreement.

'Well, I'm not going out again to buy more litter. He can make do with what he's got for now... Next time I'll know. How long do we need to keep the litter tray inside anyway?'

'Just until Theo knows where his new home is,' Emily said.

'And how long will that be?'

'A fortnight,' Emily said. 'He's not going out before then. He's got to get used to his new home. Two weeks... That's what they say. Then we'll need to butter his paws...'

Theodore stared up at her, his eyes wide in disbelief. Buttering paws? What sort of barbaric nonsense was this?

'It will fly by,' Emily said, reading his feline mind, before bending down to stroke his head. 'I'm going to unpack some more boxes,' she said. 'They're not going to unpack themselves.'

Some minutes later Jonathan, still on his mobile, watched as Emily struggled into the kitchen with a box.

'This one weighs a tonne... What's in it?' she said. 'Rocks?'

'That'll be my fossil collection,' Jonathan said. 'I was going to put them in the front room.'

'We're not having rocks in the front room,' Emily said. 'They can go in the garden. You can make a rockery with them.'

'But they're valuable,' Jonathan protested. 'They took me years to collect.'

Emily opened the kitchen door. 'I think rocks belong in the garden,' she said.

She placed the box outside the kitchen door and returned inside.

There was a knock at the front door and Emily went to answer it.

Theodore followed at her heels. It may be an opportunity to gain a few minutes of freedom, he thought.

'I'm your neighbour,' a man with shaggy grey hair under a red cap said. 'I brought round a little house-warming present.'

'Oh, thank you,' Emily said, opening the door a little further to take the punnet of red tomatoes. 'They look nice and ripe.'

Aware that Theodore was standing behind her, brushing up against her bare calves, she held the door open only enough to accept the house-warming present.

'My cat,' she explained, 'I can't let him out.'

'What was that?' her new neighbour said. 'I'm a bit hard of hearing.'

'My cat,' Emily said loudly. 'I don't want him to get out.'

'Good,' her new neighbour said. 'They can make an awful mess.'

'Mess?'

'In gardens. You see, I've got green fingers and I'd prefer to keep them that way.'

He opened his mouth and laughed showing off a large gap between his middle teeth.

Emily looked down at the blood red tomatoes in the little green box and then back at her grinning new neighbour.

'They're very red,' she said, 'the tomatoes.'

'Yes,' the grey-haired man replied, nodding his head, still smiling. 'It's the bone meal. I make my own bone meal.'

'I see,' Emily said. 'How quaint...'

The man laughed.

Emily felt Theodore's fur once more, against the backs of her bare calves, and felt her skin begin to prickle. She inched the front door closed.

'The cat,' she said. 'I don't want him to get out.'

'No, he's best kept indoors,' the man said. 'Like I said... Well, I need to be on my way. Errands!'

'Well, thank you for the tomatoes,' Emily said.

'It's Walter,' the man said. 'But everyone calls me Wally.'

'Well, nice to meet you, erm... Wally. And thank you again for the tomatoes. We can have them with our dinner.'

'The pleasure is all mine... Sorry, I didn't catch your name.'

'Emily,' said Emily.

'A pleasure indeed,' said Wally.

'My boyfriend's in the kitchen,' Emily added, and then pushed the door to.

It was evident that Wally didn't like cats. He was probably a mouse in a past life, thought Theodore, staring at the back of the front door.

He stayed staring at the front door for a long minute. It was only April but his new neighbour had already managed to grow his own tomatoes. Theodore wasn't too familiar with horticulture having spent his youth in the backyards and cobbled alleys of Clementhorpe, but something did not seem right.

So far April had been a bipolar month – swinging between sunny days to others overcast with icy showers of rain. Was it possible to grow ripe tomatoes in April?

Constantine Crescent is a tree-lined street built by the Quakers mainly in the early 1920s, though construction had started in 1914 before being disrupted by the First World War. It is horse-shoe shaped, beginning and ending on York Street, Acomb – York's largest residential suburb.

The houses are a mixture of detached and semi-detached, with a few bungalows thrown in. Not one house on the street is the same as another. The Quakers understood that people are different and they like their houses to be different too. The trees that line the grassed verges are all lime. They had yet to sprout their waxy leaves.

Many of the houses had net curtains across their windows. Theodore sensed many eyes looking back at him from behind their veiled screens. A net curtain twitched from behind a display of Pampas Grass from the house in front.

Suburbia..., thought Theodore. How boring.

Then he noticed his new neighbour, Wally, mounting his bicycle and launching himself into the road; off on his errands, Theodore presumed, the bottom of his brown trousers tucked into his brown socks.

As Wally passed by, he turned and waved at Theodore, smiling his gappy smile. The world slowed down for a moment. Theodore blinked and then Wally was gone.

Then along the street, from the other direction, an ice cream van approached. It was driven by a fat, balding man, who toted a fat cigar. As it neared, the chimes played The Funeral March of a Marionette.

I make my own bone meal, Wally had said. Theodore's brow furrowed. What was bone meal made out of? he asked himself.

Bones, he answered. Whose or what's bones?

The hair along his spine began to bristle.

Perhaps he made his bone meal out of cats' bones...

2

Later, as Emily and Jonathan ate their chicken dinner, Theodore sat below the table. Emily had been known to drop the odd scrap on the floor in the past. That was before she had moved in together with Jonathan though. The dynamics had evidently changed.

He loitered hopefully, flicking his tail against Emily's bare calves from time to time to make sure she knew he was there, waiting.

Neither Emily nor Jonathan spoke while they ate. They had hoped to move into the house on Constantine Crescent before Christmas but it was almost Easter by the time they finally moved in.

The last few months their lives had been in suspended animation; their possessions in boxes in their respective homes, caught between two worlds with little to talk about apart from the upcoming move. So it was with a sense of relief that they had finally signed the papers in the solicitor's office, had a moving date confirmed, booked the removal company and, with a big sigh of relief, it was done.

As anyone who has listened to others talk about moving house knows, it is only interesting to those who are actually doing the moving, so it was also a huge relief to those who knew Emily and Jonathan that they had finally moved in.

Jonathan was chewing on a chicken wing. 'The Chinese believe the wing to be the best part of the chicken,' he said.

'I like best those little bits from underneath,' said Emily.

'The oysters?' Jonathan said.

'Is that they're called?'

'That's what I call them.' Jonathan took some salad from a bowl in the middle of the table. 'Did you use the tomatoes our new neighbour brought round?' he asked.

'Yes, why?' Emily said. 'They looked very ripe. I thought we should use them straightaway.'

'They taste a bit beefy.'

'Beefy?' Emily took a slice of tomato and chewed on it. 'Perhaps they're beef tomatoes,' she said.

'Not sure I've had beef tomatoes before,' he said.

'He said something about making his own bone meal.'

They ate in silence for a minute, pondering the significance of making your own bone meal.

'I'm in Derbyshire tomorrow,' Jonathan said, changing the subject. 'Looking for sinkholes...'

'Sinkholes?' Emily said, picking up a leg and taking a bite.

Jonathan explained that the area was prone to limestone dissolution.

'Oh, sinkholes,' Emily said, licking her greasy fingers. An image of a field with buried kitchen sinks scattered around came to her mind.

'A nice walk in the countryside and being paid for it,' Jonathan went on. 'It doesn't get better than that.'

'Well, just be careful,' Emily said.

'Of what?'

'The sinkholes, stupid. You might trip up in one.'

Jonathan laughed. 'I'll be fine,' he said.

Theodore looked at the bare floorboards. Not a scrap of chicken. He flicked his tail against Emily's bare calf, aiming the tip at the back of her knee.

Emily's hand appeared below the table. She flicked the back of her fingers against his side. 'You be patient! You'll get some later...' she said.

Theodore exited from beneath the table. He headed into the hallway and then made his way upstairs. He added his own scent as he went, rubbing himself against the steps. It wouldn't be too long before his own smell dominated the new house.

On the upstairs landing he paused. There were three bedrooms and a bathroom. The front bedroom was Emily and Jonathan's. One of the back bedrooms was crammed with cardboard boxes, waiting to be unpacked. The other back bedroom he knew too well; he had spent half the day locked in it and had no desire to return. So he made his way into the room filled with cardboard boxes and navigated his way through this temporary landscape.

From the windowsill he took in the garden below.

His previous house had just a concrete yard with one raised bed against the boundary wall. He now looked out across the lawn, to the islands of daffodils and the overgrown rockery beyond. There were long grasses and euphorbia, a rhododendron and other small shrubs. Behind the plants and shrubs, there was a hedge: part privet, part hawthorn. Through a gap at the bottom of the hedge, a ginger head appeared.

The head looked from side to side, and then a ginger cat emerged. Theodore miaowed at the glass but the ginger cat did not hear, or chose to ignore him.

Hamish strutted between the shrubs. He had got used to the garden being part of his territory, the previous occupant having moved out some months before. He looked up at Theodore. He widened his green eyes, as if to say: 'What are you going to do about it?'

Then he raised his rear end and sprayed the rhododendron, before making his way through a cluster of daffodils and padding across Theodore's lawn.

Once Hamish had returned through the gap in the hedge, Theodore turned his attention to the house next door.

He spied the greenhouse, where he assumed the tomatoes had come from, though there was little sign of anything green inside. Beside the greenhouse, there was a shed, which backed onto a hedge that formed the boundary with the house behind. On top of the shed was a little pole with a little flag. A white rose on a pastel blue background: the flag of Yorkshire.

On the other side of the hedge, there was another shed. This one had the blue and white cross of St Andrew. Theodore understood that the humans were showing their territorial affiliations, as cats marked their territory by spraying.

Theodore's father was a Scottish Fold and his mother a Ragdoll, born and bred in Yorkshire. He had no qualms about his heritage. He was where he was now. Humans were a different kettle of fish, he realised, though wondered what kettles and fish had to do with questions of national identity. He blinked his eyes. He was thinking too much, too much into human nature. Perhaps a bit more interbreeding is what's required, he concluded.

Then, from down below, he heard a woman call: 'Wally! Time for tea...'

There was no response from the shed.

The woman walked to the edge of the lawn, before shouting across, 'Wally! Wally!'

Wally finally emerged from his shed, walked across the lawn, along a well-trodden path.

To the rear of the house, there was a conservatory. The conservatory was roofed in opaque plastic sheeting. Theodore made out a table and chairs, the table set for two.

'What are we having, Marje?' Wally said.

'Quiche,' Marjorie said. 'And salad.'

'What kind of quiche?' said Wally.

'Hamon.'

'Ah, ham and salmon,' Wally said. 'You know that's one of my favourites.'

'I know,' said Marjorie with a smile.

They sat down at the table, and Wally poured them both mugs of tea from the pot. He added salad to his plate.

'That reminds me,' he said with a grin. 'I went round and met our new neighbours today. Introduced myself, you know.'

'Oh, yes,' Marjorie said. 'How are they?'

'They seem nice enough. A young couple... I only met her. Well, I gave her some of those tomatoes...'

Wally began to laugh. He threw back his head, showing his gappy grin.

'What's so funny?' Marjorie said.

Wally stopped laughing for long enough to tell Marjorie that he had told the young woman next door that he made his own bone meal.

'Made your own bone meal?' Marjorie said. 'Whatever must they be thinking? You great Wally!'

Wally spluttered on a piece of celery. He coughed, and then swallowed loudly. He took a drink of tea.

Marjorie tutted. 'Why, they probably think you're here now, grinding up bones in your shed...'

Wally grinned, his cheeks red.

Marjorie shook her head. 'You silly old thing...'

'I was only joking.'

'That big mouth of yours,' Marjorie said, 'is going to get you into trouble one of these days!' She wagged a knowing finger at her husband. 'Mark my words.'

3

The next day Jonathan fell down a sinkhole in Derbyshire and fractured the navicular bone in his left foot. He was provided with an aircast boot (a large grey, plastic moon boot), and painkillers, Naproyn and Tylenol, and told that he would have to keep the boot on for at least four weeks. If he didn't, he might walk with a limp for the rest of his life, he'd been warned.

'I'm going to be laid up for weeks,' he complained from the sofa, his booted foot propped up on a little coffee table.

'I did warn you,' Emily pointed out, 'about those sinkholes.'

'I'm not going to be able to drive or anything.'

Emily was removing DVDs from a cardboard box and stacking them on a shelf below the television. 'How convenient,' she said under her breath.

'I won't be able to do anything but sit here,' Jonathan went on.

'You're not going to be much use to anyone,' Emily said irritably. 'Just let me do everything...'

'What am I going to do for four weeks? We don't even have Sky installed.'

Emily turned and said, 'You could watch some of these DVDs.'

She removed from the shelf a box set of Alfred Hitchcock films that she had just put there. 'You could start with these,' she said.

'Hitchcock?'

'Why not? They're classics.'

'I could give them a go,' Jonathan said. 'I'm going to be stuck here for weeks. If I put pressure on my foot, I could end up with a limp for the rest of my life.'

'Well, at least you've got Theodore. You can keep each other company and watch Hitchcock together. He always used to sit and watch Columbo with me. I think he liked Columbo...'

Jonathan stroked Theodore, who was sitting on the sofa beside him.

Theodore eyed Jonathan. I'm going to be out of here before you, he thought, and jumped down onto the floor and approached the French windows. He spotted ginger Hamish squatting down beside the rhododendron. He miaowed out at the garden.

Hamish finished his business. The ginger cat made a cursory inspection and then sauntered back to his own home, without bothering to cover.

Jonathan was wearing a dressing gown over an old t-shirt. On his right foot he wore an old rugby sock, dark blue and light blue hoops. On his left foot he wore the grey plastic boot.

He looked out of the French windows.

The house directly behind was at a higher level, so that from Jonathan's position on the sofa he could see over the top of the back hedge and into the two first-floor bedroom windows that faced him.

He saw a middle-aged woman in one window, the one on the right. Her face was heavily made up, large rimmed glasses on her face and a blond wig on her head, slightly dishevelled. The curtains were partly drawn and the light from a television flickered against the yellow and brown floral pattern.

The woman looked out from the window, and Jonathan watched as she raised a bottle and took a swig from it.

In the next window a younger woman in her twenties, probably the daughter, Jonathan guessed, was smoking a cigarette. She was sucking on the cigarette and then blowing the smoke up and out of the window. Jonathan realised she must be kneeling up on her bed. The room was lit up from a lamp so her figure was outlined from behind. As his eyes focussed on the woman, he realised that she was wearing only a black bra that contrasted against the pinkish white of her skin.

Jonathan noted that she was generously proportioned. If he were in the field, he would have described them in geological terms as 'Off white/cream, well-rounded cobbles of alabaster…'

He glanced back at the other window. The older woman took another swig from her bottle and then adjusted her wig.

On the other sofa, perpendicular to the one Jonathan was sitting on, and facing the television, Emily sat, absorbed in some US crime drama. She was wearing a onesie she had got for Christmas, a giant pink rabbit, though she didn't have the hood over her head.

Jonathan looked at the television but soon his attention was drawn again to the French windows and the house behind. He watched as the younger woman, the daughter, dropped her cigarette from the top of the window and then pulled the curtains slowly together. Her body was perfectly outlined against the pink and blue of the curtains.

Then the curtains parted an inch in the middle and Jonathan knew that she was peering out. Peering back at him.

He adjusted his dressing gown, pulling it down below his knees.

He was no longer the watcher but the watched.

He looked over at Emily, still staring at the television and nibbling on minty Matchmakers.

He looked back at the window behind; the curtains were closed. 'We really need to get some curtains to go over the French windows,' he said.

'Full height curtains,' Emily said, 'are going to cost a fortune.'

'Maybe some sheets,' Jonathan said. 'Just for the time being.'

'There is no way we are putting sheets up.'

'It's just that,' Jonathan said, 'we are a bit overlooked.'

Emily glared across at Jonathan; then said, 'Where's Theo got to?'

Theodore was in the upstairs bedroom.

He looked out from the windowsill. He had watched the young woman smoke her cigarette through the window. He had seen her drop the lit cigarette onto the paving stones below the window. He had watched as the red glow from the cigarette end had grown smaller and smaller and finally gone out.

He heard a rat-a-tat from the garden to his right.

This garden was bigger and belonged to a long, low-slung bungalow. An extension took up the entire rear.

A grey-haired man in a dressing gown and mirrored glasses was standing in the doorway of the conservatory, shaking a box of dog biscuits. 'Lucy! Lucy!' he called. 'Are you there, Lucy?'

Theodore noticed some movement in the bungalow's garden and then a Labrador appeared in the yellow light cast by the conservatory, the reflective bands on its harness catching the light.

Lucy approached the man, wagging her tail, and the man in dark glasses attached a lead to the dog's harness. After the dog had led its owner back inside, the blind man locked the doors and retreated inside his house for the night, turning on the lights out of habit rather than need.

Theodore looked over the top of the bungalow. He made out the steeple of a church, St Stephen's, surrounded by beeches, oaks and elms. Theodore blinked as the dying light disappeared behind the church and then jumped down from the windowsill.

Downstairs Jonathan was still sitting on the sofa. His booted broken foot was propped up on the coffee table in front of him; his head was sunk back into a cushion. His mouth was open and he was snoring.

Theodore looked over at the French windows and the garden beyond, now in darkness.

The television had been left on. There was a 1980s' film on called Body Double.

Theodore watched as Holly Body, played by Melanie Griffith, gets drilled to death on the floor of her apartment, while Jake Scully, played by Craig Wasson, looks on helplessly from his own apartment window.

4

The next morning Emily left for work at quarter past seven. Before she left, she reminded Jonathan that her mother was going to pop round with some lunch for him.

'Don't get into mischief while I'm gone,' Emily called from the hallway, putting on her coat.

'That's not very likely, is it?' Jonathan called back from the sofa.

'And make sure Theo doesn't get out,' Emily called, opening the front door.

'I'll do my best,' Jonathan shouted, only to be answered by the front door shutting behind her.

Emily almost tripped over her neighbour Sam, who was bent down picking up a small dog turd from the footpath.

Sam held the turd in a little blue bag at arm's length. In her other hand she gripped a lead that was attached to a fat Chihuahua, its body the size and shape of a melon.

'I'm Sam. I'd shake your hand but, as you can see, they are both fully occupied.'

'I don't know how you can do that,' Emily said, staring at the little blue bag. 'First thing in the morning.'

'You can't leave it there,' Sam said. 'Not with the neighbourhood gestapo looking on... I'd be reported to the Council. Then firing squad at dawn.'

'I couldn't do it,' Emily said. 'I'm a cat person. Cat people don't have to pick up poo.'

'Well, I'm a dog person,' Sam said, 'and it's the price we have to pay... And this is Charlie.'

Emily looked down at the little dog. It was whipping its tail from side to side, and showing its little teeth in a fierce grin.

'Hello Charlie... I'm Emily. My cat is bigger than you.'

She bent down and was about to pat the dog on the head but Charlie, perhaps in his excitement, squatted down again and let out a sliver of diarrhoea.

Sam grimaced. 'He's got such a sensitive tummy.'

'I need to get going,' Emily said, making her way past Sam and the still squatting Chihuahua to her car. 'I'm running late...'

'I'll wash it away later,' Sam called after her, squinting down at the brown streak on the pavement.

Theodore watched from the bay window of the front room. He looked at the little blue bag and then the mess on the footpath. He watched as Emily's car made its way down the street, still in second gear.

Cat People and Dog People? He closed his eyes and imagined a world populated by humanoid cats and humanoid dogs.

When he opened his eyes again, he saw people dashing by on their way to work. Mums and dads pushed prams and pushchairs with one hand, clasping handbags or briefcases in the other. Children were bundled or ordered into cars, depending on their age, only to join the queue of traffic on York Road. Cyclists with determined faces and crust in the corner of their eyes sped past. Fashionable men strode past in brown shoes and tight trousers, their faces adorned with trimmed bushy beards. Young children were dragged along by parents who feared they would be late for work. A man who had had a stroke walked lopsidedly past, on his way for the newspaper.

Then a woman in purple emerged from the house opposite. 'What a lovely morning!' she called over to Sam and Charlie, who were returning along the street.

'Yes, isn't it, Linda?' Sam called back. Charlie the Chihuahua strained at his lead, desperate to be let off.

'Such a shame he can't be let off his lead,' Linda said, crossing the road towards Sam and Charlie.

'He'd run away,' Sam said. 'I couldn't bear to lose my Charlie.'

'I'm on my way to yoga with laughter,' Linda said. 'It's very therapeutic... You should try it. Don't want to be late!' She hurried on down the street.

Charlie strained at his lead, flicking his little tail from side to side, not wanting his walk to end. He knew that the rest of the day he would be shut in by himself.

Then a man in a suit appeared and said, 'Hurry up, Sam. You know I have a breakfast meeting. I really need to get going.'

He didn't really. He was meeting his personal assistant for some pre-office personal assistance.

'I know, Steve,' Sam said. 'I'll just be a minute... Tidying up after Charlie, you know.' She held the little blue bag in the air.

'Just hurry up,' Steve said. 'I really don't have the time.'

'Just give me a minute.' Sam yanked the Chihuahua around and began dragging him back towards her house.

Ten minutes later Steve was sitting in his car, a white Audi, blowing his horn. Steve enjoyed blowing his horn.

He blew his horn until several minutes later his wife, who had been a hairdresser in Harrogate before she met Steve in a bar in York, came out of the house.

She opened the car door. 'What's the big hurry anyway?' she said.

'I told you... I have a breakfast meeting,' Steve almost shouted. 'And now I am already late.'

He knew that if he missed his pre-office appointment he would be frustrated and bad-tempered the rest of the day.

'Well, Charlie had to go to the loo, didn't he? Wouldn't want him having an accident in the house while we were out, would we?'

'No, we wouldn't,' Steve said. 'That carpet cost two thousand quid.'

'You don't always have to bring up what things cost all the time,' Sam said, still not getting into the car. 'Have a little decorum.'

'I'm going to be late,' Steve shouted. 'Because I have to drive you to your spa. Why can't you learn to drive for heaven's sake.'

'You know I don't drive, darling,' Sam said and then slid into the Audi.

As soon as the passenger door closed, Steve sped off down the street, within seconds exceeding the twenty mile an hour limit.

All this rushing about, thought Theodore. You need to set the pace for the long haul. No point rushing towards death; it'll only come looking for you.

He stretched his body, arched his back, and then settled onto his haunches. It was definitely time for a nap.

5

Jonathan was sitting on the sofa, his foot still propped on the little coffee table. He had spent most of the morning playing random strangers at Scrabble. He was now waiting for fifteen people to take their turns.

The remote controls were laid in a row on the arm of the sofa. 'Shall we watch Rear Window?' he asked Theodore, patting the empty seat next to him.

Theodore jumped up onto the sofa next to Jonathan.

'I take it that's a yes,' Jonathan said, turning the DVD player on.

Theodore settled down against Jonathan's side, and together they stared at the Greenwich Village scene.

Jonathan had not attempted to go to bed the night before. Instead, aided by a bottle of wine, he had fallen asleep where he was sitting while watching Body Double.

He'd woken at four in the morning and couldn't get back to sleep. He retrieved a book, *The Glacial Geology of Holderness and*

The Vale of York by Sidney Melmore, coincidentally a former resident of Acomb, thinking it would help him to get back to sleep, but twenty pages later, he noticed the sky begin to lighten and the birds in full song.

On the screen James Stewart said into the telephone: 'He killed a dog last night because the dog was scratching around in the garden. You know why? Because he had something buried in that garden...'

Theodore looked over at Jonathan; the human looked deep in thought. He continued to watch the Hitchcock film, and when it had finished and the DVD returned to the start menu, he got down from the sofa. Jonathan had fallen asleep.

Theodore wandered into the kitchen and inspected his bowls. He went to the corner where the litter box was but then remembered that Jonathan had bought the wrong type of litter.

He went back into the lounge and approached the French windows. He peered out into the garden.

Hamish, the ginger tom, was sitting in the middle of the lawn. The hairs along Theodore's spine stood on end. Hamish caught his stare and held it.

Had there not been a pane of glass between them, Theodore would have seen off the intruder.

Soon as I'm out of here, he growled to himself, we'll see whose garden it is...

He was sitting on a Turkish rug that Jonathan had contributed to the house.

Jonathan had had the rug since his teenage years. It had been under his feet in his bedroom in Market Weighton, where he had lived with his parents. It had accompanied him to university in

Leeds, where it had adorned his room at Bodington Hall, and then two attic rooms in Headingley. Before he had moved in with Emily, it had been in his front room in the little terraced house he had rented in South Bank, York.

Theodore had noticed a fine fuzz of black hairs coating the carpet. He sniffed the rug and smelled another cat: Jonathan's former cat, Edward. Theodore had had enough of other cats. He squatted down on the rug.

Once he'd finished, he made his way upstairs and settled on the windowsill in the back bedroom. The window was open a couple of inches, but not wide enough for Theodore to fit through.

Apart from the birds' tweeting, there were no other noises. Most grown-ups were at work, children at school, cats napping the day away. This was as it should be. Jonathan had no right to be at home, disturbing his daytime peace. There was a limit to the hours Theodore could spend in the company of humans.

Then, in the house behind, Theodore noticed the younger woman warming soup in the kitchen.

Ellen was making soup for lunch. She lived with and cared for her mum Tessa. It was just the two of them; her father Colin had died ten years ago, and her sister Penny had moved away, to university in Bristol, and then stayed on and got a job in that city.

Ellen brought the soup to a gentle simmer. She poured some into a bowl, which she placed onto an orange plastic tray and carried it upstairs.

A minute later, Theodore saw Ellen enter the back bedroom. Her mother was sitting up in bed. A television in the corner of the bedroom was turned on to a shopping channel.

A Shih Tzu, Sandy, yapped, jumped down from the bed and ran through the open door and down the stairs.

'It's lunchtime, mum,' Ellen said.

'Is it?' Tessa said, sitting up. 'Already?'

Ellen sniffed the air. 'Have you been drinking already?'

'No, of course not,' Tessa said. 'It's only just lunchtime... Now, where's Sandy?'

'He went downstairs,' Ellen said. 'He might need to go out.'

Theodore could hear the dog yapping, out of sight.

Ellen placed the tray in front of her mother.

'What is it?'

'Curried parsnip.'

'Curried parsnip? But I don't like curried parsnip.'

'But mum,' Ellen said, 'it's your favourite.'

'Now I'm sure I would remember if it were my favourite, wouldn't I?'

She pushed back her glasses with her forefinger.

'Well, yes, mum,' Ellen said. 'You would remember.'

'I don't like curried parsnip,' Tessa said, her voice raised. 'In fact I hate curried parsnip soup. Whoever heard of such a thing? Curried parsnips!'

'But you haven't tried it.'

'I'm not going to eat that muck,' she said. 'It stinks.'

Ellen reached over and lifted the tray from the duvet, before her mother could overturn it. 'I can get you something else,'

Ellen offered. 'How about chicken? Chicken soup. You like chicken soup.'

'Yes, I like chicken soup.'

Ellen carried the tray to the door. 'I won't be long,' she said. 'I'll make you some nice chicken soup.'

'Where's Sandy,' Tessa asked.

'He just went downstairs. He probably needed to go out.'

'Well, go and let him out if he needs to go,' Tessa said.

Ellen went downstairs and Tessa turned and faced the window. She looked down into the garden to see if she could see Sandy.

Her lips were painted red, smudged across her lower face. Her blonde wig was again at an angle. She peered down into the garden. She glanced back at her bedroom door and then retrieved a bottle of Lambrini from the gap between her bed and the wall. Theodore watched as she took a swig of sparkling perry. He noticed her wedding ring, set with diamonds, sparkling in the light.

Ellen was back downstairs in the kitchen. She opened the back door and let Sandy out into the overgrown garden, where the dog defecated on the lawn. The small heap joined the hundreds of others.

Ellen poured the bowl of curried parsnip soup down the sink. She opened a cupboard and took out another can of soup, checked the flavour and then put it in a clean saucepan. While the soup was warming, she poured the remainder of the curried parsnip soup into a bowl, and sat down at the kitchen table and ate it, her face bent over the bowl.

From downstairs in his own home, Theodore heard Jonathan shouting his name. He remembered what he had done to his rug and thought it best to stay put in the back bedroom. There was no way Jonathan could make it upstairs. He closed his ears to the shouts and curses coming from downstairs. The sun had come out and he felt it warming his fur.

Later, he heard a familiar voice, now a little slurred. 'But I don't like chicken soup.'

He opened his eyes, and in the house opposite he saw that Tessa had a new bowl of soup in front of her.

'Well, what soup do you like?' Ellen's voice now had an edge of desperation.

'Mushroom,' Tessa said. 'I like mushroom soup. Mushroom soup is my favourite.'

'All right,' Ellen said, picking the tray back up from the bed. 'I'll be back in a few minutes... With a bowl of mushroom soup.' She left the room but didn't return to the kitchen.

A minute later she re-entered her mother's bedroom. 'Here mum,' she said, 'I've brought you some lovely mushroom soup.'

She placed the tray back down on the bed covers in front of her mother.

'Mushroom soup,' Tessa said. 'Yes, I do like a bowl of mushroom soup.'

'I know you do,' Ellen said. 'Now I'd better be getting on.'

'Where's Sandy?'

'He's outside.'

'Well, let him in.'

Ellen left the room and a minute later was back downstairs. She let Sandy back in and then sat at the dining table and lit a cigarette.

Theodore wondered about the conversation he had overheard regarding Tessa's preference for soups. He was still wondering when there was a knocking at his own front door.

He heard Jonathan call out, 'Come in... I'm in the lounge.'

Theodore jumped down from the windowsill and went to the top of the stairs.

'Oh dear,' Emily's mother, Trish, said. 'Whatever is that smell? Have you had an accident, Jonathan?'

'I haven't had an accident,' Jonathan said. 'Theodore has done something on the rug.'

Trish went into the lounge, her hand across her mouth and nose. 'Well, I'd better get some detergent and some gloves on,' she said and coughed into her palm. 'I don't know how you can bear it in here. You don't even have a window open.' She crossed the lounge and opened a window. 'There. That's a bit better,' she said, coughing once more.

'Thank you,' Jonathan said.

'Now let me find some rubber gloves,' Trish said. 'We'll soon have this cleaned up.'

Once Trish had gone into the kitchen, Theodore wandered in.

He took up position under the dining table, behind Jonathan. He stared up at the open window. The window was over another two-seater sofa, placed perpendicular to the one on which Jonathan was sitting. From the back of the sofa, it was a simple step up onto the window sill. Then there was a three foot jump up to the wide open window. Then a drop of no more than six feet on the other side, down to the ground below... To the Outside World. This was his opportunity.

He dashed forward, past Jonathan, towards the open window.

6

'Trish!' Jonathan shouted.

Trish hurried into the lounge, yellow, suddy rubber gloves on her hands. 'Whatever is it now?'

'It's Theodore,' Jonathan said. 'He's got out of the window. He's not supposed to be let out...'

Trish crossed to the French windows and saw her daughter's large fluffy grey cat dart across the lawn and head towards the hedge at the back of the garden.

'Oh dear,' she said. 'These windows could really do with a clean.'

She wiped her forefinger across the glass.

'Both inside and out...' she said and shook her head.

Theodore made for the gap in the hedge. Seconds later he was through it and into the garden behind. There was a yapping from the house and clashing of paws against a door. He was in Shih Tzu territory.

He stood rigid in the middle of the lawn, among a mine-field of dog shit. At least he's locked in, he thought. He can't get at me.

Then the kitchen door swung open and the little dog came rushing out, yapping. Straight at him.

Theodore just managed to make it to the boundary hedge, find a gap and dive through to the next garden.

Sandy the Shih Tzu yapped from behind, unable to squeeze through the hawthorn hedge.

Theodore took in his new surroundings. He was standing in a patch of soil dotted with young plants. The vegetable patch occupied most of the back garden apart from a large shed to his left. There was a narrow strip of lawn, and then a patio that went up to the back of the house. A man with a power spray was jetting down the flagstones.

It is said that many people resemble their dogs, or their dogs resemble them. Well, Stuart resembled his cat Hamish. He had ginger hair cropped short; the ginger hair continued across most of his face as stubble, and his eyes were green and bright.

Stuart turned and noticed the large grey fluffy cat in his vegetable patch. He raised his power spray and aimed the jet at Theodore.

'We come here with no peaceful intent, but ready for battle,' Stuart cried, quoting William Wallace, 'determined to avenge our wrongs and set our country free. Let your masters come and attack us: we are ready to meet them beard to beard!'

From behind Theodore, Sandy yapped. From in front a jet of water hit him. He turned to the side, and headed for another hedge. He was through it and up the vertical face of a shed, Wally's shed. For a moment he was relieved to feel the warm felt of the shed roof beneath his paws. Then water lashed the wooden wall of the shed below him.

'I have brought you to the ring, now see if you can dance,' Stuart cried, aiming the jet at him once more, arching it over the shed roof.

'What's going on here?' Wally shouted across the top of the hedge.

'That cat was in my tattie patch,' Stuart said, red in the face. 'I was defending my territory.'

'Well, he's not in your territory now,' Wally said, burring his r's to mimic Stuart's pronounced roll. 'He's on my shed, and I say he can stay up there.'

'We'll see about that,' Stuart said, sending another arc of water over the shed roof.

'Don't you get your bagpipes in a twist, you silly Scottish haggis!'

Stuart turned redder in the face.

'You think you can tell me what to do on my own land? Take that, English pig!'

He pointed his jet spray at Wally, catching him in the face.

'Put that spray down,' Trish shouted from over the hedge. 'That's my daughter's cat up there.'

Stuart lowered his power spray and released his grip. 'He was in my tattie patch,' he shouted across at her.

'That's no reason to soak him. He's absolutely sodden,' Trish called back. 'If he comes down with cat flu, you'll be paying the vet's bills.'

'I won't be paying anything of the sort.'

'We'll see about that!'

From the felt roof of the shed, Theodore took in the scene. There was Stuart, jet washer in hand, standing in the middle of his potato patch. Wally standing by his shed, wiping water from his face. Then there was Trish, still in rubber gloves, pointing an accusing yellow finger at Stuart from the corner of his garden. He looked over at the house behind his own. Sandy the Shih Tzu was yapping from behind the hedge, out of sight.

There was a dull crack and Theodore looked up at Tessa's bedroom window.

While the two men and Trish bickered over the hedges, Theodore saw Ellen in Tessa's bedroom. Chicken soup slid slowly down the bedroom wall across daisy-patterned wallpaper. Ellen was on her knees, picking up pieces of broken porcelain. He couldn't see Tessa but he could hear her.

'It was chicken,' Tessa was saying. 'You gave me chicken soup. You know I don't like chicken soup. It's carcass scrapings.'

'It was mushroom, mum,' Ellen said.

'Don't you mum me. I know your game,' Tessa said. 'You can't wait for me to pop my clogs; then you'll get the house. That's why you're hanging around, isn't it? Well, just you wait. You've got another thing coming. If only your dad was around to see it!'

'I never thought anything of the sort,' Ellen said.

'Well, I've been to see Mr Philby,' Tessa said. 'If anything happens to me, everything will go to the dogs' home, do you hear? The house! His stamps! Everything! Do you understand?'

'Yes, mum,' Ellen said, a stammer in her voice. 'I understand.'

'Going to the dogs! Tessa screamed. 'Going to the DOGS!'

'Please calm down,' Ellen said.

'Don't tell me to calm down,' Tessa shrieked. 'GOING TO THE DOGS!'

From below him Theodore heard Trish shout, 'You don't go near my daughter's cat ever again!'

He looked down at the people squabbling over the hedge. He looked back at his own house. Jonathan was standing in the French windows, holding himself up with his crutches.

Then he looked back over at Tessa's bedroom window.

Ellen was now standing in front of the window, looking down at the scene below. They maintained eye contact for a few seconds. Then Ellen snapped the curtains closed. They had sunflowers on them, yellow and brown.

A moment later Theodore jumped down from the shed roof, scrabbled through the bottom of the hedge, into his own garden and let himself be grabbed up by Trish.

7

When Emily got back from work, her mother had gone, leaving a tin-foiled dish of lasagne in the fridge for their dinner.

'How's your day been?' she asked Jonathan, before noticing that Theodore was sitting in front of the open French windows, his legs crossed in front of him, looking out at the garden.

The lounge had a sickening smell of Febreeze that failed to mask the underlying smell of cat shit, despite Jonathan's Turkish rug having been removed to the garage, from where it would never return to domestic duty.

Emily walked over to the French windows and closed them. 'You know Theodore isn't allowed outside,' she said. 'We've only just moved in...'

'Well, he managed to get out earlier,' Jonathan said. 'It was your mum's fault.'

'My mum?' Emily said. 'How was it her fault?'

Jonathan explained that Theodore had defecated on his rug; her mother Trish had opened the window and Theodore had escaped into the garden. He had been chased by a Shih Tzu and then jet-sprayed by an angry Scot. He had taken refuge on Wally's shed roof; then rescued by Trish.

'But what's happened to his paws?' Emily said. 'They're all greasy.'

'Your mum buttered them.'

'But we don't have any butter.'

'She used the goose fat left over from Christmas... She said it would do the same job.'

Emily walked over to Theodore and picked him up.

'I think it's worked,' Jonathan said. 'He hasn't been out of my sight since your mum greased him up.'

'No wonder. What with Shih Zhus and angry Scots about,' Emily said. 'You stay home where it's safe.' She hugged him to her chest.

Theodore wriggled from her embrace, and gaining the floor again approached the French windows. He miaowed.

'You're not going anywhere,' Emily said. 'You see what you've done. Now that he's tasted freedom, he wants to be out again. Make sure he doesn't get out again. He might try to make his way back to Clementhorpe... Acomb is his home now.'

Theodore had spent most of the afternoon trying to lick the goose fat from his paws. The taste now coated his mouth. He drank lots of water but the taste would not go away. Everywhere he went the smell followed him.

As they were eating their dinner in front of the television, Jonathan commented that the lasagne had peas in it.

'My mum always does it with peas,' Emily said. 'It was the only way she could get me to eat greens when I was younger....'

'I don't think it's how the Italians do it,' Jonathan said.

They ate the lasagne while watching television. Jonathan picked the peas out of his dinner. When Emily placed her half-eaten meal on the little table by her side, Theodore had a sniff but turned his tail up at it.

Dairy spelled poison to a cat. The smell of cheese was bad enough, but then there were the garlic and onions, and to top it off – the little green balls stirred into the sauce. What sort of cat would like lasagne? wondered Theodore. Especially lasagne with peas in it.

Emily asked Jonathan, with a touch of irony, if he had managed to find time in his busy day to watch Rear Window. Jonathan told her that he had.

'James Stewart has a more interesting set of neighbours than we do,' Jonathan said.

Theodore's eyes widened: If only he knew.

'I can't see anything much happening around here,' Jonathan went on.

He gestured towards the back garden and the houses that backed onto theirs. 'This is just plain old York,' he said. 'Not New York.'

'Well, what do you expect? This is suburbia after all,' Emily said, picking at her food with her fork. 'You're the one who wanted to move here.'

'There was one thing that happened today that was a bit odd.'

'And what was that?'

'It's probably nothing,' Jonathan said.

Then he explained to Emily that before Theodore got out and in the ensuing commotion, the curtains in the bedroom window of the house behind had been open. Then afterwards they had been closed.

'What's so strange about that?'

'Well, there's this woman in there. Probably in her fifties or sixties. Spends all day in bed, watching television and swigging Lambrini... Looks like her daughter cares for her.'

'So?'

'I saw her looking out of the window earlier. She was scary looking. Bright red glasses and make up all over her face. And she's got this little toy dog stuck in there with her.'

'How sad...'

'If I ever get like that,' Jonathan said, 'just put me out of my misery.'

Not a problem, Theodore thought, still licking his paws in front of the French windows.'

'Well, at least she's got her daughter to look after her.'

'Well, that's the thing. Before Theo got out, her bedroom curtains were open. Then there was a big commotion outside with Theo on top of the shed. And above all the noise, I heard the old woman shout: "Going to the dogs!"'

'So what? A lot of older people say stuff like that,' Emily said. 'This country's going to the dogs, you know. They're just moaning that things are different to when they were young.'

'It's the way that she said it,' Jonathan said. 'Then the curtains were closed and the window was shut... Why close the curtains in the middle of the afternoon?'

'Maybe it was all the noise outside,' Emily said. 'Her daughter probably shut the window and closed the curtains so that her mother could get some peace.'

Theodore looked at Jonathan, his brow creased, his eyes narrowed to slits.

'Could be,' Jonathan said. 'It just seems strange. And that was hours ago... They're still closed now. I hope nothing has happened to her.'

Emily walked over to the French doors and looked out at the house behind. The curtains were closed even though it was daylight.

'Oh, come on. This is Acomb. People don't just going killing people in the middle of the afternoon.'

'I'm sure you're right,' Jonathan said. 'It just seems strange.'

'She may have a headache from all the noise outside. Maybe a migraine. I get them from time to time.'

'You're probably right,' Jonathan said. 'It's probably nothing.'

They sat for some minutes, tapping at their mobile phone screens and occasionally glancing at the television screen.

After a few minutes Jonathan said, 'I think Rear Window is flawed.'

'How do you mean?'

'Well, the dog is killed because it's been digging in the garden. But then when Thorwald's arrested, he admits that he threw the wife's body in the East River. But the head he buried in the garden and then later packed it away in a hat box.'

'So?'

'Well, why would he bury her head separately? He would have dumped it in the river with the rest of her... Why would he treat the head differently? And why would you bury it in the focal point of the entire neighbourhood. It doesn't make sense.'

'You're thinking too much into it,' Emily said. 'You have to over-analyse things all the time. It's just a film.'

Theodore twitched back his ears and looked out of the French windows, across at the house behind. From inside the house, he heard the muffled barking of Sandy the Shih Tsu.

Emily flicked on the television. The programme comprised people being filmed while watching television programmes. The people were watching the latest James Bond film.

'It was Martini that killed my father,' a man in mustard trousers said, nodding at the screen.

'I thought it was Noilly Prat,' his wife, wearing a flowery dress, said.

Jonathan laughed at this last comment, and the end titles came on.

'I can't believe we are watching a programme about people watching television,' Emily said and sighed. 'What have we become? Next there'll be a programme about people watching people watching television.'

'I suppose it's in our nature,' Jonathan said. 'You know what they say about passing open windows.'

'We are becoming a nation of peeping toms,' Emily said, picking up her mobile phone again.

She tapped at the screen, catching up on what her friends were up to on social media.

Theodore observed the two of them, both staring at screens. He furrowed his brow. For the love of Bastet, he murmured. Peeping toms, we are nothing compared to you guys...

He could foresee the end of the human race. Their downfall would be an obsession with staring at screens. All cats had to do was wait. They would take over... one living room at a time. One day, the world would be theirs.

And people would just look on from their screens.

When Emily went upstairs to bed, Theodore followed. He settled by her side as she lay in bed reading. She soon put the book aside and stared at the ceiling.

He rubbed himself against her cheek and Emily turned on her side. She began to stroke him. Theodore stared into her green-grey eyes and purred.

But while Theodore was content with being in the moment, Emily was in a different place entirely.

The sun is shining brightly; the skies are bright blue, cloudless. There is a light breeze blowing from the sea.

Emily is standing behind a well-worn wooden bar, a glass of pina colada in front of her. She is wearing a denim skirt from Zara, t-shirt from All Saints and Kirk Geiger sandals. She takes a suck of the plastic straw and then grins at the two tanned, dark-haired men in front of her.

'But I haven't finished this one,' she says, shaking her head and laughing. 'And besides, I'm supposed to be working, aren't I?'

'This is Spain,' one of the young men says. 'Here we have an expression: mańana.'

'Mańana,' says his friend, taking a sip of beer. 'Why don't you close up now and come dancing with us? We are the only customers anyway.'

Emily laughs. 'Well, maybe a little later. I'll need to change into something different.'

Emily blinked her eyes. Theodore was staring at her, his green eyes wide, still purring.

'We are allowed to dream, you know,' she said to Theodore.

Theodore continued to stare into her face.

'I know I should be happy with all this,' Emily said. 'I have a house, a job, a boyfriend. And you of course... I should be happy.'

Theodore agreed.

Cats didn't have much choice when it came to houses or even owners. They made the most of what they had and got on with it. Dreaming of what life may have been like if another human had taken them in or if they lived in that house and not this house was completely futile. You just got on with what you had.

When Emily turned off her bedside light, Theodore snuggled into her side but found he couldn't sleep.

He jumped down from the bed, crossed the landing and went into one of the back bedrooms. He jumped up onto the windowsill.

The kitchen light was on in Ellen's house. The light in Tessa's bedroom was also on, lighting up the sunflowers on the curtains.

He watched as Ellen appeared in the kitchen. She had her arms under her mother's shoulders, as she dragged her body across the kitchen floor. Tessa was without her wig. Tufts of grey white hair stuck out from her scalp.

Ellen lay her mother down on the linoleum. Then she removed her necklace, ear rings and wedding ring. She placed the items in a little wicker basket on the kitchen side.

She opened the back door and then pulled her mother out into the night. She pulled her across the overgrown lawn, her mother's two feet making two long furrows, two feet part, across the lawn.

They stopped in front of the shed. Ellen went inside and began making room. Five minutes later, she shut the shed door and returned inside the house. A minute later the light went off in her mother's room and the light went on in the next window.

Theodore watched as Ellen approached her bedroom window and looked outside into the night. She was wearing a grey t-shirt that was too small for her, her chest pressing against the soft cotton. Her brown wavy hair was tied back. She looked across at Theodore and smiled. Then she drew her curtains.

Theodore looked across at the pink and blue curtains. He made out princesses riding unicorns.

And then the window went black as Ellen turned off the light.

8

The sunflower curtains in Tessa Black's bedroom remained closed all the next day. From the back bedroom window Theodore observed the house. Mid-morning, he spied Ellen in the kitchen making herself a mug of tea. She was dressed in baggy grey jogging bottoms and a blue shirt that had belonged to her father, three buttons undone.

At lunchtime she heated soup on the hob and poured it into a bowl. She carried it along with half a loaf of bread into the dining room and ate bent over the dining table.

Theodore noted several large brown envelopes on the table, an iPad, as well as a large album with a black shiny cover.

He heard Sandy yapping but there was no sign of the Shih Tzu. She must be locked in the bedroom, thought Theodore, licking his paws; the taste of goose fat still strong on his tongue.

He watched as the blind man next door to Ellen let his guide dog Lucy out in the garden for her fifteen minutes of freedom. Later he watched as the man located Lucy's morning turd, by sense of smell he presumed, and popped it in a little black bag which he popped into his black wheelie bin.

Downstairs Jonathan was watching Psycho, another Hitchcock film. Theodore settled down on the cushion beside him; he preferred black and white films to colour ones, like most cats.

'It's strange,' Jonathan said, 'but the curtains of the house behind haven't been opened today.'

I know, purred Theodore in agreement, rubbing against Jonathan's side.

'I wonder if she has done something to her,' Jonathan went on, rubbing Theodore behind the ears. 'The dog hasn't been let out today either. It's been yapping all morning.'

Theodore purred in agreement. Dogs should learn to keep quiet. Yapping and barking all the time... Disturbing the peace. There ought to be a law against it. Then they settled back and watched Psycho.

About halfway through the film, a man wearing a black beanie and carrying a yellow bucket appeared in front of the French windows. Jonathan's reaction was to take hold of one of his metal walking sticks and wave it at the intruder.

'I'm here to clean the windows,' the man shouted through the glass. He waved a window cleaning blade in the air.

Jonathan managed to get to his feet with his crutches and hobble over to the French windows being careful not to put any weight on his booted foot.

He opened the doors and said, 'I didn't think we had a window cleaner. We've only just moved in...'

There was a blur of grey by his feet and then he watched as Theodore raced across the lawn and disappeared into the hedge at the back of the garden.

'The cat,' Jonathan said, 'he's not supposed to go outside.'

'Well, it's out now,' the window cleaner said. 'I'm Norman. I had a call this morning,' he went on. 'A lady... She said the windows needed cleaning as a matter of urgency, and I was to come straight round. She told me to let myself in through the side gate and that you'd be sitting on the sofa watching telly.'

Trish, thought Jonathan. She must have phoned a window cleaner.

'Don't you have a colour telly?' Norman said, looking at the frozen picture on the television screen.

'The film is in black and white,' Jonathan said.

'I didn't think they made them in black and white anymore.'

'It's an old film. Psycho.'

'Never heard of it,' Norman said. 'Well, I don't have time to be sitting watching telly when there's windows to clean... Do you want me to do inside as well as outside?'

'How much does it cost for both?'

'Twice as much. It's twice the work, isn't it?'

'I think both,' Jonathan said. 'I don't know when they were last cleaned, but they do look a bit grimy. Inside and out.'

'It'll be twenty quid.'

Jonathan nodded, hoping that he had twenty pounds in his wallet.'

'I used to clean the windows of that house over there,' Norman said, nodding at the house behind. 'But then they stopped. After what happened... Terrible business that.'

'What happened?' Jonathan said.

'Terrible business,' Norman said. 'I'd better be getting on.'

He then went into the kitchen to fill his bucket up.

Stuart was in his garden, clipping his hedge though it did not look like it needed clipping.

Theodore watched him from the top of Wally's shed. He looked at the next garden and the shed in the corner. A grey hand jutted out from below the bottom of the door.

Ellen opened the kitchen door and lit a cigarette. She looked over at Theodore and then turned and followed his gaze. She spotted the hand sticking out from the bottom of the shed door and began to cross the garden towards it.

'Got a spare ciggie?' Stuart shouted over the hedge at her.

Ellen stopped and turned to face her neighbour. She was standing directly between Stuart and the shed. She walked towards Stuart taking her cigarettes from her shirt pocket as she went.

'You ever going to buy any?'

'I've got some baccie but it's not the same.'

He took the cigarette. 'You got a light?'

Ellen passed her lighter over the hedge, and Theodore noticed Stuart glancing at her chest that pushed against her shirt.

'So, how's Tessa today?' Stuart asked and took a drag on his cigarette.

Ellen glanced up at Theodore. 'Same as ever,' she said.

'I don't know how you do it,' Stuart said. 'You must have the patience of a saint putting up with her.'

Ellen looked at her neighbour. 'Someone has to do it, haven't they?'

'Aye. I suppose so. Well, I'd better get back it.'

Theodore watched as Stuart finished his cigarette, took one last appreciative glance at Ellen's chest; then went back inside his shed.

Ellen walked over to the small shed in the corner of her garden. She opened the door.

Her mother fell out onto the lawn.

'Let's get you back inside,' Ellen said. 'We can't have you waving at people, can we now?'

She picked her mother up and pushed her as far back as she would go. She then shut the shed door and inspected it to make sure nothing was on display.

'That'll have to do,' she said to herself. 'For now...'

Before she went back inside, she glanced up at Theodore.

'Thanks for letting me know,' she murmured over at him.

Theodore closed his eyes, believing that that would make him invisible.

He opened them again when he heard footsteps approaching.

'I've brought you a mug of tea,' Marjorie said. 'And a slice of quiche.'

'What type of quiche is it today, Madge?' Wally said from inside the shed.

'Bork,' Marjorie said.

'Ah! Beef and pork,' Wally said. 'That's my favourite.'

'I put a bit of crackling in it too.'

'You shouldn't have,' Wally said. 'You'll be fattening me up...' He laughed.

'Get away with you,' Marjorie said. 'There's not an ounce of fat on you!'

'Theo!' Jonathan called.

Theodore turned.

Jonathan was standing in front of the French windows.

'The window cleaner's gone now,' he said. 'You can come back inside.'

Theodore blinked no; he was staying where he was.

Jonathan began to make his way towards him, using his crutches trying not to put any weight on his broken foot. He reached the corner of the garden when his neighbour's head appeared above the hedge.

'That cat of yours has taken up residence on my shed roof,' Wally said.

Jonathan looked up and saw Theodore looking down.

'That's Theo,' Jonathan said. 'He came with the girlfriend. He shouldn't be out of the house.'

'That's what I told her,' Wally said. 'But I don't mind if he wants to sit up there. You see, we are allies of sorts.'

'Allies? Oh, you mean the Scot?'

'Aye, Stuart.'

Wally told Jonathan that Stuart was married to Leslie, who worked in a bank in the centre of York. They had two children, Dougie and Daisy, and Stuart was a stay-at-home dad. When the children were at school Stuart spent the time in his shed. When they weren't at school he spent most of the time in his shed.

'No idea what he gets up to in there,' Wally said. 'But he spends a lot of time in that shed of his. All you can hear is tap-tap-tapping and then a lot of cursing.'

'I wonder what he's up to in there.'

'Beats me... Have you met your other neighbours?'

Jonathan shook his head.

'Well, on your other side you have Steve and Sam. They have a little Chihuahua. Fattest little dog I ever saw.'

'I'll keep an eye out,' Jonathan said.

'Then there's Geoffrey in the bungalow over there. He was a pilot but lost his sight. Spent too long staring into the sun...'

Wally laughed and Jonathan wondered if he was joking.

'What about my neighbours behind?' Jonathan said.

'The Blacks?' Wally said. 'It's just Ellen and her mum Tessa now... Colin died some years ago. Very sudden it was. He was here one day... Then one day he was gone. Whoosh! Just like that.'

Jonathan wondered a moment at the 'Whoosh'.

'Tessa hasn't been well of late,' Wally went on. 'She has good days and bad days. Mainly bad days... She used to take her dog Sandy to West Bank Park every day. I saw her one day. It was after her husband had gone. She had a bottle in one hand and she was pulling hair from her head with the other. One hair at a time. Carried on doing that till she had no hair left. That's why she wears a wig. Pulled all her hair out.

'She never got over him. Fell apart she did... Never leaves the house these days. I don't think she even gets out of bed some days.'

'What about her daughter?'

'I suppose Ellen does the best she can. She'll be on that carer's allowance. She's never had a job. Stays at home and looks after her mum. That's not much of a life for a young girl. In your twenties you should be out and about. Gallivanting...'

Wally took a drink of tea.

'There's another daughter,' Wally said, remembering. 'Penny. Aye, Penny... Colin was a keen stamp collector...'

Jonathan looked puzzled.

'Penny Black! Like the stamp,' Wally said grinning.

'I see,' Jonathan said.

'Penny visits now and then but she moved away. Lives somewhere down south I believe. Went off to university and didn't come back. Hardly ever visits.'

'That's a pity,' Jonathan said.

'Bad it is,' Wally said, 'Ellen being left to look after her mum like that.'

'You didn't hear Tessa shouting the other day, did you? You know when Stuart was trying to jet wash our cat...'

'Can't say I did,' Wally said. 'There was all the commotion out here, and my hearing's not what it was.'

'I was just a little worried about her. I heard her shouting. Then when I looked up again the curtains were closed and the window shut.'

Walter looked across. 'She'll just be having a lie in... Watching TV in bed. Like I said, some days she doesn't even get up.'

'I'm sure you're right,' Jonathan said uncertainly, glancing up at the window with the sunflower curtains.

When Emily got home from work, Jonathan told her about the curtains not having been opened in Tessa's bedroom all day and the dog yapping from inside the house.

He had a can of beer in one hand and took a swig. 'I think something might have happened to her. I really do.'

'Are you serious?' Emily said, hands on hips. 'She's probably got a migraine and closed the curtains. And the dog was barking so her daughter shut it in another room so it wouldn't disturb her.'

'I'm not so sure.'

'Oh please,' Emily said. 'I've had a long day at work. This isn't what I need when I get home.'

She crossed to the table and picked up a packet of painkillers. 'I'm sure you shouldn't be drinking when you're on these. You're imagining things.'

'I was just telling you what happened today,' Jonathan said. 'I'm just a bit concerned about her.'

'Where is Theo?' Emily asked.

'He got out again,' Jonathan said. 'A window cleaner came and I opened the doors... He was on Wally's shed roof earlier.'

Emily crossed to the glass doors. She opened them wide and called his name. A moment later Theodore appeared from the back hedge and trotted across the lawn. Emily scooped him up and hugged him to her.

'The window cleaner mentioned something happening with the house behind, and then Wally said that the father had died suddenly. Maybe the daughter, Ellen she's called, killed him too. She might be working her way through the whole family...'

'Give it a rest,' Emily said. She put Theodore down and closed the French windows. 'I'm going to have a shower, and when I come back I don't want to hear any more about it.'

She marched out of the lounge and into the hallway.

'Just be careful of the shower rail,' Jonathan called after her. 'It's loose and needs fixing.'

But Emily was already in the downstairs shower room, the door pushed closed behind her but left ajar. A few moments later Theodore heard water. He approached the door and then noticed a white rectangle of card lying on the floor by the front door.

It was a business card from Norman, the window cleaner. He must have posted it through the front door after he left.

On the card was written:

N. BATES
PROFFESIONAL WINDOW CLEANING SERVICES
NO SMEAR GARANTIE

Theodore stared a moment at the slip of paper. Then his attention was drawn by a buzzing overhead. It was a bee.

Theodore swiped at it as it flew past him. He turned round and chased after the bee. As the bee rose in the air, Theodore launched himself, a paw held out at the intruding insect. He just missed it. He turned again and saw the bee fly into the shower room. Theodore followed, pushing open the door so that he could fit through.

'Is there somebody there?' Emily said, over the spray of the water from the shower.

The shower room was tiled in shiny white and had a white shower curtain dividing it into two. From behind the curtain, Theodore made out Emily's outline, her silhouette cast onto the plastic curtain by the window behind her.

The bee buzzed within the confined space of the shower room, unable to navigate a way out. Theodore crouched in the doorway waiting his chance.

'Is that you Jonathan?' Emily said from behind the shower curtain.

When the bee buzzed past the shower curtain the third time, Theodore chose his moment. His paws outstretched, he launched himself into the air. He saw the bee pass just in front of his paws as he dived forwards. Then his claws snagged on the shower curtain, ripping the thin plastic sheet.

Emily screamed, as the shower curtain and metal rail came down on top of her.

Not again, thought Theodore, as the shower head spun round, sending out a spray of water at him. Another soaking.

Emily stood naked and screamed again, but this time it was Theodore's name that came from her lips.

9

Most people think of Acomb as a big suburb of York, inhabited by plumbers and decorators, and retired plumbers and decorators, and they wouldn't be far wrong.

But it was once a village on the outskirts of the city, and part of the West Riding of Yorkshire. Its name came from the Old English for oak tree. It was only in 1937 that Acomb was swallowed up by the City of York and transformed into a suburb of the city.

The twentieth century saw the population of Acomb rise dramatically with housing built on the farmland and by the twenty first century Acomb had a population of twenty thousand people.

Jonathan was sitting on the sofa, reading the Pevsner guide he had picked up in Fossgate Books some years before. He glanced at the brief entry for Acomb. 'No perambulation,' he read aloud.

'He didn't even bother getting out of his car... Probably just said to his wife from the back seat, "Keep driving!"'

Theodore flicked back his good ear. Writing about architecture was the equivalent of miaowing about cat biscuits in his opinion. And besides, Pevsner might have had the right idea by not getting out of his car, he thought, thinking of some of his new neighbours. He looked out of the French windows at the houses behind and then jumped down to the floor.

Theodore paced in front of the glass doors. A woman had been killed and all Jonathan could do was to read architectural criticism.

Theodore knew that Ellen had killed her mother; Jonathan only suspected as much; Emily didn't believe a word of it. It was going to be down to him to expose Ellen.

He thought of the crime dramas he had watched on television with Emily in the pre-Jonathan days. The 'whodunnits'. Theodore knew who had done it: Ellen.

Then he thought of the Columbos he had seen, where the viewer knew who had done it but watched to see how Columbo would prove how they had done it. The 'howdunnits'.

But this was not a howdunnit. Theodore licked his paws in contemplation. This was not a whodunit or a howdunnit, but a how-do-I-prove-to-the-humans-that-she-did-it?

He paced in front of the sofa, where Jonathan sat reading his book. He wagged his tail from side to side. He went into the kitchen. His litter box was still in the corner. The wrong type of litter, he remembered.

He headed towards the litter box. He urinated in the corner and then patted the clay pellets with his front paws until they turned to sludge. It really was the wrong type of litter. He emerged a minute later, his paws coated with urine-soaked clay.

Back in the lounge Jonathan was still reading his architectural guide to York. Theodore approached the French windows again. If Jonathan had any doubts that a murder had been committed he was going to have to spell it out to him.

He began on the right hand door and worked his way to the left. As everyone knows, cats both read and write from right to left. When he had finished he stood back to inspect his paw-writing.

'She killed her mother,' it was supposed to say.

Instead it looked like a lot of muddy smears across the glass. Theodore blinked. This writing business was trickier than he had presumed. He glanced at Jonathan on the sofa. His head was tilted back and his eyes were closed. He hadn't even noticed Theodore's attempts at writing.

Theodore settled down on the other sofa. He was going to have to think long and hard about the situation, he realised. It was definitely a three-nap problem; he would need at least fifty minutes to consider the problem.

He crossed his forelegs in front of him, placed his head in the V between his legs and closed his eyes, readying himself to enter into deep analytical thought, worthy of a detective of his status.

Before his fifty minutes had elapsed, there was a tapping at the front door and then he heard a key in the lock and the front door opened.

'Jonathan?' Trish called out, before entering the lounge. 'Are you in here?'

'I haven't run off,' Jonathan said from the sofa, not bothering to turn round.

'I've brought you some lunch,' Trish said. 'Soup and a sandwich.'

'Sounds good,' Jonathan said from the sofa.

'Did the window cleaner come the other day?' Trish asked, staring over Jonathan's head at the French windows.

'Yes,' Jonathan said, 'he did both inside and out.'

'Did he now?' Trish said.

She crossed to the glass doors and waved a finger across the muddy smears. She held her forefinger in front of her face. 'They're still dirty. On the inside.'

'He did the insides,' Jonathan said. 'I was here when he did them.'

'Well, he didn't do a very good job,' Trish said. 'These window cleaners... They're a law unto themselves.'

Jonathan pointed past Trish at the house behind. 'I think something might have happened to the woman behind. I haven't seen her since the other morning. Her curtains haven't been opened. And the dog has been yapping all the time. I think it's been locked in a room.'

'Why Jonathan,' Trish said, 'are you developing an imagination?'

Trish had evidently not forgotten Christmas Day. They had all been watching The Hobbit: The Desolation of Smaug, in which a party of dwarves and their hobbit ally continue their quest to reclaim their kingdom, journeying through the forest of their ancestral enemy, the elves, and finally face the dragon Smaug that had driven the dwarves from their home, when

Jonathan woke from a post-prandial nap and said: 'Well, this is all a bit far-fetched.'

'You'll be reading Terry Pratchett next,' Trish added.

'I think the daughter Ellen snapped and smothered her with a pillow,' Jonathan said. 'I heard her mother say, "It's going to the dogs". I think she meant her daughter's inheritance. She was going to leave everything to the RSPCA...'

'You're reading too much into it... This is Suburbia. People don't commit murder in the suburbs. You want to move to a village if you want that sort of thing. We have homicides, patricides, matricides, suicides... Even the odd felinicide,' she said, casting a sideways glance at Theodore.

Theodore folded back his ears and looked at a patch of floor. He was glad he didn't live in a village.

'Well, I'd better put the soup on.' Trish said. 'I don't have all day.'

Jonathan was relieved that the soup was tomato and the sandwich cheese. He ate off a tray on his lap and watched the news on television while Trish cleaned the kitchen.

After he had finished his lunch and Trish had washed up the dishes, she announced that she was going back to Acaster Mildew, a village just outside of York, its existence known only by those that actually live there, and the postman, of course.

'I don't like to leave Pat too long,' Trish said, referring to her husband and Emily's father.

When they had met, they both went by Pat. But as everyone knows, you cannot have two Pats in a house, so rather than her husband becoming Trick she had offered to be Trish, and that was the name she now went by, though deep down she was and would always be a Pat.

'You know he's always having those little accidents,' Trish went on. 'We wouldn't want him bleeding to death in his work-shop while I'm out, would we now?'

'No, certainly not,' Jonathan said nodding.

And with that, Trish turned and left.

Norman, the window cleaner, returned later that afternoon. Theodore watched from the front window as a white van with N Bates Window Cleaner pulled up outside the house and Norman jumped out. He went straight round the side of the house and let himself in through the gate.

Jonathan managed to get to his feet and opened the French windows to let the window cleaner in.

'Didn't you clean the windows only the other day?'

Norman explained that he had been called by Trish. 'She said there were some smears. She wasn't very happy about it. I thought I'd better see for myself. I told her when I left yesterday, they were sparkling clean, but she insisted that they were covered in smears. On the inside.'

'I hadn't noticed any smears,' Jonathan said.

'The lady said there were smears. Gave me a right earful.'

Norman bent down and began to examine the glass. 'Looks like muddy paw prints.'

He pushed his forefinger through the muddy streaks and then raised it in front of his nose. 'It's like clay.'

'It's probably...' Jonathan said and then stopped himself as Norman dabbed his forefinger on his tongue. 'It's like clay.'

Theodore looked on from the doorway as Norman took a cloth and wiped the glass clean.

'There's nothing to pay this time,' Norman said once he was done and satisfied that there were no more smears.

'Are you sure?'

'Yes,' Norman said. 'No smear guarantee and all that... Besides I had finished for the day. I don't have that many customers at the moment...'

'Maybe it's down to the name,' Jonathan said. 'You know Norman Bates...'

'What's up with my name? Norman was my dad's name, and his dad's before that. It's a good name.'

'Norman Bates was the one who slashed the girl in the shower. You know in Pyscho?'

Norman shook his head. 'Don't know about him.'

'He dressed up as his dead mother. You must know it. It's the film I had on yesterday.'

'Don't know anything about slashing a girl in the shower,' he said, still shaking his head. 'Or dressing up as a dead mother...'

'It was in the film,' Jonathan explained. 'It was a Hitchcock film. Psycho... You must have heard of it. 'He's the serial killer in Psycho. Anthony Perkins played Norman Bates.'

'I've never heard of this Perkins,' Norman said. 'It was him who slashed this girl?'

'The actor who played Norman Bates slashed the girl. You must know it. It was a big film. They remade it. He kills this girl in the shower.'

'Psycho? No, never heard of it. And Norman Bates is this psycho in the film, right?'

'Yes. Maybe that's what's putting people off calling you. They see your name and think twice.'

'It explains a lot,' Norman said. 'But I've had all these leaflets and business cards printed up. They cost me twenty quid for two hundred at the service station.'

Norman took a business card from his back pocket and handed it to Jonathan.

Jonathan took the card. 'It says N. Bates,' Jonathan said, handing the card back to Norman. 'You could always change your first name to another name that begins with N.'

'Like what?'

'What about Nigel?'

'Nigel? I'm not sure about that. My family have always been Normans.'

'Nigel Bates wouldn't scare customers away like Norman does. You don't get many mass murderers called Nigel.'

Theodore's eyes widened. I think you might be forgetting Nigel 'Cat Killer' Hibbs.

Nigel Hibbs murdered up to 70 cats in the village of Newbold Verdon, Leicestershire, by placing sodium cyanide-laced sardines in his back garden in a killing spree that lasted two years. When arrested, the police found enough poison under his bed to kill 1,500 cats as well as an empty sardine tin, latex gloves, face masks and newspaper cuttings about the disappearances.

'Nigel?' Norman said. 'I suppose it sounds all right. Nigel Bates.'

'So, are you going to be Nigel from now on?'

'Yes, I think I might give it a go. Just for business like.'

While Jonathan and Nigel were discussing the changing of names, Theodore slipped through the French windows that had been left open and trotted across the lawn to the back of the garden.

10

He watched from the bottom of the hedge as Ellen dragged her mother out of the shed by her feet and laid her out on the unkempt lawn.

She then pulled the green wheelie bin next to the corpse and swung open its lid. She bent down and picked up her mother in a fireman's lift. Then she dropped her into the wheelie bin, head first.

Rigor mortis had set in, and her mother's feet stood proud of the top of the bin. Ellen pulled the lid down on the legs but the bin lid refused to close. She tried to push the legs further down into the bin but they still jutted out at odd angles, so that she couldn't close the bin lid without a foot sticking out.

She pushed the bin on its side and went inside the shed. She emerged a minute later with a rusty old axe.

She pulled her mother out by her feet until her knees were exposed and then began to hack at her shins.

Theodore heard an excited bark and then watched as Lucy led Geoffrey to the hedge that formed the boundary between his house and the Blacks.

Geoffrey stood beside the hedge and heard Ellen chopping at her mother's legs. 'Doing a spot of gardening?' he said. 'A spring tidy, is it?'

Ellen paused from her efforts. She stood up and faced her neighbour, who was wearing his mirrored sunglasses and a shirt that had been buttoned up wrong so that one collar was higher than the other.

'Just trying to get this old tree in the wheelie bin,' she said. 'Can't seem to get it all in...'

'I've got a chipper in the garage,' Geoffrey said. 'You could use that... Haven't used it in years what with my eyesight going but I'm sure we could get it going. You'd have to give me a hand looking for it... If we put it through the chipper, you won't have any problem fitting it all in your wheelie bin.'

'A chipper?' Ellen said. 'I don't think a chipper is really necessary... It's just these big branches I need to fit in.'

'Well, the offer's there,' Geoffrey said.

Lucy had her face pushed into the hedge. She whined excitedly; the dog could see the dead woman on the other side. She clawed at the ground in front of the hedge and barked.

'Lucy!' Geoffrey admonished. 'Whatever's got into you?' He yanked on her lead.

Lucy barked again.

'That's quite enough,' Geoffrey said, pulling on her harness. 'She wants her walk,' he said to Ellen. 'I'd better get her to the park. We're normally in West Bank by now.'

'You get off,' Ellen said. 'I'll soon sort this out; don't you worry about us.'

'Well, give my regards to your mother,' Geoffrey said. 'Haven't seen her for a while.'

'No,' Ellen said. 'She doesn't get out that much these days.'

'Oh, she should. A bit of fresh air would do her the world of good.'

'I think it might be a bit late for that,' Ellen said under her breath.

Geoffrey shrugged and pulled his dog away, Lucy still barking.

'I really don't know what's got into her,' he said, pulling Lucy across the lawn, back towards the bungalow.

Theodore watched from the bottom of the hedge as Ellen finished hacking through her mother's legs, threw the dismembered body parts into the wheelie bin and closed the lid. She then went back into the shed and came out with a spade. She wedged the spade down the inside of the wheelie bin and closed the lid once more.

Well at least he was not the only one to know the truth, Theodore thought. Lucy had also seen the dead woman. He wasn't the sole witness anymore. But why did it have to be a dog? A dog detective on the case! Whatever next?

Then he heard Marjorie shouting for her husband, louder as she drew closer to the shed. She was almost at the shed door before Wally opened it.

Theodore turned and looked back at his own house. Through the French windows he saw Jonathan sitting on the sofa, his booted foot propped up on the coffee table.

Wally, Jonathan and Geoffrey...

Deaf, dumb and blind...

He was definitely up against it.

He closed his eyes, deep in thought, and only opened them when he heard Emily call his name. She was standing in front of the French windows. Theodore chose to ignore her; he stayed where he was.

He looked across at the green wheelie bin that stood by Ellen's shed. Emily soon gave up and went back inside. Theodore waited.

In the kitchen Ellen was staring out of the window. Her eyes were red rimmed from crying. She took a gulp from a wine glass. She spotted Theodore in the bottom of the back hedge and caught his eye. She smiled at him.

From behind, Theodore heard Emily almost shout, 'I told you not to let him out. And what do you do? Let him out... Three days in a row.'

Theodore looked again from Ellen to the wheelie bin and waited.

Night-time came. Ellen went out the back door. She pulled the wheelie bin down the side of the house. Theodore waited for her to disappear before emerging from the bottom of the hedge and setting off after her. He followed behind her, along Constantine Crescent and out onto York Road. She didn't look back.

There were few people in the street and the people they passed took little notice of the young woman with a wheelie bin and the large grey cat that trailed twenty yards behind.

Eventually Ellen turned left and entered through the gate that led into the grounds of St Stephen's church.

Theodore paused at the gate, and as Ellen passed between two great elms, Theodore began to trot after her.

He passed to the east of the church, under the curtilage of a gigantic beech tree. Before him there was a cemetery, stretching down the hill. Gravestones stood high, low, or lay flat on the ground. There were plenty of places for a cat to hide.

Near the bottom of the hillside, Ellen had stopped. The headstones in this part of the cemetery were of hard black granite and not the softer sandstones and limestones of the ones further up the hill.

She pulled the wheelie bin to the side of a grave. She pulled out the spade and began to remove the turf from the grave and put it to one side.

Once the turf was removed, she began to shovel the sandy soil to the other side. Within half an hour she had dug a hole three feet deep.

Theodore approached cautiously, careful not to make any sound. He crouched behind a headstone. He watched as Ellen pulled her mother from the wheelie bin and laid her in the newly opened grave. She placed the bottoms of her legs at the foot of the hole.

She stood for a moment over the grave.

Theodore studied the headstone. It was inscribed in gold letters on the black background:

Colin Black
1954 – 2007
Beloved husband and father,
A light that burned bright, snuffed out too soon
R.I.P

Theodore watched as Ellen wiped tears from her eyes. Then she began to backfill the hole.

11

On arriving home from work, Steve always parked his Audi on the grass verge in front of Linda's house. He couldn't park in front of his own house, as there was a lime tree growing there and all the other spaces along the side of the road had been taken.

What had once been a little rectangle of green in front of Linda's house had been reduced to churned-up dried mud. Linda was determined to change that.

After Steve had set off to work that Friday morning, she scurried out of her house, a trowel in one hand and a large bag in the other. She then proceeded to plant daffodils in the verge in front of her house. Linda wasn't one to complain to the council; she was a believer in direct action.

Theodore watched from the front window as his purple clad neighbour squatted down and planted the yellow flowers.

12

Sandy the Shih Zhu was twelve years old. She had been utterly devoted to her owner Tessa. When Tessa had taken to her bed after her husband Colin died, Sandy had stuck it out with her.

He had watched her drink bottle after bottle of Lambrini or Pinot Grigio from her basket in the corner of the room. He had kept her company while she watched depressing daytime television. He had witnessed her wee the bed on numerous occasions.

Now the bedroom door was closed and her owner was dead. It was two days since she had been fed. She scratted at the brown carpet in front of the bedroom door. She whined. She yapped. She weed in the corner. She yapped some more. She scratted at the carpet some more. She weed in the corner once more. Finally she heard footsteps approach. Sandy yapped with excitement. Finally she would be released.

The bedroom door swung open.

'If you don't shut up,' Ellen said, entering the bedroom. 'You're going to get it.'

Sandy yapped some more.

'I've warned you,' she said and shut the bedroom door behind her.

'Is that dog ever going to be quiet?' Jonathan asked Theodore. They were sitting on the sofa, watching North by Northwest.

On the screen, Eva Marie Saint is hanging by her fingers to the rocky face of Mount Rushmore. 'What happened to your first two marriages?' she asks Cary Grant, who is playing advertising executive Robert O Thornhill, mistaken for a government agent by a group of foreign spies and chased across the country.

'My wives divorced me,' he replies.

'Why?' asks Eva Marie Saint, who is playing the part of gorgeous blonde Eve Kendall.

'They said I led too dull a life,' Cary Grant says.

Yap, yap, went Sandy from the house behind.

Jonathan paused the film.

'I really can't concentrate on this,' Jonathan said to Theodore. 'What with that racket coming from behind...'

They both looked over at the window with drawn curtains.

Theodore heard Sandy's yaps take a different, more desperate tone. He watched as Sandy's head suddenly appeared in the window, the flowery curtains parting for a moment, before coming together again, as the dog dropped out of sight.

'Did you see that?' Jonathan said.

Theodore blinked yes and sat up.

A few seconds later, Sandy's head appeared once more in the bottom of the window.

Both Jonathan and Theodore watched the window opposite, as the flowery curtains were repeatedly parted and the little dog's head appeared again. The curtains remained slightly apart, and the dog managed to scrabble up onto the window sill, only to fall back down again.

'It must be locked in the bedroom,' Jonathan said.

Theodore agreed with another blink of his eyes.

Then the yapping turned to a whimper.

Then a yelping.

Then nothing.

'Do you think something might have happened to the dog now?' Jonathan asked.

Theodore jumped down from the sofa and approached the French windows. He miaowed affirmatively.

Jonathan took his crutches and got to his feet. Careful not to put any pressure on his booted broken foot, he crossed to the French windows and joined Theodore.

The curtains were closed.

'I think something has happened to that dog,' he said.

I think that was curtains for Sandy, agreed Theodore.

'Ted Bundy started on animals and worked his way up to humans,' Jonathan said. 'Let's hope she's not working her way down the chain... Cats could be next.'

Theodore pondered his words. Working her way down the chain? I think you might have that tail about whiskers...

Jonathan opened the right hand window absent-mindedly and looked across at the house behind. It was now deathly quiet.

He didn't notice Theodore slipping through the open window until it was too late.

'Not again,' he said to himself.

13

Ellen was standing over a hole she had dug in the flower bed. She stuck the spade in the lawn and stared over at the corner of the hedge, over which grey smoke billowed. She walked over.

'That smoke is coming right at me,' she shouted across at Wally, who was standing over the garden fire, a stick in his hand, a red cap on his head.

Wally turned and grinned at Ellen. 'I can't change the direction of the wind. But you could always try standing somewhere else.'

'You're always burning stuff,' Ellen said.

'There's a lot of garden waste this time of year.'

'You could always use your wheelie bin like everyone else.'

'I'd never fit it all in,' Wally said. 'They're too small.'

Elle thought back to the difficulty of getting her mother into the bin. She agreed with Wally that they were a bit small. 'You might have a point there,' she said.

'If you want to chuck anything on, go ahead.'

Ellen glanced back at the shed, in which Sandy waited to be buried. 'I think I can manage,' she said.

'Well, if you change your mind, just chuck it over the hedge.'

'I'd better get on,' Ellen said.

She crossed the garden to the shed and retrieved the Shih Zhu. She carried it across the lawn by its paws as if it were a handbag coated in faux fur.

Theodore watched from the bottom of the hedge as Ellen deposited the dog into the hole in the garden and began to shovel soil over the top.

He turned, exited the hedge and raced back across the lawn. He saw Jonathan sitting on the sofa and Jonathan saw him. Theodore noticed a look of alarm on Jonathan's face.

He carried on running, towards him, forgetting that there was glass in the French windows that separated them; glass that had been so thoroughly cleaned by Nigel, it was invisible to the eye.

When he opened his eyes again, he was lying on the patio. Jonathan was standing over him, balanced on his crutches. He wasn't sure how long he had been knocked out. He invoked Bastet to bring about a curse upon window cleaners before getting to his paws.

Then he remembered the dead dog.

He began to make his way on wobbly legs back towards the lawn.

'Are you OK?' said Jonathan, following. 'Are you sure you don't need a lie down or something?'

But Theodore kept going, back across the lawn, weaving his way towards the hedge.

And Jonathan followed after him.

14

Jonathan saw Ellen over the hedge, digging in her garden. Theodore had disappeared into the bottom of the hedge. Jonathan approached, trying not to put any weight on his broken foot.

When Jonathan reached the hedge, Ellen was compacting the soil with the back of a spade.

She had her back to him and Jonathan surveyed her rear, clad in tight blue jogging pants, before asking, 'Have you seen my cat?'

Ellen turned, surprised, holding the spade as you would a weapon. She stared at Jonathan. 'What?' she said.

'My cat,' Jonathan said. 'He got out. I saw him going into the hedge. I thought he must have got through.'

'I haven't seen a cat,' Ellen said.

'Doing a spot of gardening?' Jonathan asked.

Ellen stuck the spade into the ground 'What does it look like?'

'I don't know,' Jonathan said. 'I suppose you could be burying something...'

Ellen took a step towards him. 'Burying something? Like what?'

Jonathan thought 'dog' but instead said 'treasure'.

'Treasure?' Ellen said, shaking her head. 'Why would I be burying treasure in the garden?'

'You know,' Jonathan said, thinking what to say next so that she wouldn't think him stupid. 'It's Easter soon. You might be planning an Easter Egg hunt...'

She shook her head and folded her arms across her chest. 'I am not planning an Easter egg hunt. I'm just doing a spot of gardening.'

Jonathan looked across at the patch where she had been digging. The soil had been turned over in just one place. The rest of the flower bed was still overgrown. The surface covered by dense weeds. He noticed that the lawn hadn't been cut for a long time. He noted the little dog turds scattered about. 'A spot of gardening?' he said.

'Yes, a spot of gardening.'

'Yes, of course... Nice weather for it.'

'Is that all?'

'I haven't heard your dog today...'

'No,' Ellen said. 'Sandy is sleeping. Must have tired herself out.'

'Right,' said Jonathan, looking up at the bedroom window. 'Upstairs.'

'Yes, upstairs,' Ellen said. 'She sleeps on my mum's bed.'

'They're both sleeping?'

'Yes. They're both sleeping upstairs.'

'The curtains...' Jonathan said, 'they haven't been opened in days.'

'No,' Ellen said, 'my mum's having a lie in. Like I said, they're sleeping.'

Jonathan couldn't think what to say next.

They stared at each other a minute.

Ellen took a packet of cigarettes from her shirt pocket and lit one. She stood staring at Jonathan and took a long drag on her cigarette, still staring at him. She blew smoke towards him.

'I had an accident,' Jonathan said. 'That's why I'm at home.'

'I see,' said Ellen, taking another drag.

'I'd better get on.'

Ellen didn't reply.

'If you see my cat,' Jonathan said, 'let me know.'

He turned and made his way slowly back across the lawn towards the French windows. He could feel Ellen's eyes on his back as he went. He was tempted to turn round but resisted.

He was more convinced than ever that Ellen had killed her mother and her dog. He hadn't seen her put the dog in the hole. He just knew that she hadn't been doing 'a spot of gardening'; she had been burying Sandy.

Theodore watched from the bottom of the hedge as Jonathan returned inside. Then he turned his attention back to Ellen.

She had left the spade sticking in the ground and was now pacing in front of the patio doors, smoking her cigarette. She kept looking at the patch of soil and the hedge which separated her from Emily and Jonathan's house. She smoked the cigarette down to the filter and then tossed it onto the top of the dog's grave.

Then she went back into her house, sliding the patio doors closed behind her.

15

Theodore approached the dog's grave and the cigarette butt that still smouldered. Sandy was buried at least two feet below the ground. He wouldn't be able to dig up the dog, and even if he did, what would he do with it then? He could hardly drag it through the hedge and drop it at Jonathan's feet.

He walked towards the house, where Ellen was now in the kitchen, vigorously washing her hands in the sink.

He made it to the wall of the house without being seen. In front of him were the sliding glass doors that opened onto the lounge. Above his head was Ellen's bedroom window.

He was standing on a patio made up of concrete paving slabs. A thousand cigarette ends littered the ground. Theodore noted that some of them had burned down to the filter.

There was a rectangle of lighter grey, measuring about six feet by four feet. Theodore noticed some dark grey marks outside this rectangle. He examined them carefully. They were charcoal. He looked closely at the bricks and mortar of the wall that flanked the sliding doors. In the small crevices, he noted particles of soot.

They extended up the wall and stopped at the windowsill of Ellen's bedroom. The bottom of the windowsill was blackened.

He looked out across the lawn, to where the shed stood.

Had there been two sheds, he wondered, or had the shed been put there to replace one that had burned down. He remembered what Wally had said, 'Then one weekend he was gone. Whoosh! Just like that.'

He looked up once more at Ellen's bedroom window and then down at the patio and the cigarette ends that lay there.

Then there was a ringing from inside the house. The telephone went straight to the answerphone.

'It's Penny. Can you answer the phone, Ellen?'

Then, 'I know you're there... Please just answer the phone. I'm starting to worry. Ellen?'

Theodore saw Ellen enter the room. He pressed himself flat against the ground; he could feel cigarette butts against his abdomen.

'Just let me speak to mum... I'm going to have to come up if you don't answer the phone Ellen... I'm worried about you.'

There was a beep. Then the doors slid open. Ellen towered over Theodore. In her hand she held a saucepan. She threw the contents at Theodore.

He was already running towards the hedge that separated the garden from Stuart's when the water hit him.

At least it's not soup, Theodore thought, as he dived through the gap in the hedge.

Stuart was in his shed. Theodore was a couple of feet away and could hear tapping coming from inside, and every so often a string of expletives.

'Rattle, rattle, tap, tap,' the shed went, and then: 'Och! Och! Mah cock's on a block... Och! Och! Mahcocksonablock.'

Theodore narrowed his eyes. I wonder what he's up to in there, he thought.

He padded down the side of the shed and into the garden. There was no sign of Hamish, the ginger tom. Theodore took the opportunity of spraying parts of the hedge and the side of the shed, expanding his territory. He had no fear of Hamish.

But suddenly there was a whirring overhead. He stopped mid-flow and looked up.

A drone was hovering two feet above him, descending on its sets of propellers.

Theodore dived sideways into the vegetable patch, just avoiding the drone as it dropped at him from out of the skies.

He was hidden by the foliage of potato plants. He could hear the drone go over head, darting up and down the rows of vegetables.

He dashed to another row and the drone descended at the same time, almost catching him with its whirring propellers whipping up the air above his head. Now's not the time for a fur-cut, thought Theodore.

He glanced up through the vegetable leaves and in the back bedroom window he saw his adversary.

Stuart's ten-year-old son Dougie was leaning out of his bedroom window, remote controller in hand, piloting the drone that hovered menacingly above Theodore, waiting for the cat's next move.

Dougie grinned with childish malevolence. To break a butterfly on a wheel was one thing; to conduct an aerial assault on a cat was a new one on Theodore.

No wonder Hamish was keeping out of sight: it was the Easter holidays...

He was going to have to make a break for it, Theodore realised, as the drone swooped low over his hiding place.

The drone came back for a second pass, its propellers clipping the tops of the plants and sending them into the air.

Theodore dashed to the edge of the vegetable patch where it joined the lawn. There was a two foot gap he would have to cross to reach the safety of the hedge.

Dougie saw the movement in the plants and sent the drone down the corridor cutting off the cat's escape.

Theodore miaowed for human intervention.

But Stuart was still tapping away and cursing in his shed; Wally was busy trying to keep his fire going, and Jonathan was back inside, probably watching the rest of North by Northwest.

The drone came down once more, clipping the leaves from above his head. He flattened himself against the ground.

He looked and saw the drone hovering in the air, just a few feet away, its blue and white plastic shell held up by its four whirring propellers. A red light flicked on and off on the underside of the drone: Dougie was recording the attack to enjoy later.

Theodore was fed up of running. He would make a stand. He chose his moment and dashed out onto the strip of lawn.

The drone came straight at him. Theodore jumped and struck out with one paw, aiming it in between the whirring propellers at a circular strip of plastic.

He made contact with the plastic body of the machine, sending it crashing into the side of the shed, where it fell to the ground.

Theodore dashed to the bottom of the hedge as the shed door was thrown open.

'What's going on out here,' shouted Stuart.

'My drone,' Dougie shouted down from his bedroom window. 'It crashed... Sorry!'

'You bloody tweeny sod!'

Stuart looked at the plastic toy lying on the lawn. 'It looks like you've gone and bust it. Forty quid that cost.'

'It wasn't my fault,' Dougie said. 'It was that big grey cat.'

Stuart looked around the garden. There were no cats to be seen. 'Cat, mah arse,' he said.

'But dad...' Dougie began.

'I may be mad north by northwest,' Stuart said and waved his forefinger at his son, who was his own spitting image. 'When the wind is southerly, I know a hawk from a hacksaw!'

And with this Shakespearean quotation, he went back inside his shed and slammed the door shut behind him.

16

Like quite a few people with overactive imaginations, Stuart McRae believed that people originated from outer space. Stuart, however, went one step further. He believed that the different races on Earth came from different planets. The Scots were from one planet, the English another.

The Scots on their home planet had limited food, so had gone in search of other planets. They had discovered Scotland and in its rich soils they had grown the oats from which they made their porridge.

He put his ideas into books: a planned series of Scottish Science Fiction featuring a band of feisty Scots who travel the universe, battling the anaemic English and other alien breeds. His first book in the series, working title: 'Scots in Space', was nearing completion and he was looking forward to the royalties pouring in. He would put the money into offshore bank accounts to make sure the English taxman couldn't get a slice of it. He was even considering opening a Swiss bank account; he admired the Swiss: they knew how to squirrel away other people's money.

In the meantime, he played househusband to two children: Dougie and Daisy. His wife, Leslie, worked for a bank in the centre of York and made enough money for them to live in reasonable comfort – just until his first book was published, he told

Leslie. Then they would leave England, return to Scotland and buy a castle by a loch, and Leslie would not have to work again.

It was just a matter of time before the literary world would bow to his pen.

He bashed another paragraph into his laptop:

The Scots of Scaramanga had long lived under the oppressive oligarchy of the English tyrants. Then, one day, a man emerged who would in time sow the seed of discontent and begin the uprising that would bring down the oligarchs. He was the chosen Scot. His name was Hamish McHaddock. Hamish would bring down the oligarchical governance that oppressed the people of Scaramanga.

Stuart liked the word oligarch. He read out loud his latest paragraph, emphasizing the arch of oligarch each time the word cropped up.

Hamish McHaddock, the hero of his book, was a younger, more handsome, more eloquent version of himself. His adversary, William Weakbladder, was drawn from his neighbour over the hedge, Wally. Though set in outer space, his novel was firmly rooted in Acomb.

He heard Leslie call his name from outside the shed.

For another minute he continued to bash away at the keyboard. Then the shed door swung open. Leslie was standing, arms folded across her chest.

Leslie's chest was quite formidable. It was what had drawn Stuart to her in their early days of courtship, when he had been the steward on the early morning Edinburgh-bound train that she took each morning. He had impressed her by his knowledge of the Scottish bard. He had quoted Burns to her as he poured her coffee each morning. It had been Leslie who had eventually plucked up the courage to ask if the lyrical train guard would like to meet up after work one day – just for a wee dram. It was Stuart's gift of the gab that won her heart.

Leslie's chest had been what had drawn Stuart to his future wife, but what had once been objects of adoration for Stuart had become objects of practical use with the birth of their two children and off limits to Stuart and then after breast-feeding had been done with, they had never returned to their former role.

'Haven't you forgotten something?' Leslie said, her arms still folded across her chest.

Stuart's intergalactic War and Peace was going to have to wait, he realised, saving his work with a control's'.

'Have I forgotten something?'

'You're supposed to be taking the kids to parkour,' Leslie said.

'I was just finishing this wee paragraph,' Stuart said.

'Well, your wee paragraph can wait.'

'Why can't you take them?'

'Because it's your job to take them,' Leslie said. 'And I'm supposed to be working. You know that.'

'I don't see why they cannot just jump about the garden.'

'Look: we've already paid for parkour. The kids have been inside all day, playing on their phones, and you went and dug over most of the lawn so you could plant vegetables, so they can't very well play in the garden.'

'All right, all right, I'll take them.'

A mobile phone began to ring from within the house and Leslie dashed back inside.

Stuart shut his shed door and entering the lounge he heard Leslie snap into her phone, 'Just power off, count to ten and then start it up again... If it still doesn't work, call me back.'

The garden and shed now quiet, Theodore ventured out from the bottom of the hedge.

There was still no sign of Hamish, so he took the opportunity to empty his bowels in Stuart's vegetable patch. He kicked some soil over and then gazed at the back of Stuart's house.

Leslie was pacing in front of the lounge window, her mobile phone in her hand. She was tapping frantically away at the screen.

Leslie was a secret gambling addict. What had started as a bit of harmless fun at the end of the working day had become an all-consuming obsession. At night she would lie in bed clicking away while her husband read a chapter of his book. Stuart wasn't aware that she had squandered most of their savings. But she knew, with a little bit of luck, she would eventually make it all back and more besides.

She used a website called Doggo Bingo. Doggo was a Yorkshire terrier with spinning pound coins for eyes and a pink tongue that slithered saliva. He wore a top hat with a pink band. A playing card stuck out from the band: the jack of diamonds.

Theodore watched her waste another hundred pounds in less than two minutes on Doggo Bingo, her fingers jabbing away at the screen of her iPhone, her forehead creased.

Humans would be better off without hands. Theodore glanced at his paws and then back to Leslie's fingers, still jabbing away at the screen of her iPhone. All pad and no claw, thought Theodore.

17

Emily was not in a good mood when she got home.

It was Good Friday, and during her lunch break she had gone out to M&S and bought a whole salmon for dinner, as she was traditionally minded enough to avoid meat on this day. She left the plastic bag containing the fish in her car when she returned to the soft furnishing store for her afternoon shift.

The shop's owner was on a three-week holiday in Thailand and Emily had been left in charge. The widow of a local fish and chip tycoon had entered the shop with the intention of furnishing a dozen properties she had bought on the Terry's site in York, now named the Chocolate Works, and was going to let them out. Emily had widened her eyes when the woman had taken out her purse and paid in cash. Almost twenty thousand pounds.

How many fish and chips did you have to sell to make that sort of money? How many hours would she have to spend working in a shop to make that sort of money?

The banks were closed as it was a Bank Holiday and wouldn't be open again until Tuesday. She knew there were such things as night safes but was unsure how they worked. So, rather than leaving the money in the till overnight, she put it in her handbag.

They wouldn't count it until the banks reopened on Tuesday anyway, so what difference did it make?

It had been a sunny afternoon, and when she got back in her car, it stank of fish. She drove home with her windows down.

Now the plastic bag containing the smelly salmon sat next to her handbag containing twenty thousand pounds on the kitchen side.

She removed the salmon and slid it into a dish. She took out a container of mashed potato from the fridge. She removed the cardboard sleeve. She took a knife from the drawer and began to stab the plastic cover, the knife going through the contents and stabbing the wooden counter surface below. She didn't notice; her attention was focussed on her handbag.

She would take the cash into the bank on Tuesday morning. What did it matter, a few days?

While she was sorting out dinner, Jonathan came into the kitchen. He sat down on a stool and rested his crutches in the corner. 'Something smells a bit fishy,' he said.

'That'll be the fish,' Emily said. 'So what have you been doing all day?'

Jonathan spread his palms, wondering where to begin. 'I think she killed the dog today,' he said.

He pointed at the back door and what lay beyond. 'First she did in her mother, and now she's gone and killed the dog.'

'Oh, come off it,' said Emily, arms folded. 'People don't go killing their mothers and dogs in the middle of the afternoon. Not in Acomb they don't...'

'But it happened,' Jonathan said. 'I'm sure of it. Both me and Theodore saw the dog jumping up in the window. Then the barking stopped. Then it was quiet. And then afterwards the curtains were snapped closed again.'

'Have you been drinking?'

'No,' Jonathan said. 'Well, maybe a beer or two...'

Emily raised her eyebrows.

'Look I'm not drunk. But I do think she's done something to the dog... And her mother too.'

'You really expect me to believe that some old woman behind, who I have never seen for that matter, has been murdered by her daughter? And now her dog's been killed?'

'She was in the garden. She had dug a hole. I reckon she had buried the dog. Or maybe even her mother's head. I never saw her putting anything in the ground. She'd already covered it over. But I'm sure she's buried something in the garden.'

'I've heard enough,' Emily said.

'And the curtains haven't been opened all today,' Jonathan went on.

'Give it a rest,' Emily said. 'I've had a crap day at work. I don't need this as soon as I get in.'

She turned and went over to the back door. She looked across the garden to the house behind.

'Well, they're open now... And the television's on. You can see the light flickering.'

Jonathan got to his feet and crossed to the back door. 'You're right. She's gone and opened them, and she must have turned the TV on to make it look like her mum's in there watching it.'

'Look,' Emily said, 'if you really are concerned about the old lady, why don't you just ask the daughter next time you see her?'

'Ask her what? Did you kill your mother?'

'You ask how her mother is.'

'I will,' Jonathan said. 'Tomorrow... I'll ask her how her mother is. See what she says.'

'She was just doing a spot of gardening,' Emily said. 'Maybe you should do something about our garden. The lawn needs cutting. It'll take your mind off all this murder nonsense...'

'I can't do the garden,' Jonathan said. 'Not with my foot.'

'Well, I don't know anything about gardening, and I'm not going to start learning now.'

'We could get a gardener.'

'Gardeners cost money and I don't see you earning any sitting there.'

'I'm on sick leave,' Jonathan protested. 'I'm still being paid...'

'Enough about gardens and dead mothers,' Emily said. 'You haven't even asked me about my day.'

'How was your day?' Jonathan said.

Emily shook her head. 'I'm going to get changed now. When I come back down I don't want to hear any more about dead dogs and murdered mothers.'

Theodore watched as she went upstairs taking her handbag with her. He followed.

When Theodore entered the bedroom, Emily was sitting on the edge of the bed. Banknotes fanned out across the duvet. Theodore jumped up onto the bed and stared at the money.

The concept of money baffled him. It was a difficult concept for most humans to get a grip on. You work so that you can gain money, so that you can sleep in a bed, eat food and maybe, if you are lucky, have one or two weeks' holiday from the tedium of work. To a cat's mind, those things should be a basic requirement of existence, not something that required eight hours labour a day.

Emily too wondered at the point of it all. She stared into Theodore's eyes and began to stroke him.

Theodore felt the tension release from her as she stroked him and a faraway look appeared in her face.

Emily is lying on a deckchair in front of a five star hotel. She is wearing a black and white striped swimsuit by Whistles, sunglasses by Fendi and hat by Melissa Odabash.

Waiters wander around with trays of drinks. She lowers her sunglasses and gazes across at the other hotel guests. None of them look like they do a hard day's work and neither does she.

She gets up and pads over the golden sand. The sun glistens on the turquoise blue of the sea.

A young bronzed man calls out to her. He looks like a young George Clooney crossed with Brad Pitt. He is standing in front of a convertible car.

'Well, are you going to jump in?' George/Brad says. 'I thought we could have a romantic dinner and then dance away the night at a little club I know.'

'Sounds fun,' Emily says. 'But I'm not really dressed.'

'I'm sure we could call in and get you a little something on the way... It's on me.'

'Well, if you insist,' Emily says, walking over to the waiting George/Brad.

She lets him give her a little kiss on the cheek before she climbs into the car, George/Brad holding the door for her while she gets in.

In the distance a telephone rings.

Then George/Brad says, 'Are you going to get that?'

But it wasn't George/Brad's voice. It was Jonathan's.

'Telephone!' he shouted again from downstairs.

Emily stopped stroking Theodore and began to gather up the banknotes. She pushed them back into a plastic envelope and put the money into the drawer of her bedside locker. She then rushed downstairs, the telephone still ringing insistently from the table in the hall. She knew who it was; only her mother called the landline.

Theodore stayed on the bed a minute. He stared at the closed drawer of the bedside cabinet. He then looked at the tower of paperbacks stacked on top, their spines facing him. He read the capitalised titles:

TOO GOOD TO BE TRUE
THE MAN ON THE BUS
THE BETRAYAL
THE GIRL YOU LOST
NO KISS GOODBYE
EAT, PRAY, LOVE
NO COMING BACK
THE NEW LIFE

He noted that she had yet to read 'The New Life' by Nobel-prize-winning Turkish author Orhan Pamuk, as the spine was uncreased; either that or she had started and soon given up. He furrowed his brow, blinked his eyes and then jumped down from the bed.

Emily was still on the phone to her mother.

'But it's only Easter,' she said, 'won't it be too cold for a barbecue.' She was then silent as she listened to her mum Trish speaking.

Then: 'Well, if he insists...'

A minute's silence, then: 'No, he's still resting his foot... I've really just got in.'

Theodore soon lost interest in the one-sided conversation. He padded across the hall and slipped into the kitchen.

A minute later Emily entered the lounge.

'My parents invited us over to Acaster Mildew on Sunday for Easter lunch,' she said to the back of Jonathan's head. 'But as you are not mobile, they are coming over here instead.'

'So you're cooking?'

'No,' Emily said. 'My dad's already bought the food in and he's insisting that he wants to cook... Surf and turf.'

'Surf and turf?'

'He likes to do it on the barbecue. Prawns for starter, then lamb cutlets. Barbecued pear and brandy snap surprise for pudding. It's sort of an Easter tradition.'

'But we don't have a barbecue.'

'He's bringing one over, along with the food.'

'I guess that's all right then.'

Emily said. 'I'd better put dinner on. It's already quarter to eight.'

She entered the kitchen.

'Theo!' she screamed.

Theodore was on top of the salmon, wolfing down the pink fish flesh. He stopped and jumped down onto the floor. He dashed at the backdoor, but then remembered there was no cat flap. He turned round and dashed past Emily, who was standing in front of the remains of the salmon.

Emily screamed, and then whimpered from behind her hands which she held over her face, 'That was our dinner...'

18

Emily slept through her alarm on Easter Saturday. She was working that day and left the house without saying more than two words to either Jonathan or Theodore.

Theodore ate some biscuits left over from the day before and then went back upstairs.

He settled on the back bedroom window. He could see Ellen in her kitchen, emptying the kitchen bin. She opened the back door and carried the bin liner over to the black wheelie bin. She threw it in and was about to return inside when Stuart appeared at the boundary hedge.

'Got a spare ciggie?' he shouted over at her.

'Are you ever going to buy any?' Ellen said, walking towards him.

She handed over a cigarette and noticed Stuart staring down at her chest. She was wearing one of her father's old shirts, three buttons undone. She knew that Stuart fancied her. He didn't try to hide it. Although he was pushing forty he was handsome in a virile sort of way. Besides, there weren't any other men who had ever shown any interest in her.

'I've a shelf I need putting up,' Ellen said, lighting his cigarette. 'In my bedroom.'

She lit a cigarette for herself.

'I can put a shelf up for you,' Stuart said. 'I'll bring my drill round later.'

'Well, I'm about to have a bath,' Ellen said, blowing smoke provocatively at Stuart. 'Give us an hour or so.'

'Righty-ho,' said Stuart. 'What about your mum? Won't all the drilling disturb her?'

'Don't worry about her,' Ellen said. 'She was up late. She'll be dead to the world.'

'Whatever you say,' Stuart said. 'I'll be round later.'

'I'll leave the back door unlocked. Just come straight up and I'll be waiting.'

'Not a problem.'

'And don't forget your drill,' Ellen said with a smile.

Theodore was distracted by a blur of black and white at the kitchen door. It was a magpie. He watched as it flapped about inside the kitchen. Another magpie stood guard on the edge of the overgrown lawn.

Theodore turned his attention back to Ellen. She was walking back towards her house. Stuart was staring at her back, at her rear end to be precise.

As Ellen reached the back door, the bird flew out of the house. She flapped her arms at the bird. 'Get out of it,' she shouted after it.

Theodore watched from the bedroom window as the magpie disappeared into the branches of an apple tree in Geoffrey's garden.

Ellen closed the kitchen door and went upstairs to have a bath. Theodore jumped down from the windowsill and trotted downstairs.

Jonathan looked out of the French windows at the house that overlooked his. The curtains in both back bedrooms were open.

He remembered that he was going to confront his neighbour Ellen about her mother and the dog; he decided to put it off. Maybe Emily was right. He was just reading too much into it.

'Fancy watching a film?' he said to Theodore.

The cat was strutting up and down in front of the French windows, miaowing from time to time, already wanting to be out in the garden.

'The Man Who Knew Too Much,' Jonathan said, waving the plastic box at Theodore. 'We might as well give it a go.'

He got to his feet on his crutches and managed to slot the DVD into the player.

Theodore looked at the television screen.

An American couple, played by James Stewart and Doris Day, and their young son, played by Christopher Olsen, are sitting on the back seat of a bus, travelling through a busy Marrakesh market place. The boy spots a camel through the side window of the bus. 'Oh, look, a camel,' he says.

And the three of them turn to look at it through the rear window of the bus.

Theodore looked through the rear window of the bus but there was no camel to be seen.

Soon, a Frenchman makes their acquaintance.

The boy says to the soon-to-be-murdered Frenchman, 'If you ever get hungry, our garden back home is full of snails. We tried everything to get rid of them. We never thought of a Frenchman!'

And they all laugh.

Theodore turned from the television screen and peered through the French windows. He glimpsed the red cap of Wally, standing over a smouldering fire. He looked across at the house behind. He saw Ellen in her bedroom. She wasn't alone.

On the television screen, Doris Day sang of being a little girl and asking her mother about her future, and her mother replying with, 'Que Sera, Sera'. What will be, will be.

Jonathan turned from the screen and through the French windows he looked across at Ellen's bedroom window. He saw Ellen's face appear in the window. She looked across at him and mouthed:

'When I was just a young woman
I took a pillow
From my mum's bed.
You asked if I held it

Until she was dead?

What do you think I said?'

Jonathan looked at the television screen and then back through the French windows up at Ellen's bedroom window. Ellen's face was close to the window. She sang the garbled chorus:

'Que paso, paso
Whatever I did, I did
The past is not yours to know
Que paso, paso
What happened is so... is so.'

Another face then came into focus from the shadows of the room. It was coated in red hairs with red cheeks to match. It was Stuart. His face moved forwards and backwards behind Ellen, in and out of focus.

Then Ellen, her cheeks pink, her mousey-brown hair hanging across her face, sang:

'When poor Sandy wouldn't shut up
You ask me, neighbour
You ask with a sigh
Did I throttle her?
Poor little Sandy
Did the pooch have to die?'

Then, from behind her, Stuart joined in:

'Que paso, paso
Whatever she did, she did
The past is not yours to know
Que paso, paso
What happened is so... is so.'
Then Ellen sang:
'Well, I've got concerns of my own
I ask my conscience
What should I do?
Shall I confess all?
Tell the police?
Why, they'd have a ball
If only they knew!

Ellen's face was now pressed to the window, her cheeks pink, as she mouthed out the words:

'Que paso, paso
Whatever I did, I did
The past is not yours to know
Que paso, paso
What happened is so... is so.'

Jonathan managed to look away. He looked down at Theodore, who was sitting in front of the French windows.

Theodore turned to him and miaowed what sounded like: 'Que paso, paso.'

'Not you, as well,' Jonathan cried and threw a cushion at the cat.

Theodore darted behind the sofa.

Jonathan looked back up at the window.

Ellen's mouth was wide, her face pressed up against the glass. Stuart was behind her, working his way frantically to a climax. They both stared down at Jonathan and sang out:

'Que paso, paso
Whatever I did, I did.'

Jonathan put his hands to his face, covering his eyes, as Ellen, Stuart and Theodore, from somewhere behind the sofa, all sang at the tops of their voices:

Que paso, paso
What happened is so... is so
Que paso, paso!'

When he opened his eyes, the curtains in Ellen's bedroom had been pulled shut and Theodore was sitting once more in front of the French windows. From outside he heard a woman call out, 'Stuart! Stuart! Are you out here?'

19

Nigel Bates returned that afternoon.

Jonathan, shaken by what he had seen in Ellen's window, was pleased to see him. He got up from the sofa and opened the French windows.

Theodore darted through the open windows and out onto the lawn.

'Just wanted to make sure there were no more smears.' Nigel watched the cat make for the hedge at the back of the garden.

'They look fine to me,' Jonathan said. 'Has work not picked up?'

'Still a bit slow,' Nigel said. 'I've started telling people to call me Nigel now. I'm starting to like it. Norman was a bit old fashioned when you think about it.'

'That's good, Nigel.'

'I'm going to change it officially by dead pool.'

Jonathan knew that Nigel meant deed poll but didn't bother to correct him; he had something else on his mind. 'You mentioned the house behind the first time you came round,' Jonathan said. 'Terrible business, you said.'

'I remember it well,' Nigel said. He took off his beanie and scratched his head. 'Not something you forget in a hurry. Must have been ten years ago.'

'What actually happened?'

'There was a fire, wasn't there? Shed went up in flames with him inside. They say a petrol can had been leaking fumes.'

'But what caused it to suddenly burst into flames?'

'That's the funny thing. The word was that the young girl had been smoking out of her window. Then lobbed her fag end out, and that's what did it. An accident like.'

'Then what happened? What happened to the girl?'

'Nothing, I don't think. She was just a young lass. It was an accident, wasn't it? They took pity on her.'

Jonathan stared at the house behind. 'I think Ellen might have had another accident...'

Nigel stared at him at moment. 'You're kidding. You only get one dad. You can't kill him twice.'

'Not her dad this time,' Jonathan said. 'This time she's killed her mum. But it wasn't an accident.'

'Well, she should be put away then. She's not a young girl anymore. You can't just go round killing your parents...'

'I know. But I can't prove anything... I think she killed her in her bedroom. Smothered her with her pillow. I didn't see it, mind you. But the old woman was screaming; then she was quiet. And then I haven't seen or heard anything from her since.'

Nigel stared at Jonathan, his face vacant.

'I think she did it for the money,' Jonathan went on. 'For the house... The last thing she cried was: "It's going to the dogs!" So Ellen thought she wasn't going to inherit anything.'

Nigel continued to look expressionlessly at Jonathan. He didn't say anything.

'You don't believe me, do you?' Jonathan said.

Nigel turned and looked at the house behind. 'The windows look like they could do with a clean.'

Jonathan's eyes widened. 'That's it,' he cried, clapping his hands together. 'You've got ladders. You could take them round and do the windows. While you're there, you could look in the windows and see if you can see her mum. That's her bedroom on the right.'

'You can't just go round and clean someone's windows unless they ask you to.'

'What if we wait till she goes out? Then you go round and wash the windows...'

'But I won't get paid...'

'I'll pay you,' Jonathan said.

'Well, as long as I'm not going to get into trouble.'

'Come on. Let's go upstairs. From the back bedroom we'll be able to see when she goes out. Then you head round.'

Ten minutes later they were in the back bedroom. They could see through the sliding doors Ellen working at the dining room table. After an hour of waiting, they saw her gather up a wad of brown envelopes, grab a hoodie and make her way out of the back door.

From the bottom of the hedge, Theodore watched her leave. Ten minutes later he saw Nigel walk along the side of the house, carrying his ladders over his shoulder.

He put them up so they reached the bottom of Tessa's bedroom window. He disappeared and then returned a couple of minutes later with a bucket. He then began to climb the ladder, the bucket in his left hand.

Theodore turned round and looked back at his own house. He could see Jonathan in the bedroom window, a pair of binoculars held to his face.

He turned back to Ellen's house. Nigel was near the top of the ladder. The curtains had been left half open. He peered into the darkened room.

Suddenly Ellen appeared round the corner of the house. 'What are you doing?' she cried.

Without waiting for a reply, she rushed at the ladder and pushed it over.

The ladder landed on the paving stones with a clatter. Nigel landed with a thump. The empty bucket rolled across the patio and came to a rest against the sliding glass doors.

Nigel cried out in pain. 'My leg! My leg!' he screamed, holding his leg. 'I've broken my leg.'

Theodore looked at Nigel's leg and noticed it was bent at an impossible angle.

'Call an ambulance,' Nigel shouted. 'Please!'

Ellen took her mobile phone from her jeans pocket. 'Hello! Hello! Yes... Police... I've just stopped someone trying to break into my house...'

Jonathan was also on his phone, calling an ambulance.

It was an hour before a police officer knocked on Jonathan's door. By which time Nigel had been taken to hospital in an ambulance, accompanied by another police officer.

'I'm Police Constable Pigeon,' the police officer said. 'You can call me Gary.'

'You'd better come in,' Jonathan said.

He made his way through to the lounge and PC Gary Pigeon followed.

When they were both sitting down, Gary said, 'I believe you are a witness to the attempted break in at 64 Constantine Crescent. The house behind...'

'Yes but no,' Jonathan said. 'I mean I saw what happened, but it was not an attempted break in.'

'Not a break in? Well, what was he doing up there? The bucket he had with him didn't have a trace of water in it.'

'He was trying to see inside...'

'A voyeur? Are you sure? It's more likely he was scoping the house. Waited until she'd gone out, and then thought he'd have a quick look. See if there was anything worth nicking.'

'No, it wasn't like that. He was checking if her mother was alive...'

'I'll stop you there,' Gary said. 'I don't think you know who you're dealing with. The suspect gave us a false name when he was arrested. Said he was called Nigel. But when we checked his driving licence, it was Norman. And then we did a quick look on our system and it turns out that he's not even registered.'

'Registered?'

'Yes, registered. Registered to be a window cleaner.'

'Do you have to be registered to be a window cleaner?'

'Of course, you do,' Gary said. 'We can't have just any-one putting up ladders and peeping through people's windows, can we?'

'I didn't know.'

'If you didn't need to be registered, anybody could set them-selves up and go peering through people's windows.'

'I wouldn't,' Jonathan said. 'I suffer from vertigo.'

'Well, maybe not you,' Gary said. 'But this Norman, he's an unsavoury character. He's a maverick. A wild card. A rogue window cleaner.'

'I didn't realise,' Jonathan said. 'I'd never heard of rogue window cleaners.'

'They are anarchists,' Gary said. 'You probably don't remember the Window Cleaning Wars of the 1980s.'

'I'm afraid I don't.'

'It was a turf war. Too many of them going for too few windows. Encroaching on each other's territories. There was fighting in the streets. Blades drawn. A lot of broken windows. Very unpleasant business.'

'I had no idea.'

'Thatcher tried to sort them out. But the NUWC, that's the National Union of Window Cleaners, was too powerful even for her. The NUWC organised a national strike and they all put their blades down. People had to endure dirty windows for weeks. They refer to it as the Summer of the Window Cleaners' Discontent.'

'I think I might have heard of that.'

Gary stood up and began to pace in front of the French windows. 'You will have heard of the Great Uprising of the Window Cleaners.'

Jonathan nodded.

'It was following the introduction of the window tax in 1696,' Gary said. 'They taxed people on the number of windows they had. So people began to brick up their windows. Now, what do you think is going to happen?'

'Less windows?' Jonathan guessed.

'Less windows to clean. Who's that going to affect?'

'The window cleaners?'

'That's right,' Gary said. 'The window cleaners. They weren't happy at all. There were protests. It began in the north. They ended up marching on London. Others joining as they approached the capital. Parliament sent the army to meet them. There was a great battle.

'That was all a long time ago,' Gary said. 'But you bear in mind: always be wary of window cleaners. Be very wary of window cleaners.'

'I will,' Jonathan said nodding. 'What's going to happen to Nigel? I mean Norman.'

'He'll be charged with unsolicited window cleaning, I imagine. Soon as he's allowed out of hospital. We can't do much till then, but as soon as he's out, he'll feel the full weight of the law.'

'I see.'

'I think your cat wants to come in,' Gary said nodding at the French windows. 'And I'd better be off. I've got a lot of paperwork to do because of this.'

Jonathan looked and saw Theodore sitting in front of the French windows. The cat miaowed to be let in.

'I'll see myself out,' Gary said, and saw himself out.

Jonathan realised it was probably for the best that he hadn't said anything to Gary to implicate himself. He got to his feet and let Theodore back in.

20

When Emily got home that evening, Jonathan told her what he'd seen that afternoon. 'She was having sex in front of her bedroom window,' he said. 'Doggy-style.'

'Are you sure?' Emily said shaking her head.

'Well, he was behind her, and she was moving backwards and forwards.'

'No,' Emily said, shaking her head. 'I meant, are you sure you're not just imagining it, like the murdered mum and the dead dog.'

'I saw them at it, I tell you. They were at it like... Well, like dogs. Her and that Scottish man.'

'Yes, you said.'

'And then she knocked Nigel off his ladder and he's been taken to hospital.'

'Who's Nigel?' Emily said, staring out through the French windows.

'He's the window cleaner,' Jonathan said. 'A rogue window cleaner...'

Emily stared outside. 'There's a card in the bedroom window,' she said, squinting

There was a rectangle of white paper stuck to Ellen's bedroom window. It read: 'VOYER!'

'It says voyeur,' said Emily.

Jonathan got to his feet and went over to the French windows. 'I don't think that's how you spell voyeur.'

'She knows that you've been watching her,' Emily said.

'She made sure I was watching her.'

'You didn't have to sit there and watch.'

'I didn't want to have to sit there and watch.'

'You are obsessed with her.'

'I am not obsessed by her.'

'You are.'

'I'm not.'

'I am going to get changed now,' Emily said. 'When I come back down, I don't want to hear any more about her. I'm sick of it.'

Then Emily left the room, leaving Jonathan standing in front of the French windows, holding himself up by his sticks.

He stared at the rectangle of white paper. Then he looked at the next window. A light was on in Tessa's bedroom.

A figure was silhouetted against the sunflower curtains. It looked like Tessa. It was her hair, or at least her wig. She was sitting up in bed, watching television. From time to time, she raised a bottle to her mouth and drank. So Tessa was alive after all.

Jonathan shook his head. He reached for the package of tablets on the coffee table. He removed the folded sheet of paper they came with and began to read the long list of possible side effects.

Theodore followed Emily upstairs.

Emily took from her handbag, several more clear plastic bags of rolled-up money and emptied then across her duvet.

'Oh, Theo,' Emily said. 'Look at all this money. There's thousands here. And that's just today's takings.'

She began to stroke Theodore with one hand and with her other she stroked the money.

'Imagine what we could do with this,' she murmured, closing her eyes.

Emily is wearing a dress by Alice Temperly. She is carrying a Mulberry handbag. On her wrist she is wearing a watch by Larsson & Jennings.

She is standing in front of a roulette table. In front of her are hundreds of brightly-coloured chips in several cylindrical towers. The wheel comes to a stop and more chips are pushed her way by the croupier.

'It looks like you can't help but win today,' a handsome man in a suit standing next to her says and smiles a bleached white smile.

'It certainly appears that way,' Emily says. 'I don't know what I'm going to do with so much money...'

'You could buy a boat with all that dough,' the man says and laughs.

A little later, Emily is dressed in an Eres Diagramme one-shoulder swimsuit and sunglasses from Oliver Peoples Sayer.

She is standing on the deck of a speedboat. The man, who is called Carlos and bears a striking resemblance to Antonio Banderas, is at the controls, propelling the boat across a bay of choppy azure. Carlos is wearing just a pair of silky white shorts by Prada and sunglasses by Dolce & Gabbana. His body is burnt caramel. The sun shines down from a cloudless sky.

'This is such fun!' Emily says laughing and Carlos laughs too.

They pass very close to a rowing boat. Jonathan is struggling with a pair of oars and not making much progress. His hair is damp with sweat and stuck to his forehead. He is wearing super-market own brand t-shirt and shorts.

As Emily and Carlos pass, a tidal wave created by the speedboat almost capsizes Jonathan.

'I think I might have splashed that pasty-looking English-man,' Carlos says.

'Don't worry about him, Carlos,' Emily laughs. 'He's just my ex-boyfriend...'

She laughs so hard, her eyes are closed.

She opened her eyes to be faced by Theodore's wide green stare.

'Oh, Theodore,' Emily said, returning from her reveries. 'There's nothing wrong with dreaming. Life can be so tedious. What have we but our dreams?'

That night Jonathan and Emily watched a film set in San Francisco, featuring a detective who follows and then becomes obsessed with an attractive woman. It was called *Basic Instinct*.

This seems familiar, thought Theodore. He stretched and got down from the sofa.

From the back bedroom window Theodore watched as Geof-frey let Lucy out, for her fifteen minutes of freedom, before he locked up for the night.

The Labrador went straight over to the hedge they shared with Ellen. She began scratting at the ground in front of the hedge, concentrating her efforts at a spot where the vegetation was sparsest.

She dug furiously, sending dirt into the air behind her. Then she put her head to the ground and Theodore saw it emerge on the other side of the hedge. She then squeezed the rest of her body through the gap she had made. She was in Ellen's garden.

She ran over to the flowerbed, where Sandy the Shih Zhu was buried, and began to dig.

Theodore glanced over at the back of Ellen's house. A dark human-shaped shadow appeared in the kitchen window.

21

Emily woke early on Easter Sunday. Within minutes she realised what day it was and her mind turned to chocolate.

Theodore was sleeping by her side. On her other side, Jonathan lay. He had managed to make his way upstairs the night before. He was still sleeping, snoring. He still wore the boot on his injured foot. It lay on top of the duvet.

After petting Theodore for some minutes, Emily poked Jonathan in the shoulder until he stirred. 'I got you an egg,' she said, placing the chocolate egg on his chest.

'An egg?' Jonathan said, rubbing his eyes.

'I know you liked minty chocolate.'

'That's very kind,' Jonathan said. 'I'm afraid I wasn't able to get you one... What with being housebound.'

'You didn't get me an egg?'

'I couldn't get to the shop to get you one.'

'Well, you'd better be prepared to share that one.'

'I'm sorry.'

'It doesn't matter really,' Emily said, but her tone of disappointment said it did.

'I'll get you one,' Jonathan said. 'Soon as I'm back on my feet.'

'Well, at least I can have a lie in,' Emily said. 'It is Sunday after all.'

Theodore miaowed from her side of the bed. It might be Sunday. He still needed feeding though, and chocolate eggs, especially minty ones, were not high on his list of favourite breakfast items.

Emily rolled over and hugged him to her.

'Yes, Theo,' she said. 'We can have a lie in together.'

Not quite the response Theodore wanted. He miaowed at her again; then crawled out from her grasp.

At that moment there came a deep rumbling from the back of the house.

'What's that?' Emily said.

'Sounds like a tractor,' said Jonathan.

'Or a tank,' said Emily.

'It must be right outside.'

He got out of bed and grabbing his crutches, crossed the landing to the back bedroom. 'It's the old guy from next door. He's cutting his lawn.'

'But it's not even eight o'clock...'

An hour later, Emily opened the bedroom curtains. That was when she saw the dead Labrador on the verge in front of their house.

'Jonathan,' she screamed.

A minute later, Jonathan approached their bedroom window. He looked out and swore; then said, 'He's only gone and parked his Audi on the flowers she planted. That's not very neighbourly.'

'No, not the car,' Emily said. 'Down there.'

Jonathan peered down and saw the dead dog on the verge, and he knew straightaway that it was Geoffrey's dog. 'It must have got run over,' he said, not so sure.

'Yes, it must have. You can't just leave it there. You're going to have to do something about it.'

'I'm not too sure what to do about it.'

'Well, you need to find out whose dog it is and then tell them to shift it. My parents are coming over later... We can't have a dead dog in front of the house. Whatever would they think?'

'I think it belongs to the blind man in the bungalow behind,' Jonathan said. 'He's not going to be happy.'

'A guide dog,' Emily said. 'That makes it even worse.'

Jonathan made his way downstairs.

He opened the front door and walked over to the dead dog. It still wore its harness. The silver identity tag attached to its collar confirmed that it was Lucy.

He looked up and down the street. There was no one around. He could hear Wally still cutting his lawn. He approached Wally's front door and knocked.

His wife Marjorie answered it.

'There's a dead dog on the verge,' he said.

'I'd better go and get Wally,' Marjorie said, peering past Jonathan. 'He'll know what to do.'

Jonathan smelled home baking coming from inside the house; then the front door closed.

A minute later Wally emerged from the side of his house. He crossed over to where the dog lay and knelt down. 'It's dead,' he said.

His eyes were moist. He blew his nose on his handkerchief.

'It's Geoffrey's dog. His guide dog. Hasn't had it a year.'

'Who's going to tell him?'

'I'll go and get him,' Wally said.

Jonathan sat down on his front wall and waited. He stared at the white Audi parked on the grass verge opposite his house and the flowers flattened below its tyres.

He heard a door creak behind him. He turned and saw Theodore saunter out of the front door. He must have left it ajar. He couldn't be bothered trying to get the cat back inside. Instead he watched as the cat approached the dead dog.

Theodore carried out a cursory examination of the crime scene.

He immediately noted the soil on the dog's paws, where she had been digging in the flowerbed.

There was dried blood around an ear and around her nostrils, the result of a single blow. Not from a passing vehicle but from the back of a spade.

He then examined the verge in front of the body. He saw two parallel lines, a paw's width wide and four cat paces apart, impressed in the grass. The lines started from the footpath and ended in deeper ruts, where the wheelie bin had been pulled over so its contents could be deposited onto the grass.

Theodore looked back to the point where the wheelie bin had been pulled onto the verge. It had come from further around Constantine Crescent, and not from York Road.

Ten minutes later, Jonathan watched as Geoffrey and Wally approached.

Geoffrey was wearing a navy-blue dressing gown and brown suede slippers. He tapped a white stick in front of him.

'She's right here,' Wally said. 'Just to your left. Two feet away.'

'I'm not blind,' Geoffrey said.

'You're not?'

'I am visually impaired.' Geoffrey retracted his stick with a click of a button, so that it looked like a little white truncheon and then knelt down on the footpath beside Lucy. He moved his hands over the dog. He stroked her for some minutes.

'I'll take her to the vet's Tuesday morning,' Wally said. 'Leave it to me.'

Geoffrey didn't say anything. He stroked Lucy.

'They won't be open tomorrow, it being Easter Monday,' Wally said.

Geoffrey got to his feet. 'She never came back in last night,' he said finally. 'I let her out but she never came back. I looked all over for her... Must have got out of the garden. It's not like her at all.'

'Must have got hit by a car.'

Wally now looked across at Steve's Audi parked on the verge in front of Linda's house and shook his head slowly from side to side.

'I'll phone the guide dogs on Tuesday,' Geoffrey said. He clicked a button and his stick extended back to the ground. 'I'm sure they'll soon be able to sort something out. A replacement...'

From below Jonathan's dark blue Volvo, parked on the driveway, Theodore looked from the dead dog to its owner. Geoffrey wore his mirrored sunglasses. The sunglasses hid his eyes. They hid his feelings. They gave nothing away.

Theodore watched as Geoffrey tapped his way back along the street. Jonathan went back inside the house and Wally left but shortly returned with a blue tarpaulin. He lifted the dead dog onto the tarpaulin; then folded it over. He carried the dog away.

A minute later, from the front door of the house next door, Steve appeared, his golf bag in his hand. While he struggled with his bag and the door, Charlie the Chihuahua shot out. Steve put his golf bag in the boot of his car. He looked for a moment at the fat little dog darting about the street. He looked up at the bedroom curtains of his house that were closed. Then he got in his car and drove off.

In the house opposite, Theodore saw the Venetian blinds snap back to the horizontal, and knew that Linda, the neighbour opposite, had been watching the proceedings.

Then he made his way along the side of the house. He squeezed below the gate and was in the back garden. He was shortly on top of Wally's shed roof: his favoured surveillance spot.

Stuart had been up early, hiding little foil-wrapped chocolate eggs in his garden while his wife Leslie had a lie in.

Theodore heard him call to his children: 'Dougie! Daisy! I believe the Wee Scottie Bunny has been.'

'Tell us the story of the Wee Scottie Bunny, please daddy,' Daisy said.

'Do we have to?' Dougie said.

'Pleeaaase.'

'All right,' Stuart said and clapped his hands together. 'It was a Sunday, an Easter Sunday like today, and Jesus had been dead a few days. The Romans had put him in a cave and rolled a big rock across the entrance to the cave. And this big old rock was egg-shaped...'

'And that's why we have chocolate eggs at Easter, dad,' Daisy said. 'Isn't it?'

'That's right,' Stuart said.

'Can't we just look for the eggs now?' Dougie said.

'No,' Daisy said, 'I want to hear dad tell the Easter Story...'

Stuart carried on with the story: 'That morning, a wee little bunny was out hopping around in the early morning sunshine, and he heard a voice coming from behind this large egg-shaped rock. "Let me out!" the voice called from inside the cave. "Let me out!"'

'It was Jesus, wasn't it?' Daisy said. 'It was Jesus in the cave.'

'That's right,' Stuart said. 'So the bunny jumped against the rock. But it didn't move. He tried again and still it wouldn't budge.

'The wee little bunny looked up to the heavens and he prayed to God that he be given the strength to roll that rock away and release whoever was trapped inside.

'Then he jumped against the rock and this time the rock moved. It didn't just move. It rolled away. And Jesus appeared, and thanked the wee bunny rabbit.'

'Did that really happen, daddy?' Daisy said.

'Of course it didn't,' her brother Dougie said. 'Can we look for the eggs now?'

'Aye, go for it,' said Stuart. 'Go and get your eggies!'

Dougie and Daisy ran into the garden in their pyjamas. Dougie was ten, Daisy a couple of years younger. They both had their father's red hair.

'I can see one,' Dougie shouted, dashing across the garden to where a speck of tinfoil caught the early morning sunshine. He wiped the soil from the little egg and tucked it into his pyjama pocket and darted after another.

'I can see one too,' said Daisy, her hands in the soil.

'I've got four!' Dougie called out.

'I've got something on my hands and it smells,' Daisy said.

Theodore looked down and saw that Daisy's hands were streaked with brown.

'Looks like cat shit,' Stuart said from the patio. 'A fresh one too.'

Daisy started crying, her palms held out. 'It smells, daddy,' she said.

'Bloody cats,' Stuart said. 'Get inside and wash your hands.'

Dougie was still pocketing the little chocolate eggs. 'Silly Daisy,' he said.

Daisy ran inside, crying. 'Mummy!' she shouted. 'I've put my hand in cat poo! Mummy! Mummy!'

'Don't wake your mother,' Stuart shouted after her. 'She's having a lie-in.'

He looked up and saw Theodore peering down at him from the top of Wally's shed roof.

'Did you do that?' he said, pointing an accusing finger up at the cat.

Theodore looked down at the angry Scot. What if I did it? You don't expect me to go in my own garden? He turned his back to Stuart.

'It might have been Hamish,' Dougie said, stuffing more eggs into his bulging pyjama bottoms.

'Hamish knows not to shit in his own back garden,' Stuart said.

Exactly, thought Theodore.

Wally and Marjorie were sitting on a bench in their garden.

'When I hear the children over there, all excited, I do wonder what it would have been like...' Marjorie said, 'if we could have had some of our own.'

'Now, now,' Wally said, 'there's no point thinking like that.'

'I know,' Marjorie said. 'I just sometimes wonder...'

'No point wondering about what never happened.'

'I suppose not.'

They both drank from their mugs of tea.

'I've got something for you,' Wally said, getting up from the bench. 'For Easter.'

He crossed to his shed, and a moment later emerged carrying a large chocolate egg.

'Oh, my favourite, Wally. How did you know?'

'We have been married for nearly forty years.'

'Well, I've got something for you too.'

Marjorie got to her feet and disappeared inside the house. A minute later she returned carrying a large chocolate egg.

'Oh, my favourite, Marge! How did you know?'

'We have been married for nearly forty years.'

Theodore looked down at the old couple sitting together on their garden bench. Marjorie's face was pink in the early morning sunshine, and Wally had a glow to his cheeks, like red dabs. They each held identical chocolate eggs.

'I might have a bit of mine now,' said Marjorie.

'I might do the same,' said Wally.

22

Penny Black had left York and gone to study at university in Bristol. After she had graduated with a first class degree in graphic design, she had stayed on in Bristol. She got a job with a marketing agency and got engaged to Tom, who she had met on her course.

Penny had a by-line: she'd say on the phone to clients: 'It's Penny... Penny Black – like the stamp!', and people remembered it; they'd ask for her by name when they called up the agency. It was a memorable name after all. She already had a stable of half a dozen clients. Her future looked bright.

Penny was glad of the geographical as well as emotional distance that existed between her and her alcoholic of a mother and psychopath of a sister. She had managed to avoid forcing her family on Tom so far; she preferred to keep it that way.

She usually called her mother on her mobile phone every few days to make sure she was all right. When Tessa didn't answer, she began to wonder. When her mother's mobile went straight to answerphone, she began to worry. In a panic she called the landline but that too went straight to answerphone. She didn't have Ellen's mobile number. She doubted she had one.

Penny went out Saturday night to a trendy bar with Tom, but she couldn't relax, no matter how much she drank in the bar, where she sat with a group of their friends.

When they got back to their flat, they watched a programme in which young couples have to convince the viewing public that their feelings for each other are genuine, otherwise they get voted off, their 15 minutes of fame over, but Penny couldn't engage with the programme. She couldn't help but think that something terrible had happened to her mother.

Sunday morning she woke early. She got dressed, and leaving Tom sleeping, a note left on her pillow, she set off for the railway station to get the train to York.

She thought she would be back that evening. Easter Monday at the latest. She would never return.

23

Emily's parents arrived shortly before midday.

Emily's father Patrick carried a large blue cool box through the kitchen and into the back garden. The cool box contained the prawns and lamb cutlets that Patrick was going to cook on the barbecue.

Patrick ordered his clothes from slim brochures that fell out of The Times. Theodore appraised his attire from the bottom to the top, as was his way. He eyed his well-worn suede loafers that were shiny with wear at the extremities. His trousers were flat-fronted, brick-red chinos, held up by a woven leather belt, acquired while on holiday in the north of Ibiza. His shirt was blue and white vertical stripes, which exaggerated his belly that hung over the aforementioned belt. Theodore finished his examination, noting his balding pink head that glistened with sweat.

Patrick got the barbecue out of the garage and placed it on the patio. The cool box was left in the shade cast by the garage wall.

They were waiting for the charcoal to heat up when Theodore heard a tapping from the garden behind.

There was a woman at the back door of Ellen's house. She had long, dyed-red hair and wore dark designer sunglasses and a red dress. She knocked again on the door, more loudly. 'It's Penny,' she called. 'Let me in... I know you're in there.'

Penny turned round. Theodore noticed that she was of a similar physique to her sister, Ellen. She wore bright red lipstick that matched her red dress. She paced in front of the door. She looked at her wristwatch. She looked up at the bedroom windows. The curtains were closed.

'I think something has happened to the woman who lives behind,' Jonathan told Patrick. 'Looks like her other daughter has turned up now. To see what's going on.'

'Trish said that you've been developing something of an imagination,' Patrick said. 'Well, just be careful... Dangerous things: imaginations.'

'It's not just my imagination,' Jonathan said. 'Something has happened to her, I'm sure...'

'Have I ever told you the story of the three-legged pig?' Patrick said, changing the subject.

'I don't believe so,' Jonathan said, shaking his head.

Patrick began to tell Jonathan the story of the three-legged pig: 'A man is driving down a country lane when he has a puncture. Not having a spare tyre or mobile phone, he finds a farmhouse and knocks on the farmhouse door. As the door opens, a pig runs out. The man notices that the pig only has three legs... "Why has your pig only got three legs?" he asks the farmer...'

But Jonathan was still looking over at the house behind, not really paying attention to Patrick's rambling story.

Penny Black was standing in the garden now, looking up at the bedroom windows, hands on hips. Then she disappeared down the side of the house and then Jonathan heard faint banging and knew that she was at the front door; she hadn't given up.

Jonathan turned his attention back to Patrick.

'Then the pig waited by her until the ambulance arrived,' Patrick said.

Jonathan looked round again. He couldn't see Penny. Maybe she had given up and gone home. But didn't she live in Cardiff, or some far-flung place. She wouldn't come all this way and leave again after five minutes.

He then noticed a patch of silver fur at the bottom of the hedge and realised that Theodore was also keeping an eye on the proceedings.

In the kitchen, Emily and her mum Trish were making salads to go with the lunch.

'I'm not sure I'm cut out for this,' Emily said, slicing cucumber.

'Cut out for what?' Trish said.

'You know,' Emily said, holding up the kitchen knife. 'All of this... The house, Jonathan, suburbia... Getting up at seven o'clock every morning. Going to a job I don't like. Coming home and sorting out dinner.'

'What you need to do,' Trish said, 'is to get married and have children.'

'I'm not sure I'm ready... And besides, Jonathan hasn't asked. He's never mentioned marriage...'

'Well, it was a mistake moving in together before marriage. All this try before you buy. It might be all right for cars or televisions but not when it comes to husbands.'

'What if I've made a mistake?' Emily said, putting the knife down on the chopping board.

'Everyone makes mistakes,' Trish said. 'You just have to live with them the rest of your life. That's why you should get married before you cohabit...'

'Why's dad weeing in the garden?' Emily said.

'He's always doing that,' Trish said and sighed. 'It's better than him traipsing dirt into the house every time he needs to go. Weak bladder...'

In the garden, Patrick turned from the hedge and said, 'Then the farmer said, "Well, I didn't want to eat it all at once".' He laughed until his cheeks were bright pink.

'I don't get it,' Jonathan said.

'I think it's time to put the prawns on,' Patrick said, struggling with his flies.

He bent over and retrieved a large bag of uncooked prawns from the cool box.

He had placed tin foil on the wire rack of the barbecue. He now carefully set out the prawns, fingering each one attentively.

'Five minutes!' he shouted across to the kitchen door.

Then Theodore spotted Charlie the Chihuahua. Charlie nipped through a small gap in the bottom of the hedge and made for the cool box. He placed his paws on the rim of the box that had been left open and tilted it towards him. He then launched himself upwards and into the box, ending up on top of the lamb cutlets, the lid snapping closed over him.

Patrick was bent over the barbecue, sweating fiercely. Jonathan was looking in his direction but also at the house behind. Penny was bashing on the backdoor, as hard as she could without doing it lasting damage.

After they had eaten the prawn starter, Patrick announced he would put the lamb cutlets on the barbecue before the heat from the charcoal began to die down. He flipped open the white lid of the cool box.

'Holy mackerel!' he exclaimed. 'There's a Chihuahua in the chiller!'

Jonathan got to his feet with his crutches and crossed over. 'Is it alive?' he said.

Patrick picked up the dog and held it to his chest. 'It's alive but it's chilled to the bone,' he said. 'I know... I'll warm it up a bit.'

He held the Chihuahua a couple of feet over the barbecue, so that the heat from the charcoal could warm up the frozen dog. The dog soon began to jerk back to life.

Just then Sam, who had been looking for her dog since she got up, put her head over the hedge.

She screamed. Then she shrieked, 'Steve! Steve! They're barbecuing our Charlie!'

Steve, just arrived back from his nine holes, appeared at the hedge. 'Hey! That's our dog you're cooking!'

Patrick removed the dog from over the heat and, realising what it must look like, said, 'I was just warming it up...'

'Animals!' Sam shrieked.

Charlie wriggled frantically in Patrick's hands.

Patrick dropped the dog, and Charlie dashed over to the hedge.

Moments later Sam was cradling the Chihuahua in her arms. 'Oh, Charlie,' she said, 'whatever would have happened if mummy hadn't saved you?'

Theodore watched the events from the bottom of the hedge. Then his attention was drawn by voices from behind.

Ellen had opened the backdoor, wearing a dressing gown.

'Why didn't you answer the door?' Penny said.

'I just did,' Ellen said.

'Before,' Penny said. 'I've been knocking for ages.'

'I was in the shower,' Ellen said. 'You'd better come in... What a surprise! Mum will be so pleased to see you.'

Ellen went inside and Penny followed, closing the door behind her.

'Where's mum?' Penny said.

'She's upstairs in bed,' Ellen said. 'Hardly ever leaves it... You know what she's like.'

'I'll go straight up and let her know I'm here,' Penny said.

'I'll put the kettle on,' Ellen said.

Penny went upstairs, but Ellen didn't put the kettle on. Instead she picked up the iron and stood to one side of the kitchen door.

When Penny returned moments later, she said, 'She's not there... Her bed's not been slept in. Where is she? Where's mum?'

Then Ellen cracked her over the head with the iron. Theodore blinked.

'Well, that was all a bit melodramatic,' Trish said, once the commotion over the chilled Chihuahua had died down.

'I think the lamb might be salvageable,' Patrick said, holding up a cutlet that Charlie had partly chewed before succumbing to hyperthermia and asphyxiation. 'I'll just need some scissors to trim them up a bit.'

'Well, at least no one was killed,' Trish said and laughed.

Jonathan stared at the back hedge. He had heard Penny bashing on the back door of Ellen's house. Now it was quiet. Too quiet.

Then he noticed that Theodore had gone from the bottom of the hedge. He looked around but he was nowhere to be seen.

Theodore made his way across Ellen's lawn, heading straight towards the shed.

The shed was six feet high but he managed to scrabble up one side, the side not facing the house. He pulled himself up onto the felted roof, and then inched towards the apex. He peered over the top of the shed roof.

Ellen had already removed her sister's body from the kitchen. There was just a large pool of blood and red smears across the linoleum where Penny had been dragged into the hallway behind and then up the stairs, red smudges across the beige carpet pile.

Ten minutes later, Ellen appeared. She filled a bucket with hot water at the kitchen sink and then began to wipe up the blood. She washed down the fronts of the cupboards onto which blood had splattered. She got into the cracks and crevices, wringing out her cloth into the bucket that she refilled a dozen times. Finally she took a mop and turning the radio up loud, mopped the floor with maniacal energy to Wham's Club Tropicana.

From time to time, Theodore glanced over at his own house. Emily, Jonathan and Trish were sitting at the patio table while Patrick was cooking the lamb chops over the barbecue, metal tongs in his right hand.

Theodore turned around. Ellen had finished in the kitchen. She had left the kitchen window and door open to dry the floor. From inside he could hear water running. She must be running a bath.

He jumped down from the shed and trotted across the lawn. He paused at the back door. Water was still running in the upstairs bathroom. He entered the kitchen.

It was only once he was halfway across the kitchen floor that he realised that he had left muddy paw prints on the linoleum. There wasn't anything he could do about it now.

He looked up at the side and spotted the little wicker basket. He jumped up and began to investigate its contents. There was a mobile phone, its screen blank, its battery no doubt dead. He pawed some pens aside but could not find what he was looking for. He furrowed his brow. The ring, Tessa's wedding ring, had gone.

He jumped down and padded into the hall.

He walked through a door into the dining room. On the dining table he noticed many beige card-backed envelopes and an album lying open. He jumped up onto the table.

The album contained stamps. Each page was a plastic envelope holding mounted sheets of stamps. There were a dozen cardboard-backed envelopes, some with names and addresses already written on in blue biro.

Then he noticed the iPad. He swiped his paw across the screen. It opened to eBay.

Ellen evidently had 98% feedback rating. Theodore looked at the items she had put up for auction.

'1841 1d Red Pl 176 NA Superb RARE PLATE with CERT Cat. £2900.00. Looking for Quick Sale'

'1840 1d Black Pl 11 JK 4m IRISH NUMERAL Matched in Red RPS Cert Cat £4730.00'

'SG. 351. N14 ½d green. "DOUBLE WATERMARK ". A very RARE superb mint'

They were all rare stamps, Theodore realised, many valued in the thousands of pounds. The auctions were due to end the next day. Ellen was set to make a small fortune.

He remembered that her father Colin had been a keen stamp collector. Ellen was selling off his collection, raising money. Money to disappear, thought Theodore. The fur along his spine began to bristle.

The running water had stopped.

He heard a door open and then steps on the upstairs landing. He jumped down from the table and trotted under the table. He saw Ellen pass in front of the dining room door. A minute later she walked past again, a pair of scissors in one hand and a carving knife in the other.

Once she had gone back upstairs, Theodore followed. He paused on the landing. He heard noises from within the bathroom. The door was pulled to but not closed. There were another three doors. Bedroom doors.

Theodore approached the back bedrooms first. He went into what had been Tessa's.

The bed was made up. The curtains were closed. There was nothing to suggest anything untoward. But a smell lingered. It was the smell of unwashed sheets, urine, sweat and perfume. The essence of Tessa Black that lingered after her death.

Then he went into Ellen's bedroom. It was very tidy: nothing out of place. A My Little Pony poster on the wall over the bed. A pink duvet pushed up against the wall. A wrinkled grey sheet. A full ashtray on the bedside table. The smell of stale cigarettes, unwashed sheets and perfume.

He jumped up onto the windowsill and slipped behind the curtains.

He looked down on his own back garden. He could see Emily, Jonathan, Trish and Patrick sitting at the patio table eating lamb cutlets and potato salad.

Theodore went into the front bedroom. This had been the master bedroom, where Colin and Tessa Black had shared the double bed, before Colin had burned to death in his shed, the fire started by a cigarette end thrown from his younger daughter's bedroom window.

On the wall facing him there was a large, framed studio photograph of Penny and Ellen, taken by Mr. Marley, the local photographer.

Penny was eight years old and Ellen five. Penny's hair was long and brown; Ellen's was short and blonde, like her mother's – before she pulled it out.

Apart from the age and hair differences, the two girls looked very similar. They had the same broad nose, brown eyes, puckered lips and slightly protruding ears.

The glass from the photo frame had shattered. Shards lay on the pink pile of the carpet at the foot of the wall, below the photograph.

A pair of short, sharp stainless steel scissors stuck out of Penny's forehead.

Theodore carefully picked his way across the pink carpet, wary of the broken glass.

He jumped up onto the salmon pink duvet, laid across the king-size bed, and then up onto the windowsill. He looked out of the window, onto the street below.

In the driveway he noticed a Ford Escort. Its tyres were completely flat, rubber black pancakes on grey concrete. The car had not been moved since Colin's death, Theodore deduced.

The toilet flushed and Theodore knew it was time to leave. He made it to the top of the stairs just as the bathroom door swung open.

He raced down the stairs, into the kitchen, skidded across the still wet floor, and out the back door into the garden. He reached the shed in the corner of the garden and scaled the side. He scrambled over the apex of the felted roof. He turned round and edged back to the ridge. He peered over.

Ellen was in the kitchen. In her hand she carried the kitchen knife, its blade coated with blood. She looked down at the paw prints on the newly washed floor. Then she approached the kitchen door. She looked out into the garden.

24

Theodore stayed below the ridgeline of the shed. He turned round and faced his own garden. Emily, Jonathan, Trish and Patrick were still sitting at the outside table. They were onto the dessert course.

He scaled the side of the shed and darted through the bottom of the hedge into his own garden. His intention was to alert Jonathan to the latest murder, this time sororicide.

But as he approached the table, he was grabbed up by Patrick, who had already finished his dessert.

'Ah, Theo. Where have you been? You've missed lunch!' Patrick petted him heavily. 'He's a bit matted,' he said. 'Needs a good brush.'

Theodore felt Patrick's soft belly beneath his paws. He began to knead his paws against the warm flesh. As human bellies went, it was one of the best he'd had the pleasure to work with. He began to purr.

He was just beginning to enjoy himself when he felt something move below his paws. Something that was in Patrick but not of him. He moved his paw following the gliding movement and then dabbed at it.

Patrick groaned.

'What is it, dad?' Emily said.

'Probably nothing,' Patrick said. 'Indigestion.'

'It's all the raw meat you eat,' Trish said. 'Steak Tartare for breakfast. That can't be good for you.'

'That's only on a Saturday,' Patrick said. 'A little treat.'

He groaned again as Theodore pushed in his other paw, trying to trap the movement inside him.

Theodore closed his eyes, deep in thought.

It was a beef tapeworm of the species taenia saginata. It had been inside Patrick for almost two years, now ten feet long.

'I think that's enough of your prodding,' Patrick said. He picked Theodore up and placed him on the ground before the cat could complete his diagnosis.

'Maybe you should get it checked out,' Emily said.

'I'm sure it's nothing,' Patrick said, his own hand on his side and a note of uncertainty to his voice.

'Please, dad,' Emily said. 'For me, if not for you.'

'You have been complaining of stomach pains,' Trish said.

'Yes, all right then. I'll make an appointment on Tuesday.'

Theodore examined the floor for any food dropped from the table. He then remembered that he had been about to alert Jonathan to the latest murder before he had been grabbed up by Patrick. He approached Jonathan's feet and miaowed.

Jonathan had already managed to manoeuvre the conversation back to his murderous neighbour. By the animation in his voice, Theodore understood that he had had more than a couple of glasses of wine. 'She's killed her mum, I swear... And now she's probably about to kill her sister.'

You're behind the times, thought Theodore.

'Well, at least it has stayed fine,' Trish said.

'Yes, it's been a lovely afternoon,' Patrick said. 'Just a shame about that little dog getting stuck in the cool box.'

'Well, never mind about that,' Trish said. 'There was no harm done.'

'A killer in the house behind,' Jonathan said, slurring slightly, 'and not one of you cares. She even killed a Shih Zhu and then a guide dog...'

'Talking of dogs, what do you get if you cross a bulldog with a Shih Zhu?' Patrick said.

'It's no joking matter,' Jonathan said. 'She's a homicidal maniac. A killer... A psychotic killer!'

Emily slammed her wine glass down on the table, causing a crack from stem to lip. 'Will you just shut up?' she said, staring at Jonathan. 'I've had enough. Enough!'

Jonathan shook his head. He didn't say anything.

Patrick filled the gap. 'Bullshit,' he said. 'It's a bullshit. Get it? A bull dog and a Shih Zhu...'

Nobody laughed.

'Maybe it's time we were going,' Trish said. 'Leave these two to it.'

'Yes,' said Patrick, gazing at the two empty bottles of Chardonnay on the table. 'We'd better be getting back to Acaster Mildew.'

25

After the barbecue had been cleared away and the washing up done, Theodore turned his attention back to Ellen. He took up position on the shed in her garden. He watched as Ellen poured come clear liquid from a bottle into a glass. She downed it and winced.

Theodore looked over at Geoffrey's bungalow.

Geoffrey was in the kitchen. He was going through his cupboards, his hands grasping at small packets and packages.

Theodore watched as Geoffrey began to pop tablets from plastic containers into a bowl, his hands shaking. When the bowl was half full of tablets, he poured a glass of water and then carried the bowl and the glass into the conservatory. He sat down at the table, the bowl and glass in front of him.

He removed his dark glasses. His milky white eyes were red rimmed. He picked a couple of pills from the bowl and washed them down with a mouthful of water. He took another handful and swallowed them too.

Theodore jumped down from the shed roof and darted through the gap in the bottom of the hedge that Lucy had made. He approached the glass doors of the conservatory.

Inside Geoffrey swilled down another couple of tablets. Then he wiped tears from his eyes before reaching for more.

Theodore scraped his claws against the glass.

Geoffrey didn't hear. He took another handful of pills and swallowed them.

Theodore scratched again against the glass.

Geoffrey turned to the doors. 'Lucy?' he said. He got to his feet. He crossed to the conservatory doors. He slid open the doors.

Theodore slipped through the opening. He jumped up onto the table.

Geoffrey was still standing at the conservatory doors. 'Lucy!' he called out to the garden. 'Is that you Lucy?'

Then Theodore knocked the bowl of pills to the floor. The bowl smashed and the pills were scattered across the floor.

Geoffrey turned. 'What's going on?'

He staggered back to the table. He felt across the surface to where the bowl of pills had been.

Theodore jumped soundlessly to the floor.

Geoffrey got down on his hands and knees. He knelt on the floor; then placed the palms of his hands together. He looked up to the ceiling, his milky eyes filled with tears, and said, 'If it be your will...'

Theodore jumped up onto the kitchen side. He looked at the empty packets of pills and wondered if it were possible to overdose on multivitamins and cod liver oil capsules. He jumped down and a moment later exited through the conservatory doors.

He glanced behind him. Geoffrey was still on his knees, still gazing up at the ceiling, his hands placed together in prayer.

26

The French windows were open when Theodore got back home. He wandered into the lounge.

Jonathan was on the sofa, watching The Birds on the television. Theodore jumped up onto the cushion next to him.

Jonathan paused the film. 'You believe me, don't you?' he said.

Theodore purred back reassuringly.

'She's a murderer,' Jonathan said.

Theodore purred his agreement.

'We just need to prove it,' Jonathan said. 'We need proof. Then we call the police and they can deal with her.'

Proof, thought Theodore; he needed to find Tessa's wedding ring. But if it wasn't in the house behind, where was it?

Theodore went upstairs to look for Emily. She was in the bedroom, sorting out clothes.

Theodore jumped up onto the front windowsill.

In the fading light, he saw Linda exit the side door of her house. In her hands she carried a jam jar of brushes, another jam jar of water, a box of acrylic paints and a palette.

Linda crouched down by the side of Steve's white Audi. The car was again parked on the verge in front of her house. Dead daffodils lay flattened beneath its tyres.

She squeezed a dollop of green acrylic onto her palette and licked the end of her paint brush.

This is going to be interesting, thought Theodore.

He turned his attention back to Emily.

She had a small suitcase open on the bed and was pushing her clothes into it.

'Guess we'll be travelling light,' she said. She looked over at Theodore. Her eyes were red from crying.

Theodore jumped down from the windowsill and then up onto the bed. He let Emily pick him up and hold him to her chest.

'This house,' Emily said. 'It's like a private trap... It holds us in like a prison. You know what I think? I think that we're all in our private traps, clamped in them, and none of us can ever get out. We scratch and we claw, but only at the air, only at each other, and for all of it, we never budge an inch.'

Clap trap, Theodore thought; a house is what you make of it. He was reminded of the sign hung on the vestibule door: A House is Not A Home Without a Cat. He was a cat. This was a house. It was their home. It was as simple as that.

Emily said, 'It's a trap... A trap of our own making. We have to get out while we can.'

You cannot run from yourself, thought Theodore.

'I just can't live like this,' Emily said. 'I can't go on like this...
pretending everything's fine. Pretending this is me. I'm not
happy. I need to do something about it.'

She put Theodore back down on the bed. She crossed to the
bedside cabinet and took out the rolls of bank notes wrapped
in clear plastic from the drawer. She pushed the money into the
suitcase and then closed the lid.

'That should last a few months,' she said.

She was pacing in front of the bedroom window and gestur-
ing at the houses and gardens of suburbia.

'I should never have come here. This isn't the life that I want.'

She put the suitcase into the bottom of the wardrobe and
closed the door. 'Tomorrow our new life begins,' she said.

27

Emily woke early on Easter Monday. She sat up in bed and
remembered that today she was going to escape this suburban
nightmare and begin the rest of her life. She looked across the
bedroom at the wardrobe, where her case waited. She glanced at
the drawer of her bedside table, where she had stashed the shop's
takings. She stared up at the bedroom ceiling. She would just
have to choose her moment to slip out and take Theodore with
her; she didn't want Jonathan making a scene.

Theodore was sleeping on the bed beside her. She stroked
him for some minutes.

When she got up she parted the curtains. The front window faced east, towards York. She could make out the Minster in the distance. In the middle ground, there were some blocks of flats and an ugly concrete water tower on stilts. On the side of the water tower somebody had painted in large red letters: 'VOYER!'

'She still can't spell,' Emily said to herself.

Theodore jumped up onto the windowsill. His attention was drawn by a commotion in the street below.

Steve was standing in front of his car, parked on Linda's front verge.

'Did you do this?' he demanded of Linda.

Linda was dressed in her purple jogging gear. 'I don't know what you're talking about,' she said with a misplaced grin.

'My car,' Steve said. 'Someone has painted flowers and trees on it... It's a bloody woodland scene!'

'I can see,' Linda said. 'How pretty!'

'This will cost a fortune to sort.'

'You could always leave it as it is. It's a big improvement.'

'It's going to need respraying.'

'Well, I need to get going. Can't stand here chatting...'

'You did it, didn't you?' Steve said.

'It's Dance How You Like this morning,' Linda said.

'You're going to pay for this...'

'You should try it! Unlock some of that aggression.'

'I would be calm if you hadn't done this to my car.'

'Don't want to be late,' Linda said and began walking away, a skip in her step, leaving Steve to contemplate his paintwork.

Emily pulled the curtains closed. 'See what I mean,' she said. 'Suburbia! Get me out of here!'

28

Theodore went into the back bedroom. It was still full of unpacked boxes. He jumped up onto the windowsill.

Wally and Stuart were arguing over the hedge. Theodore soon picked up the thread of their argument. It was over the origins of marmalade.

'It's as English as tea,' Wally shouted at his neighbour.

'It's Scottish, I tell you,' Stuart said. 'Queen Mary brought it back to Scotland. She had sea sickness and they gave her marmalade to settle her stomach. And she took a taste to it and had it brought over to Scotland in the middle of the sixteenth century.'

'I've never heard so much rubbish,' Wally said. 'It was Henry the Eighth who brought it over. Before Mary had a dodgy tummy, we were already enjoying marmalade on our toast. You Scots are always one step behind.'

'Och, och, bollocks,' Stuart said. 'You might have had a bit of some shredless jelly, but it was Janet Keiller of Dundee who added the peel to it. Her husband bought the oranges at the harbourside and she shredded the peel and boiled down the oranges to make the marmalade that we know today. They were doing that in the seventeen hundreds. What you English were scoffing back then was flavoured jelly. Not proper marmalade.'

'Absolute nonsense,' Wally said. 'Shakespeare was eating marmalade on his toast before your Janet Keiller's great grandmother was even born. Not just oranges but quinces and all sorts of fruit.'

Stuart rolled up his shirt sleeves and squared up to the hedge. 'It's Scottish,' he said. 'You never thought of putting the shred in it. That's what we Scots did. We put in the shred. Without the shred, it's not marmalade!'

'Well, it is marmalade,' Wally said. 'Just shredless.'

'Like this country,' Stuart said. 'Shredless.'

'Some people like their marmalade without the shred,' said Wally.

'Just you wait,' Stuart said, 'Us Scots will have our independence. Then Trevor Trout won't put up with your nonsense no more. We won't put up with your shredless marmalade!'

Trevor Trout was the then leader of the Scottish Nationalist Party. He carried on the tradition of leaders of the Scottish Nationalist Party being named after fish.

'Your Trevor Trout will not outlaw our shredless marmalade...'

'You prick!' shouted Stuart, escalating the argument a notch.

'Talking of pricks,' Wally said, 'you want to be careful where you go putting yours.'

'What do you mean by that?'

'Ellen Black,' Wally said. 'I know what you've been up to... Carrying on with a girl half your age... You should bloody know better.'

'What was that?'

Both men turned. Leslie was standing several yards behind Stuart, her dressing gown pulled tightly around her.

'Who's been putting their prick where?'

'I'd better get on,' Walter said. He adjusted his cap; then made for the safety of his shed.

Stuart stared at his wife. He had some explaining to do.

However, the ensuing argument escalated and less than an hour later, Stuart was in his car, Hamish in his cat carrier in the passenger seat, on their way back to Scotland.

Well at least Hamish is out of the way, thought Theodore, looking down on the scene from the bedroom window.

29

A magpie swooped down and picked up a scrap of silver from the lawn. Theodore realised that it was a fragment of tinfoil, a remnant of yesterday's barbecue. He watched as the bird disappeared into the white blossom of the apple tree in the corner of Geoffrey's garden.

Theodore thought of the basket in the kitchen of Ellen's house. The wedding ring that was no longer there. He remembered the flash of black and white feathers coming out of the kitchen.

He looked again at the apple tree and miaowed.

He trotted downstairs and miaowed at the French windows until Jonathan opened them.

He trotted across the lawn, through the hedge, and cut across Ellen's lawn. He entered Geoffrey's garden and made for the apple tree.

He ascended the four feet of near vertical trunk and gained the V of two branches. He looked up and sighted the magpies' nest up one of the branches. He climbed the branch. As he reached the nest, the branch bowed under his weight. He peered inside.

There were several scraps of tinfoil, and there in the middle was the gold ring set with diamonds. He took hold of the ring with his teeth and was about to turn around when the pair of magpies attacked.

They flew at him, pecking at his face, his body. They were everywhere. He looked down at the lawn, ten feet below. Then he dropped from the branch.

He landed but swallowed the ring on impact. He got to his feet. The magpies swooped down and pecked at his body, their sharp beaks finding their way through his long fur and piercing his flesh.

He scrambled back through the bottom of the hedge still pursued by the birds, the ring lodged in his throat.

Jonathan had suffered vertigo for as long as he could remember. It was an affliction he had learned to live with, but the condition had affected his life to the detriment.

His final year of university, he had been sent into the field to log a previously unmapped mountainside in Wales. While he had spluttered some protests, his tutor had assured him he would be fine. 'It's all in the mind,' he'd been told.

He had restricted his mapping to the lower reaches of the mountain, and on his return his tutor had given him a very low grade, resulting in him scraping a 2:2 in his degree, which meant that he was out of the running for a lot of jobs with the larger consultancies. When he was offered a job by a small consultancy on the outskirts of Leeds, he jumped at the opportunity.

He tried to explain to people that vertigo was not a fear of heights, as a lot of people seemed to believe, but an actual physical reaction to being up high.

He had placed Vertigo at the bottom of the pile of Hitchcock DVDs he was working his way through. He had now reached the bottom of the pile. He bent down and was about to put the DVD into the machine when Theodore appeared in front of the French windows, miaowing to be let back in.

Jonathan crossed to the windows and opened them. The cat stayed where it was. 'Please yourself,' he said.

Theodore miaowed up at him, a strange, raspy miaow, as though he had something stuck in his throat. He placed his head near the ground and began to heave.

Soon he had thrown up what looked like a short length of twisted grey rope.

Jonathan looked at the knot of cat fur and winced. 'Nice,' he said.

Then he noticed something glisten from within the salivary fur. He reached over and picked up the fur ball and peeling it apart, removed a gold ring, set with diamonds.

'A wedding ring...' he murmured. 'Where did you get this?'

Theodore looked back over the garden, towards the house behind.

'It's hers, isn't it?' Jonathan said. 'It's Tessa Black's wedding ring, isn't it?'

Theodore stared up at him and blinked yes.

'This is the proof we need,' Jonathan said. 'I think it's time we confronted Ellen.'

He made his way across the garden to the back hedge, Theodore following behind.

The Vertigo DVD was left on the floor in front of the television.

There was a green wheelie bin pulled in front of the back door. He could see Ellen inside the kitchen.

'Hey!' Jonathan shouted over at her. 'Can I have a word?'

Ellen pushed the wheelie bin aside and walked across to the boundary hedge. 'Yes, what is it?'

Jonathan held the wedding ring up. 'Do you know what this is?'

'Yes,' Ellen said, 'it's my mum's wedding ring. Where did you get it?'

'It's proof,' Jonathan said. 'Proof that you killed her.'

'Give it to me,' Ellen snapped.

'No. This ring is the proof! You killed your mum. Then you killed her dog. And now you've killed your sister.'

'Penny?'

'Yes. She came yesterday. I saw her... She knew something was up. Then you killed her too. Didn't you?'

Ellen folded her arms across her chest; she was wearing another of her father's old shirts. She stared at Jonathan a moment; then said flatly: 'My mum's in bed and Penny's upstairs having a shower.'

'I don't believe you,' Jonathan said.

'See for yourself.'

He looked at the hedge. He could hardly jump over it on his crutches. 'Well, that's not really possible.'

'You'll have to walk round,' Ellen said.

'It might take me a while.'

'I'm not going anywhere.'

Jonathan noticed Theodore entering the bottom of the hedge. The cat miaowed. 'I'll walk round then,' he said. 'But if they aren't there, I'm going to call the police.'

'They are both here,' Ellen said. 'I think you've got a screw loose... You think I've been murdering my family? You're the bloody psycho!' She laughed in his face.

'Five minutes,' Jonathan said, turning red in the face. 'Five minutes and we'll see who's the psycho!'

Ellen had already turned and was walking back to the house. The door was slammed shut behind her.

Jonathan turned and began to walk back across his own overgrown garden. Theodore made his way towards Ellen's back door.

30

Jonathan grabbed his mobile phone from the side. From upstairs he heard water running. 'I'm going out,' he shouted. 'I'm going to prove that I'm not imaging things...'

'Whatever,' Emily shouted down.

As soon as Jonathan had shut the front door behind him, Emily turned off the bath taps and called a taxi.

'As soon as possible,' she said into her mobile. Then: 'Twenty minutes? That's fine... I'll be waiting.'

She heard the front door open and close. She peaked through the bedroom curtains and saw Jonathan begin to make his way round to Ellen's house. It will take him at least fifteen minutes to get there and another fifteen minutes to make his way back. She had at least half an hour to get away. She just had to find Theodore and get him in the cat box.

Although Jonathan had only seen Penny at a distance over the hedge yesterday, he recognised her straightaway. She was wearing the same designer sunglasses even though it was overcast. He also noticed that her dyed red hair was still wet. So she had been having a shower, Jonathan reasoned. Ellen wasn't lying about that.

'Where's Ellen?' Jonathan asked.

'She just went out,' Penny said.

'Where?' Jonathan said, 'I need to speak to her.'

'She was acting strange,' Penny said. 'We argued and she left.'

'Where to?'

'I think she's gone to the church,' Penny said. 'It's where dad is buried. It's where she goes when she's upset. I was about to go after her... But, as you can see, I wasn't dressed. I'd just got out of the shower. I'm going to look for her.'

Penny shut the front door and began to walk away down the street.

'I'll come with you,' Jonathan said.

But Penny was already striding down the street.

Jonathan set off after her on his crutches but he soon lagged behind. He watched as she turned right at the top of the street.

He rested on his crutches for a few seconds. He took his mobile phone from his dressing gown pocket. He called Emily's mobile but she didn't answer. He sent a text. 'Come to church. I was right about Ellen. I'm onto her.'

Theodore rested below a parked car. He knew that it couldn't be Penny that Jonathan was following: she was dead. He had seen Ellen whack her over the head with the iron. It was Ellen they were following. Ellen wearing Penny's sunglasses, dress and hair.

When Jonathan set off again on his crutches, Theodore followed him, darting from car to car until he turned right onto York Road.

He waited until Jonathan was twenty yards further up Constantine Crescent before he turned the corner.

He had to pause as a taxi entered the other end of the crescent. On the side of the taxi was written Crow-Line Taxis. Theodore watched as the taxi came to a stop in front of his house. The driver beeped his horn.

A few seconds later Emily appeared, dragging behind her a suitcase on wheels. Theodore padded behind a tree. He watched as the driver got out and put the case in the boot. Emily was looking up and down the street. She called Theodore's name. She disappeared back inside the house. She came out again. She called his name again.

When he peered around the tree, he saw that Emily was standing on the footpath, holding a cat carrier. He looked across the road, in the direction that Jonathan had taken. He was nowhere to be seen.

But Theodore knew where he was going and he knew that the quickest way to get there was as the crow flies. He spied the church steeple in the distance.

He peered back down the street. Emily was standing by the side of the taxi, her head bent down, talking to the driver.

Theodore chose the moment to dart across the road and then, rather than following Jonathan along York Road, he nipped under a gate, along the side of a bungalow and dashed across a lawn.

A dog barked and set off after him but Theodore was already at the hedge; then through it and into another garden.

'I can't leave without my cat,' Emily explained to the taxi driver. 'Give me a few minutes and I'll go and look for him.'

Emily headed back inside the house. Once back inside the front door, she noticed the sign that hung from the vestibule door.

She called Theodore's name. She knew he wasn't going to come, even if he heard her. It was as if he knew.

She took her mobile from her pocket and read the text from Jonathan. 'Come to church. I was right about Ellen. I'm onto her.'

Outside the taxi driver beeped his horn.

31

Theodore climbed to the top of the church wall and surveyed the churchyard. Then he jumped down and picked his way between the headstones. Between the trees he saw a flash of red. Ellen was making her way towards the entrance of the church.

He paused beneath the giant beech tree. There was a path that led down to Acomb Green. He watched as Jonathan appeared at the church gate.

He opened it and entered the church yard. A crutch below each shoulder, he made his way up the path, swinging his broken foot in its plastic boot in front of him.

As he neared, Theodore shot out from his hiding spot and crossed to the church door, making sure that Jonathan saw him.

Jonathan followed after the cat. He hesitated in the doorway; then walked inside.

The church was empty. He called for Theodore but the cat was nowhere to be seen. He recalled from his Pevsner's guide that the church didn't have an aisle but only transepts and the tower was on the western side.

If Penny had come inside the church, she must be hiding, he thought. He made his way along the western transept, glancing from left to right, down each pew, to make sure she wasn't hiding in a pew.

He reached the altar, where two big brass candlesticks stood. He walked around it and then looked back along the transept. He was about to give up when he heard a faint miaow nearby.

He looked to his right and noticed a small door. He walked over and pushed the door open.

There were spiral stone steps leading up the western tower. He heard a miaow from overhead.

He took a deep breath and began to climb the tower steps.

As he went up, he began to feel dizzy and sweat beaded on his forehead. He focussed on placing his crutches and his left foot squarely on each step. Sweat stung his eyes and he blinked to clear them.

Ahead he heard Theodore miaow loudly, like he was being held against his will and trying to get away.

He took another step and his head was at the same level as the belfry floor. Then he made the mistake of looking down. He placed a hand to his forehead and dropped his crutch. The crutch found its way back down the stairs, clattering to a stop on the stone floor.

He looked up and saw Penny, or who he thought was Penny. She towered over him. She was holding Theodore, one hand around his throat, the other gripping his body.

'He brought you to me,' she said and laughed. 'What a clever little boy!'

She dropped Theodore onto the floor where he scrambled away.

'You're not Penny are you?' Jonathan said.

She removed her red hair, revealing her own blonde hair that she'd tied back. It was Ellen, Jonathan realised.

'You killed Penny, didn't you?'

Ellen smiled. 'You know I did,' she said. 'Like you know that I killed my mum and the dog. Two dogs actually. Oh, and my dad… but that one was an accident, so it doesn't really count, does it?'

Jonathan took a step upwards to try to get on the same level as Ellen. But Ellen took the opportunity to kick the other crutch away from under his arm. It clattered down the stairwell to join its partner.

Jonathan took another step upwards placing his weight momentarily on his bad foot. He winced with pain and Ellen kicked him in the shoulder.

'I think this is the end for you,' Ellen said.

'No!' Jonathan shouted.

She raised her foot in the air, ready to kick him again.

Theodore chose his moment. He rushed at her other leg, throwing his whole weight against it.

Ellen lost her balance. She screamed as she fell onto Jonathan. She grabbed him and they both fell down the stairwell together.

Theodore approached the edge and peered down. He had a good head for heights: he was a cat after all.

Jonathan groaned in pain where he lay. He tried to move but was pinned to the ground by Ellen. She was lying on top of him, her chest over his stomach, her head on his chest. He squirmed below her but couldn't get out from under her.

Then Ellen raised her head from his chest and looked him in the face. 'That bloody cat,' she said smiling madly. 'He's going to get it once I've finished with you…' She got to her feet and staggered towards the altar.

Jonathan got into a crouch but couldn't get to his feet: he had broken his other foot.

Ellen soon returned. She was holding a big brass candlestick in her right hand. She did a few practice strokes as she approached Jonathan, who was now on all fours, trying to crawl away.

She held the candlestick in the air, ready to bash Jonathan over the back of the head.

Then Theodore dropped from the belfry, his claws out. He landed on Ellen's head and dug his claws in.

Ellen screamed and dropped the candlestick. She raised her hands and pulled the cat off her head and threw him to the floor.

Ellen picked up the candlestick again and went after the cat. She cornered him behind the altar.

Theodore cowered.

'You are going to regret ever setting eyes on me,' Ellen said.

She held up the candlestick, ready to strike.

Theodore closed his eyes and tensed his body.

He felt a warm liquid splash over him; it was not what he had expected death to be like.

He opened his eyes. Emily was standing in front of him, the other candlestick in her hands. She dropped it to the floor.

Ellen lay on the floor beside him. She was dead. He realised that the warm splash was blood. Her blood.

Theodore inspected his fur. It was coated with red. For Bastet's sake, he swore.

He turned his attention back to Ellen. He noticed that tranquillity had descended across her face. In death she had found peace.

32

Ellen takes a last drag on the cigarette and drops it from her bedroom window, down the gap between the house and the shed, like she has done a thousand times or more, but this time, rather than smouldering out with the rest of the butts, the shed explodes with a bang.

Her dad Colin staggers out. He's on fire. He stands in the middle of the lawn. He flaps his hands against his clothes, trying to put out the flames. He turns and faces the back of his house. He looks up at her bedroom window. 'Hell,' he shouts. 'Hell fire!'

Ellen is 14 years old. She has unicorns and princesses on her curtains, pink and blue. She has grown out of them but her dad has promised her new curtains, yellow ones. She wonders if she'll get the yellow curtains now.

From the bedroom next to hers, she hears Penny scream. She is three years older, about to go off to university.

Then she sees her mum run outside, wet tea towels in her hands. 'Get down on the lawn,' Tessa shouts at her dad.

Her dad lies down on the lawn and her mum pushes the wet tea towels against the flames and smouldering clothing. Her dad has stopped screaming and she knows he is dead. His mouth is open; his gums peeled back to show off his yellow teeth.

There is a corpse, with blackened, blistered skin, clothes burnt onto flesh, lying in the middle of a neatly trimmed lawn.

Her mum shakes out one of the tea towels. It is streaked with soot. She lays it over her dad's face.

The tea towel has rolling green hills and winding blue streams on it, and bares the slogan: 'Welcome to God's Own County'.

Ellen stares down at her dad. She is too shocked to speak. Her mum is kneeling by the corpse.

Then Tessa gets slowly to her feet and turns to face the house. Her eyes are red rimmed from smoke and tears. Her eyebrows are singed off. She has black smudges across her face and clothes.

She points a finger up at Ellen, still standing in the window. 'You!' she screams. 'You've killed him... It's your fault... It's all your fault!'

Emily bent down and closed Ellen's eyelids.

'What have I done?' she said. 'I didn't mean to kill her.'

'Can you call an ambulance?' Jonathan said, crawling across the floor towards them. 'I think I've gone and broken my other foot.'

'I told you not to get messed up in other people's business,' Emily said.

'Please,' Jonathan whimpered, 'call an ambulance.'

'You stay there,' Emily said, her mobile phone in her hand. 'I can't get a signal in here.'

Theodore approached Emily and miaowed.

Emily looked down at him. 'And you're having a bath when we get home.'

Home, thought Theodore.

'Yes, home,' Emily said and began to make for the doors.

And Theodore followed her out of the church.

33

Wally was prodding at a fire with a stick. There was not even a whisper of smoke; the fire had gone out long ago.

Marjorie came over. 'What's got into you? Moping about...'

'I'm going to miss him.'

'Well, it was your big mouth that got him into trouble, you great big turnip.'

'I know that,' Walter said. 'I should have held my tongue.'

'You were always arguing, winding each other up.'

'I know that,' Walter said. 'But we got on all right, all said and done. Now I won't have anyone to talk to.'

'Well you should have thought about that before you put your great big foot in it,' Marjorie said.

Walter didn't reply.

'How about I get you a nice slice of quiche.' Marjorie said. 'That'll cheer you up.'

'What type of quiche have we got?'

'How about tunkey? I think I've got some in the cupboard...'

'Tuna and turkey? One of my favourites...' he said with the beginnings of a smile on his lips.

'I'll go and fetch you a slice, Marjorie said. 'And I'm sure that Stuart will be back.'

'How do you know?'

'Call it woman's intuition. He'll be back with his tail between his legs. Mark my words.'

Stuart made it as far as Scotch Corner services before he began to have misgivings.

As he dunked his shortbread in his cup of service station coffee, he thought of Dougie and Daisy. A tear came to his eye. He lifted his shortbread from the waxed paper cup. Half of it was left in his coffee. 'Sod it,' he said. He sat bleary-eyed for a few minutes more.

Then he took his mobile phone from his shirt pocket and began to write a message, an ode to his wife. He would win Leslie back with his words:

Oh my love is like a big thistle
From you I'll never part
Oh my love is like a great missile
That's aimed straight for your heart

I could never leave you, darling
I hope you understand
And I will love you always dear
I'll always be your man

I'll always be your man, my dear
No matter where you are
I am returning to your heart
I'm turning round this car

He pressed send, then drank his coffee. Hamish was still in his cat carrier, strapped into the passenger seat beside him. Stuart opened up the front of the carrier and took his cat out. 'I've got a treat for you, Hamish,' he said.

He took a little plastic container of milk he had swiped from Burger King and peeled the top off.

As Hamish lapped up the milk, Stuart said, 'We're going home!'

34

'Who knows how long that thing had been living in him?' Trish said.

'Well, it's gone now,' Emily said. 'That's the main thing.'

'A tapeworm? I mean how disgusting is that? I'm doing all the cooking from now. No more Steak Tartare for him. Everything's going to be well done from now on.'

'How did they get rid of it?'

'They gave him two tablets,' Trish said. 'He was two hours on the toilet... It's a wonder it didn't break in two.'

'That's a lot of number twos,' Emily said.

Trish was thoughtful for a moment; then said, 'It's always good to have a good clear out from time to time.'

Patrick was kneeling in front of the backdoor. He had drilled four holes, one in each corner where the cat flap was going to go. He took out the jigsaw and cut lines through the door between the holes. Once he had removed the rectangle of wood, he tried to fit the cat flap in the gap but it wouldn't fit.

'What's up?' Jonathan asked. He was sitting at the outside table in a wheelchair, both his feet clad in grey plastic boots.

'I think we just need to straighten up this side,' Patrick said. 'It's not straight.'

He picked up the jigsaw again and cut into the side.

There was a bang inside as the vestibule door was blown shut. Patrick lurched forward and the blade of the jigsaw chopped through the forefinger of his left hand. The finger flew up into the air in a spray of blood.

Theodore was also supervising the fitting of the cat flap from the edge of the lawn. He watched as the finger landed in front of him.

He wasn't the only animal to see it.

Charlie the Chihuahua had his head poking through the bottom of the hedge. Charlie darted forwards, past Theodore and was on the finger. Theodore got to his feet as Charlie dashed back past him, Patrick's finger gripped in his little jaws. Theodore turned and gave chase.

'I've lost my finger,' Patrick said, his hand in the air, blood running down his arm.

'Well, where is it?' Trish said.

'That little dog ran off with it. The one I shut in the cool box.'

'Well, that'll teach you a lesson,' Trish said. 'Payback... You shouldn't have shut it in the cool box.'

'That was an accident.'

'I could say the same about your finger.'

Just then Theodore appeared back on the lawn. In his mouth he held Patrick's finger, now with little rows of teeth marks in it. Theodore dropped the bloody morsel at Patrick's feet with a short miaow.

'Look, Theo's brought it back,' Emily said. 'Well done Theo! What a clever cat!'

'Quick!' Patrick said. 'Get some frozen peas!'

'I don't think we have frozen peas,' Emily said, opening the freezer door. 'Will sweetcorn do?'

'Whatever,' Patrick said. 'Just be quick about it. I want my finger back...'

'Oh, stop flapping,' Trish said. 'They'll soon sew it back on...'

Emily looked doubtfully at the badly mauled finger, before popping it into the bag of sweetcorn.

'You'll have to drive,' Patrick said to Trish, taking the bag of sweetcorn from his daughter.

'Well, don't go bleeding over the seat,' Trish said. 'We don't want blood on the upholstery.'

After Trish and Patrick had made a hasty departure to York Hospital, Emily inspected her father's handiwork.

'He's left the job half done and his tools lying around. Can you finish it?'

Jonathan wheeled himself over. 'I can try,' he said.

And Theodore sloped off into the garden.

He jumped up onto the roof of Wally's shed. Wally was bent over a fire in the corner, prodding at the embers with a stick.

'You're never going to get that going,' Stuart said from the other side of the hedge. 'Not with all that there prodding you're doing...'

'What do you know about fires?' Wally said.

'I'll tell you what I know about starting fires,' Stuart said. 'Us Scots have been starting fires since you English knew how to suck on your mother's teat.'

'Get away with you!' said Wally.

Marjorie then appeared behind the two men. 'I've made you a special quiche,' she said.

In her hands she carried a plate, the quiche already cut into triangles. 'I made it for you both to share.'

'What kind of quiche is it?' Wally said.

'It's haggis and turnip,' Marjorie said. 'To celebrate Stuart's return and to make amends for your big mouth...'

'Haggis and neeps,' Stuart said, clapping his hands together. 'You'd better pass me a slice over.'

'Don't you be taking the big bit,' Wally said.

As the English and the Scots made friends again over quiche, Theodore heard a scratting coming from Geoffrey's bungalow. He looked across and saw a young Golden Retriever at the doors of the conservatory.

A few moments later, the doors slid open and the young dog bounced out onto the lawn.

'There you go, Sasha,' Geoffrey said. 'You have a run about.'

Theodore turned to the house behind.

It was boarded up; its former occupants, a whole family, all dead.

The police had recovered Penny Black's scalped corpse from the bath. Then they had dug up Tessa Black's body from her husband's grave. The autopsy confirmed that she had died from a massive brain haemorrhage.

Theodore remembered her screaming, 'Going to the dogs,' and then the silence from the house that followed as Ellen pulled the curtains across.

He closed his eyes. Better not to think too much, he thought, and settled down for a nap.

3

The Call of the Cat Basket

Theodore did not read the newspapers, or he would have known that trouble was brewing, not alone for himself, but for every home-dwelling creature, fat or thin, hairy or furry, from New Earswick to Middlethorpe.

A protest march was planned for the city. Members of an anonymous anarchist group, who hid their faces behind Guy Fawkes masks, planned to descend on the city to protest about the government and the state of the nation. They were to be joined by several other groups: environmental protestors, students against fees, old people against death, cow welfare activists, badger cull protestors, members of a Radiohead Facebook group... You name it; they were descending on York in their thousands.

Theodore didn't like to think too much of the greater concerns of the human world, if he could help it. He was beyond caring. As long as he had food in his bowl and a warm place to sleep, he was perfectly happy. Happy to be unaware. If only humans took the same view, the world would be a better place. He yawned with sleepy satisfaction. Then something hit him on the head.

He opened his eyes and glared at the dirty nappy that was inches from his head. He sniffed the offending parcel. It smelled of human waste. Baby waste to be precise.

'Sorry, Theo,' Emily said, fastening the poppers on Joseph's baby grow. 'Didn't see you down there.'

Theodore looked up. Emily had just finished changing the baby, although Theodore preferred to refer to it as the Pink Hairless Interloper. He got to his paws and voiced his disapproval.

'Come on. It didn't hurt. We all have to poo, don't we now?'

Perhaps it's time you taught it to go outside, Theodore thought back.

Emily's attentions returned to the baby. 'You like tickles on the tummy,' she said, and Theodore heard the Pink Hairless Interloper giggle.

'You like that, don't you... don't you, Joey?'

And the Pink Hairless Interloper giggled again.

I think I'll go downstairs, Theodore thought. There might be more intelligent forms of life down there.

Unfortunately there was just Jonathan, who was staring blankly at the television in the kitchen, a mug of tea in his hand. He was watching the news, as if it mattered; as if what was going on in the wider world was actually going to affect his existence. Why couldn't I have had less ordinary humans?

Theodore padded past him and checked out the food bowl situation. His food had not been replenished since the night before. Even his water bowl did not have a cat's whisker of water in it.

He miaowed at his bowls.

'Shush,' Jonathan said, not looking away from the television. 'You'll get fed soon enough.'

Jonathan knew that cats don't miaow at other cats. Like human babies, they just use their undeveloped vocal cords to whine and bleat for food or drink from adult humans. They probably picked it up from human babies.

Theodore looked up at the television.

'In other news today,' the newsreader said, 'a cat has been found in a child's packed lunch bag on a roundabout in Tang Hall, York. A passer-by heard the cat's cries and came to its rescue. It is now being cared for by the York branch of the Cats Protection League.'

Theodore's ears flattened against his head. Best to stay indoors, Theodore thought, glancing at his cat flap. Bad things happen outside.

He looked over at his cat basket in the corner by the radiator. *Bad things happen outside*, the cat basket agreed. *As soon as you've had your breakfast, you come for a nice long nap. A good eight-hour snooze will set you up nicely for the day.*

Theodore's internal monologue was interrupted by the television newsreader. 'We have news just in... Milton Macavity, a convicted murderer, also known as 'The Napoleon of Crime,' is on the run from prison following a dramatic escape. Macavity was transferred to York Hospital early this morning, when it appears he faked an acute appendicitis.

'Before going into the theatre for an emergency operation, he overpowered two prison guards and assaulted several people, including hospital staff and members of the public, before leaving the hospital on foot, wearing only a surgical gown. The police have warned the public not to approach the ginger-haired man, but to phone them and report it immediately. He has a history of violent behaviour...'

'That's only a stone's throw away from us,' Jonathan said. He picked up his mug and had a drink of Yorkshire Gold ('a blend of 3 leaf origins from the top 10 tea gardens in the world'). 'An escaped convict in the neighbourhood... Whatever next?'

Whatever, Theodore thought. We should never have moved to Haxby Road. I think I might have said so at the time. Next?

He approached the cat flap and stared through the rectangle of clear plastic, as a precaution to exiting.

A clothes line was hung across the yard. On it there was a row of baby grows, bibs, tiny pairs of socks and then a mixture of Emily's and Jonathan's clothes. The air was damp and there was no breeze. Rather optimistic, thought Theodore.

Then a pink-faced man with short ginger hair and ginger stubble appeared. He was wearing only a hospital gown. It must be the escaped convict: Milton Macavity, Theodore deduced.

The man turned his back to the house, exposing a pair of dirty grey boxer shorts. He cast off the hospital gown and tossed it into the corner of the yard. He snatched a pair of black jeans from the line and began to put them on.

Theodore turned and miaowed that Milton Macavity, convicted murderer and escaped convict, was in the back yard stealing a pair of Jonathan's jeans.

Jonathan turned away from the television for a moment. 'You've got a cat flap,' he said. 'Use it.'

Theodore turned once more to the cat flap. Milton was now putting on Jonathan's red and black checked shirt. Theodore announced the latest development.

This time Jonathan didn't even turn round. He just said, 'I'm not going to get up and open the door. Just use the cat flap like any reasonable cat.'

Theodore looked back through the cat flap. Milton was putting on a pair of light blue and dark blue hooped rugby socks.

Theodore turned round. He saw his cat basket. It was positioned in front of the radiator. It was brown and furry with the roof stretching over to form a warm cocoon. One of Emily's old woollen jumpers lay in the bottom. Theodore had managed to knead the jumper to the point that she could wear it no longer and he had then inherited it. From the basket he could survey his food bowls, the cat flap and also any comings and goings in the house. It was the perfect place.

Humans spend too much time looking for perfect places. Moving houses in the hope of a happier life. Expensive holidays in exotic locations. They had yet to realise that the perfect place was a warm furry cocoon by a radiator. Life is oh-so-simple, if only you let it be.

Why would you want to go outside? You don't want to go chasing escaped convicts, do you now?

Theodore blinked his eyes, trying to get the voice from inside his head. He turned back to the cat flap.

Milton was wearing Jonathan's shirt, jeans and socks. The escaped convict looked down at his stockinged feet and the wet grass and shook his head. He didn't have any shoes, Theodore realised.

Then came the voice in his head again. *Just let it go*, it said. *They're just clothes. Who needs clothes after all? You come and have a sleep. This jumper is so soft. When you wake, everything will be just fine...*

Theodore knew he had to resist the call of the cat basket. There was an escaped convict in his yard, who had stolen half of Jonathan's wardrobe. He needed to begin the pursuit.

Theodore nosed open the cat flap.

You don't want to go outside, came the voice again. Bad things happen out there.

With a snap, the cat flap shut behind him.

Milton was standing just a few yards away. He caught Theodore's eye and placed a forefinger to his lips. Theodore decided it would be wise to hold his tongue.

Then Milton walked over to the boundary wall and jumped over into the next yard.

Theodore padded over to where Milton had thrown the hospital gown. He sniffed it. It smelled of Old Spice deodorant and stale sweat. Theodore inhaled the odour, committing it to memory.

He glanced back at the house. From upstairs, he could hear the Pink Hairless Interloper squealing. From the kitchen he could hear the muted outpourings of the television. He miaowed at the house.

You know you don't want to leave the comforts of home, came the call of the cat basket. *Inside is good; outside is bad. Outside bad things can happen...*

He looked at the side wall, over which Milton had gone. Then he looked back at his own house. He was going to have to go it alone.

His tail raised up behind him, Theodore set off after Milton. He jumped up on top of the boundary wall and looked across at the rows of backyards separated by brick walls. Milton was nowhere to be seen.

Theodore sniffed the dank autumn air. There was the faint smell of smoke. He picked up the smell of used nappies in the outside bin, moulding leaves in gutters, car exhaust fumes and the scent of urine sprayed by a neighbouring cat. But he could not pick out Milton's smell and from that the direction which he had taken.

You can still come back, the cat basket called. *It's warm by the radiator. You can forget what you've seen. You can sleep away the day. You can dream beautiful dreams...*

And Theodore did consider giving in to the voice and returning to the basket by the radiator. The perfect place.

But then he heard voices. Raised voices...

Theodore jumped down into the next yard and then up onto the next wall, following the voices.

You really don't want to do that, came the voice, fainter now.

But Theodore's ears were pricked back and his tail was standing up straight.

The feline sleuth's next case had begun.

2

'Just hand over the trainers,' Milton said, 'and no one gets hurt.'

'No,' said the middle-aged man. 'Why should I?'

'Because if you don't I'm going to hit you.'

'No,' said the man. 'You wouldn't dare. I have high blood pressure...'

'I'm sorry about this,' Milton said.

Then he punched the man on the nose. The man's nose gushed blood down his shirt.

'Look what you've done,' the man said.

'You can't do that,' a teenage boy said. 'He's got high blood pressure.'

'I just did,' Milton said. 'Now, hand over the trainers.'

The man began to undo his trainers. He handed them over to Milton, who tried them on.

Theodore looked down on the scene from the garden wall. There were four people in the backyard: Milton, the middle-aged man with high blood pressure, his teenage son and a teenage girl, who was taller than her brother but shorter than her dad. A football was lying on the ground and a set of goal posts were painted in white paint on the back wall of the yard. Milton must have interrupted a knock-about, Theodore deduced.

Milton put on the man's shoes. 'They're too big,' he said. 'They're no good.'

'Can't you just leave now,' the man with the bleeding nose said.

'Not until I have some shoes,' Milton said. 'I can't go around without any shoes on now, can I?'

'Here, have mine,' the teenage boy said.

The boy took off his trainers and handed them to Milton.

Milton tried them on. 'These aren't any good. They're too small.'

'What about mine?' the teenage girl said.

Milton looked down at the girl's pink and white trainers.

'They're pink,' he said.

'Beggars can't be choosers,' the girl said.

'You calling me a beggar?' Milton said. He clenched his fists.

'I didn't mean it like that,' the girl said. 'It's just a saying.'

'Well, be careful what you go saying.'

'You want to try on my trainers or what?'

'Hand them over.'

When Milton had put the pink and white trainers on, he said, 'These fit just right.'

This is turning into quite a nursery story, thought Theodore from up on the wall.

'Can you go now?' the other man said, wiping blood from his face. 'You've got your shoes.'

'I can't just go,' Milton said.

'Why not?'

'Well, I'm an escaped convict. First thing you're going to do after I go is call the cops and spill the beans. Then they'll know where I am.'

They all paused as police sirens filled the air.

'An escaped convict?' the man with the bleeding nose said.

'That's right,' said Milton. 'Three hours ago I was in Full Sutton. I'm Milton Macavity, also known as the Napoleon of Crime...'

'I've never heard of you,' the man said.

'Why don't you lock us in the outbuilding?' the girl said.

'That's not a bad idea.'

'But we might be in there for hours,' the man protested. 'And I've got high blood pressure.'

'You shut up,' Milton said. 'Now get in there, the lot of you!'

The three of them walked into the outbuilding and Milton shut the door and then locked it. He tossed the key into an overgrown bit of garden.

The police sirens were louder and Theodore could hear the whir of a helicopter approaching.

Milton didn't hang about. He jumped over the goal posts on the back wall and ran off down the alley.

Theodore jumped down into the yard. No sound came from within the outbuilding. He trotted to the back of the house. He jumped up onto a windowsill. He looked inside.

A middle-aged woman was sitting on the sofa, reading a magazine. Theodore miaowed and dabbed at the glass. The woman got to her feet.

'Go away,' she said. 'I don't like cats.'

Why do I bother? Theodore wondered. Your husband has been assaulted and is now locked in the outbuilding with your two children while you sit and read magazines.

'I told you, I don't like cats. Stop miaowing at me and go away.'

She looked past Theodore and her eyes widened in alarm. She shook her head.

'Adrian?' she said. 'Sophie...William?'

A moment later she was out in the yard.

'Adrian!' she called, panic rising in her throat.

There was bashing on the door of the outbuilding and muffled cries from inside.

'Linda... We're locked inside,' Adrian shouted through the door.

'Where's the key?' Linda said. 'It's not in the lock.'

'He must have thrown it somewhere,' Adrian said, 'or taken it with him.'

Theodore miaowed from the flowerbed, where the key lay.

'Oh, shut up,' Linda shouted across at him.

'You what?' shouted Adrian. 'You telling us to shut up?'

'No, there's a cat,' Linda said. 'And it keeps miaowing at me.'

Theodore closed his eyes for a moment. Then he picked up the key in his mouth and dropped it onto a paving slab, so that it chimed out when it landed.

Linda turned round and spotted the key. She dashed over and grabbed it. 'I've found the key!' she shouted.

'Well, hurry up and let us out!'

Before Linda did, she turned her attention to Theodore. 'Scram!' she said and clapped her hands together.

That's all the thanks I get! Theodore turned and ran towards the back wall.

It's not too late to come home. The radiator's nice and warm.

He jumped up onto the wall and looked down the alley.

He's gone. You might as well come home now. There'll be biscuits in your bowl. And then you can have a nice nap!

Theodore stared down at the wet alley. In a grey mist he could make out the Minster in the distance.

Before his cat basket could try to call him back again, he jumped down into the alley and set off in pursuit of Milton Macavity.

'Where's Theo got to?' Emily said.

'He's about,' Jonathan said. 'He was miaowing at the cat flap earlier.'

Emily looked at the backdoor. Overhead there was the whirring of a helicopter.

Jonathan said, 'Someone's escaped from prison. Milton Macavity. They call him the Napoleon of Crime. He faked an appendicitis; then overpowered his prison guards at the hospital... He's on the run.'

'I've never heard of him.' Emily passed the baby to Jonathan. 'Could you take Joseph while I feed Theo? His bowls are completely empty. No wonder he was miaowing. You know you could feed the cat rather than just sitting there watching television all morning.'

She filled his bowls and then opened the backdoor.

'Theo!' she called. 'Breakfast's ready.'

She looked out at the yard. Theodore was nowhere to be seen. A faint drizzle hung in the air. She called again for Theodore but still he didn't come. She looked at the washing line, thinking that the clothes would never dry in this weather. Then she realised that there were gaps on the line.

'That's strange,' she said. 'I'm sure there was more washing than that when I hung it out.'

'He killed somebody during a jewellery shop robbery. Ran them over. A hit and run...'

Emily glanced over at the television. The weather was now on. Grey clouds covered Yorkshire. It was typical autumn weather.

'Don't forget we're having lunch in town with my parents,' Emily said. 'Caesars, the Italian place. My mum swears by the saltimbocca in there.'

'I haven't forgotten,' Jonathan said.

Emily turned to face the backdoor. 'I'm surprised Theo hasn't come in for his breakfast.'

She took the box of cat biscuits and shook them.

'He'll come when he's hungry,' Jonathan said.

'But he's always hungry.'

Then Joseph began to cry.

'He'll want his porridge,' Emily said.

'They say he's very violent,' Jonathan said, holding baby Joseph to his chest and jigging him on his knee.

'Who?'

'Milton Macavity. The escaped convict...'

'I'm sure the police will soon catch him,' Emily said, and went to make some porridge for Joseph.

'Let's hope so,' Jonathan said. 'He could be hiding anywhere.'

3

Near to Monk Bar and behind the beer garden of the Keystones public house, there is a small building that looks like a stone igloo and is known as the Ice House.

It was built in the early 1800s on the northern rampart of the city walls. Below the structure a hole was dug into the earth and in the hole ice was kept in warm months to stop it from melting.

These days it serves no purpose and is off the tourist trail. The entrance is covered by a metal grille that, until recently, had been padlocked. The padlock had been removed by homeless Oliver Bartholomew, who was using the Ice House as a makeshift shelter.

Unfortunately for Oliver, he was about to meet escaped convict Milton Macavity.

Theodore was standing in the remains of St Maurice's graveyard, a small grassed area with several gravestones, either standing erect or lying flush with ground.

He had managed to catch a whiff of Milton and follow him to this spot, but here at the junction in front of Monk Bar, the traffic fumes had obscured any trace of his quarry.

To his right there was an advertisement painted onto the gable end of a building. It announced in beige and brown:

'Nightly, BILE BEANS, Keep You, HEALTHY BRIGHT-EYED & SLIM'

I don't think I'll be having any of those, thought Theodore. He looked back at the street in front of him.

He could give up the chase now, he reasoned. He had done his best. Maybe it was better to leave the police to get on with their work. He could find his way home and have breakfast. His stomach agreed that it was the best course of action.

Yes. You can come back now and forget all about your silly little adventure, came the call of the cat basket. *As if you could have caught this escaped criminal... You're delusional!*

With this last quip from the cat basket, Theodore narrowed his eyes.

He scanned the pavements. He noticed several people in a group wearing plastic masks. The masks were of a man with a white face, moustache and pointed beard wearing a black hat. Two police officers were walking behind the group. As soon as the two police officers had passed beneath Monk Bar, Theodore spotted Milton.

The escaped convict in pink and white trainers and blue hooped socks dashed across the road and disappeared behind the public house on the corner.

If Theodore crossed this junction, he would be in unknown territory. The streets were filled with people. There were cyclists and motorists whizzing by in potentially deadly weapons. It was not a place for cats.

Another police car drove by, its siren blaring, its lights flashing.

He had a duty, he reminded himself. A duty to stop this thug from committing further atrocities. He blinked his eyes. Then he raced across the junction. Cars beeped their horns and braked to avoid the large grey cat.

Theodore made it to the public house. He went down the side of the building. There was an empty beer garden.

Theodore looked at the side door of the pub. Had he gone into the building? But then he heard voices.

He looked over at the strange-looking stone building below the city walls. There were steps leading up to the Ice House. Theodore climbed up the steps. The voices grew louder.

The metal grate over the entrance was open. Theodore crept forward. There was a ladder leant against the wall, descending about ten feet into a dark pit.

'What else do you have in that bag?' a man said.

Theodore peered down into the dark.

He made out Milton and another man. The second man was bearded.

'Give me that knife,' Milton said.

'But I need it,' Oliver Bartholomew said. 'What am I supposed to eat with?'

Milton thumped Oliver on the head. Oliver fell to the floor. Milton grabbed up the canvas bag. He emptied its contents onto the floor of the Ice House. He stuck the knife in his pocket. Dozens of plastic bottles were strewn around the building. They had contained cider but now most of them contained urine.

Milton shook his head. 'This place is a right mess,' he said.

'I try to keep it tidy,' Oliver said.

'It's a disgrace,' Milton said. 'Now give me your coat.'

Oliver slowly took off his army coat. He handed it over to Milton.

Milton put on the coat. He looked down at his trainers and then at Oliver's army boots.

'And your boots...'

'Not my boots,' Oliver said.

'I'm sorry,' Milton said, 'but I need your boots. I can't go round in pink trainers. Whatever would people think? Me, an escaped convict. The Napoleon of Crime is what the papers call me...'

'You shouldn't worry so much about what others think of you,' said Oliver. 'You should learn to just be yourself.'

Milton clenched a fist and leant over Oliver, ready to strike him again. 'I'm having your boots,' he said. 'Whether you like it or not.'

'All right,' Oliver said. 'You can have my boots.'

He removed his boots and handed them to Milton.

Milton held the boots to his nose. 'They smell,' he said. 'They smell like a slab of gorgonzola left in the sauna over a summer in the Sahara.'

'I think I might have athletes foot,' Oliver said.

Outside there were more police car sirens.

'I can't wear them.' Milton threw the boots back at Oliver. 'Now get out of here!'

'But this is my home,' Oliver said.

'You're not supposed to be in here, are you?'

'Well, no,' Oliver said. 'No one should be in here.'

'I'm here now and you need to get out.'

He lifted Oliver up by his shirt. 'Now get up that ladder and clear off.'

Oliver slowly climbed the ladder. 'This is everything I have, down here,' he said.

'It's mine now,' Milton said. 'Push off and don't come back.'

Theodore caught the bearded man's gaze as he climbed up the ladder. His eyes were welling up with tears.

Theodore backed away and trotted down the steps away from the Ice House and back towards the pub, before Oliver emerged, blinking in the daylight.

Oliver followed Theodore into the beer garden. He sat on a bench and began to tie his bootlaces. His hair was overgrown and his face covered by a thick tangle of beard.

He spotted Theodore. 'Here, pussy cat!' he called.

Theodore kept his distance.

Oliver called again to him.

Theodore approached cautiously and then allowed Oliver to stroke him. He was just a homeless man who had been kicked out of his shelter, Theodore thought. He seemed harmless enough.

Oliver picked him up and put him on his lap. Theodore rubbed up against him. I'm sure Milton will soon be on his way, he tried to reassure Oliver, purring. Then you can have your home back.

He looked across at the Ice House, in which Milton now hid. It was unlikely that the police would look in the stone igloo for the escaped convict. Not unless either he or Oliver alerted them. Maybe he couldn't apprehend Milton by himself, he thought, but now he had a human by his side, they might together bring him to justice.

He puzzled over how to alert the police to Milton's presence in the Ice House while Oliver messed with his bootlace. He didn't realise that Oliver had removed the lace from the boot and formed a noose until it was around his neck. Oliver pulled on the end of the lace and it tightened.

Theodore protested loudly and tried to wriggle free but the waxed cord tightened with his struggles.

'Now you be quiet, little cat,' Oliver said. 'We're going to be a team, you and I. We're going to make lots of money on the streets of York. Just you wait and see!'

I'm no Street Cat Bob, Theodore thought. I have a house and a family waiting for me. I have food in my bowls and a garden to use as a toilet. The street is no place for a cat. Especially not a cat of my pedigree.

'Yes, you're coming with me!' Oliver said. 'You're going to make me rich!'

He held Theodore up in front of him and laughed. His breath was sour.

Theodore closed his eyes and held his breath. I should never have left the safety of the kitchen, he thought. I should have stayed by the radiator and let the outside world carry on without me.

I told you so, came the knowing voice of the cat basket.

Now, see what trouble you've got yourself into... This is what happens when you don't listen to reason. You may never return home again. Yours will be a life spent on the streets. You've really messed up this time.

4

Monk Bar is one of the four gateways into York. Today it houses the Richard III Museum. The top storey was added by Richard III in 1484. Below Monk Bar, Theodore lay beside his new companion. Oliver had placed several pieces of cardboard onto the ground. He had swiped a pint glass from the pub and placed it in front of them. In large letters on the cardboard he had written:

'MONEY FOR CAT FOOD
MUCH APPRECIATED'

The pint glass rang out every minute or so as people tossed in their coins. More generous people popped in fivers or tenners, which Oliver retrieved and stuffed into his pockets. His plan to make money by using the cat was working.

Theodore had struggled at first to get away but the bootlace around his neck that was tied around Oliver's wrist tightened every time he pulled against it. In the end he lay down on the cold slab of stone and feigned sleep. His brain, however, was more alive than ever. He needed to escape this terrible situation and deal with Milton before he could hurt or kill anyone else.

While the escaped convict hid out in the Ice House, the people of York were safe. But Milton would get hungry before long and then come out. Prowling the streets of York. The next person he came across might not get off as lightly as the football-playing family or Oliver Bartholomew.

A girl's voice said, 'What's your cat's name?'

Theodore opened his eyes just enough to see a young girl standing in front of him.

'Smoky,' Oliver said. 'He's called Smoky.'

'Because he's grey?'

'That's right,' Oliver said.

'That's a rubbish name for a cat,' said the girl. 'Can I pet him?'

'It'll be a pound for a pet.'

The girl's mother rummaged in her handbag and produced a pound coin. She popped it into the pint glass.

Theodore allowed the girl to pat him on the head but he didn't purr. Smoky? What sort of a name was that?

Worst were the dogs. If they noticed Theodore, they would strain against their leads to get at the cat. Oliver had to pick him up several times and shield him from the excited canines.

And so it went on, for at least an hour. By which time the pint glass was half-full of coins and Oliver's pockets held half a dozen crumpled fivers and tenners.

'I think it's time for you and I to go shopping,' Oliver said.

He grabbed up Theodore in one arm and the pint glass in the other and made his way to a small supermarket on Goodramgate.

Several minutes later, he exited the supermarket, a plastic bag in each hand.

Emily, Jonathan, Trish and Patrick were sitting in Caesars Italian restaurant. They had been seated in front of the large window, looking out onto Goodramgate. Emily and Jonathan on one side, facing the window; Trish and Patrick on the other, facing the restaurant. Baby Joseph was in a highchair at the head of the table, by Emily and Jonathan.

Emily looked out of the window and took in the street. She noticed a man walking by in a green army jacket. Probably some homeless guy, she thought. She noted that he was wearing the same red and black checked shirt that Jonathan had and also jeans that looked similar to Jonathan's and were too small for him.

She looked across at Jonathan. He was wearing a dark denim jacket, some rock band T-shirt and beige cords. The cords were worn down at the knees.

'I think we should go to the Designer Outlet and get you some new clothes,' she said.

Jonathan glanced down and said, 'There's plenty of life in these yet,' he said, slapping his thighs where the corduroy was worn flat.

'I think I might have the saltimbocca,' Patrick said staring at the menu.

'Yes, you can always gauge an Italian by its saltimbocca,' Trish said. 'I think I'm going to have the same.'

'I fancy a Hawaiian,' Emily said, 'but it's not on the menu.'

'That's because this is an Italian restaurant,' Patrick said.

As everyone knows, the Hawaiian pizza is actually a Canadian invention. Along with paint rollers, peanut butter and Celine Dion, it ranks highly in the list of Canada's contribution to civilisation.

'I'll just have a margherita,' Emily said.

'I'm going to have a pepperoni,' Jonathan said.

'We need to order a bottle of wine,' Patrick said, his forefinger running down the wine list.

'Did you hear about the escaped convict,' Jonathan said. 'He escaped from York Hospital. Milton Macavity, he's called. He's supposed to be very dangerous...'

'Never heard of him,' Patrick said.

'Sounds like he should be on the stage,' Trish said. 'With a name like that!'

'They call him the Napoleon of Crime. He attacked a family on our street,' Jonathan went on. 'It was on the television just as we were leaving. They said that the police are looking for a man wearing pink trainers.'

'You'd've thought they'd be wearing more sensible footwear,' Patrick said and laughed at his own joke. Then, 'The merlot, I think.'

Trish tutted. 'That's not going to go with the saltimbocca.'

Patrick turned his attention to the whites.

Joseph scrunched up a napkin and threw it onto the floor and then laughed.

Emily stared out of the plate glass window. Raindrops slid down the glass. The road outside was black with rain. People wearing Guy Fawkes masks passed; they all bore the same malevolent smile. A shudder passed through her.

'Those people in masks give me the creeps,' Emily said, still staring out of the window. 'I bet half of them don't even know he was born in York.'

'The only man to enter Parliament with honest intentions,' Patrick said, still studying the wine list.

'Excuse me?' Trish said.

'Guy Fawkes,' Patrick said. 'These postmodern anarchists have taken his image to demonstrate their own protest and anger at the government. They feel let down by politicians, who say one thing to get in, and when they do get in, do nothing but claim expenses.'

'Oh, rubbish,' Trish said. 'They just fancied a day out.'

'Maybe they have a point,' Jonathan said. 'Politicians aren't doing enough. If we don't start changing our ways, our children are not going to have a planet left. Man has altered the Earth to such a degree that in geology, we even have a new name for it: the Anthropocene Epoch...'

'Have you chosen a wine to go with the saltimbocca,' Trish said. 'Now where is the waiter?'

She understood that it was poor etiquette to bring up sex, politics or geology at the dinner table.

'Perhaps the chardonnay,' Patrick said.

The Holy Trinity is the only surviving church in York with box pews. The Victorians took a dislike to the old box pews and threw most of them out; they preferred people to sit in rows. Within one of these box pews, Oliver made himself as comfortable as he could in his damp clothes and began to swig from a two-litre bottle of cider.

The partitioned-off room had been historically reserved for lepers. They would sit in the wooden enclosure, segregated from the rest of the congregation, and observe the service through a peephole in the screen.

'Not a bad start to our career,' Oliver said. 'What do you say, Smoky?'

Theodore voiced his opinion that any form of career was beneath him and he objected strongly to being called Smoky.

The back of Oliver's hand put a swift end to his protestations.

Theodore stared at Oliver's fingers. They were pink and swollen from the cold. They looked like big pink sausages. He took his chance and sunk his teeth into Oliver's fat forefinger. He held fast but Oliver's other hand grabbed him by the skin of the neck. He let go of the finger.

'You little blighter!' shouted Oliver.

He held the cat at arm's length in front of him.

Theodore struggled.

'Not so fast, little cat,' Oliver said. 'We're business partners, remember? You need to learn the ground rules.'

He grabbed at Theodore's collar. 'What do we have here then?'

He picked up Theodore's silver name tag that hung from his collar. The silver disc was engraved with his name and Emily's mobile number.

'Theodore, is it?'

Theodore tried to cry for help but no sound came out.

'Well, it's Smoky from now on.'

Then Oliver went to work with both hands. It took him some minutes to remove the cat's collar with his fat fingers. He threw the collar as hard as he could across the church.

With his hands around Theodore's neck, he said, 'We are colleagues, you see? Me and you. A team...'

Theodore struggled once more to break free. It was hopeless he knew. He still had the bootlace around his neck that was tied to Oliver's wrist.

With the loss of his collar, he had taken another step away from his former life of safe domesticity. A few hours ago, he had been complaining about the tardiness of his food bowls being filled and dirty nappies being dropped on him from small heights. Now he had been stripped of his sole vestige of civilisation.

His collar told the world that he had owners, a home, a human family. Even if he managed to escape from Oliver and the life of the street, he wasn't sure that he could find his way home. I should never have left the safety of the yard, he thought, not for the first time that day. He let his body go limp.

There'll always be another cat to fill the basket, the voice in his head said. You will be forgotten and replaced by a new kitten, who will appreciate the basket more than you did. He will not venture into town after escaped criminals. He will be content to stay by the radiator and wait patiently for his bowls to be filled. You will soon be forgotten. Emily will move on.

Even Oliver noticed the change in Theodore's attitude. He put the cat down on the seat beside him.

'Oh, come on. It's not all that bad,' Oliver said. 'Life on the streets has its rewards. You'll see. We are free souls. Wanderers of the world. Free from the trappings of society. Unencumbered by mortgages, debts and taxes. We are free to come and go as we please...'

Well, I beg to disagree, Theodore thought, straining against the bootlace tight around his throat. I was free before. Free to lie in my cat basket all day.

Oliver took another swig of cider. 'You'll get used to it. You'll have to. You're with me now. We're a partnership, right?'

Theodore closed his eyes defiantly. I will never get used to this life. The street is no place for a respectable cat.

'I've even got you a little something.'

Oliver reached into his plastic bag and took out a pouch of cat food. He ripped it open along the top. He tried to tear down the side of the pouch but it wouldn't open out. He squeezed the pouch onto the wooden floor. Then he placed the cat on the floor facing the small mound of cat food.

'There you go, Smoky.'

Theodore sniffed the food. Carcass scrapings was his verdict.

He closed his eyes and feigned sleep.

'You have a nap,' Oliver said. 'We'll earn ourselves a bit more money later on.' He took another swig of cider.

After drinking two two-litre bottles of cider, Oliver fell asleep and began snoring.

Theodore felt the bootlace slacken from around his neck. He tried to duck out of it but it got stuck on his head. He pulled against it but then Oliver snorted in his sleep and jerked on the bootlace. Theodore was dragged closer to the drunken Oliver.

He managed to place a paw across the bootlace so that it was held tight in front of his face. He began to chew against the waxen black thread, grinding it between his teeth. A minute later he had freed himself.

He darted into the corner of the box pew. He glanced back at his adversary. Oliver had jerked erect. He stared at the cat. Seconds passed as he realised what was going on. Then he got to his feet.

Theodore jumped up on top of a wooden partition. Oliver lurched forward. Theodore darted along the partition, narrowly avoiding Oliver's grasping hands. Oliver fell to the floor.

Theodore navigated the wooden partitions of the box pews, making his way to the entrance.

Oliver managed to get to his feet. He picked up a bottle of cider he had half filled with urine. He threw it at the cat.

Theodore jumped down onto the church floor.

The bottle of amber fluid hit the stone wall with a thump.

'You damned cat!' Oliver shouted.

Theodore exited the church, into the grey autumn day, and ran.

5

Oliver sat on a bench in the churchyard. It was raining steadily and his shirt was wet through. On the bench was a little brass plaque. It read:

'Benjamin Bartholomew
Liked to Sit in this Churchyard.
R.I.P.'

From time-to-time Oliver Bartholomew glanced at the little brass plaque and took a gulp of cider.

'Daddy,' he said to himself, as there was no one else to hear him, 'I miss you.'

And he sat on the bench in the rain and cried to himself.

Kings Square was once home to a church, its yard used to keep flocks of animals before their slaughter by the butchers that were located on the Shambles. Blood and guts would flow down the middle of this little street. On this dull November day, blood would once more flow. But this time it would not be the blood of animals but human blood.

Theodore spotted Milton as he entered Kings Square from St Andrewgate. He had spotted the pink and white trainers Milton wore along with Jonathan's blue socks. Otherwise he would not have realised it was him, as he was now wearing a Guy Fawkes mask like many of the people in the street.

Milton had avoided the more popular streets, heading down Aldwark and then St Andrewgate, before he was faced with the crowd that thronged Kings Square.

An escapologist entertained the crowd. Many people had come for the protest march that evening, that had been dubbed the Million Mask March, but in the meantime they were playing tourist in the city. Milton was now one of the anonymous faces in the crowd, indistinguishable apart from his footwear.

As Milton made his way through the people he jostled a pair of Japanese tourists.

The woman said to her husband in Japanese, 'It's him... the escaped convict, Takeharu. Remember we saw on the news. They said he is wearing pink and white trainers, remember?'

'You're right, Yoshi,' Takeharu said. 'We must stop him.'

So Takeharu set off after Milton. He caught up with him on the Shambles.

He placed a hand on his shoulder. 'I know who you are,' he said to the masked face. 'You are the one the police are looking for. It is your trainers that give you away.'

Meanwhile Yoshi called the police on her mobile phone.

Milton turned to face the tourist. He was over a foot taller than him. 'Get out of my way,' he muttered from behind his mask.

'No,' Takeharu said, 'you will wait here until the police arrive.' He placed a hand on Milton's shoulder. 'My wife is on the phone to them now.'

Milton glanced around. There were many people wearing the same mask that he had found discarded in the beer garden of Keystones. Some of these masked faces were now turning to him.

One of them said, 'Is this man bothering you?'

'Well, yes,' Milton said.

'You leave off him,' a masked man said.

'Excuse me?' Takeharu said.

'You leave him alone,' the masked man said. 'He's with us.'

'You don't understand.'

'Sod off, suit,' a masked woman said.

'You don't understand. This man must be arrested,' Takeharu protested.

'Who do you think you are?'

'I am a surgeon,' Takeharu said. 'A paediatrician.'

'What did he say?'

'I think he said he's a paedo.'

'A paedo? Let's have him!'

The masked woman pushed Takeharu. A man jostled him. He was surrounded by masked faces. He fell to the ground. People piled on top of him. Then there was a punch to his face. Blood gushed from his nose. He raised his hands to protect his face.

The masked crowd kicked at his body. Some of them began to chant, 'One solution, revolution!'

Yoshi was pushed to the edge of the fray. 'Takeharu!' she screamed.

'Yoshi!' Takeharu gasped from beneath the scrum of masked protestors.

Theodore looked on from the windowsill of a shop. In the window there was a hand-written notice that read:

THIS WINDOWSILL IS OLDER THAN YOU. PLEASE DO NOT SIT ON IT

I'm sure it doesn't mind, thought Theodore.

He watched as one of the masked men broke away from the melee and carried on down the Shambles, past the queue outside a Harry Potter shop. He was wearing pink and white trainers. Milton turned left at the end of the street and disappeared down St Crux Passage into Whip-ma-whop-ma-gate, which can be translated into Modern English as, 'Neither one thing nor the other', and is supposedly where husbands once brought their wives to be flogged.

Takeharu had given up trying to protect himself. He lay slumped in the middle of the road. The crowd began to lose interest and parted around him. Yoshi ran to her husband's side.

Two mounted police officers entered the street from Pavement, their horses' hooves clipping the sandstone flags.

Theodore's gaze followed the mounted police officers, as they approached the Japanese couple. He noticed a street sign.

'SHAMBLES,' it read.

Yes, Theodore agreed: 'Utter Shambles!'

He jumped down from the windowsill and set off again after Milton.

Back at Caesars Italian restaurant, Emily, Jonathan, Trish and Patrick were looking at the dessert menus.

'Isn't that Barbara from Scarborough over there,' Trish said, glancing at a woman at the next table.

Patrick looked up from his menu. 'I doubt it,' he said. 'I thought she'd moved to Market Harborough.'

'No, Trish said. 'You've got her mixed up with Shirley from Wortley.'

Just then Emily's mobile phone rang.

'I think I might have found your cat's collar,' a woman said.

'Where was it?' Emily said.

'In Holy Trinity Church,' the woman said.

'That's not far from us. We're on Goodramgate. Can you wait there? I'll be there in two minutes.'

'I don't have time, I'm afraid,' the woman explained. 'But I'll leave it on the altar, so you can find it.'

'OK,' Emily said. 'Thanks for letting me know.'

Once Emily had returned her phone to her coat pocket, Jonathan asked, 'What is it?'

'Somebody's found Theo's collar. It's in a church just off Goodramgate...'

'Theo must have followed us into town.'

Emily got to her feet. 'We need to go and look for him. He can't be far away... We need to find him.'

'But we haven't had dessert yet,' Patrick said.

'Dessert can wait till we get back to Acaster Mildew,' Trish said. 'Now you sort out the bill. We will go on ahead to Holy Trinity Church.'

Emily had already crossed to the pram, where Joseph was sleeping. Jonathan got to his feet too. A minute later they had set off to retrieve Theodore's collar and search for the cat, leaving Patrick by himself at the table waiting for their bill, the dessert menu still in front of him.

6

Theodore stopped on the corner where the Shambles meets Pavement. Pavement is actually a street, so called because it was the first bit of road to be paved in York, back in 1378. Before then, it was known as Marketshire and was probably a bit muddy.

There was a small rectangle of grass adjacent to St Crux Church Hall. A low stone wall provided some protection against the passing hordes of humans. The top of the wall was studded with silver circles, where the former iron railings had been sawn off to be melted down as part of the war effort in the 1940s. However, most of the iron collected was not required, and the government of the day quietly disposed of the metal rather than admit it was more for propaganda they had stripped our cities than bullets.

Theodore stood up on his back legs and peered over the wall. He scanned the passing people but saw no giveaway pink and white trainers.

You might as well give up the chase now, came the voice of the cat basket. *Cut your losses and come on home. Who knows what else might happen out there? Oliver might be out looking for you. And if you do manage to locate Milton, he will probably stamp on your tail and not give it a second thought.*

Behind the wall someone had left a half-eaten chicken burger even though there was a bin only yards away. He looked across the road and spied the Yummy Chicken shop from where the burger had originated. Behind the wall there was other human debris, mainly disposable coffee cups. Have you ever known a cat to litter? thought Theodore. We leave the world as we find it. If only humans behaved the same...

Theodore pawed at the grease-proof wrapper, exposing the remains of the chicken burger in a bread bun. He pawed away the bread. He noted that the chicken was smothered in white sauce.

Mayonnaise! If there is one thing Theodore could not abide, it was mayonnaise. Yummy Chicken! I don't think so.

There are fresh biscuits waiting in your bowl, the cat basket said temptingly, *and fresh water in your bowl.*

Theodore blinked his eyes to rid his mind of the image of his food bowl. But his stomach growled insistently. He had not eaten all day. This was no time to be picky. He needed nourishment if he was going to continue the pursuit.

He took a bite from the burger and tried to chew without smelling. He gulped down the meat. This was not eating. This was survival. Survival on the streets of York. At this rate, he would be devouring mice, tails and all, by the end of the day.

With each mouthful of chicken, he realised he was moving further away from domesticity, further away from the comforts and boredoms of civilisation. He was stepping towards the life of the street. A life of constant danger. A primordial existence.

A man was sitting further along the wall. He wore a pin-striped suit and a pink shirt. The pin stripes of the suit were pink to match the shirt. The suit was crumpled and the shirt creased. There were flakes of dandruff on the shoulders of the suit. The man had a dried smear of white on his stubbly chin. Mayonnaise, thought Theodore. It had to be the litter lout.

Theodore narrowed his eyes and folded back his ears.

The man had a bulky rucksack on his lap. He was bent over the rucksack, fiddling with something inside. His eyes were narrowed in concentration.

A young girl wearing a Guy Fawkes mask approached. She veered towards the suited man. As she got near to him, she spat on the ground.

The man looked up. Then he looked down at his shoes. Spit coated the toe of his right brogue. He looked at the girl who had spat on his shoe. On the back of her black jacket were the words painted in white, 'CAPITALI$M $UCKS', and a portrait of Che Guevara.

She may have a valid point, thought Theodore. We cats do all right without money. I have yet to see a cat carrying a purse around.

Theodore's attention was drawn by a siren. He watched as an ambulance with flashing lights entered the Shambles. The ambulance slowed right down, as the Shambles is very narrow, the first floors overhanging the footways on either side of the street. Pedestrians pushed themselves into doorways and through the alley into Shambles Market. The ambulance came to a stop halfway down the street, by the chapel dedicated to Margaret Clitheroe, who was a Catholic crushed to death below a door in 1585 for attending mass and hiding priests.

Paramedics jumped out and rushed to the Japanese tourist's side.

In all the commotion, Theodore saw a pair of pink and white trainers dash across the street to the other side of Pavement, where they disappeared inside a shoe shop. The shoe shop was located on the ground floor of Herbert House, a large black and white Tudor house that had once been home to a family called Herbert.

Theodore glanced at the remains of the chicken burger; then jumped down from behind the wall and set off after Milton.

'I need a pair of shoes,' Milton said. 'These ones stand out too much.'

'Have you seen any you like?' the shop assistant asked, smiling. Her name badge read Becky.

'Well, I need some running shoes,' Milton said. He was on the run after all. 'Ones that don't stand out.'

'Well, if you sit down over there, I'll bring you some to try on.'

Milton sat down where Becky indicated.

'Are you here for the protest?' Becky asked.

'I suppose I am,' Milton said.

'I was going to go down later,' Becky said quietly. 'Once I've finished here. I'll go and get you some trainers.'

Milton realised he was still wearing the Guy Fawkes mask. He took it off but kept it on his lap. He removed the pink and white trainers and pushed them under his chair.

Becky returned with a trainer. 'Do you like this style?'

'Yes, they'll do,' Milton said. 'Just give them to me.'

'You need to try them on, don't you?' Becky said with a smile. 'Do you know what size you are?'

'Yes, a 10.'

'Well, I'll just go and get you a pair of size 10s to try on. I won't be long.'

Then Becky disappeared into the back of the shop, leaving Milton sitting on his chair. He turned his face away from the window and the world outside.

Theodore stared through the glass window. He noticed the sweat dripping from Milton's head. Police officers passed by but did not glance inside the shop.

Then he noticed a police van. It had stopped in front of the Golden Fleece. Two police officers got out and approached the shoe shop. Another police van pulled to a stop in front of Pizza Hut and two more police officers approached.

Theodore looked through the window.

Milton was trying on the size 10 sports shoes.

'They're fine,' he said. 'I'll take them.'

'Do you want them in their box?'

'No, I'll wear them.'

'What's happened to the shoes you were wearing?'

'Don't worry about those.'

He stood up, pushed Becky aside and walked to the back of the shop.

'Hey! Where are you going? You need to pay for those.' Becky started after him.

Theodore looked to his left and then to his right. The police officers were still waiting to make their move.

There must be a back exit, thought Theodore. He padded in front of the shop and stopped in front of a passageway. It was sign-posted Lady Pecketts Yard. Theodore began to gallop down the passageway.

Ahead of him, he heard a cry.

He rounded the corner.

Milton had Becky up against a wall. She was crying. Milton had a hand across her mouth.

'Look, I'm not going to hurt you,' he said.

Becky whimpered.

'You need to tell the police,' Milton said. 'Tell them there's a plot. Something big is going to go down tonight. They need to send for reinforcements.'

Then he let her go and ran off down the alleyway. As he turned right onto Fossgate, Theodore noticed the blue stripes of Jonathan's socks in the space between the bottom of his jeans and the top of his new white running shoes. Milton must be quite a bit shorter than Jonathan, Theodore deduced.

Then Becky screamed.

At Holy Trinity Church, Emily found Theodore's collar on the altar. She pushed the pram back to the entrance. She called her cat's name. He did not come.

'He's not in here,' she said.

'He could be anywhere,' Jonathan said.

Outside a firework went off with a loud bang.

'I keep forgetting it's Bonfire Night tonight,' Emily said.

'It's really not a night for a cat to be out,' Jonathan said.

'We need to find him.'

They exited the church. They began to search the graveyard. There was a sign tied to a tree that said, 'Phineas Bull'. Emily wondered who Phineas Bull was and why his name was on a sign tied to a tree. She heard a belch from behind her. She looked round and saw a man sitting on a bench, a bottle of cider in his hand.

She walked over to him. 'Have you seen a cat?'

Oliver stared at her with bloodshot eyes and belched. 'No. I haven't seen your cat,' he slurred.

She turned away from Oliver and called out for Theodore.

'Come on,' she said to Jonathan. 'Let's go this way.'

She pushed the pram towards Lund's Court, formerly Mad Alice Lane; Alice confessed to crimes she did not commit and was executed at York Castle in 1825, or so some say.

'I'd better wait here for your dad,' Trish called after them, 'or he won't know where to find us.'

Trish paced the church path. She wanted to get back home to watch Gentleman Jack, a BBC drama series about Anne Lister: a nineteenth century landowner, lesbian and diarist, whose union with her companion Ann Walker was sealed by taking the sacrament at Easter 1834 in the church in front of which she paced.

It was half an hour later when Patrick entered through the church gates, a redness to his cheeks and a sheen of perspiration to his brow.

'You took your time,' Trish snapped. She was sheltering from the rain in the entrance to the church by a large brass bell, which was engraved with the words: 'Ring for Peace'.

'I had to wait to pay, didn't I?'

'You had dessert, didn't you?'

Patrick looked guiltily at his wife. 'Well, I couldn't resist the tiramisu.'

'You can never resist the tiramisu!'

'Sorry.'

'I've been standing here for half an hour while you stuff your face with tiramisu.'

Patrick looked away, his cheeks reddening. 'Why isn't that Oliver Bartholomew over there?'

'Stop trying to change the subject,' Trish said but looked over at the forlorn figure on the bench. 'Young Oliver? It can't be.'

'I believe it is,' Patrick said.

He walked over to Oliver. 'Oliver? It's me... Pat.'

'Pat?'

'Yes. You remember? We were neighbours. I was friends with your dad.... Terrible what happened. A terrible business that...'

'Yes, Oliver said. 'Terrible...' and his voice faltered.

Patrick looked Oliver up and down. 'What on earth happened to you?'

'I suppose life has not treated me kindly,' Oliver said, defeat in his voice. 'Since dad had that... accident.'

Patrick sat down on the bench beside Oliver. 'Let me tell you a little story,' he said.

And then he told Oliver a little story.

7

'Many years ago, I was down on my luck...

'Penniless... Homeless... Destitute...

'I had lost everything. One business after another had failed. I thought I would never recover. I was drinking. I was smoking. I was doing whatever drugs I could lay my hands on.

'I was sleeping in the doorway of an empty shop. I didn't even have a sleeping bag.

'One day a little old lady appeared.

"Here,' she said. 'I've made you some dinner. We can't have you going hungry when I've got food in the larder..."

'She handed over a large parcel wrapped in tinfoil. She then handed me a plastic spoon.

'I unwrapped the foil package. There was a whole Sunday roast dinner inside a giant Yorkshire pudding. No plate. Just a big Yorkshire pudding.

"I couldn't be giving away my crockery, now, could I?' the old lady said. 'So I put it all in the pud!"

'She then said, "Would you like salt and pepper? My husband would never eat owt without".

'And I said, yes, I would.

'So she put her hand in one coat pocket and took out a salt cellar and from her other pocket a pepper pot.

'After I used them, I handed them back and she popped them back in her pockets.

'I smiled my gratitude and the little old lady scuttled away.

'I looked down at the Yorkshire Pudding.

'Inside there were slices of roast beef, mashed potatoes, roast potatoes, peas, cauliflower, all covered in rich onion gravy. There was even a smear of horse radish.

'A whole Sunday roast dinner inside a giant Yorkshire pudding! Who would have thought it?

'I smiled to myself. And then I laughed.'

'Oh, get on with it,' Trish said. 'We're going to be here all day at this rate...'

Oliver stared at Patrick. 'Why did you laugh?'

'I laughed because I saw my way out of the hole I had dug,' Patrick said. 'That Yorkshire pudding gave me the seed of an idea.

'I managed to borrow some money. I went round all my old friends. I begged them. I said I would pay them back.

'Within six months, I had set up The Olde Yorkshire Pudding Shop. I took on the lease for the shop on Micklegate, the same shop whose doorway I had slept in for weeks. Every morning, as I stepped over the threshold I would remember my nights attempting to sleep in that doorway.

'By the end of that year, I had shops on every street that leads into this city. Micklegate, Fossgate, Goodramgate and Gillygate, and a flagship shop and restaurant on Coney Street.

'As you know, there are now Olde Yorkshire Pudding Shoppes in almost every town in this country. And I own them all!'

'You do?' Oliver said. 'I didn't know. I thought they'd always been around.'

'That's because I spelled Olde with an 'e' on the end and Shoppe double p, e.'

'That was clever of you.'

Patrick waved a hand with a flourish. 'And you know what the bestseller is?'

'The Sunday Roast in a Giant Pud?'

'That's right,' Patrick said. 'The toad-in-the-hole is a close second though. But that's because I use only the finest Yorkshire sausages. And then there's the Full English in a Giant Pud. That's the bestseller before eleven o'clock. People come from all over the world to sample my puds...'

'Can you hurry this along?' Trish said. 'We do have a home to go to...'

'Well, that does bring me to the point I am trying to make. You see, it was all down to that little old lady giving me that meal in a Yorkshire pudding... One act of kindness and my life was turned around. And I said to myself, that if ever I was in a position to help somebody, then I would.'

'You would?'

'Yes, I would. You are coming home with us, Oliver Bartholomew. To Acaster Mildew.'

'He is?' Trish said.

'I am?' Oliver said.

'You are,' Patrick said.

'Well, he can stay in your den.'

'Yes,' Patrick said, 'he can stay in my den.'

'I can stay in your den?'

'Just till you get back on your feet.'

'Just till he gets back on his feet,' Trish said.

'I'd better get my things,' Oliver said.

Patrick slapped Oliver on his thigh. 'What matters most is how well you pick yourself up after you fall.'

Oliver nodded. His eyes had welled up with tears at this unexpected kindness.

Patrick got up from the bench.

'I think a hot bath is first on the agenda,' Trish said.

'I just need to get something,' Oliver said.

He got up and went inside the church.

'What a lot of codswallop,' Trish said. 'You've never been down and out in your life.'

'I said at the start that it was a story,' Patrick said and smiled.

They watched as Oliver returned. He carried a plastic bag containing a bottle of cider.

Patrick shook his head.

'What is it?' Oliver said.

'The deal is,' Patrick said, 'that you leave that bottle behind.'

'But it's almost full,' Oliver said.

'You leave it behind. You leave it behind with the rest of this sorry little chapter of your life.'

Oliver nodded.

'When we get back, we'll have a nice cup of tea,' Patrick said. 'I've got some Yorkshire Gold.'

'Yorkshire Gold?'

'They select teas from the top ten tea gardens in the world to make a rich, smooth and incredibly satisfying brew... A proper cup of tea, in other words.'

'Sounds good.'

'Well, let's get going,' Patrick said. 'A new chapter is about to begin!'

'It is?'

'If you want it to.'

Oliver nodded. 'I want it to.'

He put the bottle of cider down on the bench. Then he followed Patrick and Trish out of the churchyard.

A new chapter was about to begin.

8

Theodore raced down Fossgate. The pavements were crowded and he soon lost sight of Milton. But then he picked up his scent: aftershave, sweaty socks and new shoes that had been sprayed in formaldehyde.

He passed over a bridge and stopped. The scent had gone.

Theodore turned and looked back the way he had come.

There were several police officers coming his way. One on a bicycle whizzed by. Two more on horses galloped down the middle of the street, the horses' hooves clacking on the cobbles.

Theodore began to retrace his steps until he picked up Milton's scent once more. He was standing next to the balustrade of the bridge. He stood on his hind legs and put his head through the balustrade. He looked down on the dark swirling waters of the Foss. Fifty yards downstream he saw Milton, wearing the Guy Fawkes mask, swimming silently away.

Police officers rushed by. He tried to stop them by calling out to them but they ignored him.

He looked down at the black water. He jumped up between the stone columns of the balustrade. Then he dropped into the Foss.

If you have ever tried to bath a cat, you will know that they don't like to get wet.

When Theodore surfaced, he coughed out a stream of grey water. He felt the cold currents pushing him along. He worked his legs. He was soon moving rapidly along the river, his ears folded back against his head.

Ahead of him he spied the Guy Fawkes mask that Milton wore. He was also being carried along by the fast river water.

On his right, he passed by York Castle Museum and then under another bridge. Ahead there was a crashing of water. He closed his eyes as he was carried over a sluice into the Foss Basin.

When he opened his eyes again, he saw boats tethered to moorings. He heard some splashing behind him. He turned and saw Milton swimming away from him.

He began to swim after him.

Patrick had parked his car in St George's Field car park, which abuts the River Foss in parts.

He clicked open the car doors and told Oliver to get in the back. Then he spied something in the river.

'Well, look at that,' he said. 'There's a giant rat swimming in the Foss.'

Trish squinted. 'They say you're never more than ten feet away from a rat,' she said with a shudder.

'Yes. They do that.'

'Come on. Let's get going. The sooner we get back to Acaster Mildew the better.'

Trish got in the car and Oliver got in the back.

Patrick stared after the large grey rat. It was as though there was something familiar about it. Something he couldn't quite articulate.

'Hurry up and get in,' Trish shouted. 'And open the windows.'

Patrick shook his head. It would come to him, he thought. And if it didn't, it probably wasn't important. He burped and tasted tiramisu.

He got in the car and they set off back to Acaster Mildew.

Theodore was fast approaching Foss Dam. The dam's purpose is to stop water from the River Ouse backing up into the Foss and flooding properties upriver. Today the dam was not lowered and Theodore was carried straight through. He saw Milton pass under a little blue bridge ahead of him. Carried along by the currents he had no choice but to follow.

Two figures in black wearing Guy Fawkes masks watched as he approached. One of them pointed a finger at him. The other was holding a can of spray paint. He had just sprayed his tag on the side of the bridge in dripping red paint. At least when I leave my mark, there is little visible evidence, he thought, though olfactory evidence was another matter.

Then he met the black waters of the Ouse. He was dragged below the surface. He took in water. He was spun around. This would be his end. Drowned in the dirty Ouse.

His body would be washed ashore on some remote river bank, where his remains would be feasted on by vermin. Or carried out to the North Sea, where fish would nibble on his bloated corpse until there was no meat left and then his bones would descend to the sea floor where they would become one with it.

Everything became black. Everything became silent.

This was the end. The end of Theodore.

9

Theodore was not the lightest of cats. Rather than being dragged along by the currents, he descended through the water until he reached the sludgy bottom of the Ouse.

Among the near surface sediments, there was recent waste: shopping trolleys, rusted bicycles, bottles, cans, plastic debris and branches of trees brought downriver.

Further down he sank. There was an unexploded bomb dropped by a German bomber as it followed the Ouse back to the Humber Estuary in 1942.

Even further down and further into the past, there were watches, lighters, bottles, clay pipes, ceramic fragments, all dating from the early twentieth century.

Then, from the long reign of Queen Victoria, there came more bottles, jam jars and a ceramic doll thrown from a pram into the river by a spoilt Victorian child.

Images flashed through Theodore's mind as he sank deeper into the river sediments. He remembered the newsflash that morning, announcing the escape of convicted murderer Milton Macavity. He remembered being hit on the head by a dirty nappy just before he went downstairs to check on his food bowls. He remembered waking that morning.

Broken pipe fragments were all that marked the seventeenth century. Theodore sank back deeper into his own past.

He dropped through the air and landed on the woman's head. The woman screamed. She dropped the candlestick onto the floor with a clang. She roughly pulled him off her head and threw him to the floor.

Then the woman picked up the large candlestick she had dropped. Theodore ran into a corner of the church. He cowered behind the altar.

The woman held the candlestick in the air. 'You are going to regret ever setting eyes on me,' she said.

She held up the candlestick, ready to strike.

Theodore closed his eyes and tensed his body, waiting for the end.

He felt a warm liquid splash over him; it was not what he had expected death to be like.

He opened his eyes. Emily was standing in front of him, the other candlestick in her hands. She dropped it to the floor.

Ellen lay on the floor beside him. She was dead. He realised that the warm splash had been blood. Her blood. Emily had rescued him from Ellen.

That had been back in Acomb when Theodore had tracked down and brought murderer Ellen Black to justice.

That had been a close call, Theodore thought, reflecting on this previous outing into bringing a criminal to justice. He had come close to having his brains splashed against the church walls. One of his nine lives spent. Theodore sank further into the riverbed.

Passing through the medieval age, there were fragments of pottery: French jugs, German cups and mugs, Dutch cooking vessels; remnants of medieval York's trade links with Europe. There was a leg bone of a goose carved into a whistle. York at play was symbolised by dice and gaming pieces carved out of bone and jet.

Theodore passed further back into his own past.

He could see Emily and Jonathan crossing the road ahead. He waited until they had reached the footpath on the other side before approaching the kerb.

He didn't bother looking in each direction before stepping out into the road. His technique was to dash across as quickly as he could. So far his technique had served him well. He was alive, wasn't he?

Emily and Jonathan were walking along the footpath on the other side, further and further away from Theodore. He couldn't lose sight of them. He chose his moment and dashed into the middle of the road.

There was the screech of car brakes and the smell of burned rubber.

Theodore was lying flat against the tarmac. He opened his eye. A little blue car had driven over him and come to a stop several yards in front.

'Theodore!' he heard Emily cry.

She ran over and picked him up.

Theodore stared back into Emily's face, his eyes bulging, his heart thumping. He tried to wriggle himself free.

'I think he's all right,' Emily said, holding onto him tightly.

The door of the car swung open and a woman with short dark hair got out.

'Is that cat yours?' the woman asked, her voice high-pitched, verging on hysterical.

'He must have followed us,' Emily said, still clutching him.

'I could have killed him,' the other woman said.

Emily hugged Theodore to her chest, beginning to cry. 'I'm sorry,' she said.

'He gave me the fright of my life.'

'I'm sorry,' Emily said again.

Theodore tried to wriggle from Emily's grasp but she held onto him. 'You're not going anywhere, young man,' she said.

That had been another of his lives used up, Theodore realised. He should really be more careful with them.

He then began his descent through the sediments of Viking York. There were wooden cups, knife handles and combs carved from antlers, a leather shoe, wooden panpipes, beads and rings made from amber and jet, metal pins and fish hooks, a silver brooch, a handful of silver coins, some showing Thor's hammer or Odin's raven; others dedicated to St Peter, patron of York's cathedral. Theodore sank deeper, travelling further back into his past.

He was trapped in a metal cage. The cage was in a darkened room, the curtains were never opened. He had been separated from his mother but still had some of his siblings for company. They were content to sleep most of the time, devour the food when placed in the corner and play among themselves. Theodore would stare out from the cage, between the thin metal bars. He wanted out. He knew there was more to life than this prison he was kept in.

Then one day the human came and carried the cage downstairs. There was a large dog in a cage at the foot of the stairs; Theodore's fur bristled. Then there was a room flooded with white light. The door to the cage was opened. Here was his chance.

He pushed past his siblings. He flung himself out into the world. Here I come! he thought, rolling across a soft carpet, before finding his paws. He heard the human's scolding voice. He began to run. In circles around the room, he ran. The door was closed so he carried on, circling the room. He didn't want to be put back in the cage. But there was no way out of this room.

After circling the room for some minutes he came to a panting halt. He lay on the carpet to get his breath back.

Then he heard a different voice. A different human.

'He's adorable,' a voice said. The voice was soft and kind.

He allowed the new human to approach him. He was ready to set off any second and begin his circling of the room again. But when a hand slipped beneath his stomach and another was placed on his back, he allowed the new human to pick him up.

'He's certainly a lively one,' the usual human said.

'Hello, little man,' the new human said.

Theodore pushed himself against this new human instinctively on hearing the voice.

'Can I take him home today?' the new human said.

Theodore looked up at her face. It was Emily's face. He purred with happiness. He knew he was getting out. He knew he had found his life partner.

Where was Emily? Theodore wondered. She was the only one who could save him. Down and down he went. He had taken his last breath several seconds before. He sank deeper.

Roman times were represented in the muddy bottom of the Ouse by a silver denarius embossed with the head of Emperor Septimus Severus, a bronze helmet that had once belonged to a Roman legionnaire killed in a gladiatorial battle with a lion, a gold earring missing its partner, a fragment of an amphora bearing part of a human face. Then there were seeds and fruit stones: all that remained of the foods that had been brought from the Mediterranean to feed the Romans resident in Eboracum, their name for modern-day York.

Theodore sank deeper into the muddy bottom of the Ouse and further back into time. He was near the end of his journey. His thoughts were of his earliest memories.

He was beside his brothers and sisters, the siblings he would know only for a few weeks. They snuggled together against the warmth of their mother, vying for position against her furry body, trying to get at the soft nubs that gave them liquid life.

He felt a peace begin to consume him as he drank of his mother. He breathed in the scent of his family. A calmness transcended. Life was but a struggle. Peace was found in death.

He realised that this was not another one of his lost lives playing out in his head. He had returned to the beginning of his life, to the very start of his existence. It could only mean one thing.

Then came a familiar voice: *You should never have left me. You should have stayed at home where it was safe. Now you will visit the Great Cat Basket in the sky. There can be no return from the heavenly bed. You will be watched over by Bastet. You will sleep the longest of naps. That's right: this is the Long Nap, from which there is no return. The Long Nap will give you the peace that you did not find in life.*

But before Theodore could give in entirely to the serenity of death and the voice of the cat basket, he was yanked upwards, up through two thousand years of history.

10

A short distance beyond the Blue Bridge, there is a well, known as the Pikeing Well. Over the well, there is a building called the Well House.

The Pikeing Well and the Well House were built in the eighteenth century for promenaders along the then fashionable New Walk. The water was said to possess medicinal properties, so many would come and drink it and even wash their eyes with it.

It wasn't until 1929 that they realised that the water was poisonous and the Ministry of Health declared it unfit for human consumption. Following this announcement, the well was neglected and abandoned until its restoration in recent years.

Theodore felt his senses begin to return. He didn't know where he was. He only knew he was not in the river. He was not drowned. He was alive. There goes another life, he thought. I really need to be more careful with them. Bastet can only allow nine lives per cat, which is plenty more than what humans are allowed.

Then he heard a voice.

'Ding, dong, dell,' it sang. 'Pussy's in the well.'

Theodore opened an eye.

'Who put her in?'

There was Milton Macavity squatting in front of him. 'Little Tommy Thin,' he sang.

His knees were pulled up below his chin.

'Who pulled her out?'

He stared past Theodore, at the stone wall that surrounded them both.

'Little Johnny Stout.'

He was hugging himself to try to keep warm.

'What a naughty boy was that,' he sang in a high, broken voice, 'to drown the poor, poor pussy-cat...'

He twitched and blinked. 'Who never did him any harm... But killed the mice... in his father's barn.'

Milton jerked his head up, returning to the moment. He noticed that the cat had come to its senses. It backed away from him against the opposite wall of the Well House.

'I saved you, little pussy cat,' he said. 'You would've drowned if it weren't for me. I pulled you out. Are you not going to say thank you to your Johnny Stout?'

Milton's whole body was shaking from cold. At least he had found temporary shelter, in this old well.

In the debris on the floor of the well, he spied an old box of matches. There were also some cigarette ends. Kids, he thought.

He then remembered a short story his teacher had read to the class when he was at school.

It was set on the Yukon trail. A man walked alone to join his camp. It was so cold his spit crackled before it met the ground.

Bad luck struck when his feet smashed through a skin of ice, into the freezing water below. If the man didn't light a fire, he would die.

So the man gathered twigs and moss and managed to light a fire using matches and a scrap of birch from his pocket. But he built the fire beneath the boughs of an overhanging spruce tree and his actions caused the snow to cascade from the boughs and the fire to be extinguished. The man desperately tried to light another fire, but his fingers were too numb, and he dropped his matches into the snow. He lost the ability to move his fingers but he managed to light the whole bunch of matches. Ultimately his final attempt at a fire failed. He ran along the trail on frozen feet in desperation. He collapsed into the snow. Finally he succumbed to the cold and died, out there in the vast snowy whiteness.

As the teacher read the story, it was as though the temperature in the classroom had dropped.

Milton felt a shiver run through him and the hairs on his bare arms stood erect. He looked out of the classroom window. It had begun to snow outside, and it was only the beginning of November.

Now, that's a writer, the young Milton had thought: a writer who could make it snow.

He couldn't remember the writer's name. Jack or John Somebody. Johnny Stout? No, that was something else. He glanced over at the sodden grey cat he had pulled from the Ouse.

He needed to get warm and dry out his clothes. He looked at the discarded box of matches. He glanced around the well house. There was dried moss on the walls, and twigs and leaves that had found their way in to this gated cave of stone.

'I'll light a fire,' he said. 'That'll keep us warm!'

He grinned at his companion.

Theodore agreed that it was a good idea with a raspy miaow of approval from his side of the well.

But what if Milton was planning on cooking him? If he had missed his morning porridge, he would be starving by now.

You're going to be barbequed, came the voice of the cat basket. *Roasted on a spit over a campfire. That's what comes of your getting involved in human affairs. You must learn to let them do what they do.*

Theodore looked outside. He heard fireworks in the distance. The skies were already beginning to darken. He got to his paws and made for the entrance of the Well House.

'Do you not want to get warm?'

Theodore turned. Milton had gathered up the materials with which to build a fire and placed them within a square hollow in the middle of the Well House.

Milton placed a lit match at the base of the fire and within seconds it had taken hold. 'Well, that was easier than in that story,' he said. 'We'll soon be nice and warm... And then, as soon as darkness falls, I'll be on my way. I'm on a bit of a mission, you see.'

Theodore looked at Milton with apprehension; then inched closer to the fire. He could feel its warmth on his fur. Through the flames, he eyed Milton cautiously.

Milton noticed his nervous stare. 'You got me wrong, little pussy cat,' he said. 'I'm not really a bad sort. The press made me out to be much worse than I am. All that Napoleon of Crime business...'

Theodore widened his eyes. Oh, yes?

'Well, inside it worked to my advantage. The other inmates didn't bother me. They kept a bit of a distance. I guess I started to cultivate the image of a hard man so that the others would keep their distance.'

Theodore continued to stare at the convicted murderer.

'I'm not a bad sort really,' Milton said. 'I am just a victim of my environment.'

Theodore could understand that one's environment could affect one's behaviour and attitude to life. He had learned that from his few hours on the street.

'In prison, it was beat or be beaten,' Milton went on.

On the street, it was eat or be eaten, Theodore agreed with a slight nod of his head.

Milton removed his socks and shoes. He placed them close to the fire. He then removed Jonathan's black and red checked shirt, so that he wore only his prison-issue underpants. The pants were shapeless grey boxers, with the stains of a hundred other inmates of Full Sutton. Milton had never earned the privilege of wearing his own underpants while inside.

He then noticed a triangle of pink plastic poking out from beneath a heap of leaves.

'Now, what do we have here?' he said.

He picked up the pink corner and recovered a half-eaten bag of marshmallows.

'Well, that's a bit of luck,' he said with a grin. 'Must have been the kids, hiding goodies...'

He grabbed a twig, broke it into two and speared two marsh-mallows.

Theodore stared at the grinning pink man with ginger stubble on his head and chin, squatting over the camp fire in just his prison-issue underpants, toasting pink and white marshmallows. When I woke up this morning, I never expected this, he thought to himself.

'There you go!' Milton said, tossing a toasted marshmallow towards him.

Theodore sniffed at the toasted sugary offering. Marshmallows were not near the top of his list of favourite foods, but it was energy. Energy that he had expended while on the trail and energy that he would need before the day was done. He wolfed down the sticky marshmallow.

Then he noticed the crescent moon of an appendix scar on Milton's lower abdomen. Milton followed the cat's stare.

'That's how I knew how to fake an appendicitis,' he said. 'Problem was, as soon as they saw the scar, they knew I had faked it. You only get one appendix, don't you? That's why I had to make a quick getaway from that hospital.'

Theodore narrowed his eyes. Probably not the greatest of criminal minds we are dealing with here.

'I should never have been put away in the first place,' Milton went on. 'I'm an innocent man.'

That's what they all say, Theodore thought, staring into the flames.

'The judge said it was "Joint Enterprise". That's what he called it.

'But I didn't intend to kill anyone. We just wanted his car. I wasn't even the one who was driving.

'He should have just let us take it. Instead of trying to stop us. Who would have thought he would try jumping onto the bonnet. It would have been insured...

'Well, I've cleaned up my act now. I got clean in prison. And I started studying a degree in law with the Open University... And I know I'm not guilty of murder. It was a robbery that went wrong. Manslaughter at the most. I didn't know he was going to try to stop us, did I?

'I didn't kill nobody.'

That's a double negative, Theodore thought; meaning you probably did.

Milton shook his head. 'That's the other thing about being inside,' he said and laughed. 'You end up talking to yourself!'

Theodore's mind was racing. All crime was the result of human weakness, he realised; human greed became human misery. Crime was the symptom of humanity. All humans were criminals...

I must be having a sugar rush, he thought.

'He doesn't look the sort to shop in Urban Outfitters,' Jonathan said.

Emily looked over and saw the middle-aged paunchy man in a pin-striped suit with a rucksack on his back enter the clothes shop on High Ousegate, which describes itself as a 'hip retailer for apparel and home décor'. 'Maybe he wants a new look,' she said.

'He'd be better off at M&S,' Jonathan said. 'People should dress their age...'

Emily's mobile phone beeped. She took it from her pocket. 'It's my dad,' she said. 'He never usually texts...'

'What's it say?'

'Just: "Might be worth checking the river. Theo might have fallen in".'

'The river? Is he drunk?'

'He can only just have got home,' Emily said. 'Maybe he has a hunch about Theodore.'

'Oh, come on. A hunch? You want us to go and search the River Ouse for your cat? He's probably back at home by now. On our bed...'

'Maybe,' Emily said. 'But I think we should split up. You go home and check if he's there and I'll keep looking in town. I might just have a walk down to the river. You never know.'

'What about Joseph?'

'He's going to have to stay with me, isn't he? He'll want a feed when he wakes up.'

'You're right,' Jonathan said. 'I'll head off back home.'

'Let me know if he's there,' Emily said. 'Or if he's not, for that matter.'

'Will do,' Jonathan said.

He noticed the worried expression in Emily's eyes. He gave her a hug. 'I'll see you soon,' he said. 'We will find him.'

'Yes,' Emily said. 'We will find him.'

Jonathan turned and began to walk the other way.

Emily put her mobile back in her pocket and pushed the pram past Fat Face, provider of 'casual clothing for an outdoor lifestyle' for people who don't like going outside very much.

Standing in front of her, there was a little man dressed as a fireman with lipstick marks stamped on his cheeks. He smiled at her as she pushed the pram past.

Ten minutes later, Miles Macavity exited Urban Outfitters.

Miles was wearing a black corduroy Sherpa jacket and black jeans that he had only just managed to squeeze into. Over his shoulder he carried the large blue rucksack.

Next he went into Lakeland ('kitchenware chain with innovative gadgets and cooking utensils, plus homewares and garden products'), bought a knife with an eight inch blade and tucked it into the side pocket of his rucksack.

11

Emily pushed the pram over the Blue Bridge, which connects St George's Field to New Walk at the confluence of the Ouse and the Foss rivers. There were two people wearing Guy Fawkes masks loitering in the middle of the bridge. It was late afternoon, the skies grey, overcast, the ground wet from the earlier rain.

Could Theodore really have ended up in the river?

She stared at the ground as she passed the two Guys on the bridge. Somebody had spray-painted 'Death to the Capitalist Pigs,' on the bridge's wooden deck in red paint.

Where did all this anger come from? Emily asked herself. The world's not perfect, she understood, but why were people so hostile to each other? It was like nobody could agree on anything anymore.

She stared at Joseph's innocent face, staring up at her from his pram. Noticing her gaze, he began to cry. His face turned a touch red and his eyebrows moved closer together.

Emily knew what it meant. He needed changing. Where am I supposed to change a baby round here?

She pushed the pram onto New Walk and looked to her right at the river.

Even if Theodore had somehow managed to get in the river, what were the chances that she would be able to spot him? Jonathan might have been right. Her dad had had two large glasses of wine with his lunch and probably another as soon as he got home.

Joseph's cries became more insistent.

'I know, I know,' Emily said.

But rather than turning round, she carried on, pushing the pram along the northern bank of the River Ouse.

She would find somewhere discrete where she could change Joseph. Then she would turn round and walk back to the city centre.

A firework went off in Rowntree Park on the opposite back. It screeched as it whizzed across the grey skies, bright green and then red. It exploded with a bang.

'You shut it!' Milton said, raising a warning hand at the cat. 'Don't you be giving us away now. Not after I saved you and then fed you marshmallows.'

Theodore had smelled Joseph. His nappy contents were like a fingerprint to his highly developed olfactory senses. Unfortunately the firework had masked his cry for help.

There were several repeated bangs from outside the well. Theodore's heart pounded in his chest. Bonfire Night was certainly not a night for a cat to be out. The smell of Joseph's nappy began to recede into the distance.

'If I get caught,' Milton said, 'something serious is going to go down tonight. That I am sure of. I'm the only one who can stop it.'

Theodore's eyes widened.

'It's my brother, Miles,' Milton said. 'He's planning on doing something, something big. Bonfire Night's going to end with a bang. That's what he said. I'm not a hundred percent sure what he's planning. But he told me that he was going to make a stand. Against the hypocrisy. Against the bullshit. Against the system that destroyed his career...

'That's why I had to get out of Full Sutton. They didn't believe me. The guards laughed at me when I tried to tell them. But I knew. You see, some spice head had had a mobile phone smuggled in... Flew it in by drone.

'I paid to borrow it. I phoned Miles and he told me. He knew I couldn't do anything about it. That just made him happier. "There's nothing you can do about it," he said, laughing down the phone at me.

'I knew I had to do something about it. You see, I'm not a bad guy. I've had my troubles. But I know right from wrong. Miles, on the other hand, is a deviant. He's malicious. What he has in mind could be anything. I know he means war though. War against the anti-establishment that destroyed his banking career.

'That's what he said to me. This is war. He's going to target the protest. The Million Mask March.'

Theodore stared into Milton's face. It was pink and stubbly. His eyes were ringed in grey. Was he telling the truth?

He's making it up, came the voice in his head. And besides, even if his brother Miles was planning some terrible atrocity, do you really think that you could stop him? You're just a big fluffy cat!

Outside the Well House, Theodore smelled Joseph returning, the smell still there but now only faint. She must have changed him, Theodore deduced. The nappy bagged and riding in the undercarriage of the pram.

He heard Emily call his name outside.

Just go to her and you'll be home in a matter of minutes. You could ride home with little Joey in the pram, nice and snug in there. You could have a nice snack of biscuits when you get in and then get warm by the radiator. I'm here waiting for you!

Theodore looked back into Milton's pink face. He made his decision.

There was truth in what Milton had told him. Why else would he have broken out of prison as he had and missed his breakfast? He would no doubt be caught sooner or later. He had broken out to stop his brother Miles committing whatever act of revenge he had come up with.

Emily pushed the pram back along New Walk towards the Blue Bridge. She had managed to find a secluded spot to change Joseph, who was now quite happily staring out of his pram at his surroundings; the dirty nappy tucked away in the bottom of the pram until they came across a bin. A firework exploded in the sky overhead and Joseph clapped his hands and laughed at the shooting colours in the darkening sky.

She carried on and as she approached the Blue Bridge, she saw two police officers on horseback.

As she drew near, one of them said, 'You haven't seen anything suspicious up there, have you?'

'No,' Emily said.

'You do know there's an escaped convict on the run?'

'Yes, I heard,' Emily said.

'It's best that you weren't out,' the police officer said. 'Especially by yourself... He could be anywhere.'

'I was looking for my cat.'

More fireworks went off from the opposite bank of the river.

'It's not a good night for a cat to be out,' the police officer said. 'It should be locked inside...'

'I could say the same for your escaped convict,' Emily said under her breath.

Joseph was staring up at the horses with wonder. Then another firework went off, a string of colours appearing in the darkening sky.

'Ohhhh,' Joseph said and clapped his hands together.

'You get yourselves home,' the police officer said to Emily. 'Your cat's probably there waiting for you.'

'I was thinking the same,' Emily said.

'And you haven't seen anything suspicious up there?'

Emily glanced back the way she had come.

'There was smoke,' she said, 'coming out of an old building, up there on the left.'

'How far?'

Emily gestured into the distance. 'Back there,' she said. 'Not far. Five minute walk at most.'

'We'd better check it out,' the police officer said, and the two mounted officers trotted past Emily and Joseph towards the Well House.

Theodore heard the clack of hooves approaching. He looked across at Milton, who was putting on his now dry clothes and shoes.

The fire had died down but wisps of smoke still curled from it and out through the entrance of the Well House.

He miaowed at Milton that the police were on their way and no doubt they would be interested in what was the cause of the smoke from this old well.

'You shut it,' Milton said. 'I've told you...'

But Theodore carried on miaowing, staring at the entrance to the Well House.

'Horses?' Milton said, hearing the clacking of hooves. 'Well, why didn't you say? I think it's time we made a move...'

Milton pulled on his shoes and got to his feet.

The horses were almost at the Well House.

Theodore realised that if they didn't make it out, Milton would be arrested with no chance to get away.

But then what about his brother Miles? Only Milton knew of his brother's intention to carry out some heinous event later that day. With Milton put back inside, there would be nobody to stop him. Theodore didn't know what Miles looked like. He had to make sure that Milton stayed free long enough to stop his brother.

Theodore could smell the musk of the horses as they neared. He slipped through the metal bars of the Well House gate. But it was too late.

The mounted police were upon them. In front of him there were two enormous beasts, their hooves capable of smashing the life out of him with one blow. Behind him he heard a rusty squeak as Milton swung open the metal gate, ready to make his escape.

Theodore raised his tail high. His fur stood on end, making him appear bigger than he was. He stared into the big dark brown eyes of the horse that loomed over him. He opened his mouth and hissed.

The horse looked down and noticed the small furry animal at her feet. Something inside her told her it would be a mistake to harm this creature that some humans took into their homes. The rider on her back urged her on, but he didn't know about the cat in front of her. So she reared up on her hind legs and whinnied.

The police officer was caught unaware and lost his balance, grabbing onto his colleague. They both fell to the ground.

Theodore looked on as the riderless horses whinnied excitedly and the riders began to get to their feet. I didn't know I had it in me, he thought.

'Quick,' Milton said. 'This is our chance.'

He slipped out of the Well House and darted back along the path. Theodore set off after him.

The police officer got up from the ground. 'Not sure what got into her,' Paul said, helping his colleague to her feet.

'Something must have spooked her,' Maria said grabbing the reins of her horse.

Wisps of smoke were still coming from the Well House.

'We'd better check out that building,' Maria said. 'It must have been what the woman with the pram was on about.'

She drew her horse over and peered inside.

'Anything in there?'

'There's a fire. An empty bag of sweets... Looks like they might be marshmallows. Some burnt sticks...'

'Sounds like kids,' Paul said. 'They must have scarpered when they heard us coming.'

'Here, hold this,' Maria said, handing her horse's reins to her colleague. 'There's something else...'

She stooped down and pulled open the metal grill.

'What is it?' Paul said.

'Only one of those Guy Fawkes masks. One of those that the protesters are all wearing.'

'There's going to be trouble tonight; I can feel it in my bones.'

'They've bussed up a thousand of them from London to cause trouble. Anarchists. Radicalists. Animal rights activists, badger baiters, Radiohead fans... You name it. We've got it coming.'

'We've got twenty extra officers from Leeds, mainly PCSOs. It's a bloody joke. If it kicks off, how are we going to cope?'

'And on top of everything, we have an escaped convict on the loose...'

'I did hear that if things get out of hand, they are going to issue us with Heckler and Koch water blasters.'

'I've always wanted to have a go with one of them. Wash the grins off their faces!'

'Well, let's hope it doesn't come to that.'

Maria shook her head. 'I say we get them all in a narrow street like the Shambles and teapot them.'

'You mean 'kettle' them, don't you?'

'Isn't that what I said? Kettling... Tea-potting... Tea-bagging... Aren't they the same thing?'

'I think tea-bagging might have another meaning,' Paul said. 'Are you sure you didn't bang your head when you fell?'

Maria raised a hand to her helmet. 'I don't think so.'

'All this talk of teapots and kettles, how about we have a nice cup of tea,' Paul said. 'I brought my flask. A cup of Yorkshire Tea and you'll feel right as rain again.'

'A proper brew,' Maria said. 'Now you're talking!'

'I double-bagged it,' Paul said, getting out his flask.

'Well, better to be safe than sorry.'

'I meant my flask,' Paul said. 'I put two teabags in it.'

'Sorry,' Maria said, 'I thought you were talking about something else.'

12

The Kings Arms on King's Staith is a public house famous for flooding. Whenever York floods, which is quite regularly, library images of the pub are shown on the television news. But the pub located next to Ouse Bridge is well prepared for such flood events.

It has been well and truly flood-proofed. Electric points are at least four feet off the ground. Soft furnishings and furniture can be quickly removed to higher ground, to be returned once flood levels go down.

However, as the pub is so famous for being flooded, tourists expect it to be flooded all year round. They arrive with their wellies on, and the pub does not disappoint. The pub now retains the floodwater year round, so customers have to wade to the bar.

Theodore peered through the window from the stone windowsill. Milton was standing beside him, also looking in. There were several regulars sitting on bar stools, their boots dangling in the black water that stood two feet above the floor. Tourists and out-of-towners had also come prepared, wearing waders and waterproofs, taking photographs of themselves with their feet below water. Sodden beermats floated on the water's surface. In the corner by the door, there was a flood marker, showing the highest levels the floodwaters had reached.

2000 had been a particularly good year, Theodore noted. If you were into flooding, which he certainly wasn't.

A customer at the bar, his back to them, ordered a pint of bitter and the landlord went to pour it. But the barrel was almost empty and the glass was left with just an inch of foam in it.

'Can you go down and change the barrel?' the landlord said to the barman.

The barman looked up from his book. 'I'm reading,' he said.

'That's not a book,' the landlord said. 'That's a comic.' He laughed.

'It's not a comic,' the barman said. 'It's a graphic novel.'

'It's got pictures in it. Therefore it's a comic. Now go and change the barrel.'

The barman snapped his book closed. Theodore noted the Guy Fawkes mask on the cover.

The barman put on a diver's mask and tanks on his back. He opened a trapdoor in the floor. Then he dropped down to the flooded cellar to change the barrel.

The customer at the bar, who had ordered the pint of bitter, held up something brown between his thumb and forefinger. 'I have a pig's nipple in my pork scratchings,' he said.

'Not so loud,' the landlord said with a laugh, 'everyone will want one.'

'It's not a laughing matter,' the man said. 'I paid 79p for them.'

'There's probably a phone number on the back of the packet,' the landlord said. 'If you want to complain, complain to them...'

'I might do just that,' the man said.

He had a rucksack perched on the barstool next to him. He unzipped a side pocket and removed a mobile phone. He scrutinised the back of the packet of pork scratchings and then tapped a phone number into his mobile.

He swivelled round on his stool and placed the mobile to his ear.

'It's Miles!' Milton said. 'What a stroke of luck!'

Theodore stared at the man with the phone.

'I have a pig's nipple in my pork scratchings,' the man said into his mobile phone.

He remembered the man with the rucksack from outside the Yummy Fried Chicken, the litter lout. So that was Miles, Milton's older brother. The one who might be plotting some terrible event for this evening.

'It's not a laughing matter,' Miles said. 'I paid 79p for them.'

Milton was already making his way to the front door. Theodore jumped down and followed Milton.

On the door of the pub was a sign that read, 'Don't Open this Door! Use Side Door!'

But Milton didn't read the sign. He opened the door and the floodwater poured out onto King's Staith to be reunited with the Ouse.

Theodore braced himself as a tidal wave of black water passed over him. When he opened his eyes, he spied Milton standing in the entrance to the pub, his trousers drenched from the waist down.

'Look what you've gone and done!' the landlord shouted. 'You've only gone and let the floodwater out...'

Milton ignored the landlord. 'You!' he shouted across the bar room at Miles.

Miles, recognising his brother, smiled to himself. Then he slipped his mobile phone into his jeans, grabbed his rucksack and made for the side entrance.

Milton was straight after him.

'Not so fast!' the landlord shouted, his hand on Milton's shoulder.

Milton spun round and hit the landlord across the head with his fist.

The landlord went down and hit the wet floor.

The barman stuck his head up out of the trapdoor, removed his breathing apparatus and said, 'the water's going down.'

Theodore looked him in the face, eye to eye. You don't say.

'Did you not lock the front door?' the landlord shouted, still lying on the floor. 'I've told you a thousand times. The front door must always be kept locked... Otherwise something like this will happen!'

Then Miles slipped out of the side door, Milton close behind him.

As the barman struggled up through the trapdoor, Theodore noticed something small and brown on the stone floor on front of him. It was the sodden, deep-fried pig's nipple. Theodore wondered for a second whether to eat it or not. He decided not.

Outside he heard footfalls on cobblestones passing by the front entrance of the pub.

He glanced again at the pig's nipple and then made for the door.

As he exited onto King's Staith, he turned to see Miles taking the steps up to Low Ousegate, two at a time.

Milton was not far behind. But on reaching the bottom of the steps he stopped.

Theodore looked back up at Miles. Miles slowed down as he passed between two police officers standing at the top of the steps. Then he disappeared into the crowd, many of whom were wearing Guy Fawkes masks.

Milton turned away. He met Theodore's questioning gaze. Then he held his hands up to his face. He had left his Guy Fawkes mask behind, Theodore realised; back in the Well House. The police would no doubt recognise the escaped convict. Milton could not continue the pursuit. The police would recognise him and arrest him again. He would be back at Full Sutton by nightfall.

Milton turned and retreated towards Theodore, a look of hopelessness in his eyes.

Theodore walked forwards to meet Milton. When they were a couple of feet apart, Theodore sidestepped him and continued towards the steps.

He knew what Miles looked like. If Milton could not follow him and stop his brother's Bonfire Night Plot, it was down to him.

Don't do it, came the voice of the cat basket. *You have no idea what you're getting yourself caught up in. Miles is probably just going to let some fireworks off... You should keep out of it and come home now. Bonfire Night is not a night for pets to be out. It's a night to stay at home and be glad you're not outside...*

Do be quiet, thought Theodore. I'm not afraid to stand up to tyranny. If somebody has to, then let it be me.

His tail held aloft, though sodden and bedraggled, he made his way across the wet cobbles towards the stone steps.

13

As you may know, the collective term for buskers is a cacophony. In recent years a cacophony of buskers has descended on Coney Street, many of them with very little talent. Some of them have also brought amplifiers in order to compete sonically with their neighbours and amplify their lack of talent.

As Miles passed the Spurriergate centre, he noticed the old guy on the stool with his guitar. He hadn't seen him for maybe twenty years. Back then he had two Border Collies; they would whine and howl at appropriate parts of the song. He used to have a blow-up doll dressed up in ladies clothes beside him. His little entourage had a name too. On a rectangle of cardboard, he had printed Heartbreak Candy.

'More like Deadbeat Shandy,' his father had muttered as they passed by one day.

The teenage Miles had paused to watch the performance. The busker had been playing How Much Is That Doggy in the Window, and after every time he sang the title, the two dogs would begin whining and barking. Miles thought it very clever. He had a fifty pence piece, his weekly pocket money, in his trouser pocket. He reached in and withdrew the coin.

The busker finished the song and people approached and threw coins into the guitar case on the ground. Miles looked at the coin in his hand and then at the guitar case. Then he felt his father's hand on his shoulder.

'Don't you be giving your money away,' his father Maxwell said.

Miles looked up at Maxwell.

'You go giving it away,' Maxwell said, 'and you'll never have any. It doesn't grow on trees.'

Miles nodded and slipped the coin back into his pocket.

Over forty years later, the middle-aged Miles noticed that the busker no longer had the dogs or the doll. He no longer had the Heartbreak Candy sign. His band was no more. There was just a man struggling to be heard above the noise of the rival buskers.

He was playing The Man Who Sold the World, the Bowie song that Nirvana had nailed, many, many years ago. Both Bowie and Kurt Cobain were dead, Miles thought, but this busker, who had been or he had supposed had been old when he was just a boy, was still alive. In fact the old busker didn't look any older than he did forty years ago. How did that work? Miles wondered.

Miles stopped in front of the busker, thinking about aging and death. He didn't notice the grey cat that had darted into the doorway behind the busker.

Theodore stared across at Miles. He noticed that Miles was mouthing along to the song, deep in thought. When the song ended, he reached into his pocket and plucked out a silver coin. He approached the busker and dropped the 50 pence coin into the guitar case. He turned and walked away.

Theodore followed.

Further down Coney Street, there was a Tina Turner tribute act. She was singing along to Private Dancer. Miles didn't stop and give her any money. She wasn't even singing in tune.

Then there was a group of students, playing to a large crowd. They even had a drum kit set up in the street. They were playing Don't Look Back in Anger, as Miles walked past.

'Don't look on with languor...' Theodore thought he heard him say.

Miles paused in front of the Starbucks on the corner of Coney Street and New Street.

This building used to be a branch of the National Westminster Bank. It was where his father Maxwell had begun his career, aged 16, as a clerk; before he had departed for London and a career in investment banking; a career that Miles would also pursue.

On the building's corner, there was still the moulded, red and gold painted shield of arms, with two boars standing on either side of a shield bearing a further three boars' heads and the motto PRODESSE CIVIBUS. Maxwell had told Miles that the boars symbolised hospitality and the motto meant 'to benefit the citizens'.

His father had evidently been misguided. Boars were far from hospitable, from what Miles knew about them, and banks were not set up to benefit the citizens; they were created to benefit the bankers.

He glanced at St Martin's clock, which overhangs Coney Street; the Little Admiral standing on top, pointing his strange instrument at the sky. It was almost five o'clock. It was time he had tea.

As he turned right into St Helen's Square, he was almost run over by a pram.

'Hey!' he shouted at the young mum. 'Watch where you're going!'

He stepped around the pram and carried on his way with an angry shake of his head.

Emily stood and let the crowd pass around her. What was it they said about never feeling more alone than when in a crowd?

Then baby Joseph began to gripe. She was going to have to find somewhere to feed him.

She took her mobile phone from her coat pocket. She had a new message. She opened it.

'Theo not here,' Jonathan had texted. 'Have you had any luck?'

She messaged back. 'No. Nothing. I am really worried now.'

Before she could put her mobile away, Jonathan messaged back. 'Come home.'

'But what about Theo?'

'He'll come back when he's ready.'

'He's probably terrified. I can't believe he's disappeared on Bonfire Night.'

'He'll be hiding somewhere... I think you should come home now. It's getting dark.'

'I can't,' Emily texted back. 'Not until I find Theo.'

Then she put her mobile back in her pocket.

Joseph looked at her and sucked his thumb and Emily knew that she would have to find somewhere to feed him.

Theodore had lost Miles in the crowded street. He took refuge in the doorway of an empty shop. He stared out at the passing people, trying to locate the man with the rucksack.

Then he heard a whisper above the noise of the crowd. 'That way,' it murmured. 'He went that way.'

Theodore looked across the street. On the second floor windowsill of the building facing him there was a sculpture of a black cat.

The cat had been installed on the windowsill by York architect Tom Adams in 1979. In the same way that Leonardo da Vinci signed his sketches with a mouse, Tom Adams bestowed a cat upon the buildings he worked on. These days there are many Tom Adams cats adorning the city's buildings and more erected after his death in 2006 by others wanting to carry on the tradition.

'He went that way,' the cat murmured to Theodore, flicking its tail further down Coney Street.

Theodore blinked his eyes in disbelief; there is a lot I do not understand about this world, he thought.

He emerged from the doorway and carried on down the street in the direction that the stone cat had flicked its tail.

Up ahead he spotted Emily pushing Joseph in his pram. Her face was creased with worry. Her eyes darted from left to right but she failed to see him. He stopped in his tracks. He watched as she passed by. He turned round and watched as she disappeared among the crowd. He had to carry on the pursuit. He turned and made his way into St Helen's Square.

Another busking band was playing and a large crowd had formed, many of whom were wearing Guy Fawkes masks, others were wearing cow or badger masks.

He tried to navigate a way through the hundreds of feet. A cigarette end landed in front of him and he darted to the side, narrowly avoiding the smouldering butt. A toddler in red wellies spotted him and made towards him stamping his little feet. Fortunately he was reined in before he could stomp on Theodore.

Theodore closed his eyes a moment. He wished for an empty bedroom. A windowsill in the sunshine. A laundry basket of newly-dried and folded clothes, preferably woollens. He wished for his cat basket by the radiator in the kitchen of his home. He wished he was far from this madding crowd.

I told you so, the voice of the cat basket said. *You should never have left the safety of home. What did you hope to achieve? The humans will always wreak havoc upon the outside world. They cannot be stopped.*

The humans will eventually destroy themselves by their selfish and destructive nature. But until that day comes, you must wait. You must wait patiently until you hear the call.

Theodore opened his eyes, only to see a large burgundy Dr Marten's boot about to come down on his head. He dashed to the right but the boot landed on his tail. He cried out in pain: Bastet!

He took refuge in the doorway of the Edinburgh Woollen Mill, beneath a rack of woolly jumpers. He took the opportunity to examine his tail. It was kinked. His wonderful tail was deformed; he would never be able to hold it up with pride again.

He peered back at the crowded square. He needed to get back out there or he would lose Miles. He crossed the shop entrance and hugged the side of Bettys. There was a queue that snaked around the corner. He watched as Miles walked past the queue. He darted after him. Between the shoes and boots he ran. He was closing in on him.

Then he stopped. Miles had entered Bettys Café Tea Rooms.

14

Milton walked down High Ousegate and stopped in front of a stall that had been set up in front of the Spurriergate Centre. The stall sold cheap plastic Guy Fawkes masks, aimed at those attending the march that evening. The plastic mask had become an icon of popular culture, used to protest around the world against tyranny and the status quo. Cashing in on anticapitalism, Milton thought with a sneer.

He asked how much the masks were.

Five pounds, he was told by the Chinese man. They probably cost five pence to produce in China, Milton thought, remembering he didn't have any money.

A teenager approached and also asked how much the masks were. As he was rummaging in his coat pockets, Milton snatched one of the masks and began to make his way into the crowded street. But he'd been spotted.

'Tony!' a Chinese woman shrieked. 'He's taken one without paying...'

Milton heard footsteps behind him. He turned and raised his fist.

Tony came to a halt in front of the raised fist. He had only paid fifty pounds for a thousand masks. Five pence each. He had taken over five hundred pounds already and sales were increasing as the day went on and the streets became more crowded. He looked at the clenched fist held inches in front of his face.

Then he heard his wife Sue yell from behind him, 'Get it off him! He is a thief!'

Tony thought of the bills he had to pay. His daughters were at the Mount School. Not only had he the school fees to pay but also the costs for boarding. Then there would be their university fees to come. It was not easy having girls at the Mount School.

'Police! Police!' Sue screamed from behind him.

Tony felt a bead of sweat trickle down his face. Was it worth being hit in the face over five pounds? He took a step backwards, away from the man with the clenched fist and troubled stare.

'Take it,' Tony said. 'Please just take the mask.'

Milton lowered his fist. He turned and walked away, pulling the Guy Fawkes mask over his face.

Sue screamed, 'Don't let him get away! Police! Police!'

'Let it go,' Tony said. 'We have plenty more.'

'That's not the point,' Sue snapped. 'It's the principle. Whatever would the twins think if they knew what you were really like? Weak! That's what you are! Weak! Weak! Weak!'

'That's enough, Sue,' Tony said, walking back to his makeshift stall, where a queue of people had begun to form. 'Enough...'

The streets were crowded but Milton knew that Miles was carrying a large rucksack. He couldn't be hard to spot in the crowd.

He noticed that British Home Stores had closed down. An Eastern European man was squatting down in front of the empty shop. He had created a dog out of sand. Milton was impressed.

This young man had taken a bag of sand and with only a little knife he had created a sculpture of a labrador. What skill and talent had gone into that? The young man was making the final touches to the dog's head, absorbed in his task, a little pile of sand in front of him.

Milton reached into his pocket but remembered he had no money.

The young man looked up at him. He tilted his head at the little basket next to him that was half full of coins. His eyes were full of hope.

Milton raised his palms. He would have liked to help this young man who had such great talent. Such potential! No doubt he would go on to succeed in life. A life in which he had so terribly failed.

The young man, understanding that Milton wasn't going to give him any money, turned away and carried on with his monumental work.

Milton turned away, an ache in his heart.

He turned right into New Street, then up Davygate towards Parliament Street.

By the side of the disabled toilet in St Sampson's Square, he noticed another sculpture of a dog created out of sand. That's some coincidence, he thought, approaching the young man.

The sculpture was again of a Labrador, identical to the one he had seen on Coney Street.

Then it dawned on him. The sculptures were not the hand of the young men. They probably were plastic shells with a coating of sand stuck on. It was a con and he had been fooled.

He looked at the little basket of coins by the man's side. 'You're a fraud,' he said.

The young man, who had been pretending to make some final touches to the dog's face, turned. 'Excuse me?'

'This,' Milton said, tapping the dog with the toe of his shoe, 'is a fraud.'

'I not understand you.'

'You did not make this,' Milton said. He tapped the sand dog again with his foot, so that it moved two inches. 'You are a fraud!'

'Please, no!'

'It's a con!' Milton said.

He looked at the people around him. They were staring at him.

'Don't you understand? He hasn't made this. He's conning you. He's a fraud!'

A middle-aged man tutted, dropped a pound coin in the basket of coins and walked away.

Probably a Liberal, Milton thought. He shook his head. 'Don't you understand? It's all a con. The sand dogs aren't real!'

He raised his foot and brought it down on the sand dog. The plastic shell crumpled beneath his foot. 'See! I told you...'

'You are an ass hole man,' the young man said, a tremor in his voice. He got to his feet and faced Milton.

Milton pushed his Guy Fawkes mask to the top of his head. 'And you are a liar and a cheat.'

Milton assessed his opponent. Although skinny, he was taller, younger and fitter than he was. Maybe he shouldn't have picked a fight with this guy.

Then he heard a voice to his right. 'It's him,' a woman's voice said. 'The escaped convict...'

'You sure?' a man's voice said.

'Yes, I'm sure. I remember his face off the telly. And he's wearing the clothes they said on the radio. A red and black checked shirt. I remember.'

Milton turned to face them.

'It is him! Milton Macavity!' the woman shrieked. 'Police!'

Milton felt a hundred eyes upon him. He turned and began to run through the crowd.

Back at home, Jonathan stood at the back door, a box of cat biscuits in his hand. He shook the box, so that the biscuits rattled inside.

'Theo! Theo!' he called.

But Theodore didn't come.

He walked across the kitchen and peered inside the cat basket for the twentieth time. 'The Cat Cave,' he liked to call it. One of Emily's old jumpers was laid in the bottom, coated with grey fur. He wondered if Theodore would ever find his way back to it.

He went again to the backdoor and opened it. He stepped outside and surveyed the yard.

He noticed the clothesline. Emily should have hung the clothes in front of the radiator. They were as wet as when she had hung them out, several hours ago.

Then he noted that there were gaps on the clothesline... Gaps where his shirt and jeans had been.

Jonathan remembered Theodore miaowing at the transparent cat flap while he watched the news. That was when there was the newsflash that Milton Macavity had escaped from custody while at York Hospital.

He then noticed the green smock that lay discarded in a heap.

'Theo,' he said, shaking his head. 'What have you got yourself mixed up in now?'

He knew he would have to return to town to continue the search.

His denim jacket was soaked through. He took it off and hung it over the kitchen radiator to dry. On his way out, he grabbed his corduroy jacket from the coat stand and then headed back into town.

15

Emily had managed to find a table in the Spurriergate Centre, where she could feed Joseph. In his highchair, he played with his plastic spoon, flicking pureed parsnip at passers-by while Emily tapped away on her phone.

She requested to join a Facebook group called 'Pets – Lost & Found – York-UK'. Seconds later she was accepted. She selected a recent photograph of Theodore and then wrote, 'This is Theodore.' Her eyes became blurry and she had to stop herself from crying. 'He's been missing since this morning,' she wrote. 'Haxby Road area. I'm so worried as it's Bonfire Night and he's out here somewhere...'

Joseph gurgled. She looked over and watched as a bubble of pureed parsnip appeared at the side of his mouth, only to pop a second later.

'If anyone sees him, let me know,' she typed and then posted it.

Seconds later her post had been shared several times by good-natured strangers.

Then a message arrived from Jonathan. 'I'm coming back into town,' he wrote, 'to help look for Theo.'

'I'm at the Spurriergate Centre,' Emily texted back.

'Stay there. I'll be with you in twenty mins.'

Emily returned to Facebook. She found another group. This one was called 'York C.R.U.D. – Cat Rescuers UniteD'. She requested to join this group too though it didn't sound as good.

Then she got a comment back from her first post.

'I saw a cat like this by Monk Bar. A homeless guy had him tied to a bit of string. He said it was called Smoky.'

Then someone else commented. 'I saw them too. He was begging for cat food. That's what the sign said.'

'I saw them in the Tesco on Goodramgate. The homeless guy was buying cider.'

'I know that guy. He drinks in the little churchyard off Goodramgate... Behind the Happy Valley Chinese restaurant. He's a proper piss head.'

The homeless guy on the bench, Emily thought. He must have taken Theodore and used him for begging. She swore under her breath; then she called her dad.

Patrick put his mobile on the kitchen side and took a bottle of Chablis from the wine rack. He poured himself a large glass. He then went into the den, where Oliver was sitting on the sofa, wearing Patrick's second-best dressing gown. A mug of tea on the coffee table in front of him.

Oliver's face lit up when he saw Patrick holding the glass of wine. 'Can I have a glass?' he asked.

'No,' Patrick said and took a large gulp of wine.

'But that's not fair,' Oliver said.

'Life's not fair, Oliver,' Patrick said gravely. And then, 'Did you take my daughter's cat?'

'Cat?' Oliver scratched at his head. His hair was still wet from the bath Patrick had run for him. 'I didn't steal any cat.'

'People saw you with him, Oliver. You were out begging with my daughter's cat.'

'That cat? It was your daughter's? I had no idea... I just borrowed him for a couple of hours.'

'Yes, it was my daughter's cat... And she is now frantic with worry. Now tell me: when and where did you last see the cat.'

'In the churchyard where you found me. It got away from me and ran off.'

'And that was the last time you saw him?'

'Yes, that's right. Now how about that glass of wine? I've told you all I know.'

'You are not allowed any wine,' Patrick said sternly. 'I have made you a mug of Taylor's finest Yorkshire Tea. From now on, you will drink only tea. You are teetotal while you are in this house. If you relapse, you will be out. Back on the streets. Do you understand me?'

'Yes,' Oliver said. 'I understand.'

Patrick put his half-empty glass of wine down on the coffee table. 'I have given you a great opportunity... don't forget it. This could be the beginning of the rest of your life. If you want it to be...'

Oliver nodded, staring at the cream pile of the carpet.

'Now, I am going to call my daughter and let her know what you have told me.'

Patrick turned and left the den.

Back in the kitchen, he called Emily's mobile. 'It was Theodore,' he said. 'Oliver borrowed him for a couple of hours for financial gain. Theo managed to escape from him.'

'Does he know where he is now?' Emily asked.

'Last time Oliver saw him was back in the churchyard.'

'Jonathan's on his way back,' Emily said. 'We are going to keep searching for him... He's still in the city centre, I know it. I'm not going home till I find him.'

'Tell her she needs to get herself and Joseph back home,' Trish said. 'Theo will find his own way home. There's trouble brewing in York.'

'Your mum says...' Patrick began.

'I heard,' Emily said.

She heard the chinking of pots in the sink; then her mother in the background saying, 'All this fuss over a cat.'

She could picture the scene. Her mother standing in front of the kitchen sink, her apron spotless as she did the washing up. Her father standing by the Welsh dresser, mobile phone in hand. Bess, the border collie, lying in her basket. It was the perfect world she had grown up in. She raised her hand to her head. She felt something wet. It was parsnip, beginning to harden in her hair. She looked at Joseph. He was splatting his food with his hands on the plastic tray in front of him and grinning like a little demon. Her world was so less than perfect.

Her dad was saying, 'He'll turn up. I know he will,' in an attempt to reassure her.

'I know,' she said. 'I have to go now.'

She hung up and started to cry.

Back in the Patrick's den, Oliver stared at the glass of wine that Patrick had left on the coffee table. He picked it up and took a tiny sip. Then another sip. Then a gulp. Then it was empty.

16

Frederick (Dickie) Belmont, a Swiss confectioner in search of his fortune, arrived at King's Cross railway station in London and accidently got onto a Yorkshire-bound train. He never looked back.

It wasn't long before Dickie opened his first Bettys Café in Harrogate in 1919. Why it was called Bettys, nobody knows for sure. But one story has it that during a meeting by the directors to discuss the choice of names, a child accidently wandered in. When asked her name, she said Betty. "That'll do,' Frederick said.

By 1927 afternoon tea was being served and ten years later Frederick opened the famous Bettys Café Tea Rooms on St Helen's Square in York. The interiors of Bettys were inspired by the rooms of the Queen Mary ocean liner; Frederick and his wife Claire had been on the Maiden Voyage the previous year. If you like wood panelling, it's the place to go.

These days tourists queue round the corner in all weathers to have the Bettys experience. Miles strode past the queue and into the shop.

He glanced at the counters. They were selling off Halloween stock: gingerbread bats, ghost-shaped lebkuchen and chocolate pumpkins. He spotted a basket of Fat Rascals. He used to like them when he was a kid.

He took his rucksack off and held it by the handle at the top. He looked back at the queue that snaked out of the door. He strode over and pushed his way in near to the front.

'Excuse me!' an old man said. 'There is a queue.'

Miles glared at him. 'I know. I'm in it, aren't I?'

A woman tugged at the man's coat sleeve. 'Don't make a fuss,' she hissed.

Theodore navigated the many pairs of feet. He made it into the shop part of Bettys without being seen. He saw Miles being led to a table inside the tea rooms. He would have to follow. He kept close to the wall.

He could see dozens of tables, all covered with bright white table cloths that reached almost to the floor. If he could make it inside, he could hide below the tables and make his way from table to table until he located Miles. Then he could find out what was in the rucksack.

He chose his moment. Any moment was as good as any other, wasn't it? He sprinted past the queue and into the tea rooms, making his way to the nearest table.

He made it below the table and was met by a pair of shiny red shoes. There was no commotion. He had done it. Now he just had to locate Miles and his rucksack.

He remembered that Miles was wearing shiny back slip-ons with silver buckles. He peered out at the nearby tables. He would have to make his way to the next table.

Again he chose his moment and dashed below another table. This one had several pairs of shoes but the men's shoes were all lace-ups.

A waitress went over to the duty manager. 'I think there's a cat under table 47,' she said.

'A cat? In the tea rooms?'

'Yes, I saw it. It dashed from table 14 to table 47. I don't think anyone else saw it.'

'But how did it get in?'

'I don't know.'

'We need to get it out,' the duty manager said. 'Before someone notices it. Leave it to me.'

The duty manager approached table 47. 'Is everything satisfactory?' she said, stooping and tilting her head to try and see under the table.

Theodore positioned himself in the centre of the table.

'Could we see the desserts' trolley,' a voice said.

'Yes, of course,' another voice said. 'I'll have it sent over straight away.'

Miles was sitting by the rain-specked window. He hadn't been in Bettys for over twenty years. Then he had been with his brother Milton and his father Maxwell. It was the lunch that had decided their fates.

Memories slowly surfaced.

He had ordered the chicken schnitzel. He always ordered the chicken schnitzel when he had dinner with his father Maxwell and his younger brother Milton on the first Sunday of each month. That was how often he saw his father. Once a month. Twelve times a year.

That day, they all had ordered the chicken schnitzel. When the waiter had brought out the three plates, one cradled into his elbow, he had dropped Milton's. The chicken schnitzel ended up on the floor, cheesy side down. Milton looked down at it, a lump in his throat. The waiter promised to return shortly with a new one.

'Well, there's no point in letting ours go cold,' Maxwell said and proceeded to tuck in.

Miles did likewise and they had both almost finished their meals before a replacement chicken schnitzel could be brought for Milton.

Miles realised that Milton, ever the sensitive one, looked like he was about to cry. He smiled to himself and then popped a very thin chip into his mouth.

'There is something I've been meaning to tell you,' Maxwell began, his voice serious. 'Something I've been meaning to tell you for quite some time, as a matter of fact.'

Miles knew that their father had an important job in the City but wasn't exactly sure what he did. He knew he commuted from the London suburbs but wasn't exactly sure what suburb. He knew that his father lived with someone down in London but wasn't exactly sure with whom. There was a lot he didn't know about his father; he had never taken the time to ask.

'Well, I think the time has come that you know some home truths,' Maxwell said. 'I feel that this has dragged on for far too long.'

'Well, what is it?' Miles asked.

'I am going to divorce your dipsomaniac mother and then marry my partner Cheryl. I am fed up of living a lie. Up to this point in my life that is what my life has been... A lie. And that has got to change.'

Just then the waiter reappeared with Milton's replacement chicken schnitzel. He slid it in front of him and said, 'I'm sorry.'

Miles wondered if he was apologising for the dropped schnitzel or for the state of their parents' relationship. The waiter turned and walked back to the kitchen doors.

'You will be starting at university in London,' Maxwell said, looking at his elder son. 'So perhaps we could meet up for lunch from time to time. You could meet Cheryl.'

'I don't know who Cheryl is,' Miles said. 'First I've heard of her.'

Maxwell turned to his younger son. 'I'm afraid you will have to go to York College and take your A levels there. I am not prepared to pay the fees for St Peter's for another two years. Like I said: I feel that this has dragged on for far too long already. Running two households takes its toll. And I am not prepared to do it any longer.'

Milton stared at his plate of food, the chicken schnitzel untouched.

'Don't look so glum,' Maxwell said. 'When I was your age, I was already working. I didn't have the benefit of a private education. You need to make your own way in this world.'

Milton stared down at his food. He thought of saying, 'But that isn't fair,' but decided against it.

Miles broke the silence. 'I didn't know you had a woman down there,' he said.

Maxwell looked at his elder son. He nodded. 'Yes, I do. We have cohabited for over ten years. Your mother knows.'

Miles noticed that his father's face was the colour of gammon. He hoped he wouldn't develop such a reddened face with age. But he did take after his father. He had the same dark brown hair and eyes. He glanced over at his ginger-haired brother, the chicken schnitzel left untouched in front of him.

'Shall we have dessert?' Maxwell said.

Milton got up from the table. 'I have to go out,' he said.

Miles looked out of the plate glass window and saw Milton hurry off in the direction of the Museum Gardens.

'I think Milton hasn't taken it very well,' Maxwell said. 'We'd better go after him.'

That day had been the turning point in Miles's life. It had been a day of fateful consequences. Miles gazed out of the window and wondered how lives can be decided so whimsically.

'Are you ready to order?' a waitress asked.

Miles turned. 'Sorry,' he said. 'I was a million miles away.'

'I can give you some more minutes if you like?'

He looked at the waitress in her starched white apron and white long-sleeved blouse. She looked like something from an Agatha Christie television adaptation.

He glanced down at the menu. He hadn't even opened it; his mind had been fully occupied in the past.

'The chicken schnitzel,' Miles said, 'and a pot of Tea Room Blend.'

The waitress scribbled in her pad and then left.

Miles got to his feet.

He picked up his rucksack and carried it with him downstairs. He needed to make some final adjustments.

Theodore noticed his shiny black shoes as he passed by the table he was hiding under. He crossed to the edge of the table but there were several waiters walking up and down, trying to peer under tables; they were on to him, he realised. He didn't know where Miles was going but he was going to have to follow him. He couldn't let him get away.

Then he saw his chance. The sweets' trolley was being pushed between the tables, laden with Fat Rascals, chocolate tortes, frangipane, eclairs, tarts and brightly coloured macaroons. The trolley had a shelf a few inches above the floor. Transportation, Theodore thought. As the trolley passed by his table, he hopped on board.

He heard a voice nearby say, 'Russell. I think this wine has gone to my head...'

'But you've only had the one glass, Barbara...'

'But I've just seen a large grey cat riding the cake trolley!'

'It must be your medication,' Russell said, 'mixing with the alcohol... We'd better get you back to Scarborough.'

17

Randy Dickman had been handicapped by his unfortunate name his whole life.

There are others with even worse names. There is a resident of Los Angeles called Russell Wankum, a Belgian politician called Luc Anus and a Arun Dikshit living in San Jose. If you are a Wilson or Smith, you should feel grateful.

But Randy was loath to change his name as he was named after his paternal grandfather, who had been a hero during World War Two. Like many American and Canadian fighter pilots, he had been stationed outside of York and flown many missions over Germany. He had eventually got shot down one night over Cologne, his body never recovered.

His grandson Randy was looking for Dickmen in the mirror at Bettys.

During the war the mirror had been upstairs in Bettys Bar. This was where the American and Canadian pilots stationed in Yorkshire drank between missions. They nicknamed the bar 'The Briefing Room' or 'The Dive'. Many pilots signed their names on the large mirror using the diamond-tipped pen set aside for that purpose. By the end of the war, the mirror contained 568 names, many belonging to dead pilots.

Randy had searched every inch of the mirror but had not been able to trace a Dickman among the signatures. He had read that the mirror had been damaged during an air raid. The surviving sections had been taken down and put back up downstairs in what is now the corridor outside the toilets. Randy wondered if his grandfather had written his name on one of the sections that had been destroyed, his signature blown into a thousand thin splinters of glass.

He was examining a section of the mirror for the third time when he was jostled. He turned and saw a bulky blue rucksack heading towards the door of the gents'.

'Hey!' he called after the disappearing figure.

The person with the rucksack didn't even turn to acknowledge him. The toilet door closed silently behind the man.

Randy then made a split second decision that would cost him his life. He followed the man with the rucksack into the gents'.

Milton passed by the large window of Bettys. He halted at the corner and stared in through the rain-flecked glass. There in front of him was a table set for one. An untouched plate of chicken schnitzel, pommes allumettes, salad and roasted cherry tomatoes had been placed on the table along with a pot of tea for one. It was as though the place had been set for him. His stomach growled with hunger and his mind raced back to that Sunday when he had lunched with Miles and his father Maxwell for the last time; he had not entered Bettys since that eventful day.

He remembered looking down at his untouched plate of food while Miles and his father decided what they would have for dessert. He felt sick. He felt like he was actually going to throw up. Dessert... His father was deserting them.

He had always suspected that his father favoured Miles. Miles was like his father. He was more like his mother. His thoughts turned to his mother. She had probably been drinking since Maxwell had called round for them that morning. When they returned, she would be passed out on the chaise longue in the conservatory. 'Just having a nap,' she would slur. Then she would get up and fix herself another gin and tonic. It was so predictable.

That day, some twenty-odd years ago, he had left the tea rooms, his eyes blurred by tears, and made his way to the Museum Gardens. He needed to be by himself.

He walked through the gates and passed between two strutting peacocks, their feathers fanned out behind them. Fortunately the gardens were almost empty of people. He found a bench by the museum that looked down over the gardens towards the Ouse. Thoughts raced around his head. His father and brother were no doubt tucking into their desserts back in Bettys. Then his father would get the train back to London and carry on with his life down there. He realised that nobody cared about him. He closed his eyes and hugged himself. In the distance he saw the dark water of the River Ouse. He might as well throw himself in. His life was over before it had even started, he realised. He closed his eyes and wished he was already dead.

'What's the matter with you, young sir?' a man said. Milton opened his eyes. A tramp had joined him on the bench. He looked like what you would expect a tramp to look like. Red veined bulbous nose, large grey straggly beard, yellowed eyes. But his voice was more that of a gentleman.

'Do you want to talk about it?' the tramp said, leaning towards Milton. 'I can be a good listener.'

Milton shook his head.

'Well, I'm just going to sit here and enjoy the view. Don't mind me.'

The tramp reached into a carrier bag by his feet and took out a can of Special Brew. He cracked it open and took a large swig.

Milton looked at the man. He didn't seem to have a care in the world. He would probably just roll under a bush that evening and sleep beneath the stars. He glanced from the tramp's contented face, to the can of beer he held and then back to the tramp's face.

The tramp turned to face him. 'You want a can?'

Milton nodded.

His drinking up to that point had been largely confined to finishing off bottles of wine that his mother left out; she never seemed to realise. He had tried the gin and tonic she always had in the house but he hated the taste.

'You got any money,' the tramp said.

Milton reached into his jacket pocket and took out his wallet. He handed his new companion a crumpled five pound note. The tramp smiled and handed Milton a can of Special Brew.

After Milton had had a few sips, he began to tell his new friend his troubles. By the end of the first can, he felt his troubles receding into the distance; in fact, he struggled to remember why he had been so upset. By the end of the second can, he was having a good time. His troubles were gone and he was riding a wave of drunkenness, laughing at the absurdities of life. By the end of the third can, he was throwing up in the bushes, his new friend gone.

He staggered out of the Museum Gardens and into Museum Street, straight in front of the No.1 bus. What happened next was a blur.

He heard his father shout his name.

Then his father was lying beneath the driver's side front wheel, pinned to the road.

People were shouting. A child screamed. A crowd gathered. His brother Miles swore at him.

They tried to lift the bus off his father.

Milton looked on helplessly.

His father looked at him, the bus wheel on his chest. Then he said his surprising dying words: 'Sylvia...,' he said. Then: 'Please forgive me.' Then he died.

Sylvia was the name of Maxwell's estranged wife and Miles and Milton's mother.

'Look what you've gone and done,' Miles said, under his breath.

Milton turned to his brother.

Miles shook his head. He said, 'You've gone and killed dad.'

Tears streamed down Milton's cheeks.

The crowd backed away leaving the two brothers standing by their dead dad.

Then a peacock approached from the entrance of the Museum Gardens. It strutted into the empty circle in front of the bus. It looked at the dead man under the bus wheel. Then it screamed, 'Bu-kirk!'

A quarter of a century later, Milton stared at the untouched plate of food on the table in the window of Bettys. He had to find Miles and stop him. Whatever foul plot his brother had come up with, there was only Milton who could stand in his way.

So, with a knot of hunger and misery in his stomach, he turned and made his way to the Museum Gardens.

Theodore was downstairs, in a wood-panelled corridor lined with doors on one side and a mirror on the other. He located the gents'. He pushed against the door but it did not open. He heard footsteps behind him. He turned and saw two waiters, a man and a woman, coming towards him. He flattened himself into the door recess.

Then the door swung inwards. Theodore was inside the gents'. Before the door could close behind him, he saw Miles, rucksack on his back leaving. In the seconds before the door closed, Theodore heard the rucksack tick three times in three seconds. A ticking bag, he thought. There must be an alarm clock in it.

He looked at the closed door. He knew he had no means to open it from the inside. From the other side of the door, foot-steps grew nearer.

Then there was a knock on the door and a voice called, 'Are we all right to come in? Hello? Hello?'

When nobody answered, the door swung open.

Theodore fled into one of the toilet cubicles. There was a partition separating his cubicle from the next. There was a gap below the partition about four inches high. From the next cubicle, a pool of blood had spread.

Then there were footsteps in front of the cubicle door. As the door was pushed open, Theodore ducked under the partition and into the next cubicle.

A silver-haired man lay slumped on the floor, his throat cut.

Theodore padded across the toilet floor, his paws dabbing at the pool of warm blood.

There was a rapping at this cubicle door.

'Please open the door!' a man called.

Theodore noticed that the door was locked from the inside. How the man had been murdered was a locked toilet cubicle mystery, but Theodore did not have time to try and figure it out.

Outside, someone was hammering on the door. 'I'm going to have to kick in this door,' the man said, 'if you don't open it now.'

Theodore didn't have long. He inspected his surroundings.

Behind the corpse, there was some boxing covering pipework. The boxing had a hatch in the corner for access. Theodore pushed at the hatch but it did not give. He realised that it must lift up and outwards. He then noticed a slot at the bottom, where someone could slot in a screwdriver and lift the hatch out.

Theodore went to work with his claws. He managed to prise out the hatch and lift it an inch but it fell back into place before he could get his head below it. The second time he managed to get his nose below it. There was more hammering on the door behind him. He pushed himself through and up into the boxing. He managed to pull his tail through behind him just as the cubicle door was kicked in from the outside.

There were some pipes running along the wall and a gap above them. He squeezed himself into this gap and crawled along. He turned a corner and the gap became wider and higher. He began to trot along the pipes.

But then the pipes disappeared into a hole and Theodore fell into blackness.

18

Beneath York there is a network of underground tunnels built by the Romans some 1,600 years ago. This culverted drainage system is still operational in part today.

During the siege of York in the seventeenth century, legend tells that people were smuggled into and out of the city through this subterranean network of tunnels. Only a certain blind man knew his way about the unlit passageways. As he walked through the tunnels, he played a violin so that people could follow him in the dark.

Theodore opened his eyes. He could make out sandstone blocks on either side of him. Beneath him there was soft silt. At least he had had a soft landing. He peered upwards. There was a grey circle of light. There was no way he could scale the circular stone walls and make his way back to the surface.

He realised that he was lying on a raised platform. Beside him there was a channel in which water trickled. He knew that all water flowed to the sea. If he followed the flow of the water, he would come out at the river. Theodore decided to go the other way. One dip in the Ouse was enough for him.

He got to his paws and began to make his way along the culvert. Side passages led off to the left and right, some of them were vaulted, others had flat slabs of Millstone Grit for a roof. In places, he had to wade through ancient silts, at other times he had to make way for rats that used the drainage system like an underground road network.

Smaller channels extended off this passage, many of them filled with dry soil. In one of them he spied a pile of bones. They were the remains of a slave child, sent down into the network of tunnels to clean them out, only to get lost and never find his way out again. Theodore plodded on, against the trickle of water.

Then he stopped. He looked up at the vaulted arch over his head. Emily was there, ten feet above his head. He couldn't see her, hear her or smell her; he just knew she was there; call it cat sense, if you like.

Theodore miaowed as loud as he could.

A drop of cold water fell from the roof of the channel and landed on his head.

Emily stopped. She looked around her.

'He's here,' she said to Jonathan. 'I just know it.'

Jonathan had returned to the city centre to help look for Theodore. He looked around him but the streets were crowded and he knew that the chances of finding him, if he was in the middle of York, were small. A cat would undoubtedly find a quiet place, out of sight, and lay low until things died down. Any ordinary cat would not be in the middle of York on Bonfire

Night of all nights. But Jonathan knew that Theodore was far from ordinary.

As they walked past Lendal Post Office, he said, 'Let's try the Museum Gardens. He might be hiding there.'

Emily agreed. 'Yes. Theodore's like me. Doesn't like crowds...'

There were many others heading towards the gardens. Many of them wore masks or horror make up. Among the many Guy Fawkes, there were zombies, witches, ghosts and ghouls, and others dressed up as cows and badgers. The odd local caught up in the melee wore a determined expression, wanting to be home before the Million Mask March started. The demonstration was scheduled to begin at six o'clock and converge on the Minster at nine o'clock.

As the crowd marched, they began to chant, 'One solution: revolution.'

'Let's hope there's no trouble,' Jonathan said.

'I doubt it,' Emily said. 'It is a peaceful protest. They just want a fairer world. I think they are right about a lot of things. We need to think about what sort of world we are going to leave behind for our children, don't we?'

'You're right,' Jonathan said, 'but there's always a few who ruin it for the majority. A handful that will have come just to make trouble.'

'Let's hope nothing happens,' Emily said. 'I just want to find Theo and get home.'

'Isn't that your dad's car?' Jonathan said, as they approached the gates to the Museum Gardens. 'I thought they'd gone back to Acaster Mildew.'

'I did too,' Emily said, and pushed the pram across the road to the car.

It was Emily's mum Trish who wound down the window.

'What are you doing back in town?' Emily asked. 'I thought you'd gone back to Acaster Mildew.'

'Oliver relapsed,' Trish said, a tone of 'told-you-so' in her voice. 'He demanded to be brought back to York. No doubt to buy cheap bottles of cider and pass out under a tree.'

'Oh dear,' Emily said, but she did not care too much about Oliver. He had used her cat to profiteer from begging.

'Your dad has had a few glasses of wine so I thought I'd better bring him back.'

'I see.'

'Your dad said he could use the Acaster Mildew community bicycle, but I said I wouldn't want a guest of ours to be seen riding the village bike. Who knows who's been on that saddle!

'And your dad said Oliver is no longer a guest of ours. He is a disappointment. He said he didn't care if he caught something fatal from the village bike.

'So I said that I would drive him back to York and your dad should have a good strong cup of tea. He should never have brought Oliver back to Acaster Mildew in the first place. The man is beyond hope. But you know your father. When he gets something in his head...

'So here I am. Would you like some parkin?'

'Parking?' Emily said.

'Parkin,' Trish said. 'It's traditional. On Bonfire Night.'

'Oh, parkin,' Emily said. 'No, I think I'm all right.'

'I made a batch this morning. Your father and I were going to go to the village bonfire this evening.

'Any luck finding Theo?'

Emily shook her head. 'I'm so worried.'

'It's awfully busy,' Trish said. 'All these people... There were hundreds more coming out of the station when I drove past.'

'It's an awful night,' Emily agreed.

'How about I take Joseph back to Acaster Mildew with me? You know your dad would love it. They can watch Mr Bean DVDs together. We have the car seat plugged in and ready to go.'

'Would you? That would be so kind. We could pick him up in the morning.'

'You'll need to fold up his buggy,' Trish said. 'You know I'm hopeless with that.'

Five minutes later, Joseph was strapped into his car seat, the pram folded up in the back of the car, and on the way to spend the night at his grandparents. He gurgled happily in his car seat and even managed a wave through the car window at his mum, as the car pulled away.

Emily and Jonathan entered through the gates of the Museum Gardens.

Milton wondered what had happened to the peacocks that used to live in the Museum Gardens. Then he thought of his brother Miles. No doubt he was lying low until a decent-sized crowd had gathered in front of the Minster. He would want to maximise the damage.

He shivered. His jeans were still wet from the King's Arms. He needed to get warm. He needed to build another fire.

He found some dried leaves and created a large pile. Then he went into the shrubbery and emerged minutes later, his arms laden with twigs. He placed them over the leaves and then went looking for branches. Once he had built a fire, he realised that he needed a light. He spotted some people in the distance and from the orange dots, knew there were smokers among them. He approached and asked for a light.

Taking the proffered lighter, he said, 'I'll be back in a minute.'

As he was lighting the fire, the man whose lighter it was approached.

'What are you doing?'

'I'm building a fire,' Milton said.

'A bonfire?' the man said. 'What a good idea. Let me help. We'll go and get lots of wood. We'll make a massive bonfire!'

He walked back to his friends. 'We're making a massive fire!' he said. 'A bonfire! Come on! We need wood!'

Twenty feet below the ground, Theodore heard a movement behind him. He glanced back. He saw a pair of red eyes glow in the darkness. The creature had a glistening black coat and white fangs. It was a giant rat.

He began to run. The rat gave chase, its claws scratching against the stone floor behind him. It was gaining on him. Ahead of him, Theodore saw a light coming from the roof of the tunnel.

19

The Roman Bath is probably the only public house to have a Roman bath in its basement.

During renovations to the tavern on St Sampson's Square in 1930, the remains of the Roman bath including a caldarium, or steam room, and also a plunge pool, were revealed. Two thousand years ago, Roman soldiers would come here to relax and leave cleaner than when they arrived.

Miles had ordered his meal at the bar and was sitting nursing a pint waiting for his meal. It was a pity that he hadn't got to eat the chicken schnitzel back at Bettys. It was a pity he had been interrupted while he was making the final preparations for this evening. It was a pity he had had to cut the American's throat and leave his body in the toilet cubicle. Well, you can't make an omelette without breaking eggs, he thought.

He glanced at the rucksack on the floor by his feet. Then he glanced at his watch. He wanted to make sure that it had the maximum impact. He planned to wait until the crowds of protestors converged on York Minster. At nine o'clock these protestors would realise that their protests were a waste of time. Direct action would always win the day. He grinned to himself.

Miles had spent five years in prison for manipulating bank-reported interest rates, in order to enhance his own trading results; he had been sent down for ten. His brother Milton had got less time for aggravated robbery and manslaughter. The world was truly unfair.

Five years is a long time to stare at the walls. He was separated from the other prisoners for his own protection. The guards had also taken an instant dislike to the overly-educated banker, who had earned more in bonuses in one year than they would earn in a lifetime.

Miles suffered severely from boredom but he never regretted anything he had done. In his mind he had done nothing wrong, except for trusting his colleagues and managers. They didn't say anything when he was making money for them. He had done what was expected of him at the time. He had been no different to the hundreds of others working in finance and lining their pockets. Why else would you work in finance unless you wanted to make some money?

When the system finally came unstuck, he got no support from any of them. He must have had scapegoat tattooed on his forehead. They singled him out and made an example of him. It was his face on the cover of the papers.

Miles kept his head down while inside, conformed to the rules and was released on licence three months ago. His wife had already moved on, filing for divorce within months of his being put away. When he was finally released, he had nothing but a letter from the Child Support Agency setting out how much he was to pay his ex-wife for the maintenance of their three children.

That was also the time when he had got a letter from his brother asking for money. The letter went straight in the bin.

A week later he got another letter from his brother Milton. This letter also went straight in the bin. Then he had a phone call from an unknown mobile number. He answered it. It was

Milton. He had somehow managed to get a mobile in prison. He asked for money again; that he wanted to take his case back to court and was going to represent himself. Miles told him what he could do. Then he told him he was coming up to York to pay a visit soon. He had his own plans for the night of the Million Mask March. Bonfire Night was going to end with a bang, he told his brother. Then he hung up.

And now his brother had somehow managed to escape from Full Sutton prison and was no doubt going to try to put a stop to his plans.

A plate of sausage, mash and peas was put down in front of him. 'There you go, love,' the barmaid said. 'Knives and forks are on the bar.'

At least he had a decent meal in front of him, he thought, thinking back to the grub back inside.

Downstairs Theodore emerged from a hole in the basement floor and stepped into the caldarium. The floor of the steam room had been removed, exposing the short stone columns that had once supported the floor. The giant rat emerged a moment later, drool hanging from its sharp fangs.

Theodore weaved between the stone columns, the rat snapping its teeth at his tail. He saw steps leading upwards. He flew up them.

He was in a crowded bar room.

Someone screamed: 'There's a stray cat!'

Someone else shouted: 'There's a giant rat!'

'I've never eating here again,' someone muttered.

Theodore ran under a table. He was face to face with a large blue rucksack. He had seen it somewhere before. The rucksack ticked.

Then the rat was upon him. It locked its jaws onto his tail. Theodore swung around and hissed at the rat.

The man whose table they were under jumped to his feet.

The cat and the rat were battling it out on the pub floor, jaws biting into furry flesh.

Miles raised his foot and kicked out at the skirmishing animals. He caught the rat below the belly.

The rat flew through the air and landed on the bar, in front of several barstool drinkers. Stunned, it lay on a beer towel and closed its eyes.

There was shouting, screaming and cursing. People began to make their way outside.

In the ensuing confusion, Miles picked up a sausage from his plate, popped it into his mouth like a cigar, picked up his rucksack, slung it over his shoulder and then made for the door.

Theodore followed.

20

The peacocks of the Museum Gardens are no more.

For over seventy years they resided in the gardens: loitering in the ruins of St Mary's abbey, strutting about in the botanical gardens, screaming at people from the safety of trees, stopping the traffic on Museum Street when they decided to go for a wander down Coney Street.

In 2000 there were four birds: two males, a peahen and a chick. But the peahen decided to relocate with her chick, leaving the two males by themselves. For a peacock to be happy, he needs a harem of six peahens, so to ensure the continued presence of peacocks in the gardens, it would require a total of fourteen or fifteen birds to sustain the population.

The city was divided on the issue. Many didn't like the screaming the birds made. Many didn't like their journeys interrupted when they decided to stray onto the roads. Bus drivers didn't like it when the birds decided to hop a lift on the bus roof to visit their peacock friends in Bootham Park. Even the gardeners complained that they scratted up their plants. So it was decided after some debate that new birds would not be introduced and the remaining ones would be left to dwindle and die. It is unclear who made this final decision regarding the fate of the peacocks. They were evidently not peacock fans.

In February 2001 one of the peacocks was found dead in the gardens. The other carried on a solitary existence until 2009. On the fifth of November, the local paper reported that the last peacock had died.

That is what happened to the peacocks of the Museum Gardens.

Milton wished they were still there. They had brought colour to the gardens even in the middle of winter. When he was a teenager, drinking cider in the bushes, he would listen to them calling out to each other in the darkness, and he would copy them, calling out, 'Bu-kirk! Bu-kirk!' It had made him feel better.

He looked into the flames of the fire he had built and screamed, 'Bu-kirk! Bu-kirk!'

Some younger people who were standing by his fire backed away from him and made their way back into the darkness.

'We need a guy,' a man said.

Milton turned to his companion. It was the same man who had helped him collect firewood.

'A guy?' Milton said.

'You know... A penny for the guy and all that. A figure to burn on the fire. We should make a guy and then parade it through the streets. We might make a bit of money.'

'There will be no guy on my bonfire,' Milton said, staring into the flames.

Milton had attended St Peter's School on Bootham until his A Levels, when his father had refused to carry on with the cost and then ended up under a bus. It was St Peter's policy not to burn a guy on their annual bonfire as Guy Fawkes had gone to St Peter's some four hundred years earlier. It is usually not a good school policy to burn effigies of your former pupils on bonfires each year.

Milton stared into the flames, remembering. 'Remember, remember...' he murmured, 'the fifth of November.'

'A toast!' Sylvia slurred from her sofa, her Dachshund Dolly on her lap. 'A toast for my big boy!' Both Milton and Miles referred to the worn pink chaise longue as 'her sofa', as their mother spent most of her waking as well as sleeping hours on it, either sprawled out watching television or sitting up reading Hello magazines.

Milton took a sip of tea. He had always been an avid tea drinker. And he knew that Yorkshire Tea was the best.

Sylvia, undeterred, raised her glass in the air. Dolly squirmed to her paws and jumped down from the chaise longue. Miles raised a can of lager to his lips.

'I can't believe you are going off to university,' Sylvia said. 'It doesn't seem like yesterday that I was bottle feeding you, right here on the sofa.'

She patted the seat beside her and managed to spill some wine on the upholstery. Dolly scampered under the sofa.

Milton noticed several dark brown chipolatas on the parquet floor beneath the sofa. Dolly needed to be let out more often, he realised. He looked across at his brother. It was three weeks since they had seen their father put into the ground.

Miles was pacing up and down, distracted. He was taking a train down to London the next day. His mother didn't drive, so he had little choice in the matter.

'I'll have to come down and visit one weekend,' Milton said. It was his attempt at making the peace; he doubted he would ever go and visit; he had never been to London.

'I don't think so,' Miles said.

'Don't be like that, Miles,' Sylvia said. 'Not on your last night at home.'

She got up and went into the kitchen to pour herself another glass of wine.

'I meant it,' Miles said. 'I never want to see you or her again.'

'Whatever,' Milton said. He shrugged.

'You don't get it,' do you? Miles said.

'What's that?'

'Don't you see? You're ginger...'

'So?'

'Did you not do biology in school?'

Miles took a drink of beer and stared out of the window, at the house opposite. 'The Ginger Ferret... That's what dad used to call him.'

Milton was confused. 'Who's this Ginger Ferret?'

'He was the neighbour,' Miles said. 'He upped and left. You're not one of us.'

Sylvia came back into the lounge.

'Now, where were we?' she said. 'A toast! That's right. A toast to my son. A toast to my big boy!'

Miles stood up. 'Oh, do be quiet,' he said. 'I'm going to bed.'

'But it's not even nine.'

'I've had enough,' Miles said. 'Of you. Of him. Of this house. I'm going to bed now.' Then he went upstairs.

Milton sipped his tea. His mother would be dead by Christmas. He would be seventeen and left to live on his own in that awful house. He would never sit on her sofa though. It was left like a forgotten museum piece.

Twenty-five years later, he stared into the flames of the bonfire. The fire was dying down. He was going to have to find some more firewood. He turned his back to the fire and made his way over to some trees.

'Do you really think he might be in here?' Emily asked.

'If I were a cat,' Jonathan said, 'it's where I'd come.'

A firework went off with a bang and the sky was momentarily lit up with white light.

'It's very smoky,' Emily said.

'There must be a fire.'

'In the gardens?'

'Somebody must have started a fire. A bonfire... It'll be one of the protestors. Come on. We need to look in the bushes. That's where I'd hide. In the darkest places.'

Jonathan headed off towards some dark shrubbery. Emily followed.

It was only once Jonathan had entered the shrubs did he realise he was not alone. A man was stooping down, picking up sticks. His arms full the man turned and came towards Jonathan. It was only when he was almost on top of him did the man see him.

He was wearing a Guy Fawkes mask pushed back on top of his head, an old army coat, a red and black checked shirt and jeans that were too short for him.

Jonathan recognised the man from the news that morning. He also recognised his shirt and jeans.

'I know who you are,' he said. 'You're Milton Macavity.'

'That's my name,' Milton said. 'Don't wear it out.'

Milton moved to the side to step around Jonathan.

'Not so fast,' Jonathan said. 'I'm making a citizen's arrest.'

Milton shook his head, looked Jonathan up and down. 'Well, well, well. Who do we have here? The Corduroy Kid...?'

Jonathan looked down at his clothes. He was dressed entirely in beige corduroy. When he had returned home to check for Theodore, he had taken off his denim jacket which was soaked through with rain. When he had left home again to join Emily he had put on his corduroy jacket, not realising he was doubling up on the corduroy.

Suddenly he was angry that his fashion faux pas had been called out by this escaped convict.

'You're right,' he almost shouted. 'I'm the Corduroy Kid and you're under arrest!'

Milton laughed. He dropped his pile of firewood. Then he punched Jonathan in the nose.

Emily screamed.

Jonathan dropped to his knees, blood spilling down his corduroy jacket.

Milton pushed his way past. 'Nice meeting you,' he called out, disappearing into the smoky night.

'I can't believe how bad this day is turning out,' Jonathan said.

'Well, we all have our sartorial mishaps,' Emily said, crouching down beside him. 'I was going to point it out earlier but I was more concerned about Theodore.'

'I meant being punched in the face by an escaped convict.'

'You mean that was Milton Macavity?'

'Yes,' Jonathan said. 'And he was wearing my shirt and jeans, I'm sure of it.'

'We need to find the police and let them know,' Emily said. 'They need to catch him... Then you can get your clothes back. We can't have you going around in double corduroy, can we?'

21

There was a huge explosion. Then the sky lit up green. Then a high-pitched whizzing went overhead. A star exploded, pink and green. Then came a volley of short sharp bangs, like machine gun fire. It was as though Theodore was caught up in the middle of a warzone.

Whoever invented fireworks should have a rocket inserted up their rectum, Theodore thought, flicking his tail from side to side.

He saw the bulky rucksack passing through the crowd on Stonegate. Theodore dashed after it, giving a purple man on a purple bicycle a wide berth.

The man in mauve was a living statue, who made his living by posing as a windswept cyclist on Stonegate. He also collected money for charity. His mission was to spread love and happiness throughout the world. He had been to war-torn Syria, where he had handed out a thousand soft toys to the surprised children.

They were surprised to see him as they had never seen a purple man before.

Miles stopped and Theodore stopped.

Miles was staring down at a crumpled, dirt-streaked Guy Fawkes mask, lying in the gutter. He picked the mask up.

A man wearing a Guy Fawkes mask approached.

'They're selling them on Coney Street for a tenner if you want one,' the man said.

Miles stared at the masked face. 'What do you know about Fawkes?'

'They're cutlery, aren't they?'

'Fawkes... Guy Fawkes,' Miles said.

'That Fawkes,' the man in the mask said, who happened to be studying seventeenth century history at York University. 'Well, he was born around here, someplace. He went to St Peter's School in Bootham. His father died when he was a teenager. Guy was executed outside Westminster, the place they had planned to blow up rather ironically, on the thirtieth of January 1606...'

'He was a scapegoat,' Miles cut in.

'He was responsible for placing the gunpowder and guarding it. He was culpable.'

'He was just one of thirteen conspirators. It was Thomas Percy who funded it. Catesby and Percy were the ones behind the scheme. Fawkes was just employed because of his military background. His knowledge of explosives.'

'Well, why don't we hear more about this Percy?'

'Well,' Miles said, deliberating. 'It doesn't have the same ring, does it? "A penny for the Percy." "Let's put a Percy on the bonfire."'

'I wouldn't want my Percy burning on a fire.'

'This is not a joking matter,' Miles went on. 'When arrested, Guy Fawkes claimed he was John Johnson, servant of Thomas Percy... It was Percy who had put him up to it. It was Percy who had financed the plot. It was Percy's name which appeared first on the arrest warrant.'

'So what happened to this Percy?'

'Percy fled to the Midlands where he met up with Catesby. They engaged with government forces and, they say, Percy and Catesby were killed by the same musket ball. They were buried but later exhumed, so that their heads could be put on spikes outside of Parliament. They got off lightly...'

'So why do we only hear about Guy Fawkes then?'

'Fawkes was tortured. His torture was so cruel that he could hardly sign his name to his supposed confession.'

'The Attorney General told the court that each of the condemned would be "put to death halfway between heaven and earth as unworthy of both. Their genitals would be cut off and burnt before their eyes, and their bowels and hearts removed. They would then be decapitated, and the dismembered parts of their bodies displayed so that they might become prey for the fowls of the air..."

'So, on the last day of January 1606, Fawkes and his fellow plotters were dragged from the Tower to the Old Palace Yard at Westminster. Fawkes was the last to be sent to the scaffold. Weak from torture, he was helped by the hangman to climb the ladder to the noose. He managed to climb so high that the drop broke his neck, and he was saved the agonies promised him. He was taken down, quartered and his body parts sent out to the four corners of the kingdom...'

For Fawkes' sake, thought Theodore. This is turning into a horrible history lesson.

Theodore, like many cats, was not keen on history. In fact it had been his worst lesson at school.

He turned away and looked down High Petergate. There were many shop signs hanging over the crowd of people. One sign read: 'The Cat Gallery'.

I didn't know cats could paint, he thought. We cats are a species of many talents.

Then he felt hands tighten around him.

22

'I've got him,' Becky said. 'It's that cat that's missing. I saw it on Facebook.'

'Looks like a street cat to me,' her friend Sam said.

Sam backed into the doorway of the National Trust gift shop still clutching the cat. 'I'm sure it's him. His name's Theodore.'

'He doesn't have a collar on,' Sam said. 'Just put him back down. You can tell he doesn't want to be picked up.'

Theodore struggled in Becky's grasp. His manhunt had been halted by millennials. Excuse me, he thought, but I have the important business of catching escaped convicts and bankers who would prefer you dead.

'Just leave him be,' Sam said. 'He'll find his own way home.'

'This woman on Facebook was really worried,' Becky said. 'What with it being Bonfire Night and all. Pets shouldn't be allowed out. I need to contact her.'

'But we're missing the protest. And I heard that there's going to be a gig in the gardens later on.'

'Then the sooner we get Theodore returned to his owner the better. Here you hold him and I'll find the post on Facebook. She's probably around here somewhere looking for him.'

Becky passed the cat to Sam.

Her day had not gone well. When she had arrived at the shoe shop on Pavement that morning, she found out that the shop was due to close. Herbert House was to close for renovation and the shop's lease was not being extended. Then she had been man-handled by Milton Macavity in the alley behind the shop. She had had to go with the police to Fulford Police Station, where she had made a statement.

She had told the police what Milton had said to her about there being some terrible plot for that evening and his brother being behind it, but the police hadn't seemed to take it too seriously. The escaped convict was trying to take attention away from himself and what better way than to claim there was going to be some form of terrorist plot planned for the centre of York. They probably had a point, she'd thought once she had managed to get home.

'This protest is a bit of a let-down anyway,' Becky said. 'I mean there aren't even any TV cameras. If it's not on the telly, there's no point in doing it, is there? We need exposure.'

'But we have to make a stand now,' Sam said, taking Theodore. 'Before it's too late. There is no Planet B, remember?'

Becky was wearing a T-shirt that read, 'There is no Planet B.' It showed a forlorn polar bear heading towards a pine forest, a mountain range in the background.

Theodore struggled in the hands of his new captor.

Sam held onto him, pulling him tightly against her chest. Her T-shirt read, 'Help More Bees. Plant More Trees. Clean The Seas.'

Get Off, Please, thought Theodore, still struggling.

He understood that the two young women were trying to help reunite him with Emily. Unfortunately they were impeding his attempts to stop Miles.

Becky took out her mobile and opened Facebook. She searched her groups until she found the 'Pets – Lost & Found – York-UK' group. She scrolled down until she found Emily's post.

'I think we've found your cat,' she wrote. 'We're outside the National Trust shop near the Minster. Please come quickly! Not sure how long we can hold onto him...'

'You take him back,' Sam said. 'I don't think I can hold onto him much longer.'

She passed the struggling cat back to Becky. Becky slipped her mobile into her jeans pocket and then took Theodore. She held him with both hands so that he faced away from her, his hind legs dangling down.

'We'll be missing the speeches,' Sam said.

'We can't let him go though,' Becky said. 'He's scared shitless. We need to reunite him with his owner.'

Emily and Jonathan made their way back to the entrance of the Museum Gardens. More protestors were entering the gardens and they had to make their way against the flow.

'I need to get home and lie down on the sofa,' Jonathan said, holding his nose between two fingers to stem the bleeding.'

'You can go and lie on the sofa,' Emily said. 'I'm not going to return without Theodore.'

By the entrance someone was handing out flyers. Jonathan waved one away when it was pushed towards him.

Emily felt her phone vibrate in her pocket. She backed up against a wall and clicked on the alert.

'Someone's found Theodore,' she said. 'They are holding him by the Minster. He's at the National Trust Shop.'

She typed, 'I'm on my way. Five minutes max. Please don't let go of him.'

Then she said to Jonathan, 'Come on. We're going to get Theodore.'

And she pushed into the crowd on Museum Street.

Becky felt her mobile pulse in the back of her jeans.

'Sam. Get my phone from my back pocket. I think she might have responded to my message.'

Sam took Becky's mobile. 'You have an alert,' she said. 'She's responded. She's on her way.'

Looks like you're coming home whether you like it or not, came the voice of the cat basket. *Your little adventure is at an end. I'll be seeing you soon no doubt. Then we can get reacquainted...*

It's not over 'til the fat cat miaows, thought Theodore. He kicked backwards with his hind legs, catching Becky in the stomach with his claws.

'That hurt,' she gasped, but she did not let go. 'Your owner is on her way. Just stay still, will you?'

Theodore stared out into the crowd, expecting to see Emily approach. But instead he saw Miles with his bulky blue rucksack hurry past.

He kicked out with his legs again but this time Becky pulled her body backwards and managed to avoid his claws.

He glanced from side to side. He spied some flesh on her arm that he could just about reach. He twisted in her grasp.

This is going to hurt you more than it's going to hurt me, he thought. Then he twisted to one side and bit Becky on the arm.

She cried out in pain and dropped Theodore to the ground. She looked at her arm that was bleeding just above the wrist.

'This is turning out to be the worst day of my life,' she said, staring after Theodore's grey tail as the cat disappeared into the crowd.

23

Milton knew he had to return to the crowded streets and find Miles, before his brother could carry out whatever fiendish act he had in mind.

He pushed his way through a large group of people at the entrance to the Museum Gardens. He noticed some protestors lying down in the road in front of Pizza Express, stopping the traffic from passing through the city. Police officers stood by the protestors. Car drivers blew their horns in frustration. Milton watched as a police officer stopped a taxi driver from dragging a Radiohead fan from the road.

He stared at the crowd for his brother. There were so many masked faces. There were those in Guy Fawkes masks. Then there was a smaller group of people wearing cow masks, their black clothes daubed with white paint, so that they resembled Friesian cows. They carried a banner that read, 'Dairy is Scary!' Then there were people wearing badger masks and also dressed in black and white. They carried a banner that read, 'Innocent Till Proven Guilty!'

His brother may well have got a mask. He might even be dressed as a cow or badger. He shrugged his shoulders in despair; perhaps he should have stayed put in prison.

Then he remembered his brother had been carrying a rucksack. A large bulky rucksack. He needed to find the rucksack and his brother.

He turned, pulled his Guy Fawkes mask down and set off towards the Minster. That was where most of the crowd seemed to be drifting. That would be where Miles was heading.

As he walked, he remembered the last time he had seen his brother.

He had caught the National Express down to London. His trial was coming to a close and he was about to be sentenced.

On the coach, he noticed other travellers reading tabloids. His brother's face was on many of the front covers. The headlines read:

'DISGRACED FINANCIER'
'BANKER WANKERED'
'GREEDY SWINE'
'TIME TO PAY THE PRICE'

The general public had no sympathy for the former banker. Scapegoat or not, he epitomised the hated public school-educated City figure who received massive bonuses while they worked their hours without fair rewards.

Outside the court, Milton watched from the crowd of onlookers as Miles was brought out. His eyes darted among the crowd.

'Miles!' a woman shouted.

Milton looked across and saw Carol, Miles's wife. Milton had never met Carol Macavity but he recognised her from photographs in the newspapers. Miles's former personal assistant and then trophy wife.

'Carol?' Miles said, uncertainly in his voice.

The crowd quietened down, suspecting some outburst of emotion. Cameras flashed. Television cameras turned from husband to wife and back again.

'I'm divorcing you!' Carol cried in a Cockney accent. 'And I'm going to take you for every penny you own.'

A cheer went up from the crowd.

Miles didn't respond. He let himself be led to the waiting Amey van.

As he passed, Milton called out, 'I'll write to you!'

Miles turned and caught his brother's eye. 'Don't bother,' he called back.

Some of the crowd had begun to chant, 'Wanker Banker! Wanker Banker! Wanker Banker!'

Milton watched as the van doors were closed; then he turned and began to walk back to Victoria Coach Station. Miles was the only family he had in the world. The only other Macavity. But then if what Miles had implied was true, they were only half-brothers. His own father was a ginger-haired former neighbour he had never known. He felt very alone as he walked along the crowded streets of the Big Smoke.

He pushed his way through the crowd, looking for that big blue rucksack. Then he saw him, just ahead of him.

Miles was making his way down Stonegate towards York Minster, the rucksack on his back.

He glanced at the faces of the young people around him, in their T-shirts with slogans and cheap plastic masks.

It is easy to be idealistic when you are young, he thought. These kids would have it kicked out of them before too long.

By his forties, Miles had already spent twenty years in the dog-eat-dog world of finance. It was trample or be trampled on.

The traders were known as fat cats but they were more like feral cats, fighting over the meagre scraps dropped from the dining table of the top cats, the few who really ran everything.

Under his breath he quoted:

'Remember, remember the fifth of November,

Gunpowder treason and plot.
We see no reason
Why gunpowder treason
Should ever be forgot!'

He pulled on the straps of the rucksack. There was quite a weight in the bag.

I'm going to give you fifth of November fifth to remember!

Then he heard a shout from behind him. He turned and saw a man wearing a Guy Fawkes mask coming straight at him.

'Miles!' Milton shouted. 'Stop there!'

Miles turned back round but he didn't stop. He carried on, past the purple man on his purple bike. He pushed people aside, shouting at them to get out of his way. The crowd parted, pushing themselves to the sides of the street.

Milton saw the purple man on his purple bike. One of those living statues, he thought. Another person trying to make a living by not doing much of anything.

He pushed the purple man off his bike. A purple pot of coins crashed onto the pavement; silver and gold coins spilled out onto the flagstones. The bike fell to the ground. Milton snatched it up. He would soon catch up with his brother on this purple bike.

He jumped on it and pressed the pedals. But they did not turn.

'Bloody useless thing! he shouted, as Miles turned a corner and disappeared from sight.

'It's a prop!' Purpleman shouted from the ground.

Two men approached. They were dressed in black shirts and trousers but wore purple ties.

They were security guards employed by Purpleman to protect him from drunken racegoers, stag and hen parties and football fans. It wasn't the first time that Purpleman had been pushed off his bike.

One of the security guards helped Purpleman to his feet; the other turned to Milton. 'What do you think you're playing at?'

'I needed to borrow a bike...'

Milton threw the bike back onto the ground. 'It's bloody useless...' A purple toy dog fell from its purple basket at the front of the bike.

'I know you,' the security guard said. 'You're Milton Macavity... The so-called Napoleon of Crime. Been reduced to stealing bikes, have you?'

Milton raised his hands to his face. Somehow he had lost his Guy Fawkes mask.

The security guard had a walkie-talkie. 'Come in, come in,' he said. 'I'm going to need some assistance.'

Purpleman replaced his purple hat which had a small purple camera mounted on the top. 'I've had enough!' he shouted. 'I've been sworn at, spat at... had things thrown at me. I've been pushed off my bike. I've had enough.'

'Sorry,' Milton said.

'Sorry?' Purpleman said. 'You're sorry? I have tried to bring some love and laughter to this city. I have tried to bring out the awesomeness in everyone. But look at them.' He waved his hands dramatically at the crowd around him. 'All I see is hatred. I have failed in my mission. Now I am going home. I quit... No longer will Purpleman be the object of ridicule. No longer will he bring smiles to the faces of those both young and old. I am going home.'

Purpleman threw his purple hat onto the ground and then walked away. The crowd stood in silence, knowing that they would never see him again and that they were partly to blame.

Milton watched as Purpleman disappeared into the crowd. He then turned and began to make his way in the opposite direction, after Miles. But a hand grabbed his shoulder and spun him round.

'You're not going anywhere,' one of the security guards said. 'There's a police van on its way. You're going back inside...'

'You don't understand,' Milton said. 'There's a plot to blow up the Minster. My brother Miles is behind it. We need to stop him.'

'You want us to believe that?' The security guard laughed. 'You're going back inside, mate.'

The other security guard approached. On his jacket he wore insignia that read, 'Eboracum Security'. 'Not such a big shot, are we now?'

Milton pushed the security guard squarely in the chest so that he fell against his partner. Then he spun round and began to run.

24

Theodore followed Miles into the crowd that was heading to-wards the Minster. The shoes and boots drew ever tighter around him. He slipped between the protestors, dodging footwear from all sides while trying to keep sight of the blue rucksack as it moved through the crowd. But soon the rucksack disappeared.

He kept to the side of a pub. He noted that the pub was unimaginatively called the Guy Fawkes Inn, for it was here that Fawkes is reported to have been born in 1570, in the shadow of York Minster and across the street from the church where he was baptised, St Michael Le Belfrey.

Ahead of him, Theodore spotted a very tall man wearing a top hat standing on the lawn off College Street. He must have been ten feet tall. In front of the very tall man there was a large crowd. He must be wearing some contraptions on his legs to be so tall, Theodore realised.

Theodore spied Oliver Bartholomew leaning against the trunk of a large tree in the shadow of York Minster. In his hand he had a two litre bottle of cider. Theodore slipped among the crowd gathered in front of the very tall man. He didn't want to be snatched by Oliver again.

People were packed tightly around him. He spotted a raised plinth about two feet above the ground. He jumped up on top of the bronze plinth.

A plan of York Minster was portrayed on the plinth. Theodore padded across a bright red circle that had 'YOU ARE HERE,' written below it. The red circle had an aureole of shiny metal around it from people putting their finger on it; it looked like an obscene nipple.

Theodore entered the Minster from the east end. He paused a couple of moments in the crypt before settling down in the nave, his tail extending into the south transept of the largest Gothic cathedral in northern Europe. I never realised I was so big, thought Theodore, to be able to fill the nave of York Minster.

The tall man in the top hat began to tell a story, a ghost story.

'Some sixty years ago,' the top-hatted man began, 'a family moved into the house over there. They had acquired it at a bargain price. A house in the shadows of the Minster... Usually they don't come cheap.

'But they were not aware of the house's horrible history...' The man paused for dramatic effect.

Not another horrible history, thought Theodore.

'Weeks after they had moved in,' the man continued, 'strange things began to happen. The parents heard the wails of a young girl. When they went to their children's bedroom, they found them wide awake, the light in their bedroom turned on. They asked them what the matter was...

'The children said that they had seen a young girl sitting at the foot of the bed. When they had turned the light on, the girl was gone. The children refused to sleep in the room.

'The next day the parents began to ask questions...

'They discovered that during the plague, a husband and wife and their daughter had lived in the house. Both the husband and wife had contracted the disease. They were sealed in their house, so as to stop the spread of the disease within the city; their doors and windows were nailed shut. They quickly succumbed to pestilence. They were fortunate. Their daughter was not so fortunate.' Again the tall man paused for dramatic effect.

'Unfortunately for her, she was immune to the disease...

'With her parents lying dead in the next room, she tapped at her little window, trying to get the attention of those passing on the road outside. She saw the carts of corpses being drawn by, being carried to the pits where they were covered in lime. She called and called at the passing people. But the people ignored her cries. They were worried that if she were released, she would infect them. During times of plague, there is little time for compassion.

'So, without food or water, she eventually died. But, as you know, the human spirit does not give in easily. For weeks she fought death. Eventually she succumbed. When death did finally come, it was a blessing...

'The house is now occupied by another family,' the tall man said. 'They do not believe in ghosts...'

The man turned and pointed at a small rectangular window set into a limestone block wall. 'In that window, some people claim that they have seen the girl's face. And on quiet nights, some people claim that they have heard the girl's cries.'

The man paused and the crowd stared at the small window. A silent minute passed.

'Now, we will make our way to our next haunted location. Please follow closely behind. York is very busy tonight... I wouldn't want to lose any of you.'

As the crowd followed the top-hatted man on stilts towards their next haunted location, Theodore stared up at the window.

Suddenly a girl's face appeared. Then he heard a wailing noise, a young girl crying out within the prison of her house.

He glanced around him. Oliver was still leaning against the tree. He was staring wide-eyed at the small window.

Oliver shook his head in disbelief. He lifted his bottle of cider to his mouth and took a big gulp. Then he staggered off towards the Minster, his head bowed.

Theodore watched him depart. Then he looked back up at the little window. He didn't believe in ghost stories. He knew they were based on human superstition and had their roots in the humans' misunderstanding of the world. There was always a feline explanation to most things, he understood.

He heard a peel of laugher and then excited voices. He looked back up at the little window.

He saw the young girl's face staring out into the night. Then it was joined by the face of a young boy. They were both giggling.

'Did you see that silly man,' the boy said.

'Yes,' the young girl said, 'he fell for it, hook line and sinker!'

'We really put the wind up him!'

And both the children laughed.

Theodore blinked. I told you that there would be a simple explanation, he thought. Then he set off after Oliver Bartholomew towards the Minster.

25

The war between the bovine and the badgers had been going on for many centuries.

It was a distant memory to both creatures when they had peacefully shared the British countryside; before the humans had sided with the cows, understanding that they could be cultivated for food on a commercial scale while the badgers were harder to catch and didn't taste as good.

The badgers were driven to ever-diminishing areas of woodland, as the land was given over to the ever-increasing herds of cattle. The dominant cows were mostly ambivalent about the matter; many of them did not even know there was a war: they spent so much time munching grass and farting clouds of methane that they had little time to philosophise.

Sensing defeat, the badgers resorted to biological warfare: spreading bovine tuberculosis among the herds of cows.

The cows launched a propaganda war in response: Rumours abound that they were using their methane farts like napalm, wiping out huge areas of the remaining woodland indiscriminately. But on hearing this false news, the badgers knew it was just bullshit.

Then the humans got wind of the badger fightback and intervened, culling badgers in Gloucestershire and Somerset. The badgers retaliated, laying siege to Stroud with a network of sinkholes, resulting in a nationwide shortage of green baize for covering snooker tables and tennis balls. The manufacture of baize is one of Stroud's few remaining industries, along with organic banana cake and Damien Hirst artworks.

Some humans sided with the badgers. They tended to be people who didn't like the idea of trained marksmen shooting down our remaining wild animals. Their numbers included in many veterinarian surgeons, many of whom were veterans of the Stroud offensive. They called themselves the Badger Protection Squad, or the BPS for short.

Others sided with the cows. They tended to be those who enjoyed eating steaks and drinking milk. Their numbers included many snooker players and tennis fans. They called themselves the Bovine Preservation Society, or the BPS for short.

There were also cow supporters who didn't enjoy steaks or milk; they objected to the treatment of the cows by the human farmers. But they quite liked badgers too, so were undecided when it came down to which BPS to support.

So, on this Bonfire Night, the warring BPS factions met in front of York Minster. It wasn't long before skirmishes broke out between those dressed as cows and those dressed as badgers.

In the middle of the melee, a cow furry faced off a badger furry. The cow furry was flanked by angry snooker players and tennis fans wielding snooker cues and tennis rackets. The badger furry was flanked by angry vets, sporting elbow length gloves.

'You disease-ridden creature,' the cow furry shouted at the badger furry. 'You should all be stood in front of a wall and shot!'

'You're full of hot air,' the badger furry shouted back. 'Get back to eating grass and farting in your field.'

'At least I don't root about in the dirt and eat worms and slugs...'

'At least I don't have suction cups stuck on my tits and my milk sucked out.'

'You've gone too far with that one,' the cow furry said, coming at the badger furry, her hooves raised.

The badger furry pushed the cow furry back. The cow furry responded with a swipe of her fluffy hoof to the badger furry's black and white striped head. The badger furry jabbed the cow furry in the belly with his clawed paw. The cow furry doubled up.

Other furries piled in. Scuffles broke out between the snooker players, tennis fans and elbow-length-glove-wearing vets.

The York mounted police decided to intervene. They had been armed with police-issue water blasters in case of just such an event. They knew that furries didn't like to get their fur wet.

They rode into the centre of the melee and held out their blasters. Some of the protestors stopped skirmishing. They stared at the mounted police carrying firearms. Some stood their ground; others slunk off into the shadows, not wanting to get wet. Then someone threw a banger. It went off at the horses' feet, scaring the animals.

'Right,' Paul said, 'let them have it.'

Maria pulled the trigger on her water blaster. 'Take that!' she cried. A spurt of water shot out and hit a cow supporter in the face.

Paul sprayed a group of retreating badger supporters. He laughed and then jetted more water over the crowd.

'Hey!' one Radiohead fan, who had until recently been lying on Lendal Bridge stopping traffic, shouted, 'Lay off, you pig!'

One BPS member removed her cow mask and wiped the water from her eyes. She noticed that the black paint had started to flake away from the water blasters, revealing garish yellow, orange and blue plastic underneath. She turned to the crowd, who were rapidly dispersing.

'Hang on,' she shouted. 'They're just water pistols. They're not real guns... They're just Nerf water blasters, painted black.'

Paul examined his water blaster. It was true: they were just cheap, plastic water shooters, painted over with black gloss paint. 'Bloody cutbacks,' he muttered.

The crowd had started to regather. They began to surround the two mounted officers.

Maria aimed her water blaster and tried to soak a girl dressed as a badger. The badger girl laughed at her. Maria sprayed over the crowd that were closing in on them. The water pressure began to go.

'I think I'm running out of water,' she said, panicking.

'Me too... Come on, let's get out of here! Leave them to it!'

'Yes,' Maria said. 'Let's get back to the station and have a nice cup of Yorkshire Tea!'

Theodore watched as the mounted police cantered off into the night, horse hooves clipping on the flags of Yorkstone.

He was crouched at the base of the statue of Constantine the Great, located by the southern entrance to the Minster. He stared out at the crowd of masked protestors from between the great man's legs. He spotted a police dog, a German shepherd, running amok among the crowd, its handler nowhere to be seen.

Then, from the direction of Minster Yard, Miles appeared, his rucksack strapped to his back. Then, from the direction of Minster Gates, Milton appeared. Such convenient synchronicity, thought Theodore.

The two brothers saw each other at the same time. Milton headed straight for Miles. Miles ran behind the Roman Column. When he emerged seconds later, Theodore noticed that he was without his rucksack.

Theodore remembered Miles fiddling with the rucksack when he had been sitting in Pavement. Then in Bettys toilets, the rucksack had ticked three times as the door closed behind him. There had to be a bomb in the rucksack, he realised.

Miles began to push his way through the crowd, away from his younger brother. But Milton caught up with him and grabbed him by the shoulder, swinging him round.

'You're too late,' Miles cried.

Milton removed his Guy Fawkes mask. 'You what?'

'You heard,' Miles said. 'You're too late!'

He then hit Milton in the face. Milton staggered backwards and fell to his knees. The crowd parted around the fighting men. Milton got to his feet and the two brothers squared up.

Theodore looked across at the Roman Column. Miles must have put his rucksack behind the huge column. The bomb might go off at any minute. The explosion would cause the column to topple onto the crowd in front of the Minster, flattening the protestors.

He looked back at Miles and Milton. Milton punched his brother in the face. Blood spurted down Miles's shirt. Miles wiped the blood from his mouth and then kneed his brother in the groin. Milton doubled up in pain.

Then Theodore heard a bark. It was the police dog that had got loose. It had picked up his scent and was circling the great stone plinth on which Theodore was standing.

Theodore glanced at the Roman Column, back to the brawling brothers and then down at the barking dog. How was he going to get off this statue and through the crowd to the column to defuse the bomb before it went off, killing and maiming innocent people?

Then he remembered the police on their horses and had an idea.

He stared down at the police dog as it did another lap of the statue. Then he approached the edge of the plinth. The dog did one more lap. Theodore chose his moment and then dropped from the plinth, as the dog came round again.

26

Oliver was leaning against the old Roman column; he liked to have something to lean against. He took a swig from his bottle of cider and gazed out dreamily at the crowd. He wasn't sure what all these people in masks and costumes were doing in front of the Minster and didn't really care about finding out. He was enjoying the fireworks that went off over the crowd every few minutes, the coloured flares of light blurring into the night sky.

Then the crowd before him suddenly parted and a cat riding on the back of a German shepherd appeared. It was the same cat he had been begging with earlier that day.

'It can't be!' he muttered.

The dog-mounted cat was heading straight for him.

'Please no!'

It was coming for its revenge.

Oliver glanced at his bottle of cider and then at the advancing cat. The dog barked, the cat wailed and Oliver collapsed onto the stone flags with a scream. His last thought before he blacked out:

I never knew justice would take the form of a big fluffy cat riding a devil dog.

When he woke in a hospital ward the next day, he vowed never to take another drink, and the Theodore 'treatment' he had received would prove effective: The reformed Oliver Bartholomew would never have another drink in his life. After that Bonfire Night, he would be completely teetotal.

Fifty yards away, the Macavity brothers were still fighting. As anyone who has been in a fight will tell you, punching and taking punches is tiring. They stood bent over, their hands on their thighs, trying to get their breath back.

'Isn't that Milton Macavity?' one of the protestors said. 'The escaped convict?'

'And isn't that Miles Macavity?' another protestor said. 'The disgraced banker?'

'Bloody scum! Let's get them!'

And the crowd descended on the two brothers.

Theodore stared down at the ticking rucksack. He had managed to dismount his steed by the Roman Column, the dog returning to the crowd, its job done.

Theodore used his paws to lift the flap on the rucksack. There was a drawstring with a toggle attached. Theodore bit into the toggle and pulled it down the string. He then loosened the opening at the top of the bag before peering inside.

The ticking box inside was covered by many brightly coloured wires: red, green, blue and yellow. There was an LED, which ticked down the seconds until the bomb went off: 058, 057, 056, 055...

He realised that he had less than a minute to defuse the bomb. He flexed his claws and stared at the many wires and cables.

047, 046, 045, 044...

He knew that if he chose the wrong one, he would be cremains.

033, 032, 031, 029...

He thought briefly of Emily; he would never see his human ever again.

021, 020, 019, 018...

He wondered at the state of his food bowls; he would not be around to find out.

013, 012, 011...

He needed to focus on the situation. He stared at the network of wires and cables. Then he reached in a claw.

007, 006, 005...

Red, green, blue or yellow?

He reached inside.

003, 002...

He grabbed several cables in his claw and clamped down his jaws.

001...

The LED flashed 000.

Nothing happened. No big bang. No toppling column. No flattened protestors. No screaming people. Just the absence of ticking.

Theodore had saved hundreds of lives. He was a hero. Then he felt a jab in his side. He pulled his head out of the rucksack.

'Out of it!' a man in a Guy Fawkes mask said, and tapped him in his side again with his boot.

Theodore hissed at the masked man.

The man raised his foot. 'Get out of it!' he said. 'I'm having that bag and whatever's in it.'

Then Theodore was pushed aside and the masked man grabbed the rucksack. He didn't bother looking inside. He pulled it over his shoulder and disappeared into the night.

Theodore watched as the rucksack disappeared.

Now you can come home, came the voice in his head. *You managed to stop Miles killing the protestors. Your job is done. You are a hero! You can come back and have a long rest now.*

I will, Theodore thought back.

You will?

Yes, as soon as I've found Milton. I need to make sure he is returned safely to Full Sutton. We can't have him left wandering the streets.

Oh, please yourself, you foolish cat!

27

Emily and Jonathan watched as Miles and then Milton Macavity were dragged by the angry mob through the Museum Gardens, where a big bonfire awaited the brothers.

'Well, I guess those two are going to get what's coming to them,' Emily said.

'They can't throw them on the fire,' Jonathan said.

'Why ever not?'

'Milton's got my jeans and shirt for a start,' Jonathan said, shaking his head.

'Well, maybe it's time you got yourself a new wardrobe,' Emily said. 'The Corduroy Kid!'

'Don't you start.'

'Isn't that Brian May over there?' Emily said, nodding at an old man with long, wavy grey hair.

'What would the famous guitarist from Queen and astrophysicist be doing in the Museum Gardens on Bonfire Night? I'm sure he's got better things to do. Like badger watching…'

'Yes, I'm sure you're right,' Emily said, watching the figure disappear into the crowd in front of the museum.

'I'm a victim!' Milton shouted as he was dragged towards the fire. 'A victim… I'm the one who was trying to stop Miles from blowing you all up.'

'He's lying!' Miles shouted at the crowd. 'He's trying to save his skin. He was the one who was going to blow up a bomb and kill and maim you all. That's why he escaped from prison this morning. He is a violent criminal.'

'It's not true,' Milton protested, as he was pulled through the gates of the gardens. 'If anyone was going to blow anyone up, it was him.'

'He's a liar!' Miles shouted.

'Let's just burn them both!' a Guy Fawkes said and the crowd roared in agreement.

'Stop!' Milton cried, as he was pulled towards the pyre.

'Murderer!' a voice called out.

'Burn him!' another shouted.

'Throw them both on the fire!'

Milton gazed out at the masked faces in the crowd. Cows, badgers, Guy Fawkeses and kids in Radiohead T-shirts.

'This is a farce,' he called out. 'A farce!'

More of a tragedy, thought Theodore, trying to get to Milton. But the crowd had a million booted-feet that stomped the ground around him.

Then a combat boot came down on his tail. He let out a yowl. 'That's my tail!' He yowled again.

As the combat boot lifted, he pulled his tail out and beneath his body.

He looked around. He saw a stone stump: the remnant of one of the old columns of St Mary's Abbey. He made for it.

Jonathan and Emily were searching in the shadows of the ruins.

'We're never going to find him,' Jonathan said. 'There are too many people about.'

'He must be around somewhere,' Emily said. 'We can't give up on him now.'

'Isn't that Willie Nelson over there?' Jonathan said, pointing at a short man with a ponytail.

'Looks more like Tom Yorke,' Emily said.

'Don't be stupid... What would the lead singer of Radiohead be doing at a protest demonstration in the Museum Gardens on Bonfire Night?'

'I could say the same about Willie Nelson.'

Just then they heard a yowl.

'Did you hear that?' Emily said.

'It sounded like a peacock,' Jonathan said.

'There hasn't been a peacock in the gardens for years,' Emily said. 'It was Theo. He's in trouble... Come on!'

Emily pushed her way through the crowd towards the fire. Jonathan followed.

'I knew nothing about a bomb,' Milton protested as he was dragged towards the fire. He could feel the heat on his face.

'He's guilty,' a Guy Fawkes shouted. 'I found the bomb. It was in a bag by the Roman Column. He had set it to go off and kill us...' He held up the blue rucksack.

'The monster!' a Radiohead fan called out.

'I managed to defuse it,' the Guy Fawkes said. 'Before it exploded.'

'You're a hero,' the Radiohead fan said.

'Burn him! Burn him! Burn him!' the crowd chanted at Milton.

'I never put it there,' Milton protested. 'I wasn't even sure there was a bomb.'

'Of course you did,' Miles cried. 'He planned to kill you all. He phoned me from Full Sutton and said he had plans for this evening. I was trying to stop him. When I found out he had escaped from prison, I knew I had to find him and stop him. Burn him!'

'Burn him! Burn him! Burn him!' the crowd chanted, pushing Milton towards the flames.

Then a flare went off. The ruins of St Mary's Abbey were lit up in blue-white light.

Milton spotted Theodore standing on the stump of an old column.

He pointed at the cat. 'That cat knows the truth,' he cried. 'He knows that I was trying to stop Miles. I wasn't the one who planted the bomb...'

The crowd turned to look at the cat.

Theodore stared out at the masked faces and then at Milton. He knew that whatever he said, it wasn't going to save Milton. He miaowed out Milton's innocence knowing that it would fall on deaf ears.

Then Miles said, 'It's just a big fluffy cat!'

There were loud murmurings among the crowd.

'Maybe it's not just a cat,' a girl in a cow costume said.

Theodore miaowed again.

'It seems to be trying to tell us something,' a badger-faced boy said.

'Let's put it to the test,' a Radiohead fan said. 'Form a space between the cat and these two...'

The crowd parted to create a corridor between the cat and the two brothers.

The Radiohead fan now addressed Theodore. 'Now, let us know which of these brothers is telling the truth. Is it Milton, the escaped murderer? Was he actually trying to stop his brother from setting off a bomb this evening?

'Or was Milton indeed trying to stop his brother, the disgraced banker Miles Macavity, from setting off a bomb in the crowd?'

Theodore stood on the column. He looked from the face of one brother to the other.

'Here kitty, kitty...,' Miles pleaded.

'You remember me, don't you?' Milton said. 'I'm the one who saved you from the river. I'm the one who made a fire and warmed your fur. I'm the one who fed you toasted marshmallows...'

With that, Theodore jumped down and trotted over to Milton. He brushed against his legs.

'The cat says Milton is the good guy,' the badger boy said. 'So Miles must be the bad guy.'

'Then it's Miles that we'll burn on the bonfire,' the cow girl said.

And so Miles was dragged off to be burned on the fire.

'Well, I guess I owe you one,' Milton said to the cat.

Theodore miaowed up at the escaped convict. He narrowed his eyes.

'What's this?' Milton said. 'You want me to give myself in?'

Theodore miaowed again.

'Well, we did stop Miles and that's why I broke out. I guess you've got a point.'

'And I think you should give me back my shirt and jeans,' Jonathan said, pushing his way through to the front of the crowd.

'Well, I did just borrow them from your washing line,' Milton said. 'I'll make sure they're returned as soon as I've handed myself in...'

Then Emily approached Theodore. 'Theo!' she cried.

Theodore raced towards his human and jumped into her arms. As they hugged, more fireworks lit up the sky.

'I'm so glad I've got you back,' Emily said, staring into his big, green eyes. 'Whatever were you thinking: going out on Bonfire Night?'

Then floodlights lit up the whole of the Museum Gardens. Everyone turned towards the light.

'What's going on?' Emily said, clutching Theodore to her chest.

Jonathan noticed a huge banner hanging down the building's façade: ROCK FOR UNITY!

Then Brian May appeared on the museum roof, his guitar strapped over his shoulder.

'It is Brian May!' Jonathan said.

He was shortly joined by Radiohead singer Tom Yorke.

'It is Tom Yorke!' Emily said.

'No, that's Willie Nelson,' Jonathan said.

The crowd burst into applause.

'And that's Phil Collins on drums!' Jonathan said as a huge drum kit was picked out by a spotlight and Phil did a drumroll to thunderous applause.

I knew there was something in the air tonight, thought Theodore pushing himself against Emily's chest.

'I didn't know that there was going to be a rock concert,' Jonathan said.

'Me neither,' Emily said.

Brian approached the microphone, set up on the edge of the building. 'Take off your masks!' he called out to the crowd. 'We must unite to be strong. Together we are stronger. Together we can fight the system. Together we can make a difference...

'We must act now for our planet. We must act now for the cows, for the badgers, for the polar bears. Climate change is real. We cannot be complacent. But we must do it together.'

The crowd applauded.

Then Tom Yorke/Willie Nelson joined Brian May at the microphone. 'We must stop hiding behind masks,' he said. 'We must stop fighting amongst ourselves. We must forget our differences... We must work together!'

The crowd cheered.

'Cast off your masks and be yourselves! Now is the time to come together! Together we are stronger!'

People in the crowd began to take off their masks.

'Now burn your masks and outfits!' Brian cried. 'Throw your shackles onto the bonfire!'

Members of the crowd began to approach the bonfire and throw on their masks and costumes. There were whoops and cheers. People began to hug one another.

The cow furry and the badger furry who had been fighting in front of York Minster minutes before took off their fluffy heads and threw them onto the bonfire. They turned and faced each other.

The cow furry smiled at the badger furry. 'Hug?' she said.

The badger furry smiled back. 'Hug,' he said.

They hugged each other and soon they were kissing.

I wonder what their offspring will look like? wondered Theodore. Compact cows with stripy noses and pointed hooves perhaps.

'What's that awful smell?' Emily said, wincing.

'I think it's the smell of burning flesh and plastic,' Jonathan said, his hand across his mouth and nose.

'It stinks,' said Emily.

Theodore miaowed impatiently. Can we please go home now?

Probably the most sensible idea you've had for quite some time, came the voice of the cat basket.

'Yes, come on,' Emily said, looking down at Theodore. 'Let's get Theo home!'

'Yes,' Jonathan said, 'I think a large mug of Yorkshire Tea is in order after the day I've had.'

'After the day you've had?'

'After the day we've had.'

I think a 12 hour nap is in order, thought Theodore as he was carried through the crowd.

As they approached the gates to the Museum Gardens, the band on the roof of the museum began to blast out The Beatles' Come Together.

Theodore glanced down and saw a flyer on the ground, creased and smeared with mud:

ROCK FOR UNITY – 5 NOVEMBER
Super Group Tribute Band!
Featuring...
Brian Maybe-May on guitar
Thom York (without an 'e') on vocals (Radiohead tribute
and Willie Nelson lookalike)
Phil Collings (with a 'g') on drums
Plus Very Special Guests!!!

It wasn't Willie Nelson or Thom Yorke, Theodore thought disappointedly. Just some copycats...

As they neared home, Theodore heard a voice.

I'm here waiting for you. Come on then!

Theodore realised it was his cat basket calling. He struggled in Emily's arms.

'I think he knows he's near home,' Jonathan said.

'Yes, I think he does,' Emily said. 'I wonder how they always know how to find their way home?'

'Beats me,' Jonathan said, 'but I'm sure there's a scientific explanation.'

She put Theodore down on the pavement.

Come on then! Your bed is nice and warm and waiting for you...

Theodore began to run. He dashed down the side of a house. He jumped over boundary walls until he reached his own back-yard. He darted through the cat flap into the kitchen. There in front of him was his cat basket. He dived inside.

Welcome home, Theo!

By the time Emily and Jonathan unlocked the front door Theodore was purring from within his fur-lined cocoon.

'I think he's glad to be home,' Emily said. 'I know I am.'

'Yes,' Jonathan said. 'I'll put the kettle on.'

'And after a nice cup of Yorkshire Tea, we could have an early night,' Emily said. 'We don't need to be up in the morning now my parents are looking after Joseph...'

'Perhaps we could skip the tea?'

The Case of the Clementhorpe Killer was started on a Sunday morning in May 2012, on the dining table of a terraced house on Scott Street, York. Theodore was sitting on the table as I wrote down the first ideas in a blank notebook. The idea of a pet detective was nothing new. There were even talking ones. Not in these books though.

The idea of knowing what your pet was thinking was something that most pet owners have wondered but never know. 'If only they could talk,' is a common expression. But if the reader knew what they were thinking, there could be a different narrative voice, and that was the basis of *The York Cat Crime Mysteries.*

Originally there were to be nine books, the idea being that cats have nine lives, and in each book Theodore would lose a life. However, Theodore only had one life. He died in the streets of Clementhorpe, run over by a car. A tap on the front door late one night...

We moved to cat-friendly street in Acomb, worried our other three cats might meet similar ends. The second book in the series, originally titled *Rear Garden*, was set in these quiet suburbs. It was more difficult to write without Theodore by my side, but as a novel much stronger than the first. And darker – reflecting my own personal experiences of that period.

The Call of the Cat Basket came easier. Having allowed Theodore to roam into the city centre (in my imagination), there was a wealth of material to call on. It was written quickly, without impediment, one paragraph leaping to the next. If I hit a wall, I would wander the streets until inspiration came. I would like to think of it as the most accomplished of *The York Cat Crime Mysteries.*

Since the books were written, much has changed in York. There are now locked gates barring entry into the back alleys of Clementhorpe. Acomb is succumbing to gentrification with a bakery, decent greengrocers, and soon, a wine bar. Many shops have closed in York city centre (especially during the pandemic) but others have opened in their place. Purple Man is seldom spotted these days. The Harry Potter shops on the Shambles are down to one, the others closed for copyright infringement.

This book is the complete set of published Theodore books presented as a trilogy. The first has been edited heavily, the other two to a lesser extent. The local details have been left as they were when I wrote them.

There are now three new cats in my life. Two Norwegian Forest Cats: Hank, a boss-eyed grey silver stripy dude of a cat, and Walter, a dark smoke who looks tough but is a real softie when you get to know him. Then there's Wilbur, a Birman who has a knack of getting into trouble...

Maybe now is the time to begin to write of their adventures.

J.B. York. June 2022

'The First of Nine: The Case of the Clementhorpe Killer' was first published through CreateSpace in 2016. The book was republished in March 2017 by Severus House with cover art by York artist Matt Dawson.

'Rear Garden: The Cat Who Knew Too Much' followed in November 2017. The cover image was done by Robert Clear and graphic design by Burak Bakircioglu.

'The Call of the Cat Basket' was published in September 2019, graphic design also by Burak Bakircioglu.

This book 'The York Cat Crime Trilogy' comprises the aforementioned books, edited by the author for this omnibus volume.

This edition is published by Severus House

ISBN 978-0-9956571-8-2

This book is dedicated to Theodore (RIP)

Lightning Source UK Ltd.
Milton Keynes UK
UKHW040740100822
407113UK00002B/592